# Lover IN CHAINS

## A NOVEL OF THE DARKEST KYND

### S. C. Dane

5

A DARKEST KYND NOVEL
LOVER IN CHAINS
Copyright © 2017-2018 by S. C. Dane

First Printing: 2017

ISBN: 978-1-68046-592-1

Published by Satin Romance
An Imprint of Melange Books, LLC
White Bear Lake, MN 55110
www.melange-books.com

Published in the United States of America.

Cover Design by Caroline Andrus

## THE DARKEST KYND SERIES

*Lover in Stone*
*Lover in Darkness*
*Lover in Chains*

# THE KYND ONES

*O*nce the Kynd existed under God's grace, bearing witness to all things passing. Until the Schism when God and Lucifer clashed and the archangel was flung from the heavens. Refusing to choose sides, the Kynd were damned, too, forced to bear witness without the touch and comfort of another, their honorable name disintegrating into the dust of history. Now they are remembered merely as gargoyles and chimeras, and in their deaths, they become monsters of stone—Grotesques. Their Chosen Ones can save them. But after enduring centuries of solitary madness, who could love something so doomed.

# CHAPTER 1

*I*f *you love something set it free?* Clearly, the fucktard who said this didn't know his ass from his armpit, or jack shit about Kynd and their Chosen Ones.

Granted, Urick had kidnapped his "love," but hey. Watching her suck blood from a sick child's vein had kicked him off the ledge of sanity he'd been gripping. That she was his Chosen One, a woman God—in his infinite wisdom—had seen fit to pair him with, was the diarrhea icing on his crapper of a cake.

This leech was the female destined to release him from his curse of turning to stone every day of his pathetic existence. Yay for him. Talk about the short straw and the short hairs.

Speaking of which, right then the short hairs on his balls were feeling the sting as his heretofore flaccid dick unfurled its length, while he glared at the stone around his neck—his Chosen One.

A vampire. She had to be a frigging vampire. Of all the creatures, beasts, and what-have-yous roaming these realms, he got paired with a bloodsucker. If he'd had the choice, he'd have bonded with…oh, Medusa maybe, or Typhoid Mary.

Urick scraped his palm from forehead to nape and back again. Pressing the heel of his hand to the bridge of his nose, he fought the roar climbing his throat. It didn't help that his peepers stole a look across the cave floor to the very thing he loathed.

The female was curled up on the ground across from him, her legs folded up to her chest. She had one arm bent under her head as a makeshift pillow to keep her hair out of the dirt. The other arm she had clasped around her shins to hold her knees to her belly.

The classic fetal position. A pose meant to illicit sympathy and pity.

*She can rot there.* The pang flaring in his chest was as short-lived as the strike of a match, but no less of a burning bitch. It reminded him that he needed her, that they were inescapably connected. That the coiled piece of feminine flesh on the ground in front of him was the key to his salvation.

So, yeah, no. As much as he loathed the fact she was meant to be his, Uri wouldn't be setting her free and *hoping* she came back to him. He needed to be absolutely certain she did. As much as the idea wrung his guts into all kinds of pain and sickness.

She was supposed to be the one to even his keel, to keep the cheese on his cracker. God knew, his slice of Velveeta was slipping off its little square of carbohydrate.

As a chimera, he should be exulting in the triple whammy strength of being three creatures balled into one. Instead, he was gargoyle, grizzly, and cock-sucking vampire. Which, maybe he could deal with if he hadn't been—

"Quit looking at me like that, perv."

Uri's hand fell from the bridge of his nose. "Say what?"

"You heard me. And if you think I'm going to let you lay your filthy paws on me, you're going to be the recipient of a new asshole." The woman propped herself up on one arm and tossed her head like she was flinging her long tresses over her shoulder.

Which she wasn't. Her hair was cropped chin length, slightly longer in the front than the back, showcasing the different tints of blonde. Her hair was everything from platinum to rose gold to sunny yellow. In the shafted moonlight of the cave, it made him think of salty beaches and long stretches of hot sand. The kind of fine granules where you could wriggle your ass into, then flake out to bake your bones.

"Hey!"

Uri blinked like he'd been staring at the sun. When had the woman gotten to her feet? Fumbling like he wore ice skates, he found some altitude, the sudden launch to vertical dropping his blood pressure. He jabbed a finger at her. "Stay put."

The woman narrowed the prettiest eyes he'd ever seen. True liquid amber, and somehow the party-mix blonde of her hair set her irises off like they were coins from ages past. Uri ground his back teeth to keep his mouth from flopping open.

"Like I can go anywhere." She jutted her chin as she put her hands on her hips. A defiant stance worth nothing, not when he could hear her pulse flicking quicker than a hamster's wheel. Besides, he'd chosen this cave for the metals embedded in the earthen walls. After what had been done to him, he cherished the safety of a place no vampires could teleport into. Or out of, as the case was now.

"You dug your own grave." His lip curled off his right fang.

"I dug my own—?" She launched at him so fast he yanked his hands up to keep her from clubbing him in the puss. But just as he was expecting contact, she dropped from view and the next thing he saw was the jagged ceiling of the cave as she swept his legs out from under him.

He landed on his ass with no fine-grained sand to cushion the landing. As his breath punched out of his lungs, her face loomed into his field of vision, her pale cheeks smudged a dusky pink, her little fangs…beguiling. "I did not ask for this. You kidnapped me, remember. Or is stupidity a Kynd trait right along with—"

With a snag and grab, he muckled her and flipped to his stomach. On her back, her long legs stretched between his, their pelvises locked like Legos so his frigging erect shaft nestled into the soft flesh of her lower belly despite their clothing. Her wrists felt tiny and fragile in his big hands, and the feel of those small bones turned something inside him like a key tumbling a lock.

Damn him, but it felt right to feel her against him. Fundamentally sound for her body to be so close to his. Maybe he should give her a chance, share with her why vampires made him want to bellow and decapitate them for the evil things they'd done to him.

She was his Chosen One. She deserved a shot at finding a place in his heart. He could do that for her, at least. After all, she was right. He'd kidnapped her, and after three days he still hadn't tried to talk to her, to explain. Pegging her as a typical vampire, he hadn't asked why she'd been feasting on the blood of sick children before he'd grabbed her and brought her to this hole in the Earth.

Yes, good idea to share. Her gold eyes were shimmering as though she held back her tears. With his heart cramping up in his chest, Uri eased his grip and lifted his hips.

She kneed him in the balls.

As his lungs clocked out, he sagged, curling himself around the car bomb of his midsection. Fists gripped like grim death to her wrists, he dragged her into the spiral of his pain, cloaking her with his big body so she couldn't run.

He wasn't sure if when he opened his mouth he'd vomit something other than words, but he gave it a go. "What the hell?" he croaked, blessedly chunk-free.

She stiffened inside his embrace then jabbed an elbow into his ribs. His reflexes forced him to squeeze the little bones of her wrists. "Cut...it...out."

"Let me go!"

Scrubbing his hot face against the back of her head, he snarled, "I can't." As she squirmed in his arms all he could feel was the delicateness of her flesh and the incongruous strength in her muscles. Her hair felt as soft as the powder from a butterfly's wings.

"You can't, or you won't?" She scissor-kicked, nearly freeing herself with the momentum. Ignoring the shrieking pain in his ball sac, he locked his legs around hers so they were laying on the cave floor like two angry spoons.

"Damn it, female! Stop!" She wiggled more, her butt cheeks cranking down on his erect dick. Stiff-arming her, he pushed away from the tempting sensation, the scent of her heated skin washing over him. She took advantage of the space between them, twisting fast to free her right arm.

He blocked the punch, but the back of his hand over her fist still hit him under the chin.

"Son of a bitch." Those skinny arms had some horsepower behind them. And what do you know? He could feel her tensing for another shot at his face. As they grappled, he grew acutely aware of the subtle shifts of her body, the slide of her muscles against his.

With their body heat mingling, her scent grew stronger, and Uri gripped her tighter. "Stop," he rasped, surprised by how breathy he sounded. He didn't want to hurt her, not even in retaliation. She was his Chosen One— regardless of how he felt about it—the urge to do her harm was non-existent.

She, however, had no compunction. His balls were singing the proof of that.

Still, he watched her pulse throb under the pale skin of her neck, mesmerized by the tempo thumping with the beat of his own, her skin jumping at the small pulse point. Numb as a pounded thumb, he dipped his head to flick his tongue against the fluttering vein.

*Oh, God.* Huge mistake. All he did was spank it, make it ready. Nostrils flared, he slanted for another taste—

"What the fuck! You're a vampire?"

Uri reared back as if she'd slapped him with the peen end of a hammer. "No!" he roared, the sound vibrating across his lengthening fangs. In his empty, aching gut, though, he felt the heaviness of his denial. "I am Kynd! I am no bloodsucker!"

$\mathcal{F}$or a split second, his hold loosened and Violet wrenched her arms downward, hoping to slip from the shackles of his fists. True to what he was, the demonic Kynd closed his fingers tight as a hangman's noose. She'd heard they were unpredictable and violent, killers without compassion, but the chimera's speed caught her by surprise.

As did the fact of what glared back at her with such hatred, she figured his face was a mirror of her own. So there. She despised him, too. Right down to his fucked-up eyeballs that switched from gray to black to gray again so fast it frightened her. Never mind the stone hard glower, as if his eyes were made of granite even when he wasn't playing rock statue.

With his hands clapped tightly to her wrists, she felt him tremble as if his spine was a lake someone had thrown a boulder into. The vibrations eddied outward, and the harder he shuddered the tighter he gripped.

"Oh, shit." She knew what this was. The end of night had arrived, and its FTD florist ass brought the rosy fingers of dawn. As he'd done for the three days since her capture, this horrid beast was turning grotesque. His handsome visage…

Fine. She'd admit he had certain physical qualities that attracted her eye, until dawn that was. Every time night ceded to the day, he did this trembling thing, his muscles bulging as his attention lasered for the ceiling, his face contorting with utter rage. Lips peeled back from long fangs, he'd roar upward as if cursing the Heavens. Like it was God's fault this monster existed.

As adrenaline flooded her veins, her body went all human Parkinson's, shaky-shaky as panic hopped in behind the wheel. Fuck her calm, inner voice when surrounding her was the embodiment of fury. The grotesque was hardening, and because they'd been fighting he was holding her even tighter than usual. No way he wasn't going to crush her.

Violet started pummeling him with girlie fists, all Fay Rae in *King Kong* and just as helpless. "You're going to kill me, you stupid fuck!"

Too intent on whatever drama was unfolding in his head, he didn't look down. He bellowed instead as if her words echoed in that empty skull of his and they pissed him off even more.

His grip eased just as his body surrendered to the stone. The transformation seemed to ooze from the inside out as though it consumed him. The utter, freaking stillness that followed was…utterly freaky. Tough shit for her lack of eloquence. Panic still held the reins and she was playing *what's the first word you think of when you see this…*

After all the fighting and screaming, the heaving breaths and grappling, it felt like sitting in the eye of a tornado. Queerly still and quiet, the receding panic making her giddy.

Survivor's rush?

Maybe. Since she was trapped in his stone arms and couldn't move, she inhaled and punched out a couple of quick breaths to displace the shakes as the adrenaline abated, and took her bearings. They were on the floor of the cave. At some point, he'd risen to his knees, dragging her with him.

She hadn't even noticed. She was not a small woman, but this male had moved with her like she was a Barbie doll. Hell. His strength had reduced her to a flighty girl who'd ineffectively whacked at him as he did whatever he wanted.

Like, cradle her.

He fucking cradled her again just before he turned to stone. Like he worried she'd be uncomfortable while he played statue for the next twelve hours. Damn him. He was a monster, one of the legendary Kynd that mother ghouls told their children about to scare them.

Laying in his arms like she'd been doing for three days now, Violet got a real up close and personal view of the Bogeyman. Maybe because of the dopamine floating in her bloodstream, she took the time to really look at him. Not just scan the thing holding her captive, but study *who* was holding her.

Forget the huge, muscle-straining body locking her in. What made him hideous were the tendons bulging in his neck, his stretched lips revealing fangs that would span the width of her palm if she slapped him upside the head.

No wonder they were called Grotesques. Not that his strong jaw or sharp cheekbones were ugly. Or that his ears had morphed into bear ears—which fit him somehow—as if there was a beautiful symmetry to the three beings making him what he was. Gargoyle, bear, and…vampire.

He denied being vampire, but *duh*. She'd know one when she saw one. Kind of like a homo sapiens seeing himself in a fellow human. Like recognized like. Why he denied it as if she'd called him Satan, she could guess. Anger like his was personal, so it wasn't a huge leap in logic to suspect he'd been victimized somehow.

Or maybe his vampire mother had abandoned him. Who the hell knew?

What she did know was she could use these lapses of consideration against him. Okay, bucking against the legends, this monster seemed to have a speck of decency. An anomaly, sure, but she'd stretch it all the way to freedom, thank you very much. She was getting out of this cave and didn't care if she had to lie, cheat, or kill to do it. But what did she know about him or his Kynd other than the dust mote of civility he seemed to possess, and the legends she'd grown up hearing about them?

So far, he hadn't sucked the marrow from her bones, but he seemed too busy roaring at the cave's ceiling or glaring at her with disgust.

*Disgust.* Yeah, she despised being vampire, too, but she'd be damned if she'd let some monster make her feel worse than she already did about it. Especially since she lived every day atoning for the fact—killing other vampires who'd gone rogue, helping the sick kids at the hospital by giving them drops of her blood. Blood that gave them a little boost in fighting their cancers. It wasn't much, but any help was something good.

Now this deranged beast had taken her away from the things that made her long existence worthwhile, made her feel a little bit worthy when deep down she hated herself, hated what she was. So, feeling disgusted? Right back at you, asshole.

At least she wasn't the one so arrogant in her power she'd snubbed both God and the fallen archangel Lucifer. She wasn't the hideous being forever perched on the side of an old building, rotting from the inside out with her volatility and arrogance.

Though he didn't seem very arrogant at the moment. Turning to stone could probably shave off a few layers of superiority, what with being helpless and all. She could gawk at him all day if she wanted to, and he couldn't lift a finger to stop her. Heck, she could make googly faces, stick her thumbs in her ears and wag her fingers while she teased *nanananana*.

"You'd know, though, wouldn't you?"

The beast kept looking heavenward.

"Oh, yes, you would, you would, you big lug, you." He wasn't a Pomeranian puppy by any stretch, but she bet the baby-waby tone pissed him off. She'd pay when the sun went down, sure as shit, but hey, she had to pass the hours somehow.

The looking around had been done the first day he'd trapped her, which was, technically, her second. The first day she'd spent in what had turned out to be her only friend's cellar. She'd had no idea Daniela Salvai was mixed up with these creatures. If she had, she'd have warned her away.

Not that the woman had been afraid. In fact, now that Violet had hours upon endless hours to spend thinking about it, one of those Kynd beasts had stepped between them as if protecting Daniela from Violet. Her human friend had seemed more stunned to find out Violet was a vampire than afraid to be so close to the savage gargoyle.

Or, that there was an Other convention going on in her basement. Which was totally whacked. She must not be remembering that scene right. Besides, the confrontation hadn't lasted long before her captor had come to life, his stone body fluid once more. She'd had about ten seconds to wonder why her captor was stone when the other Kynd weren't, but then he'd bellowed like he should be the outraged one, and disappeared them. To here.

Beauty was in the eye of the beholder because it didn't matter that *here* had walls that glittered under the gold and blue rays of the sun and moon's beams stabbing down from the vaulted height of the cave. As if disco and the '70s, or a rainbow acid trip, were time-capsuled in this godforsaken hole. She was still trapped no matter how pretty her surroundings.

She turned her gaze upward to that horrible face. "I guess I'm not the only one trapped here. You're not going anywhere either, are you?" Good. She'd plant the seed of discontent, pretend to see his side of things. Trick him into trusting her. Granted, with his anger thicker than a blood clot this was going to take a while.

Speaking of which, she'd need to feed at some point or she was going to get too weak to rescue herself. Fucking vampires and their dilemmas.

---

*U*rick desperately wanted to bite something, but couldn't. *You're not going anywhere either, are you?* The female's words sliced deep into his gut, making him feel like they were spilling down his lap. He wanted to shred that horrible truth, clamp his grizzly-strong jaws on them and render them to harmless confetti.

Except it wasn't going to happen while he was frozen in stone. He could shriek his outrage in his head, but none of the anguish would actually escape. Without an outlet, it would spin and grow, feeding on itself. Until his body was once again his own and he could strike out, destroying everything he touched.

Even his Chosen One, his blessed salvation. His strength could pulverize things, and she might be long-lived, but she'd never survive a crushed skull or amputated limbs.

Inwardly he shuddered as the image of her ruined body flashed into his frontal lobe, the effect as debilitating as 500,000 volts cutting off his internal roar as decidedly as a switch. He'd take a deep breath if his lungs weren't currently stone moorings.

Instead, he substituted the sigh with the span of a few serene seconds, the equivalent resulting in a calmer perspective. In his periphery, he caught the flurry of shadows at the same time he felt the little vampire female wiggling against his skin. She was moving in his grasp. Not trying to escape, but to...

His visage, frozen in its grotesque rage, no longer reflected the curiosity stirring in his quieted mind. Uri concentrated on the press of her body against his stone muscles as she shifted to…

Shake her head? What in hell was she doing? He couldn't look down, but he sensed she was trying to get up in his face. To mock him?

That's exactly what she was trying to do, and it made him feel like a little boy flopped in the middle of a litter of puppies—all wriggling, giggling and squirming. Holy hell, his granite lips were going to crack into a smile.

Her antics reminded him of Kallen, his brotherkynd he'd left back at the safe house. A place and its people he missed terribly now that he had the Kynd version of family back together again. A pall settled over his mirth sure as if a dark cloud rolled in over a sunny picnic. No forecast of rain, but the mood better suited his situation.

When his body began to soften, he automatically curled around the female in his arms, as if in just three days it had become second nature to keep her close. She fell still immediately, the tension in her muscles unmistakable. As if she expected violence from him now that he could act on the anger and betrayal he'd been feeling as dawn had descended.

*I won't hurt her despite what she is.*

She couldn't know his change of heart, that his thoughts had finally settled around the truth of her being his Chosen One. He still felt as if he'd been dealt the shitty hand, but at least he'd been given the cards. Unlike Kallen, Drakus, and Kronos, who also suffered from the abuses and tortures they'd been enduring before answering Darken's call to forsake their God-given punishments.

At least Uri had his Chosen One.

After coughing out the cobwebs in his throat, he looked down at the female in his arms. She glared back, her butt wedged between his thighs, her long legs spilling over his arms. "I won't hurt you."

Distrustful, she narrowed her eyes.

"I swear it to you," he said as his insides coiled queerly. His outrage at what had been done to him mixed like oil in the water of his resolve. Somehow, he had to make it work with the one being on the planet made specifically to bring him peace. Maybe even joy someday, as Merrick and Darken shared with their Chosen Ones.

"What is your name?" She frowned as if pissed by the tremor in her voice.

Uri dragged a look down the length of her, as though truly seeing her for the first time. He noticed how lithe she was, her muscles toned under soft, pale skin. The set of her chin and the level look in those amber eyes.

They took in every exit, every object to be used as a weapon, every weakness.

He would remain wary in spite of the olive branch he offered her. She was vampire, after all. Not to be trusted. Granted, the ancient Vampyres of the Triumvirate, the Kynd's benefactors, hadn't betrayed them. Yet.

"I am Urick, the Chimera of the Kynd." As the words left his mouth, his chest grew tight, as though pride was a steam expanding inside him. "And you are...?"

That stern chin of hers hardened. Seconds passed like heartbeats as she searched his face. As though satisfied by what she found, she clipped out, "I'm Violet and that's all you need to know."

Uri let himself smirk. So like Kallen, she seemed, not even realizing how naturally funny she was. "Well, Violet That's All You Need To Know, if I let go of you, will you promise not to kick me in the balls?"

She bit her bottom lip, then shrugged. "Probably."

"Probably what? Promise, or knee my nads?"

Did she chew her lip to keep a smile from blooming? "I promise not to harm your testicles for now."

"I'll take it." Still holding her, he stood up, easing his hold just enough so she slid down the front of him as she gained her feet. *Ah, God.* She felt like the jolt of lightning to his rumbling thunder. Again, those twin feelings rose up within him, warring with each other. He hated that she was vampire, but at the same time revered that she was his Chosen.

He stepped back, resisting the urge to latch ahold of her again as she swayed on her feet. Those very feet that had found their home in the cushion of his tender ball sac. He eyed her warily, his hands surreptitiously folding in front of him.

"Nervous?" Her grin would rival that of Lewis Carroll's Cheshire Cat.

"A little."

His honesty coaxed another grin from her, this one as cagy as a coyote in the suburbs. They inched away from each other like boxers in the ring until she found the corner she preferred. He went to his just as if the bell had rung, ending their match. She watched him for so long he got itchy, suddenly not knowing what do with himself. Stand up? Fold his arms?

"I'd heard the Kynd had gathered. Now I know it's true." Her voice washed over him, smooth as the hairs on his grizzly belly. "How many have come?"

*Nowhere near enough.* "Enough for now." Any more and the safe house wouldn't be standing. As it was, they'd incrementally destroyed the beauty of the place with their outbursts. His fear that he would accidentally hurt Violet when she was in his arms wasn't without precedent.

There wasn't a room in that sprawling safe house that didn't bear evidence of claws and fists. Oh, and spiked tails, compliments of Drakus, the dragon chimera. He was responsible for the gashes in the ceilings, too, but Urick was in no place to find fault. A grizzly could do his own damage, thank you very much.

Violet raised one eyebrow, the chip calling the poker bluff.

"Six of us," he begrudged. "Plus, two Chosen Ones."

"Chosen Ones. You keep referring to that. I'm supposed to be one?"

How much to reveal? If he told her too much, she could use it against him. But if he didn't tell her enough, he could lose her. Or, be tied to a female who could, literally, hate him for ages upon ages.

And maybe she was truly curious. Maybe, being Chosen, she felt some of the attraction he felt for her. A reluctant enticement, but there nonetheless. After all, having watched Angelia and Merrick, there wasn't a doubt in his mind she was as knocked stupid by love as the lion chimera was. Surely, there was some mystical bond at work.

"Yeah," he shrugged, although he pinned her with a challenging glare.

Lashes flicking upward and her voice a little shaky, she asked, "What does it mean to be your Chosen One?"

"It means," a bag of dust landed in his throat. Inching toward the door in case she tried to run, he braced off, ready for round two. "It means you were made for me by God. That you are my other half."

She rolled her eyes. "Made for you."

Nodding, Uri prepared for the worst. She was strong, and when she lashed out he needed to be ready to deflect expert blows. His heart beat faster, excitement blending with the fear that if she fought too fiercely he would hurt her.

"Okay. I'll accept that."

Uri blinked. "What?" Surely, he heard wrong.

"Since you haven't killed me—not that you could—I'll buy that you might have a thing for me. And maybe you're telling the truth, that God ordained this. But you didn't have to kidnap me. You could have asked me on a date."

No matter how much his eyelids clapped like an appreciative audience, he couldn't comprehend her turnabout of attitude. Surely, she was feeling their bond. A twinge of giddiness stuck its wary head out, tender as a nascent sprout.

He let his stupid-ass grin quiver its unsteady way to his lips. She smiled back, the tips of her fangs resting on her lower lip. The seedling of happiness he'd been feeling got pancaked by a semi-truck load of hatred. In his head, the air horns blasted and he shook as though the eighteen-wheeler sped by so close, the wake wobbled him on his shitkickers.

*Vampire.* He'd almost forgotten she was vampire.

"What? What'd I say?"

His molars gnashing, he gritted out, "Nothing."

"It wasn't nothing. You're shaking like you do just before you turn to stone." She pushed her back up the wall as she got to her feet.

His gaze followed her. "Don't run."

She threw her hands up. "Oh, for the love of all that's holy, I'm not. All right?" Then she jabbed a finger at him. "But I'm getting pretty sick of your mood swings. You're like a playground in hell, you've got so many."

Surely, she was Kallen's long-lost sisterkynd. The thought tempered him. Somewhat. Enough so he didn't state the obvious and put them back at square one. To prove they'd moved beyond that, he settled into his corner.

Distrustful, she sank back down into hers.

Elbows on his knees, he let out a defeated sigh. "Okay. First off, I didn't ask you on a date because I wasn't sure you were my Chosen One. Second, I didn't ask…" Fuck him, he couldn't do this. Rubbing his hands down his face, he peered at her over his fingertips.

She sat about ten feet away from him, no expression whatsoever on her face. The distance between them may as well have been ten miles. Or ten inches. To trust her, or not to trust her? Well, here went nothing. "I didn't ask because I'mstarvingandIhavenocontrol."

His Chosen arched a blonde eyebrow. "Say that again, only this time pretend you're not eight years old."

---

*S*he had him dead to rights and felt positively devilish that his brows knitted as if he was worried and irritated at the same time. So complicated. Such an onion to peel. There just might be some entertainment in this hole in the ground after all. Perhaps getting to know this Kynd was going to have its ups.

Urick punched the wall beside him, stone puffing around his fist in stony bits. *Or downs.*

Undeterred, Violet stepped forward. She had a plan and couldn't afford to get to the point where she, too, was *starvingandnotincontrol.* Inwardly, she laughed at his expense. Outwardly, she got to within a foot of him and crouched to touch his knee.

Odd that her mirth fizzled out at the contact. She snatched her hand away, suddenly afraid that maybe the guy-beast wasn't talking out of his ass about her being created for him by God. They'd been touching all along, but her reaching out seemed to trigger something.

Black eyes flashed as he swiveled his head to look at her. *Holy shit.* Not your average predator by a long shot. Willing her hand not to shake, she touched her fingers to Urick's knee again. She couldn't afford to pull away. Time wasn't on her side.

She could do this. She could look into those intensely black eyes and act like he wasn't freaking the shit out of her. She had to if she was going to convince him to trust her so she could get her ass away from him.

"Hey, I didn't mean that."

Slowly he lowered his arm, his bleeding knuckles coated in rock dust. She felt a slight tremor in his fingers as he placed them atop hers. Gray swirled into those black eyes, the gargoyle of his chimera overpowering the vampire portion. Or mixing with it to make it infinitely stronger. Who the fuck knew.

"You okay?" Not that she cared, but she'd better act like she did.

He nodded, casting his eyes down as he gave his head one hard shake. "Yeah," he said again, glancing up. "I'm all right."

When he looked at her, it was with eyes that were almost fully gray. Black still bled into the whites of his eyes, but it was receding even as she watched. "You want to tell me why you're starving?"

He coughed a bitter laugh. "No. No, I don't."

Ookay, then. Maybe he'd talk about something that didn't tickle his hair-trigger. "How about if I share something about myself. And then, if you want, you can tell me something back."

Those expressive eyes narrowed and peered too close for comfort. She'd heard how observant the Kynd were, that they'd been God's witnesses before He'd banished them. Which meant they were canny bastards, and she'd have to tread carefully. Like landmine cautious. "Honest," she lied. "You aren't going to let me go because of who…what…I am to you, and somehow that pisses you off despite how awesome the gift of me is, so…" she shrugged. "I figure we might as well do something to break the stalemate, right?"

He tilted his head away, but she caught the barest hint of a grin.

"What d'you say? Deal?" Unsure what skin to skin contact would do, she squeezed his knee instead. When he gave a sharp nod, she took a deep breath, as much to steady her nerves as to buy some time. She needed to throw him a bone, not give him ammunition he could use against her. Plus, her reveal had to be loaded. She needed ammunition to use on him.

"Okay, so you know my name is Violet. I bet you didn't know Daniela and I are friends." Or, *were*. After what had happened in the cellar, she wasn't sure.

Aw, hell. Mr. Beastie perked up. "Daniela is my brotherkynd's Chosen One." He looked at her expectantly, as though he had five of the six winning lottery numbers.

Violet's guts migrated south. "Is that so?"

"That is so," he mocked, seeming smug that he'd scored a point in his favor.

"Fine. She's very nice." *And I can't imagine what in God's name she's doing mixed up with the likes of you and yours.* Violet pasted on a smile.

"It's your turn again." His fingers squeezed hers, and damn if the pressure didn't give her a little lift. Like it made her lighter somehow. Ignoring it, she looked over her shoulder to where water bled out of a worn crag in the wall to form a shallow pool.

"That looks inviting." Steam rose from the surface in little wisps. She wasn't lying about that, at least. She hadn't bathed since she'd been… relocated against her will. How was that for subterfuge? Pretending was a good strategy, especially if it was the means to a liberated end. And speaking of ends, the question game was a dead end—too many landmines.

His blushing cheekbones were not endearing, damn it. "Ah, yeah. I should have let you—"

"Yeah, you should have." She was going to seduce him, instead. Get him all foggy eyed, then slip out. After she kneed him in the crotch so he couldn't do anything but curl up and die. A far better plan, and one with quicker results. But she had to be real, so she couldn't play too nice. Pretending to like a grotesque's touch? She should get an Oscar if she pulled this off.

When she headed over to the little pool, he moved to block the entrance. He didn't trust her? The jerk was too smart for his own good. Not really. His smarts were keeping his balls, and her, right where he liked them. But it was time to switch that around. She was going to have the upper hand as soon as she seduced him into lowering his guard.

Arching a look over her shoulder, she watched his glittering gaze follow the path of her shirt as she drew it up over her arms and let it dangle and swing on one finger. "I can't very well bathe in my clothes, now can I?" She almost winked but caught herself.

As before, her seduction had to seem realistic. Peppering it with scathing remarks would remind him she didn't like him, but not so much she wouldn't take a desperately needed bath in front of him. Oh, and hey, sure I'm so caught up in this luxurious bath I'd love for you to touch me.

Or something like that.

Her back to him, she let her shirt drop into the dirt, then sauntered toward the steaming pool, all runway model, placing her steps suggestively in a strut meant to kick her hips out. At least, she hoped it had that effect. She might just be toddling like a penguin.

When she peered again over her shoulder, her captor's gray eyes were hooded, his skin pale in the shafts of moonlight beaming from small holes in the cave ceiling. Breath catching in her lungs, she faltered to a messy stop.

He was surprisingly beautiful as he stood watching her; not grotesque at all. His clawed fingers were spread, his wide chest heaving over narrow hips. His legs were spread as though he braced himself. She dragged her gaze down the front of him. Or to make room for the growing bulge in his black jeans?

Mission accomplished. Almost. She had his undivided attention, at least.

Preferring to ignore the switch in her opinion about his beastliness, she resumed her path to the pool. She exaggerated the unbuttoning of her pants, making a show of it so he'd know what she was doing even though she had her back to him. She could swear she felt his gaze heating her bare back. And her ass.

Without looking back at him, she hooked her thumbs in the waistband of her pants and worked the leather down her thighs. Too late she realized her boots were still laced, that her pants would get stuck mid-shin.

Not very romantic at all. God, seduction was so foreign to her, she couldn't even map out how to go about it. She wasn't a virgin, but all of her sexual interactions had been of the wham-bam-thank-you-sir variety. Her lifestyle didn't encourage intimacies. Intimacy led to questions and then answers she wasn't willing to give.

Murder was the kind of hobby you didn't share, not if you wanted to get away with it.

Still feeling the Kynd's rapt attention on her now bare ass, she willed her heart to remain steady while she sought a clever way out of this pickle. How to get him to let his guard down by using feminine wiles she didn't possess?

With her knees practically tied together by her gathered pants, she turned to face her captor. His legs were still braced, only now his arms were folded across his puffed chest, his lips quirked in an indulgent grin. Mocking her. That look on his face said he knew exactly what her predicament was.

Asshole.

Fine. She was no temptress, but she sure as shit knew how to get herself out of a jam. Raising one eyebrow in a challenge, she lowered herself to the ground, hoping to accentuate the curve of her hips as she sat down, her legs stretched out in front of her.

Bear-man's grin disappeared.

Heartened, she pushed her pants all the way down, letting the gathered leather collect at her ankles. Knees freed, she let her thighs flop open, revealing the red silk of her underwear.

His heavy arms dropped to his sides, his smugness falling with them.

Arching her pinkies like a dainty female, she loosened the laces of her boots, making sure when she leaned back up she traced the belly of her right boob with her finger. She could see him swallow from ten feet away.

When she stood back up, his eyes locked on the triangle of her panties.

"Like that, do you? Well, tough shit." As if put out, Violet spun around, putting her back to him once more. And giving him a full shot of her thonged ass, your welcome. Knowing she had him as good as a bass on a hook, she kicked off her boots and pants and stepped supermodel-like into the shallow pool, moaning and closing her eyes like she'd lowered her naked body into paradise.

There'd been no need to pretend. The water was deep and warm, surrounding her with its darkness as if she'd returned to the womb. Dunking under, she swayed her head back and forth, letting liquid fingers work through her short locks.

She forgot all about seduction as she surrendered to the pleasures of the bath. The warm water soothed her muscles, aches she hadn't realized that had gone deep into her bones. Buoyant in the water, she floated with her eyes closed, her arms outstretched.

*W*hen the female arched her back, her breasts protruded like island paradises where gentle waves lapped upon mounded beaches. Urick's cock strained to shred his zipper. Hand cupping the painful swelling, he stepped toward her, his feet shuffling as if they were still made of stone.

Kneeling at the edge of the pool, he freed his squashed staff with an absentminded dip and flick of his hand. The relief was instant, if short-lived. Now another kind of desperation assaulted him. Somehow, he needed any part of her to touch the thing stabbing out in front of him like a flagpole. Any part of her. Her hands, those creamy breasts, her mouth...

The groan oozing from his lungs was just another kind of torture and did nothing to deflate his need.

She lifted her head from the pool and splashed to the far side, as though she'd forgotten his presence, and his moan had spooked her.

His neck heating, Uri covered himself with his hands and hung his head between his slumping shoulders. In all the years he'd been held captive by vampires, he hadn't once grown hard. No matter how much blood they'd taken from his shackled body.

He had felt a feeble flicker of pride from that when all around him he'd watched the bloodsuckers grow aroused, their flesh ruling their minds, their hungers controlling them. Now here he knelt, his body rebellious of his will, his hunger for this female stark.

And blatantly obvious. As a shape-shifting chimera, nudity was simply another stage, a normal phase of the body changing from one shape to another. Among his brethren, they no more noticed bare skin than they did the fur of his grizzly or the scales of Drakus' dragon.

But here, now, in this cave with this vampire female and his never before hardened sexual organ—until he'd met her—he felt shame bore deep into his Kynd soul. Because unlike Merrick and Darken with their Chosen Ones, Urick didn't just want to physically join himself to this female. He wanted to drink of her. He wanted to sheathe his fangs in her flesh while he plunged his manhood between her welcoming thighs.

Binding himself to Violet in a way that wasn't how he'd seen his brethren bond themselves to their Chosen. Tainted as he was, Urick's urges were vile. His lusts as filthy as those of his vampire enslavers, as far from the beauty of being Kynd as he could get.

His shame lay heavy as a sodden cloak upon his back, and he couldn't move under its oppressive weight. Not until he heard the lapping of water against the rock edge of the little pool. When his Chosen's fingertips touched upon his knee, he fell back, as startled as she'd been earlier, scrambling for a safe distance while he fought with his past, his present, his future.

"No!" He shouted past his aching fangs stretched long and thin in his mouth, as sensitive as the cock he hid behind his hands. He shook his head, still unable to look at the vampire who was his Chosen One.

"Urick." Water dripped as she lifted herself from the pool and walked over to him. Crouching at his feet, she tilted his chin up so he'd look at her. "I thought you enjoyed the look of me. I still disgust you."

He felt his lids widen. "No." He could easily pull his face from her hand, but he didn't want to. For all his anguish that his Chosen One should be a creature he reviled, he craved her touch. Especially now when she reached for him voluntarily, when only a short time before she had been as disgusted with him as he'd been with her.

It seemed passion and compassion made strange bedfellows, allowing them to see the endearing qualities, where before they appeared as nothing but monsters to each other. "You do not disgust me."

This time, it was she who lowered her face, tilting it away from his searching gaze.

Like her, he pressed his fingertips to her chin, lifting it until their eyes met. "I think you are pretty."

She blushed, a hank of darkened wet blonde hair falling across her cheek. In the cave, the sound of water lapping echoed as loud as raindrops on a cottage roof. "If I said you were handsome, you would think it lip-service. Payback for your compliment."

"You think me handsome?" His grin broadened to a shy smile when she nodded. "Well, then. I've never thought of myself in that way." He didn't lie, exactly. Bound in chains and coveted for his blood, he had never considered himself attractive beyond that as a food source, a decadent cake to be gorged upon.

And left as a dirty plate afterward.

"You aren't as much of a brute as I'd first thought."

"No? I am a beast, though."

"You're chimera. It goes without saying."

He shrugged, willing to let the backhanded compliment roll off without stinging. He'd been jesting, she hadn't.

Leaning close, she licked her lips. "I would kiss you."

She smelled of the crystalline water she'd been bathing in. She smelled warm, of flesh. And of blood. He shook his head, afraid to put his mouth anywhere near her.

"Just a kiss, nothing more." Maybe that was all she wanted, but he wasn't sure that's all she'd get. His skin felt as if it had caught fire. His heart beat faster, his newly risen shaft kicked once against his stomach.

"Just a kiss," he rasped, feeling foolish. People kissed all the time. It wasn't a big deal. When Violet leaned in closer, her scent flooded his head, then curled through him as if she were the blood in his veins. It streaked down pathways like plasma trains, throbbed through tunnels of arteries. Uri panted as his nostrils flared, and still, she drew closer. He could see the pores of her pale skin, the bloom of roses on her fair cheeks.

Her breath brushed against his.

Now he felt the warmth of her skin it was so close, and she drew nearer, their noses touching. His eyelids fluttered closed, and the bump of her lips to his reminded him of bumblebees and flowers and other beautiful things. He leaned in to meet her.

The rush of something swift passed between his thighs just as the universe exploded behind his closed lids. Fast as the pop of a firecracker, his nuts blew apart and the roar he bellowed fought with the bile racing up his throat.

Thoughts sizzling like a sparkler against the night sky, he watched Violet's bare ass grow smaller as she ran through the cave toward the only exit.

---

*B*are feet slapping against the dirt, Violet raced like a greyhound, the bait she chased not a fluff of rabbit zip-lining just out of reach, but a tunnel that grew smaller and curved the farther down it she went, like one of those Thanksgiving cornucopias. Or someone's fucking colon because she sure as hell felt like excrement.

Her plan had nearly backfired. She'd been so into that damned bath, floating like a parsley flake in a bowl of soup, she'd left her urge to run laying in the pile with her leather pants.

And then that fucking near-kiss. Holy hell, talk about spacing it. When she'd seen Urick crumble under the weight of his shame, her body had moved to him before her brain realized it wasn't driving the bus. By then it was too late. She'd reached out for him, igniting that connection, the same pistons firing in her engine as when she'd reached out for him before.

Urick hadn't been kidding. Holy Jesus Christ, he hadn't been kidding about her being his whatever the hell he called those women made for the condemned Kynd…Chosen Ones. That was it. Chosen Ones. Women apparently just as doomed as the beasts who sought them. Sharing their breaths, his scent may as well have been a cast iron frying pan for how hard it had knocked into her head.

She'd practically tasted him on her tongue, an appetizer meant to tantalize her for the real meal. His blood. A mother-effing Kynd's blood she'd burned to taste, to draw down her throat as if it would be the sweetest ambrosia. Her fangs had grown long in her mouth, her breaths even now rasping back and forth across them as she chugged like a locomotive.

"Violet!" The roar hit her like a blast of scorching air. If she hadn't been bent over already, it would have flung her to her knees. Oh, wait. Fuck. She was on her knees!

"Oh, Jesus, Jesus." He'd recovered too quickly. Panicked, she patted the dirt floor like she'd lost an earring or some shit. "Get on your fucking feet!"

What in hell was wrong with her? *Run!* She'd just assaulted a beast known for its violent destruction, its penchant for blood and ruin.

A brute so base he was going to rip her arms and legs off while smearing her blood all over himself. Chimeras did that. She'd grown up hearing the horrific tales from the old ones, who'd heard it from the older ones and so on and so on through the ages.

Legs as uncoordinated as a newborn fawn's, she teetered upright just in time for an arm with the tensile strength of a tree limb in a hurricane wind to whip around her waist. "You are mine, Chosen," hell itself snarled into her ear.

Violet screamed.

# CHAPTER 2

*D*riving a car was pretty much the same as one of those modern day games of Twister, a feat in the physical that couldn't possibly be possible. Put your right foot here, your left hand there and now your left foot there while placing your right hand on someone's stick.

"Kallen, the road!"

Yanking the wheel counterclockwise, Kallen juuust missed crunching the nose of the truck into a snowbank. "Oh, man, Darken would have my favorite sweater if I bent his Ram." Laughing hard enough to throw his head back, he caught Kronos braced off in the passenger seat, shaking his. "Aw, come on. You know how he loves pink cashmere."

Kronos managed to crack his lips into what for him was the Grand Canyon of a happy face. Any more and the guy might actually smooth out some of the wrinkles in his stern puss.

Pushing harder on the accelerator, Kallen fishtailed the truck on the icy road, slopping his hands all over the wheel like the ring was greased, pretending he had the comedic coordination of Buster Keaton. "Whoa, whoa, whoa. Hold on, bro!"

"Would you cut that out? Darken really will be pissed if he finds out we took his truck, let alone had an accident with it."

"Wow, Kronos. I think that's the most you've said in like…the past thousand years. Way to heal thyself, brother."

"Shut the fuck up." But the Grand Canyon stretched again, easing the shadows of the crags etched in Kronos' face. Man, but it felt awesome to see

23

it. And viewing that reluctant if tiny grin made all of Kallen's antics so worth it. Hey, sometimes even he laughed at himself.

The mask of humor sometimes inverted to heal the healer, and Kallen loved those rare moments even if they did scare the piss out of him. They were a double-edged sword. They eased the ravages of the isolation forced upon him for those oceans of centuries, but they reminded him of that terrible loneliness at the same time. Besides, if he got better, maybe his humor would abandon him, and he wouldn't be able to help his brethren anymore.

A possibility that did more than scare him; it paralyzed him.

"Tell me again why you think asking Kristov for help is a good idea." By now he'd taken control of the wheel for real and nosed the borrowed truck down a thin, dark, icy drive.

"He offered."

Kallen smirked at the short answer. "Fine. But just because he's one of the Vampyres of the ruling Triumvirate, it doesn't mean we should trust him."

Kronos shrugged. Yeah, that was the gargoyle Kallen knew and tried to exorcise from his beloved brotherkynd. Being short with his answers kept Kronos' mouth shut, ergo endless shrieks from spewing out. And by endless, he meant endless. It was a fucking miracle the man wasn't just forming words, but actually responding coherently.

Five months before, Kronos would spread his cracked lips and screams would blast forth. Screams it took hours for them to shush unless those shrieks triggered their own scars and all hell broke loose. Five Kynd going ape-shit with their own horrors. So…lovely.

"What does he want in return?" He could see the glow of lights ahead, a muted halo resting atop the dark spruce forest in the distance.

"Nothing, Darken says. Just companionship."

Okay, he could believe that. Just before Uri pulled his disappearing act, Darken had answered Kristov's summons. A summons given in the name of helping a fellow vampire, aka their brotherkynd Urick. Who was starving himself to death because he refused to feed, denying the vampire third of his chimera as if he could kill it without killing himself.

"Companionship? Sounds fishy." He turned to his passenger and waggled his eyebrows. "See, the way I see it, is why would an ancient Vampyre—a leader of all the vampires, no less—want to hang out with us? I mean, come on, we're not exactly BFF material."

"Darken said he has his reasons."

"Well, Darken should be here for this meeting." Eyes front and center on the road, he still caught his brotherkynd's grimace. "Fine. He needs to lick his wounds. But, I still don't understand how he could just let his Chosen One go. I mean, come on! That Daniela is one fine..." The words *piece of ass* evaporated on his tongue like cotton candy. Like all of his brethren, he worshiped the females who were their salvation. Not his specifically, but his Chosen One was out there somewhere.

And fine, Kallen would let his go, too, if that's what she wanted. Because those women were sacred, and he and his brethren would give them every fish in the sea if they asked for it. Disrespecting them just wasn't in their DNA.

"He is hoping that by letting her go, she will come back to him."

"Yeah? Well, that's shitty logic. Have you seen the guy lately?"

Taking him literally, Kronos said, "I have. He was talking to Angelia about some meeting with the Others."

Kallen almost veered off the road. "What? He has lost his mind. The Others want only one thing from us. To see our stony asses stuck forever on a building in some place like Siberia. Darken's wasting his time."

"Most likely." Folding his arms, Kronos crunched down in his seat to stare out into the darkness.

"Yeah, most likely." As silence filled the cab, Kallen thought about how Darken and the rest of them had gone nuts when he'd had to tell them Uri had found his Chosen One—a Chosen who had turned out to be a vampire —but had teleported her to God only knew where. When dawn arrived with no Uri, fear had blown into the safe house like an arctic wind.

The Others weren't to be trusted, and Uri's Chosen One could have hurt him, or worse.

They were all still shell-shocked by Uri's absence. Hence this meeting with Kristov, leader of the Others, vampires included. With the Chosen One being vampire, maybe Kristov would know who she was and any other personal information they could use to hunt her down.

As Kallen's thoughts ran along the lines of figuring out ways to torture information from a Chosen he couldn't hurt, their destination loomed ahead about a tenth of a mile down a drive that had turned to flagstone. He leaned into the windshield to gawk, taking in everything about the huge estate.

The home was one of those federal style brick things, complete with a hundred small windows and the front door smack dab in the center. Real creative and about as staid as Kristov. The only time Kallen had ever seen the Vampyre's dander up was when the Kynd had first gathered together to answer Darken's call to help Merrick. They'd reunited in Anton's home—the second leg of the Vampyre Triumvirate, who now happened to be Merrick's father-in-law—after two thousand years of being apart.

Anyway. When the Kynd had shown up, they were all wrapped looser than a kitten's ball of yarn. Crazed and disoriented, they'd almost had a bloodbath when the third and biggest asshat of the Triumvirate got up in Darken's grille. Kristov had been Robin to Godrick's Batman. Anton had wound up being the one who stalled the near-disaster and now look at them all. Making friends.

If he and Kronos could get their asses into the house. Sure, they'd stolen Darken's truck with the intention of helping Uri. But now they sat staring out the windshield, stalled out by the fear that if they managed to get inside, one of them could lose his shit over the least little thing. Somehow, smashing the furniture of the guy who wanted to help you with a problem seemed…gauche.

And a tad unforgivable. Given their circumstances, they actually, really couldn't afford that. Fuck a duck. He glanced over at the other half of this dynamic duo. "Suddenly, my ass feels heavier than a tractor tire. Got a pry bar, Kron?"

"Yeah, but I can't move my arms to use it."

Laughter burst out of Kallen so hard it shifted him out of the rut he was sitting in, and he used the momentum to push himself out the truck door. "That should have been my line, you serious fuck." He walked around the hood and opened the passenger side door. "Come on. We're going to be fine." *I hope.* Keeping hold of the giggles like popcorn to see him through a scary movie, Kallen pasted on a brave face for his brotherkynd as he led them like Sacagawea up the curved—and wouldn't you know—brick walkway.

Their first official trip out of the safe house to visit someone and they were both skittish as teenage girls approaching a haunted house. Resisting the urge to hold his brotherkynd's hand, Kallen pressed his finger to the glowing button at the side of the front door.

The slab of welcome yawned wide, the man of the hour standing on the threshold, a silk smoking jacket custom fit to his impeccable frame. "Kallen, Kronos, so good of you to come." The Vampyre beckoned for them to come in with a wide sweep of his arm.

"Kristov." Kallen stepped inside with a silent Kronos on his heels, who gave their host a sharp nod, but otherwise kept himself at Kallen's elbow. A place of refuge. Not too far away should the gargoyle need a stabilizing touch.

As though recognizing their need to stay close, Kristov escorted them to a formal sitting room and gestured to the sofa, not the pair of chairs arranged across from it. "Have a seat and I'll get us drinks." He came back with crystal tumblers with a few inches of Perrier in the bottom and a glass of red wine for himself.

The guy had a knack for hospitality, he'd give him that. Still cursed with turning to stone every dawn, neither he nor Kronos ate or drank anything. Kristov's offering of a beverage was nothing more than a symbolic gesture of goodwill.

Sitting himself in the brocade chair across from their settee, the Vampyre leader got right to it. "I understand Urick has yet to return." The lamps in the room cast a warm, yellow light on the furnishings, most of which were rose in hue, or softer, feminine colors. Little touches which made for a welcoming environment despite the sitting room's formal designation.

The only thing marring the feel of nestling into a woman's bosom was the heavy oak bar. A beard hair in a chardonnay spritzer. Kallen wrangled his attention off the décor and back onto his host. A bachelor as far as he knew, but the house said otherwise. He tugged the corner of a silk throw pillow out from under his left butt cheek, at the last minute adjusting it under his right arm rather than wedging it between himself and Kronos, who didn't seem to notice that his leg had fallen open so their knees touched.

Kallen didn't move away, but laid his big hand on his brotherkynd's lower thigh, silently challenging the Vampyre to make some faggot comment. When Kristov didn't even flick a glimpse, he said, "No, he hasn't come back and it's been almost two weeks."

Eyebrows practically kissing each other with his frown, Kristov asked, "He has been fighting the vampire part of himself, yes? Does he know what that part will expect to do with a mate?"

"You mean like a vampire mate, not a Chosen One?"

Kristov nodded. "As far as I know, Merrick never claimed Angelia in the way of vampires."

Well, duh. Even though Angelia had been raised by vampires, she was human and Merrick was Kynd, so he wouldn't... "Oh, shit." Kronos fell utterly still beside him as if his brotherkynd could read his thoughts. "Look, with all due respect, Uri can't stand you guys. Vampires? You're pretty low on his list of likes, feel me? And if he's going to do something really strange— something only vampires do—then he's going to lose it. He already feels like he's not one of us, so if he's going to have the urge to...," he finger-quoted *mate*, "...like one of you, then shit's going to get downright nasty."

They shared looks back and forth along the lines of '*So now what the fuck do we do?*'

Kristov fell back in his chair, studying the contents of his wine glass as if the answers were swimming in the grapes. Out in the foyer, a grandfather clock chimed a pretty rendition of the Westminster Quarters, and Kallen relaxed as the tones washed over them.

Exactly fifteen minutes later, on the first quarter bells, Kristov's voice floated to him. "We know of the woman who is your brotherkynd's Chosen One. She has no family, I'm sad to say. No way to really trace her. She kept to herself, rarely interacting with her kind at all."

So much for feeling relaxed. Kallen straightened up. "And you know this, how?"

"Godrick, Anton, and myself made discreet enquiries. On your behalf, of course." Kristov sat forward. Hands steady, he set his goblet down on the low table between them with a scraping clink. The bastard knew he and the Triumvirate were skating close to yanking the leashes they had on the Kynd —a dangerous maneuver given what was on the collar end of those ropes.

"She has an apartment in Portland, but no one in the building knows her. Most aren't up when she is."

Of course, the humans wouldn't be. Night for them meant beddie-bye time. "Did they know if she worked anywhere? Had any friends?"

"Nothing. It's as if she lived off the radar as much as she could in this day and age. Her only acquaintances were people she ran into at Maine Medical Center."

Humans like Darken's Daniela. "Well, isn't this delicious. Uri's female is a ghost who feeds on sick kids." Kallen fell back on a sigh. "Brilliant."

"We did take the liberty of looking through her apartment."

"And?"

"She's got enough weapons to make a drug lord look like a kindergarten teacher. Hand to hand stuff mostly, a few guns, that sort of thing."

"Christ almighty, whatever for?"

"Godrick thought she hunted. There was blood on some of the clothes in her hamper."

Well, that got their attention. Kronos even joined in the conversation, his muscles drawing up tight. "What kind of blood?"

Kristov ignored the gargoyle's ramping temper. "It wasn't human if that's what you're wondering."

"So what, deer? Pheasant?" *Please don't let it be—*

"Other."

"Jesus fucking Christ."

"Just so." Was that a smirk on the Vampyre's lips?

Whatever. There were more important things to clog his brain with. Like, if this female couldn't kill Uri, she could sure as shit fuck him up—their greatest fear looming as a definite. Kallen's grip on Kronos' thigh dug in deep as his muscles locked down on his bones. At the same time, his lungs decided it was a good time to take a vacay, which was just as well. Puffing for a scrap of control would prove he wasn't, in fact, in control.

Like he'd done about five hundred times already tonight, he stole a look sideways at Kronos. The poor fuck sat so rigid he could have been stone even though dawn was still a few hours away. God, one of them was going to lose it. Proving to their keepers the leashes were necessary. Fuck. Fuck, fuck, fuck.

Remind him again why he thought this visit had been a bright idea.

Surprising the shit out of him, Kristov acted like a butler tuned to every nuance of his patron. He rose and stuck his fingers into the glasses on the low table between them, lifting them as he straightened. "I'll get you a refill from the kitchen."

Like he knew he and Kronos needed the space. "Yeah. Yeah, that'd be good." Kallen glanced up, surprised to see a spark of warmth in the otherwise flat eyes of their host. As if the guy knew what it was like to be gripped by a fear so great your adrenal glands started working like a blender without a lid.

He. Could. Not. Lose. It. Kronos needed him to be an anchor, and he really wanted to be that anchor. "Hug me like you mean it, man."

Kronos gripped him without an R.S.V.P., his brotherkynd's weight counterbalancing the impulse to strike out, to hurt something as bad as they were hurting. They sat on the sofa, pulled so close together Kimberly-Clark couldn't wedge a piece of paper between them.

Kristov eased back into the room discreet as Jeeves as they were peeling themselves off each other. "You guys good? Sorry I had to drop a bomb like that."

"Yeah, well." Standing up, Kallen scraped both palms across his scalp. Kronos, though, was way too quiet. "Listen, man. We're…ah…going to go, all right." Gripping Kronos' elbow, he didn't wait for the good-bye escort to the door.

Of course, once they were in the truck, his hands started shaking so god-awful he couldn't turn the key. He sat there staring out at nothing while he figured out how to get them home without having to call for a rescue from his family back at the safe house. He and Kronos were trying to take a step forward into…who the fuck knew…healthy living or some shit. The last thing he wanted to do was phone in an SOS.

"I don't know about you, but did you think Kristov went a little heavy on the pink?"

Jaw locked, Kronos grazed him with a *you can't be serious* look. Then he smiled. So tight his lips looked like wax strips. If he laughed he'd most likely scream instead, but that was all Kallen needed.

It was all they both needed.

As the Dodge Ram roared to life, Kallen draped his arm over the seat to back the truck around and stretched his fingers to touch his brotherkynd's shoulder. His fingertips barely brushed the male's coat, but the gesture carried the weight of a lifeline.

---

*F*ive days and Urick's fury still pulsated long after the pain in his nuts had disappeared. Of course, adding to the give-you-the-shits combo was a dash of resentment, a pinch of hatred, and oh, yeah. Bile. He wanted to puke his guts out because he felt guilty.

Guilty, of all frigging things. Like he'd been the deceitful one. Leave it to a rotting bloodsucker to be so cunning. To get him to let his guard down, to try putting his past behind him for the female who was supposedly made for him by God.

Well, if the past two thousand years of torture had meant anything, then sure as shit she was the perfect match. What were two thousand more years of misery? He'd wind up as whacked as Drakus, but what the hell. Hats off to God, he had his Chosen One. Who was currently crouched in her corner, pale as the underbelly of a carp.

Looking at her, Uri's guilt spiked, pissing him off. Yet again. He couldn't look at her without tapping out his altimeter, his anger blasting skyward like Chuck Yeager worked the controls.

But she was starving to death under his care. Not to mention rumpled. She still wore the same clothes he'd kidnapped her in, and hadn't bathed since the night she'd made her best bid for freedom.

She had almost made it, the treacherous leech. She'd had him so caught up in her, so hungry for that connection buzzing in his blood. All he had to do was taste her, to feel her bare skin upon his. To open himself to the sensation of her reaching for him.

So fucking desperate to be normal once again, he'd forgotten his past and thought maybe, just maybe, this one vampire would be different from all the rest. After the comet blast behind his eyes subsided, he had been kind of surprised she hadn't gone for the whole shebang and sucked down a good gutful of his blood before she'd hightailed it. God knew, pun intended thank you very much, other vampires had had their share of it.

The guilt engulfed him, though, because she needed it. Every day that passed she grew more and more ashen as if she lost blood because she didn't drink it. Just the day before he'd caught her absently rubbing her wrist under her chin as if the smell of her own blood had become alluring.

He'd been so transfixed by the sight of it, he'd felt as if his muscles were prying themselves off his bones so they could get him closer. To lay himself wide open for her taking. To feed her, to give her life.

Even now, after what she'd done to him, he wanted to.

*She's yours to take care of.* And wasn't he doing a wonderful job? She might be long-lived, but she could starve to death. His Chosen One would die and it would be his fault.

He could release her. Hell, he should let her go. Keeping her against her will meant he was no better than those who'd held him captive for all those years.

Oooor…he could feed her. Even if he could control his shakes at the mere thought of it, he highly doubted she would take of his vein. His relief, of course, got trampled under his guilt. He should lay his well-earned fears aside for her sake. Ignore the screaming of his soul when her little fangs punctured his skin.

As if he'd backed his bare ass up to an electric fence, he started to twitch, his memories of biting pain in his skin cranking up his heart rate. Chained to a stone slab, he hadn't been able to move as the vampires hovered over him, crawling and lapping like snakes. So many snakes sliding and writhing and biting…

With a yell, he bolted to his feet, slapping at himself as if to fend off the horrors stuck to his skin. Across the way, Violet lifted her head and watched. Ashamed, he turned his back, although his nape burned red hot, and she could see it.

Despite her growing weakness, she eyed him with a calculation a cat would envy.

"You take pleasure in my tortures, leech?" He turned just enough to see her over his shoulder. She remained in her corner, her mien quiet. Not lethargic, but conservative.

"As you take pleasure in mine." That her response would be without sharpness tweaked his heart hard enough he scraped his palm over his left pec. She grew so weak.

*I will feed her.* He didn't need to see the bruises under her eyes to make up his mind. She was his to care for. No matter the cost to himself. No matter that she would use her newfound strength to escape him.

With his knee joints as loose as a ball of worms, he approached her, halting the instant she lifted her chin to glare at him. "What do you think you're doing?"

When he opened his mouth, nothing came out of it.

She didn't waste her energy to lift an insulting eyebrow but sat at his feet waiting for him to say something.

Or, she was contriving ways to kill him. The look she was giving him could mean either.

"I…" The rest of his words clogged in his throat, the blockage strangling him.

---

"*Y*ou what? Want to let me go?" Violet conserved her energy, raising only her chin to get a gander at the fidiot standing before her like some kid with the stutters who needed to ask his teacher for a bathroom pass. In front of the entire class.

Jaw locked so tight the muscles bulged out past his ears, he shook his head. Then opened his mouth to say…absolutely nothing again. His ears flamed bright red as if his frustration was incendiary.

If things had been different between them, she might've felt sorry for the guy. Yeah, she had a heart's load of compassion always threatening to swamp her boat, but she spread it with an indulgence that leveled her out. Giving of herself to those sick kids made her think she was making up for the vampires who only took. Her way of giving back, of dispelling some of the evil of her kind.

Watching the male in front of her, she shifted her traitorous body, like her engine moved to comfort him whether her brain thought it a good plan or not. Bless her heart, the damned thing actually panged as she watched the beast struggle.

"What?" She ground her ass cheeks into the floor of the cave, reminding them to stay put.

"I…I would…you need…"

She'd laugh at him if he wasn't so pathetically brave. Damn him. Damn the Lord, too, for saddling her with a monster who tugged her—pun intended—God damned heart strings. Hello! She was the one starving here! She was the one taken against her will and forced underground.

She was hungry, filthy. Yet, she didn't just look at her captor. She saw him.

He was hungry and as filthy as she was. He hadn't eaten or bathed since her capture either, and he'd confessed from the beginning his hunger had him teetering on the brink of control.

Not that she'd know by looking at him. The male was still strong.

In everything but this…whatever he was trying to do right then.

"You would, what?" When he stuck his bare arm out, her gaze dropped to the vein roping the inside of that tree trunk. Before she could stop it, her tongue slipped along her bottom lip. "It's not enough to hold me captive, now you taunt me?" She sat up on her knees.

"No, no taunting." He thrust his arm forward again.

"I'd believe you if you didn't look like you'd rather rip my head off. So, no thanks. I'm good." She wriggled back into her corner away from him. Just as she got settled, he deflated as if the weight of his relief was too much to bear.

Though the look in his eyes said something altogether different. He'd been serious?

"Please, my…Violet. Take of me." He raised his forearm to his mouth, the bulk obscuring most of his face. But those eyes! Flat slate but for a few erratic heartbeats when they plunged like swirling mercury, revealing an anguish he quickly hid behind the wall of his gray stare.

A tendril of blood coursed downward to his elbow.

"What are you doing?" The viscous trail of blood attracted her attention like a train wreck, the smell of it as loud as screeching metal.

Once again, he lay his arm open for her. "Take of me." When he looked upon her, his eyes were black as obsidian. The vampire third of his chimera awake and at the forefront—from the smell and taste of his own blood.

*I'mstarvingandIhavenocontrol.* Yet, he was offering to feed her? "I think you need it more than I do. Suck on yourself." The last thing she needed was for him to get worse. That he still seemed so damned strong was proof positive the Kynd should be as feared and reviled as they'd been centuries before.

He fell to his knees, his arm still spread in front of him like a banquet.

Feared and hated? Urick, blast him, looked anything but. His hair tousled and his body shaking with a low tremble, he seemed vulnerable. As though his offer lashed him with a thousand whips. Or brought up horrific memories.

Violet eyed him closer. When her gaze dragged across the length of him and stopped at his face, their gazes stuck onto each other like Velcro straps. She couldn't glance away. Apparently, neither could he.

"Take me," he rasped again. A bead of blood pooled at his elbow, bulbous and heavy and ready to drop. To be wasted when they both were starving? It was like letting pallets of rice rot, while the refugees looked on from behind barbed wire fences. A frigging travesty.

"O-only if you stay still."

His lids slid shut and he squeezed them as if her words pained him. His free hand gripped the growing bulge in his pants. *Oh, shit.* She knew what this was. With his vampire in the driver's seat, this offer of blood meant more than sustenance.

It was a male giving all of himself to his mate. As if that wasn't bad enough, this was a Kynd offering sustenance to his Chosen One. What were the ramifications of that?

The bead of blood grew pregnant; heavy and ponderous as its neck thinned, thinned…then snapped. She caught the free-falling droplet midair, her body twisting at an uncomfortable angle.

The bead upon her tongue hit like dry ice, the burn spreading outward and seeping into her flesh, her taste buds tingling to life as if they frantically stretched for more of this promise. A promise of strength that even now oozed through her, one droplet of this Kynd's blood, as though the Grotesques were fueled by high octane.

No wonder they were so powerful, so out of control. If this was swimming through her veins, she could do anything. She could save every sick child, she could slay every vampire who flaunted the rules—those who perpetuated the myths that all vampires were cruel, bloodsucking parasites.

With her thoughts flying the invisible jet of her Wonder Woman airplane, her body reacted. Greedy for more of this elixir, she dragged her tongue along Urick's forearm as her hands lashed out to grab hold. She swallowed around a moan, her fingertips gripping harder as more of his strength passed into her.

Eyes closed, she opened her jaw as her fangs grew long, ready to pierce the vein she'd followed the blood trail to find. Just as the needle-sharp points pressed to his skin, she glanced up from his inner wrist. The reality of what she was about to do punched her in the gut, as though opening her eyes awakened her conscience.

She was rubbing her pelvis along his thigh, her body supremely and instinctively seeking its...shit. Like him, she hungered for her mate. Not just the blood she could take from any male, but Urick's specifically. Her captor. Her tormentor.

Though now that she arrested the flush of this feeding, she saw that he seemed far more tormented that she'd ever been. Yeah, she'd been his prisoner, but this anguish altered his features on a level that reminded her of what he was. Chimera. A beast of three. And all three had exploded to the fore. Black eyes and a vampire's fangs, the bulging muscles of the gargoyle, and the claws of a grizzly. Claws he raked across the wall of the cave while he held the other arm still, the arm she still clutched.

Face thrown ceiling-ward as if in agony, even as his hips rocked in a timeless and obvious rhythm, he gritted out, "Take."

He wanted her to have his blood even at such a cost? What the hell? He was fighting himself with everything he had and was barely winning. He wanted to mate with her as her kind did, but wouldn't. This was fucked up. She felt like one of the vampires she killed for stealing blood that wasn't theirs to take. She felt like the transgressor, not the other way around.

Stupid compassion. Her Achilles heel.

Releasing his arm, she leaned back. "No."

He rolled his chin downward to look upon her, his anguish stark in those black eyes. "Please," he rasped, his fangs prominent, "take of me."

She shook her head. "Why? When this isn't what you want."

"Not right."

Not right that he suffered, or not right that she wouldn't accept his offer?

"Drink of my blood, and know me. Feel me." Though it seemed to kill him to say it. "Protect you," he pushed out, his breaths heavy. "When I'm near, you will know." Another labored breath. "And you can run."

What?

He thrust his wrist at her mouth, but she didn't miss that with his other razor clawed hand, he crushed the huge bulge between his legs. "Do it!"

Without thinking, she broke his skin, his hot blood gushing into her sucking mouth.

Again, her body responded as though it knew this male to be her mate. Below the filling heat of her stomach, her womb twisted, coiling tight to wring her deep, to make her clit throb with need. Her legs scissored to ease the sensation as her pelvis rocked, seeking relief.

Oh, God, the blood. The smell. Of him, whom she held in her tightening grasp. She wanted him. Needed him. *Touch me*, she begged inwardly, as she wriggled her body against the sheer bulk of his. Craving his touch, his submission, his dominance.

---

*A*gainst all expectation, Uri gloried in the carnal press of their bodies, the tug of her little fangs under his skin. His cock kicked in time to her gulps, throbbing for release. He pressed the heel of his hand against the painful bulge to assuage the need, but it maddened him more. Giving up, he sought soft skin and closed his fingers around Violet's hand.

A hand she'd been running up and down his shoulder as if she petted him while she took of him. *I like that.* A quick thought, popped like a bubble as his hunger grew more earnest. He pushed her hand between his legs as he rolled his hips, urging her with his body as though he could no longer think, just act.

She didn't need a translation. His relief flowed through him as she released the button of his jeans, the singing of his zipper a joy to praise to Heaven. As she shoved her palm along his tight sac, he knew Heaven had come to him. Moaning, he curled around her body, pushing his face against the softness of her neck.

His heart thumped maddeningly against his breast bone as he licked her pulse then bit, puncturing skin, releasing her life force. She tasted like nothing he'd ever known. The flavor of her doing more than dance upon his tongue. It careened itself through his bloodstream. It coiled itself throughout him, encapsulating his very soul. It was like a shroud of warm silk wrapping around him.

Binding to him.

*Not how it was supposed to be!*

With a roar, he ripped his fangs from her flesh, the sudden thunderstorm of his mood awakening her. She blinked as though only now realizing what she'd been doing, her hand clasping to her neck. With a look of horror fast dawning upon her pretty face, she released him to scramble backward out of harm's way.

"Run!" he roared again, the pain at physically hurting her swamping him. "For the love of God, my Chosen, *run!*"

Shocked, and clamoring farther away, she managed to wrangle her limbs into awkward control, forcing her feet to do as he said even as they slapped around like frightened rabbits, her arms flailing like the heart he heard thumping fast in her chest.

But she did run. As fast as her petrified self could go. She ran for the only entrance, seemingly confused but running still. Out into the night, where a navy sky awaited her, vast and brilliant with a billion stars. So limitless, a body could lose itself. For better or for worse.

*Better this way.* Uri slumped to the earthen floor. He had released his Chosen One as he had never been. To free himself, he had had to rip the flesh down to his bones to escape. Violet, on the other hand, was nourished and stronger and out of this cave. With enough time and fed as well as she was, she could dematerialize to her safe and comfortable home.

Groaning with regret, he rolled to his back, draping the arm with twin, tiny punctures over his eyes. It would not be long before he learned where her home was. He had sought to sever her from himself, from this God-decreed hell of being bound to a ruined creature.

Now? He had tasted of her blood as she had of his. She would not only know when he neared, he would sense her, too. And as he well knew, there was no freedom in the fear that those who'd fed upon you could easily find you through the essence of your blood.

Just as his Chosen would fear he would come for her again.

Yet, even now with her gone, he could feel her hands upon him. Hands small and strong, he'd felt their latent power as her palm had caressed him. She'd wanted him. As he had wanted her.

As he still did. The hole in him yawned wider and deeper, growing into a pit of despair he curled his body around. Cheek in the dirt, he let his tears fall. Viscous, they traced a snail trail across the bridge of his nose, a red aura in his vision. Blood tears. The tears of the bloodsucker he now was. His gargoyle and grizzly hovered comfortably close, never absent.

*Never absent.* Uri's breath hitched, and he fell still to let the truth sidle through him, to allow his soul to pick up on the vibrations of his Kynd self. Contained, quieted. Allowing him to feel another vibration. One like he'd felt several months before in this same cave when he'd despaired.

The call of a brotherkynd, Kallen. He recognized the waves unique to the gargoyle, as he had identified Darken's those many months ago. A giddy twinge rooted in his heart. Though he lay now as a rejected vampire, his Kyndness was close, as were his brotherkynd. They called for him, needed him now just as they had before they'd learned of his hungers.

Such comfort when only moments before he'd thought himself lost. Sitting up, Uri's muscles moved fluidly, his thoughts clear. He was stronger. Not much, but there was a difference in how his body moved.

His Chosen's blood had done this to him. Just a sip, yet he felt different.

How different would Violet feel with his blood coursing through her veins? She had taken so much more, as he'd wanted her to. But would it affect her as it had his captors? Would she act the craven vampire as he'd seen happen so many other times?

Skin prickling with sweat, Uri vaulted to his feet. He'd seen vampires do horrific things when drunk on his Kynd blood. By feeding Violet and letting her go, had he unleashed a monster?

Onto those sick kids sleeping in their tidy hospital beds? Innocent. Vulnerable. She had fed on them before, what would she do to them now that she had Kynd blood amping her vampire nature?

Holy God, what had he done?

Comfort and need forgotten along with the vibrations of Kallen's call, Uri raced from the cave, his body attuned to the path of his Chosen.

# CHAPTER 3

"*H*e's not answering." Kallen strode into the library and let his ass fall onto the sofa, wedging himself between Darken and Kronos. Huge males, they were squished together, their thick shoulders bunched up, their thighs sticking out big as logs.

Nobody bitched, though. They needed the proximity, especially at a time like this when there was more torment than usual. Kallen leaned a little left, his weight falling more onto Darken.

God knew the guy could use the extra comfort. Dickweed beside him had let his Chosen One go because he didn't want her around the violence of their uncontrolled outbursts. Couldn't say he blamed him, but Daniela was still coming around. Skewing Darken's logic, but hey, you couldn't say the male wasn't giving her every chance to run away. The asshat.

"What do you mean he's not answering?" Angelia, Merrick's beautiful blonde Chosen, sat up straighter. Which put her closer to the edge of the desk she was perched on. Merrick stiffened too, his hands all up and be careful as if she might fall off and hurt herself.

Totally amused at how pathetic a Chosen One could make her Kynd, Kallen answered her. "What I said. I sent out the vibe, but he didn't respond. It's like he fell off the grid."

Drakus, from his usual spot on the window sill with the sheet of plywood behind him instead of the glass, whined as he curled around his folded arms. The poor bastard wasn't having a good night. He hadn't been having good days either since learning Uri had gone AWOL, so sharing what Kristov had told him was going to sink the guy's battleship.

Shit. How in hell did you put a funny spin on the fact that Urick's Chosen One killed Others? Or, to be more frank, Others like their brotherkynd Uri.

"He's probably too weak to hear it."

"Oh, you think."

Merrick growled. "Start something. Go ahead." As he went all Mike Tyson and rounded the desk, he put his bulk in front of Angelia, protecting her. Even though his wings had been shorn off in Hell, the chimera wasn't defenseless. "Angel, you're going to want to leave now." The black mane of his lion sprouted down the sides of his neck, proving he had other toys in his arsenal besides his wings.

Angelia hopped off the desk and shoved him to the side. "Oh, for Pete's sake, you two. Chill out. You're upset, we get it. But fighting isn't going to bring Uri back."

"No, but the way Merrick fights would feel like dancing. And that always makes me feel better."

Angelia pursed her lips to squash her smile. "Kallen, seriously?"

"Yeah. Your mate fights like Tinkerbell, all sproingy and shit."

"Sproingy and shit." Merrick planted his fists on his hips.

"Like you're doing now. Going all Queen Latifah."

"Queen La-Whofa?"

"Brother, you need to get out more. See more of the twenty-first century."

Beside him, Kronos yipped out the start of a laugh, then locked his jaw around it. Big hand covering his mouth, he squirmed deeper into the couch cushions. Every gray eye in the room and Angelia's blue ones riveted on the gargoyle. Every face shared the same miniscule smile, the tilt at the corner of their mouths. Like they looked at puppies playing or something.

Much better. That's what he liked to see on his family's faces. He was about to slash the Norman Rockwell painting with the news from Kristov, but it wasn't as if that was new. Seemed any sunshine they found, God backed his ass up to it and shit all over it.

So, without further ado... "Kristov told me and Kronos the Chosen's name is Violet."

That got everyone's attention. "She's a hunter. And wait for the drumroll. She hunts us."

Drakus' dragon wings exploded from his back, pushing so hard against the plywood the force flung him to the floor. Which of course just gave his wings more room to spread, as if they needed runway clearance. The wind blew papers off the desk. Knuckles and knees grinding into the hardwood flooring, he didn't lift his head as he stammered out, "S-sorry."

Kallen's troika on the couch kept their butts planted on the seat cushions. Any extra activity could set the dragon off more, so they were happy to sit like puppets. All stationary like they had hands up their asses.

"Drakus, love." Angelia went to him while Merrick fretted behind her, the word *Careful* written all over him. Of course, he'd learned not to say it out loud. Angelia would scald him with a look, and the male's nuts would shrivel. There was no getting between Angelia and her connection to the Kynd, at least, not while things were still salvageable.

"Glad I didn't replace that window yet," Darken said behind his fist. Since he'd put his Chosen's needs above his own, he'd been playing Home Improvement, complete with the bloody mishaps. Good thing the Kynd were fast healers. The only thing missing was the laugh track.

"The house looks great by the way." Merrick changed the subject because an audience was the last thing you needed when you were trying to screw your head on right.

"Thanks. You'd have thought figuring out sheetrock mud needed several layers and to dry in-between was astrophysics or something."

"Worth it." A comment from the Peanut Gallery.

"Glad you like it, Kron. Check this out." They heaved themselves off the sofa to fawn over Darken's handiwork with the library shelving.

"I didn't even notice when I came in. When did you fix this?"

"A couple of days ago. It took me ages to match the varnish. But there's this old man at Home Depot who…" And away they went. Every frigging one of them thrilled to be acting normal, even if one of their loved ones was trying not to lose it behind them. By the time Darken finished explaining the math behind the angle cuts he'd made on some of the boards, Angelia was giggling about something Drakus said.

Good. Good. The dragon chimera had reeled himself back in. A first. Though no one congratulated him. Sometimes you just needed to be ignored. A molehill made out of a mountain.

"So, anyways," Kallen sat himself back on the center cushion of the leather sofa just as Kronos and Darken flanked him like before. "The mighty Triumvirate—no offense, Angelia—went to Violet's apartment. They found some of her clothes with Other blood on it. Hence their deduction about her hunting."

"But they didn't find Kynd blood, right?" With Darken sitting so close, Kallen had to dip his head to talk to him or they'd kiss noses.

"Well, no."

"So, why do you think she'd harm Uri?"

"Can you say *logical conclusion?*"

"Smart ass."

"Darken's right, though." Blondie moved away from Drakus to hitch her hip to Merrick's shoulder. He'd returned to his chair behind the desk, and if she wore steeper heels, she could sit on his shoulder like a parrot.

"How so?" A guttural question from Drakus, but hallelujah! A frigging lucid one.

"There was no Kynd blood, and we all know Chosen One's have a special connection to their particular Kynd." Beside him, Darken groaned and slid deeper into the cushions like he'd lost his bones.

"Sorry, Darken, but it's true." Angelia gave him her best *I'm sorry* face. Which would melt the ice off cream and make it all soft and gooey. Kind of like the gargoyle looked right then.

"He's safe?" Kronos asked, but they all looked to Angelia as if she were their guiding star.

Unable to lie, she squirmed, attaching herself tighter to Merrick, who wrapped an arm around her hips and tugged her closer. Protective, he took charge. "He'll be all right. We'll go to Kristov's tomorrow night, and get the Chosen's address then search her apartment. We'll see things the Vampyres missed."

Once they had more clues, then what? Find her before she hurt Uri, of course. But if they were too late? Kallen's gaze slid to Drakus, who'd gone back to his home base on the window sill.

Uri was the nicest frigging male he knew, even with his hungers riding him. If that Chosen so much as laid a blade against his skin, she'd learn an unimaginable definition for "unhinged." Because watching Drakus struggle with the news of the bear chimera, he'd bet the farm the dragon would lose his shit and harm Violet.

Thank fuck he wouldn't be going on this excursion with them.

"I'm going this time, to find the Chosen." The determined growl echoed off the sheet of plywood.

Aaand there went his case of the reliefs. Kallen deflated into the couch cushions alongside Darken, a cold ball of dread forming in the pit of his stomach.

---

*W*ith Violet's blood tickling through his navigation system, Uri's teleporting worked top-notch. He landed on the fire escape just outside her kitchen window. Cupping his hands to the long pane, he peered in. Then wished himself inside.

Just like that, with the now-familiar wonky drag and spins, he was standing on her linoleum. The kitchen was narrow and long, so he didn't need to throw his senses out to learn she wasn't there. He took his size thirteens into the hallway, ears homed for the slightest sound.

Nada. But the farther down the hall he went, the thicker her scent grew around him, filling his nose and winding straight for his heart. The organ fluttered, excited to be surrounded by her. Uri pressed on.

The hallway was narrow like the kitchen, with doors on each side and a window at the end to give the illusion of more space. He peered around open doorways as he traveled, noticing the sparseness of each room. Two-thirds down, he stopped and sniffed. Hand trembling as he turned the knob, he pushed the door open.

What the hell? Adrenaline goosing him in the ass, Uri strode into the room, doing a slow circle to take in the four walls. "Hoooly shit." Moonlight gleamed on knives, guns, throwing stars; the armament representing the eras of their evolution. All mounted and polished like museum pieces.

No wonder his Chosen had nearly gotten the upper hand with him. Violet was a fighter. It didn't register until that moment his boots were squishing into the floor. Fighting mats. Where she could tumble and practice without bruising her bones or waking the neighbors below her.

As he scanned more of the room, his gander snagged on the man-sized punching bag hanging in the corner like a corpse. By the looks of its canvas skin, it had been playing crash test dummy with Violet's fists for a long time. Scuffed and stained as if the thing had seen happier days, it hung in battered contrast to the gleaming collection of lethal metal on the walls.

She took great care of her weapons. How it must have killed her to grow weak! Remembering how pale she'd grown, humiliation swam in Uri's guts, tightening his skin. He hadn't taken care of his Chosen. In fact, he'd done everything to make her as miserable as he was. If only he could teleport back in time, to when he'd taken her from the hospital in his fit of rage, his memories swamping rational thought. Maybe he wouldn't have been so hasty?

Maybe he should've asked her on that date like she'd suggested.

No. It had seared his pride to tell her, but he'd been honest about his hunger and not having control. Hell, the difference was streaming in his blood right now, his little brain cells all wakey-wakey like they'd made a pit-stop at Starbucks. The difference from then to now was shameful. It was wrong of him to have tasted of her, to cave to his weakness and become the very thing he detested. A blood sucker. *Not Kynd.* Uri squeezed his fists like he could strangle the thought.

And what do you know? It worked. While he put a choke hold on his demons, he could recall the feel of her little fangs working on his wrist. His knees loosened as the memory engulfed him. So easy it was to feel again how her body had moved in rhythm with his. Their lusts taking control so they were as one.

A shudder rippled through him, and Uri shook like his fur was on the outside. Not wholly united, no. He'd derailed that train with his fears. A good thing. He could have lost himself—

"Shut the fuck up, Bear." Man, the needle was wearing a groove and he'd lost—what?—a half hour standing in the middle of a room that should be tripping all kinds of warning flags. Violet was a hunter, not just a fighter. None of the weapons on her walls were for self-defense. So, he needed to get his ass in gear and latch onto her while her trail was still warm.

Those children at the hospital needed him to focus and get moving. His Chosen's blood in his veins wasn't going to last forever. Except the boats on the ends of his legs sailed him back into the hallway, where it was a short walk to where her scent pooled thickest. Pressing his fingers to the door, he pushed it open slowly as a low roar flared up in his gut.

Her bedroom. Her bed. Top sheet and blankets twisted together, bottom sheet rumpled. His Chosen suffered nightmares? He was on his knees sniffing the evidence before he came to his senses. Like he needed to have his face so close to where she lay vulnerable. Where her scent pooled thick even though it was cool. His trembling hands skimmed the mattress as though his palms might pick up a hint of her.

As though she lay before him and he dared caress her bare skin while she let him. *Loving Christ.* Uri shoved himself upright and gave his head another shake, even as he wished like hell she was right in front of him. Not laying down but facing him with her fierceness, acting like the tough, little vampire she was.

Why in hell did he keep thinking of her in terms of precious and little? She wasn't. Violet was a grown vampire female with curves and lethal tendencies. If that combo didn't rouse him to action, then he needed to find the nearest ledge and park his stone ass on it permanently.

All right then. Now that he'd given himself a mental slap on his puss, he was ready. Pulling up the awful scene where he'd watched her stalk into a ward full of sleeping children, Uri surrendered to the atom-fizzies and imagined himself there once again.

*O*f all the places she should be fleeing to, Violet found herself back at Maine Medical Center. Stupid. Stupid. Stupid. Even dumber was the fact she was riding in an elevator after materializing outside the cafeteria behind the row of dumpsters. Her landing pad as it were. One she relied on every night she visited the kids. It was private as hell in that back lot. By the graveyard shift, most of the cleaning of the kitchen had already been done, the trash taken out and awaiting pick up in the morning.

The added benefit of this location was the wall of windows. At night, patrons couldn't see out, but she could get a good long gander in. It's how she'd first seen her friend Daniela. The woman had been sitting alone at a corner table, stirring a cup of coffee as if her thoughts were elsewhere.

Turned out, they were. Daniela was the liaison between the hospital and police department for domestic abuse cases. That particular night, she'd had to interview a mother who had had most of her teeth knocked out of her head protecting her daughter. The two were sharing a room, the little girl with her broken arm too upset to be apart from her mom.

For some reason, Violet had been drawn to the woman who seemed to take in the pain of her clients and wear it openly in private moments. As if she removed it from her shoulders to hold in her hands, worrying over the quilt of bruises stitched together with the heavy thread of violence. They'd spent that first night sharing each other's company and not much else. But the silence between them had been the fertile ground in which to build a friendship. On Violet's side, at least.

She knew human friendships were supposed to involve more than just sitting together with few words spoken. Nights out, shopping excursions and the like, though Daniela never seemed to want more, either. Over time, she'd become Violet's only friend. A friendship she cherished.

*And is probably lost.*

Now as she leaned against the wooden hand rail inside the elevator as it climbed upward, it didn't seem like quite an oddity that she and Daniela should bond over shitty, day old coffee. Daniela was a Chosen One for the Kynd just like she was. No wonder there'd been a connection. Like maybe God Himself had engineered their meeting, putting them together, and Violet that much closer to Urick.

The elevator pinged, announcing her floor. Before the heavy doors slid open, she rubbed her hands down the front of her coat, ironing out the jitters more than trying to straighten her appearance. As if she could mask the fact her body was singing so fiercely with the Kynd's blood raging through her veins. She doubted humans would hear the low-grade humming, but what if she bumped into one of the Others? What if Urick was following the vibrations even now?

Which was why she launched her ass out of the elevator. Yeah, it had a second door opposite the one she exited, but it was still a box, ergo a trap if the chimera found her. No way would those sliders open faster than that beast could move. Boots quiet on the buffed tile, she resisted looking down the dim lit corridor behind her.

She had other things to do. Namely, figure out how to filter the sharpness of her senses since taking Urick's blood. Was this what it was like to be Kynd? No wonder they missed so little. She might as well be a satellite station, receiving signals from planet Nebulon. The bear chimera's blood was some potent shit, which was why she'd gone hasty pudding in getting her butt to the hospital.

If she shared this with some of the more critical kids?

Talk about a boost onto the main deck of the S.S. Screw You, Cancer. Her excitement over the prospect of those kids getting just that much better put her heart into Fred Astaire territory. Steps quickening but not growing louder with the hurried pace, she beat feet for the place where…Urick… had…kidnapped…her.

She slowed to a stop like a wind-up toy, her palm flat on the metal plate that with one push would open the heavy wooden door onto the ward lined with human children. Surely, he would follow her here. And then what, kidnap her again?

Not likely after he'd ordered her to run. She was being ridiculous and paranoid, the time spent as a captive gnawing at her self-confidence like mice on a bar of soap. He'd freed her, damn it, he wouldn't hunt her down.

Would he?

Who gave a shit! She was wasting time with these insecurities. Time that was fast metabolizing the Kynd blood in her system. Blood she wanted to share with sick children who would die otherwise. Making her existence as a parasite much more bearable.

Right. Squaring her shoulders, she pressed on the paddle and cracked the door just enough to squeeze through. Unlike the other times, though, her heart tapped a soft shoe dance in her chest. With short breaths like she'd run up all those flights of stairs instead of taking the elevator, she went straight for the fourth bed and managed an even exhale when she saw Jaime still in it.

A beautiful young girl despite the absence of hair and the bruising under her closed lashes. In the two weeks Violet had been gone, new machines had been added. Not a clue what they were for exactly, but she knew their gist.

With her sense of smell so much stronger now, she could smell the rot of the cancer as it ate deeper into the girl's bones. If Urick had kept her longer…

Resentment grew like a water blister as she knelt at the edge of the bed and was struck by what she was about to do. *Bite*. No pretty way to say how she was going to pierce that fragile skin, the veins running stark and blue under the surface of such pallid skin. The pulse was weak but regular, at least. She'd arrived in time to help the girl, by taking some of the sewage out and replacing it with a pure distillate from a heavenly being. Frowning, Violet sat on her heels and ran her palms down her thighs.

Shit. Now was not the time to have a moment. She wasn't going to go all Hallmark over what Urick had given her, and by turn, she could offer to this dying human girl. The frigging beast had given his essence to her freely. She knew that, and it didn't take her anywhere but right back to him. The beast from Heaven who was fucked up seven ways from Sunday, but who had still, in his messed up way, put her first.

"Don't do it." The raspy whisper came from behind her. Every tic and pulse point in her body fell quiet as her muscles stiffened. "Please. Don't harm the girl." The growl was one of desperation, and it chewed up the skin of her back like a chainsaw. Violet's heart broke free of its fetters, smashing itself against its bony cage.

Throat dry, she scratched out, "What?" Her frightened stare glued itself to the inside of Jaime's delicate arm, yet she felt the warmth of Urick's bulk as he neared. God almighty, he was big looming up behind her, his presence too much.

"She's an innocent, Violet. You don't have to do this."

"What in hell are you talking about?" Her voice sounded like it scraped up the business side of a cheese grater, and she flinched when big hands curled around her upper arms. They squeezed without force, more of a mini-hug than a grab. When her body relaxed into it, she stiffened against the allure of surrendering.

"Come with me. We'll talk about this." The grip never changed, but somehow, she knew he was losing an inner battle. And then what? He'd hurt the children?

"No." If she went with him, she would inadvertently hurt the children. Jaime did not have many weeks left before her body would be overwhelmed by the invader. It would grow too weak to fight the cancer while she was held captive once again. Both of them prisoners with different wardens.

"Come," he bit out.

"No, the girl—"

"Will die in her own time."

Not on her watch, damn it. As she craned her neck to finally look at the male who held her, Violet's shoulders twisted, tightening the grip he had on her. "I won't let that girl die!"

The spot between Urick's eyebrows made a vee. "What?"

"The girl." When the descriptive came out of her mouth, Violet's throat closed up and she felt the sting of tears building at the back of her eyes. Pushing through it, she lanced the chimera holding her with a hard glare. "She'll die if we don't help." *We?* Freudian slip, surely.

Urick, apparently, was just as perplexed by the pronoun as she was. That vee splitting his forehead in half etched deeper. "What are you talking about?" His gaze searched her face as if the answers lurked on her cheekbones, her chin.

Gray eyes. She'd never seen him so clearheaded. Her blood had done this to him? He had admitted to being starved, but could so little do so much? "Y-your blood and mine. It will make the girl stronger so she can fight the disease."

"This is what you were doing?" His harsh tone didn't match the shame flaring in his stare. A stare that now marbled with streaks of black. Should she trust him when clearly, he wasn't wrapped as tight as she'd just thought?

Or was the vampire dominating because it was pleased?

For once in her life, she wasn't sure how to go about getting out of this scrape. Trust the Kynd in front of her? Have faith in a male vampire's mating instincts? If she fought him here, would he hurt the children? He hadn't during their first altercation, but then he hadn't wasted words when he'd done the grab and teleport.

This time he seemed to be giving her a choice. And wasn't it just her luck she couldn't figure her ass out from her elbow. Ducky. Nothing like taking the first step off an unfinished bridge...

"We'll talk, yes?" She gripped his elbow and noticed then how wet he was, though his skin was blazing hot. His hair still had crystals of snow, which winked in the light of the monitors.

He was also naked as sin. Violet slipped from his grasp, putting distance between them. Urick's now empty hands cupped his manhood. God damn, what a specimen. She couldn't help but notice his long, thick thighs growing out from the point where he hid himself. Above his folded hands? An. Eight. Pack. Chiseled and glistening from melted snow. Licking her lips, her gaze traveled upward and over his wide shoulders, tripped on his bobbing Adam's apple before falling flat on his lips.

Full lips even though they were pressed tight over fangs. Vampire fangs, not bear teeth, as he'd clearly been just moments before teleporting into this room.

"Are your clothes on the roof over there?" She nudged her chin at the window behind him.

In the muted light of the ward, she could see his cheeks flush. Man, that Kynd blood had some awesome side effects. She could see in the dark before, but now it was like a layer of film had been peeled off everything.

"It was snowing," he said as if that was enough of an explanation. Though she supposed it was. He'd known she would come here and he'd waited in his bear form, protecting himself from the snow.

"You didn't dress before teleporting in here?"

"No, I…" He dipped his chin then lifted it defiantly, working those broad beam shoulders, the muscles rolling over thick bones. "I didn't think."

Because he'd been so outraged? Nope. Standing in front of her like Adonis, Urick looked luscious…*whoops*…lucid as all get out. If she could scrape her thoughts out of the gutter and remember why she'd raced to a sick girl's bedside, she'd realize she'd already made up her mind.

"Help us." Her voice came out stronger than she thought it would. She didn't want to sound like a beggar, but then did she care? No. Not with Urick standing in front of her and the sick kids surrounding them.

When had she decided this Kynd made her feel a little stronger? Not just his blood, but him. His presence.

"This isn't a trick?"

She shook her head, feeling a little bad about how many times she'd kneed him where it hurt most. Though now wasn't the time to go soft. "No trick. Not if you're going to help." Her stomach fluttered as anticipation flapped around inside it. Urick's blood in these children? Holy shit, she'd won the lottery.

"Come with me while I get dressed."

Aaaand she held only four numbers out of six. The happy bird in her belly fell still, a warm ball in her center. She eyed the other rooftop through the window, still surprised by how much her eyesight had improved. If his blood had done this to her, imagine what it could do for Jaime. She nodded as her thoughts caught up.

"You'll come because you want to." A raspy command, but a plea nonetheless.

"Y-yeah. Yeah, all right." When she looked him in the eye, she saw resolve softened by relief. The little bird in her belly fluttered.

Urick held out his big hand. As her fingertips started itching, Violet made a fist to keep from reaching for him, the urge to touch him overwhelming.

Forcing herself to stay put, she said, "If you kidnap me again, you will live to regret it."

"No, no more. I've harmed my…No, we do this as a truce between us." His level gaze razed her insides flat. Not like a bulldozer smashing a house, but like a bomb when you're standing ten feet from the site of detonation. She thought she even swayed a little, pictured her hair flying back from her face with a whoosh, and got a little giggly.

"What?"

"Nothing. It's just…" *Your blood coursing through my veins, nothing more.* "You're standing next to Winnie the Pooh." There was a poster of the yellow bear and Piglet taped to the foot of one of the kid's beds. They were holding hands and walking, wearing smiles.

"So?"

Violet shook her head. "Nothing. Like I said." As she moved closer to him she resisted taking his hand again. She wasn't Piglet, and they weren't friends. Besides, she'd bet the farm there wasn't anything cute about Urick in bear form.

"I'll see you on the ledge." With the warning clear, there wasn't anything cute about his gargoyle form, either. Then he disappeared, and she saw him materialize on the roof of the adjacent building. He shook as if the falling snow was landing on him then bent to grab his jeans.

*Holy Moses, what a bod.* As he stabbed his legs into his jeans and hiked them over his taut ass, her brain went on hiatus. Turning toward her while he wrestled his t-shirt over his head, she got to watch that eight pack flex. After dragging the tight cotton down his torso, he stood with his hands on his hips, watching her.

She watched back.

When he balled his hands into fists, she came to. He was waiting for her to follow him and she hadn't. At least, not quickly enough. Perversely, she made him wait a few seconds more, taking willful pleasure in his growing unease.

Hey, sue her, but he owed her. Big time. Riling his fur wasn't only fun, it was a good reminder that he was supposed to be kissing her ass, making for what he'd done to her. Stirring the hornets' nest? You bet. She'd give a fig when he broke her bones and supped on her marrow. Until then, she was going to make him squirm.

Just as she saw him curse she willed herself outside, the bite of the winter air enveloping her instantly.

"You like to play it loose, don't you?" His hair seemed even darker with fresh snow on it, his eyes that much more shining gray.

"So, you'll help?" The shivers took up residence, her fleece no match for the plummeting temp of a February night. Rubbing her upper arms, she glanced back from where she'd come. Jaime lay in the same position, the machines winking silently beside her.

When she turned back to look at Urick, he was watching where she'd been.

"Her name's Jaime if you were wondering."

His gaze made a slow drag back to her.

"She's ten. I've known her for about two years."

Urick sat down on an air vent, elbows on his knees. If she didn't know better, she might start thinking he regretted what he'd done. Taking a deep breath, she sat down next to him, glad that her fleece jacket covered her ass so it wouldn't get wet.

"And Winnie the Pooh?" He stared down at the snow slick tar of the roof under his boots instead of looking at her.

"I don't know." She compared their boots side by side. Hers looked half the size. "Several months."

As he gripped his thighs, his hands were pale against the dark denim.

"So, I bet it's hard to hide those beauts in public." She nudged her chin.

It was a heavy bag of seconds before he answered. "These?" Urick surveyed his claws, then shrugged. "I don't exactly have to worry about it."

"Ah." Because he hid out along with the rest of the Kynd, no doubt. Since appearing from wherever they'd been for the last couple thousand years or so, none of the Others had really seen them. It wasn't a stretch to figure humans hadn't either.

The falling snow made the silence seem that much more prominent.

Violet tucked her hands into her coat pockets.

"You're cold." As Urick leaned into her, she felt him stretch his arm out. She launched to her feet, hands at her sides and ready.

"Shit. I only meant..." He shook his head as he let it drop between his shoulders. When he looked up at her, his eyes were mostly gray, the black streaks receding.

"Your eyes change a lot."

He dropped his head again, raising his forearms to rub his head on. "Yeah."

God, he seemed so frigging harmless sitting there on a metal box in just a t-shirt. He seemed helpless, too, and a lot lost. She was going to regret this, but she sat back down beside him.

"I'm fucked, Violet. So fucked. As you know."

She didn't laugh with him. He hadn't pushed out the kind of chuckle that was funny.

Was she an asshole for what she was about to ask? Naw. He owed her. "So…about the girl. You'll help?"

He held his hands out, palms up as if all he saw in them was nothing. Not because they were empty right then, but empty all the time, worthless. Her heart did one of those little flips where it hurt for a second. Damn him.

"You said you would."

"Jesus, Ch—Violet, you just said how much my eyes change."

"So."

"They change because I'm skipping from one being to another and back again as fast as a fucking dealer in Vegas. You want me around those kids?"

"Point taken." It was a few minutes before she realized they were both leaning forward, her pose mimicking his except she'd shoved her hands back into her jacket pockets. "So, you're going to help then?"

---

"*Y*ou're not a quitter, I'll give you that." Here he was, a cocktail mixed by a drunk bartender, and she was standing her ground still asking for his help. He wasn't stupid. If he didn't help, she'd bolt.

If he helped her, he'd fucking lose it. He stood up to wrangle the trembling. Getting to her feet, too, she watched him with wary eyes. Smart woman. Why in fuck did he appreciate that? Like he needed another emotion to deal with right then. She was a vampire. He hated the parasites with a passion that spilled out of him so often he'd lost track.

Yet, he'd had a WTF moment when he caught her helping the human kids. "I gotta walk a second." He didn't wait for her reply, just started pacing as his brain played hopscotch with six rocks.

"I'm going inside while you figure your shit out. It's freezing out here."

As he twisted with a case of the Hey-whats, she materialized back in the children's ward. He'd breathe a sigh of relief if he could actually breathe.

Without removing her coat, she went straight for the bed where the girl Jaime was sleeping. His insides flared with something searing, making him think, oddly, of little men inside him with tiny clothes irons.

Jesus, he was losing it.

His brain swam in his skull all frantic like it was drowning and desperately wanted rescuing. His body kept trembling, trying to give a shit. He riveted his attention on the woman behind the glass, praying like the newly repented she wasn't going to hurt the girl. Knowing she wouldn't stabbed at him like a steel bar. Jab in, slide out. Jab in, slide out.

When she folded the blankets away from the girl's arm and bent over it, Uri lost the war. His senses honed as sharp as the edge of broken glass; he landed so close to her it was the work of a nanosecond to wrap his arms around her and yank her to his stomach. "No," he managed to bite out as he disappeared them to the one place he automatically thought of when vampires and sanctuary were his foremost thoughts.

The cave.

Ruby, Arizona. Once a thriving mining town, it was now a ghost of itself. Abandoned buildings, desert all around, and heat in February that enveloped him the second his feet hit the packed dirt. Talk about a climate change from Maine. Twenty degrees to eighty in minutes, it was like walking from a refrigerator into an oven.

"Son of a bitch! You brought me back." Pissed off words served with an elbow shot to his solar plexus. "You said you'd help."

As Uri wrestled with the viper in his grasp, he grated out, "I will." Even though he wasn't sure how he was going to pull it off. *Dig deeper for your Chosen, asswipe.* He held onto her as he navigated the tunnel into the Earth. He could feel the lead, zinc, and copper embedded in the walls of the mine shaft as he took them deeper.

Violet would be able to, as well. "You're a...a...an unethical bastard!"

*Obviously.* He set her down while she still squirmed, her body a living electric wire against him. He wanted to keep holding her just for the sensation of it. He wanted to lose himself in the touch of...his woman. Not his Kynd. This was stimulating in a way touching his brethren just didn't accomplish.

Vampire fangs dropping down, he released her. Fear crawled over his skin.

"I can't believe you brought me back here after saying you'd help. I should have known. God damned Kynd bastards. Unholy, every frigging one of you."

She was right, of course. God had damned them. Except. Rubbing his hands up and down his arms, he said, "I'm the unholy one, not my brethren."

Violet paused in her rant. "All right. Fine. I have faith that my friend Daniela isn't that stupid. I'm the unfortunate one to have gotten paired with you." She found the corner she'd used before and plunked her ass into it.

Defeated, Uri squatted, too. Unable to resist being close to her, though, he stayed within her personal space. His throat knotted like someone strangled him. All he could do was nod his head, agreeing with her.

The sound of her sigh rippled through him like a warm current, and he watched her nestle her back against the wall, preparing to stay for the long haul. Hatred burned like a living thing in her amber eyes. Even reposed, she looked vibrant, brimming with life.

Unlike the young girl at the hospital. Not like Winnie the Pooh, either, the sick kid curled into an overlarge bed like a newly hatched robin. His eyes sat too big in a thin face, his lids blue and bruised. Every fragile bone showing under pale skin.

"Tell me what you were doing in the hospital ward." His stomach felt like it had a case of the dishrags. All twisting and wringing.

Violet tensed, her intensity manifesting in her strong body. "I was helping a girl to live, you schmo. And you stopped it. You barged in with your insanity and your *I can't handle this* bullshit and stopped it like the ignoramus you are."

Welllllll. She had a point. Ashamed, Uri couldn't hold her gaze. The deep breath he took didn't go half as far as he needed it to. He took another. And another as his muscles unknotted a little, relaxing when they finally had some oxygen in their deprived cells. "You're right. I should have left you alone. I shouldn't have followed you."

"Yeah, you should've left me alone. So, why didn't you?" Not exactly a question. More like an accusation. He answered her anyway.

"I was afraid for the kids. I thought…" He managed to look at her. "I thought you were harming them. Feeding on their…" His panties got a twist and he fidgeted. "I thought you were feeding on sick kids, and with my blood in your veins, you were hungry for more."

"Well, you missed that by a mile, Captain Cripple."

*Deserved.* And at least she was talking to him. Hope ignited short and fast as a spark plug. Insults aside, her voice calmed him like nothing he'd known before. If they kept up the dialogue, maybe he could work out how to get on track with her, how to help like he said he would and bring some honor to his Kynd, if not himself.

There was no honor in being vampire. His gaze volunteered for a slow trek along Violet's curves. *Fine.* His Chosen One was the exception. She was helping kids because…shit. She exchanged blood with them, taking the illness into herself while giving them her blood. First thought? He wanted to bellow at this cancer sickness for being anywhere near this woman. The second brain fart: something good might come of his being different from other Kynd.

Uri raked his hands across his head to hide their shaking. "You rushed to them to share what I'd given you. Why would you do such a thing when my blood—"

"Is rocket fuel, restorative on a superhero level? Oh, I don't know." She waved her hand. "Maybe because it's the best shot those kids have."

"You think my blood would help them?" He couldn't have been more astonished if she sauntered over to nestle in his arms. Voluntarily.

"Of course, dimwit! You're freaking Kynd. Monster-ish, yeah, but you guys carry ambrosia in your veins."

Uri growled, his memories railroading him to the station he was all too sickeningly familiar with.

"What? Too damaged to handle a happy truth?" Violet stood up, her eyes narrowing.

That precious blood she was fond of went cold in his veins. "What would you know about it?" There had been so many fanged faces hovering over his chained body. He remembered everyone, but maybe he'd missed hers?

He got to his feet when she did. Only when she stepped toward him, he backed up.

"Afraid of me?"

"Scared I'll hurt you."

The exacerbating fiend of a woman shook her head. "No. I'm your Chosen."

*Such conviction!* His feet ran him in reverse until he hit the dirt wall. He could move sideways away from her, but he was riveted as if her approach magnetized him. "Yes," he agreed, the single word answer all he could muster as he watched the nearing fox like a pinned rabbit.

Her scent slid like tendrils up his nose, through his whole body. She was so close now she tilted her chin to keep looking at him. She parted her lips to say something then cocked her head.

"You're truly afraid."

The trembling that once resided in his hands spread all over his skin. Answer enough, he didn't need to voice it.

"Not of hurting me, though. Of what I am. What you are."

"Not…"

Her amber eyes glittered with a comprehension he'd seen only in his brethren. "Other vampires have harmed you." She halted when her body was close enough he could feel her heat, but she didn't touch him. "Who?"

He swallowed. "Doesn't matter." He'd recognize her scent even in his memories. He'd never known her while he'd been chained for feasting. "Oh, God." Memories erupted, swamping him. Obliterating the image of the one bravely standing before him. Panicked, Uri turned running back, stiff-arming Violet out of his way as he fled.

To where? He didn't give a fuck. Moving reminded him he wasn't chained to a stone slab, reminded him he was free from his enslavement.

"Urick."

The sound of his name upon her beautiful voice unhinged his legs, and he crashed to his kneecaps, palms scraping into the dirt of the floor.

# CHAPTER 4

*J*esus on a popsicle stick, this male had some serious damage. Jiminy Cricket piped up to answer who had done the damaging, and Violet's heart shriveled in the crush of her suspicions. Her thoughts leapt straight to the image of her father.

Her father and the cult of the vaJacaka—the rogue vampires she took pleasure in murdering—were most likely the ones responsible for Urick's scrambled brain. As Violet's mouth flopped open under the weight of her confession, she clapped it shut. Telling Urick she was the child of the male who might have tortured him would accomplish what, exactly?

*Nothing good, sister, so shut your yap.*

Super advice. Afraid to startle him more, Violet approached him like she would a wounded Rottweiler, all show of hands and soothing endearments.

"Urick, easy now. You're not there. You're safe in the cave." It finally dawned on her why he kept returning to this spot. It wasn't to jail her, it was to keep himself safe. Turning into his corner, he rounded his broad back as if trying to curl into himself, his muscles sharply defining the knobs of his spine.

Violet reached for him just as he spun and clung to her as if she was the stronger one. "Hey, you're squeezing too tight," she said but found her arms wrapping around him as she spoke. The strange humming she'd felt before emanated through her like a tuneless melody, and she surrendered to it, placing her cheek to his chest.

Beneath her ear, Urick's heart slowed. His grip eased, and he placed his cheek to the top of her head after brushing a kiss across it. He moved just enough to place his palm to her nape, his fingers and thumb rubbing the short locks. Seeking comfort in her. Shelter.

Aaaand it felt so right that he should. Not the other way around, where typically the female surrendered to the protection of her mate. Where vampire males claimed, then took proprietary possession.

A Kynd thing, it had to be. The truth blared out at her like an electronic billboard on Times Square: Kynd needed touch. Proving Urick wasn't just vampire, but bear and gargoyle, too. A chimera.

She'd been an obtuse idiot not to have noticed something so basic. Caught up in her own kidnapping and hatching ways to escape, she'd missed the obvious. Urick needed her, not just for blood as vampire males did but for touch.

Man, if she'd known this two weeks before, she'd have been walking free within hours of her kidnapping. How easy it would have been to trick him. She could easily do it now.

Instead, her arms hugged him tighter, as if her subconscious preferred the contact. Ah, hell, she liked it, too. If she overlooked how they'd gotten together in the first place, she could admit he felt nice against her. The way only a strong male could.

Violet closed her eyes and leaned into the touch of his hands to her hair as he nuzzled her bared neck, his breath soft and warm. When he kissed along the tendons, she surrendered to the plush of his lips in such a provocative place. "Yes, that." She grew moist between her legs.

He kissed harder, his lips parting to free his tongue. Her nipples twisted tight against the lace of her bra, and she arched to release the coil tightening through her body.

Urick growled against her skin, his teeth scraping. Violet let her head fall back upon his forearms, his weight moving on top of her as he eased her to the floor. His lips and tongue continued their exploration across her skin. Tasting, kissing as if to savor her scent.

As she caressed him, his muscles slid beneath her palms, his t-shirt a frustrating barrier. She dropped her arms to her sides, feeling the loss of their peculiar hum the instant their bodies no longer touched.

"More," he growled, grinding his hips between her spread thighs.

Violet's hands took the trip before her brain gave the green light, and she stroked the ball of his shoulders, pulling him down to her. His mouth crashed over hers, their teeth clacking as their tongues slid together like long-lost lovers.

God, he felt like a long-lost lover. Stranger still was how weird that didn't seem. Violet opened herself wider, letting Urick into the space she'd let no one ever tread before.

He seemed to realize the instant she did so. Moaning, he ground himself harder to the cleft of her thighs, releasing their kiss to suckle her neck, play biting as she writhed beneath him. She heard the rip at the same time cool air brushed her bared chest. Lifting her heavy lids, she watched him gaze upon her breasts as they heaved up and down with her breaths.

"Stunning." He swallowed hard, his black eyes burning in his handsome face, his features harsh yet reverent. For a split second, brilliant gray slid across his corneas like comets trailing through a night sky.

An answering heat spread between Violet's thighs. Urick's nostrils flared just before he dove down to suck one of her boobs into his mouth. Releasing it with a pop, he flicked his tongue across the bouncing nipple, then scraped it playfully with his sharp teeth.

Somehow, her hands were in his hair gripping and stroking, over and over. When her back arched of its own volition, Violet surrendered to the loss of control, her knees falling away to make way for the imminent penetration despite the fact they were both still wearing clothes.

Twin piercings sank deep into her breast, straddling her nipple. Moaning, she tilted her hips, making way—

They both froze in the same instant.

For a few seconds, neither of them moved. Then things went from awkward to annihilated in two seconds flat. Urick vaulted off her. Roaring, he drove his fist into the dirt wall.

Clasping her shirt together, Violet leapt to her feet. "You God damned—"

"Yeeees! I am damned!" Urick swung around to face her, teeth and fangs bloodied. "Damned to never be what I was! Damned to be this awful…thing! This horrible thing that lusts for blood, when it's—" He clapped his jaw shut like a steel trap.

He might as well have clamped his teeth down on a can of worms to open it. Violet snagged the bait, hell bent to end this seesawing of violent rages and turbulent lusts. "When it's what? So god-awful horrible to be a vampire! Well, thanks a fucking lot, asshole! Because guess what? I'm a vampire. Your precious Chosen One is a disgusting. Bloodsucking. Leech!" Leech came out as *leeeeech* as she shrieked it, her voice barely scraping out of her seizing throat.

Damn it, she would not cry!

Never before had she had to defend herself in this way. Not for being what she was, even though she'd hated it. In the face of Urick's attack? Her pride surged forth. Pride for what she'd been doing with those kids, pride for how she hunted down the rogue vampires and killed them. It made her stand straighter, so when she faced off with the prick in front of her, he didn't seem as tall as he had just moments before.

Violet rammed her finger into his chest, even as she felt blood drip from her nipple. "And another thing, if you think for one second you and your Kynd are better than me, then thinking twice better become. Your. New. Hobby."

She whirled and bolted down the rabbit hole, fully expecting him to charge after her. He roared, but it trailed off as she gained distance. He wasn't chasing her, wasn't trying to stop her from leaving. Violet slowed as she peered over her shoulder.

No Urick. No enraged chimera snagging her from behind.

By the time she reached the adit, she was breathing normally and not so fired up to teleport her ass out of there. Instead, she sat down in the packed sand. The sky spread so black above her the stars were a trillion diamonds smeared together, a wash of Milky Way.

Violet tipped her head back, playing her tongue over her fangs. They tingled under each pass as if attuned to her mood. Dental barometers, they sprang forth when she was pissed. Or tickled like they were doing now when she was ready to bite something.

Like Urick's body. Anywhere she heard or smelled a throbbing vein. In her lust, she hadn't cared any more than he had. The leaking puncture wounds on her boob were proof if she needed some.

The rat bastard. She laid back, placing her hands behind her head to keep her hair out of the sand. She was facing the stars, but all she could see was the chimera's head under her chin, then the comet tail of gray across his vampire eyes.

Urick. A male she couldn't deny she had an attraction to. It had felt right to be so close, touching him, opening herself.

Screwing her to Gibraltar because she wanted more.

More from a male who would despise her if he ever learned the truth about her. She was falling for someone who would hate her worse than she hated herself. Then he wouldn't just lose it, he'd probably break.

How was that for an image seared onto her heart? She couldn't do it to him, not when she had every intention of killing her father—as soon as she could pin him down long enough to push her blade through his black heart.

She'd been trying for centuries, but eventually, she would succeed. So, problem solved. Urick didn't have to know of the tainted blood in her veins.

Besides, maybe it was someone else who had tortured him. There were other vampires out there capable of such sick shit.

*Yeah.* She could totally board that plane of denial. Violet relaxed into the warm sand as much as the knotting muscles in her shoulders would let her. God, she hoped Uri could pull it together. She wouldn't even mind if he emerged from the safety of the cave to sit with her.

Just so it would feel like they worked this Chosen thing out together. Proving just how far her heart was cracking its precious little self ajar.

---

*U*rick watched her run with his feet planted and his soul stretching like a billion elastics behind her. Until she'd gone too far and they snapped, flinging him back onto his ass. He sat in the dirt, stunned, mortified, and aching.

He'd bitten her again. Had been loving it, lost in a frenzy of righteous *rightness* that he should be clutched to her vein and seeking…so much more. His imagination following that line of carnal reasoning, Uri clenched his fists, unsure whether he should bellow in outrage at not being the benevolent, vegetarian Kynd he used to be, or fist-pump his rigid cock and high-five himself through the euphoria of having been connected on a visceral level to his Chosen One.

He'd felt her *open*. She'd lain beneath him like the doors of the Florence Baptistery and its Gates of Paradise. The vibration he felt when he connected to his brethren had revved into so much more with Violet. A rendition of the Boys Choir of Oxford, or better still, to those many, many years ago when he'd listened to the angels singing on high.

Violet had brought him as close to Heaven as he hadn't been in thousands of years.

He exulted. Yet, at the same time, he spurned. Confused, he let her go, even though her absence bore into his center like an auger, hollowing him out.

God, he needed her. The trouble was, he couldn't decide what part of him ruled the strongest, and screw him by cutting his nose off to spite his face, but he'd be damned—pun intended—if he'd let the vampire third of himself enjoy a frigging thing.

He'd given enough pleasure to other leeches, fuck you very much.

Like he hadn't been tormented enough through the ages, now he had to deal with hurting his Chosen One. He'd pierced her flesh, drawn blood…

Uri crossed his arms and curled around his middle, sick to his stomach.

Vomiting like a bulimic parasite crossed his mind, but so did the abhorrent idea of disrespecting anything related to Violet. He'd keep what he'd stolen and ride the residuals like a carnival goer chancing a trip on the Flying Circus. He'd want to puke, but the thrill would be well worth the cost of the ticket.

Maybe.

An all too familiar tingling scurried across his skin, launching him down another horrid track. Dawn approached. He felt the nearing of the sun in every cell, in the fibers of his muscles, and even in the vessels of his blood, despite the rush of being nourished.

His Violet was out there somewhere, although not far. Uri picked himself off the packed dirt of the floor and gave himself a shake, as much to throw off the dust as to get his ass in gear to find her.

She hadn't gone home. The tickle he felt in his blood wasn't just the emergence of stone. His Chosen was close. Ignoring the sluggishness, he trod down the shaft, disregarding the scrape of the narrow dirt walls along his shoulders. He stood up when the breezes of fresh desert air hit his face. In front of him, the horizon loomed gray, the few brazen stars left in the sky ceding their brilliance to the coming sun.

"Violet." She was sitting to his left, her eyes closed and her face lifted. "The dawn comes." Saying it aloud, he realized his fear was for her, not himself. He yearned to hover over her, to protect her from the morning rays even if they obliterated his stony butt to dust.

When she turned her face to him, he quit working his fists. He'd been doing it to fight the lethargy lest he succumb to the stone before his…this woman…found shelter.

"I know." She seemed strangely becalmed. As though she were at odds with her thoughts. He had expected her to be furious, and rightfully so. He'd been prepared to bear the brunt of her anger. But this? It knocked him sideways when he was already twirling.

"Come inside?" *Please, oh, please.* Just say fucking yes.

"Yeah. Yeah, I'll come in."

He almost fell down. "You will hurry? I'm almost—" Admitting his weakness stuck in his throat. He held out his open palm.

A wry smile lifted one side of her pretty lips, but she reached for him. As his fingers closed around hers, his exhalation unclogged his airway. He nearly sagged with the relief of feeling her skin upon his.

Gently, he tugged her closer, careful not to squash her to him as he desired to do. *Baby steps.* She was voluntarily coming inside with him. He couldn't ruin this fragile trust. God knew, he didn't deserve it, so he'd better well straighten up and earn it. She was giving him a gift more valuable than clean water and it humbled him. Smoothed his resentment, eased his outrage.

He kept her in front of him as they made their way into the cave. Not to prevent her from bolting if she changed her mind at the last second, but to keep his legs pushing forward, the act of walking becoming an exercise in wading through thick mud.

"Come on, faster. We're almost there." She cast a glance over her shoulder and tugged harder on his hand. She knew he struggled? Shit. He'd hoped to hide it from her. But then she'd spent more than two weeks with him, dealing with his turning to granite in her own way.

By the time they reached the cavern he was all but crawling. She slid her hand from his, effectively yanking the stopper on his basin, his pool of calm circling the drain. He fought not to raise his face to the Heavens, to bellow his rage against his Maker. It would render him grotesque, and he needed her to see him as…something not totally and utterly fucked.

Bad enough he was seconds from turning to stone and she would be as good as lost to him. Squeezing his eyes shut and digging his claws into the ground, Uri concentrated not on the crystalizing of his blood, but on the miracle of feeling Violet *inside* of him.

He scraped together what little courage it offered him and relented to the inexorable force of metamorphic rock.

---

*K*allen listened with the impatience of a tiger pacing behind bars. Daniela sat beside his stone prison, her voice deceptively melodic given the topic of their one-sided conversation.

He wanted to explode out of his granite casement and beat the ever-living tar out of the human male she was talking about, who had seen fit to nearly blind his girlfriend with his fists so she wouldn't look at other men. Holy Christ, the depths to which humanity could sink.

"She might lose the left eye if the doctors can't stem the swelling." He heard Daniela shift position. Crossing and uncrossing her legs? He couldn't fucking tell. She sat at his feet and he couldn't look down, what with his own eyes doing whatever they hell they were going to do. Like sit there, in place, staring at the same starburst in the wall near the crown molding where either he or Drakus, or Kronos, or hell, any one of them, had lost their grip and struck out, damaging what was around them.

The moral of Daniela's story wasn't lost on him. Violent outrages never ended well, whether the victim was living or inanimate.

"It makes me want to press her to my bosom and hold her, keep her safe." Kallen didn't miss the flush in her voice as if she was embarrassed to have confessed such a thing. Hell, it made him want to crush her to *his* bosom and protect her from the violence of the world.

Poor, beloved Darken! No wonder his brotherkynd wanted his Chosen One a thousand miles from this house. Though her line of work put her in the path of Hurricane Destructus, a fact not lost on the other gargoyle, who spent his time spying on her when she wasn't at the safe house.

Now there was a metaphor for the story-minded. A fable steeped in irony. How about that? Mythological beasts with violent tendencies unwilling and unable to hurt their womenkynd.

*Beauty.*

They should get an award.

"…know I can't do that. I guess I just wish they wouldn't go back to their abusers. They always seem to forgive them. Some don't. I mean, these women aren't stupid, Kallen. It's just, I don't know…they love their men. They can't imagine their lives without them."

*Darken's head must spin like that girl from the movie* The Exorcist. Complete with vomit now that he was eating again.

"You don't have to say it." As though she could hear Kallen's thoughts. "You guys are nothing like the human males I have to deal with."

He wondered if Daniela even realized she was already seeing herself as Other, separating herself by degrees with her vocabulary.

"I mean, yeah, you guys get very angry and hit things."

*Very angry.* There were some verbal calisthenics for you.

"But it's that or mutilate yourselves, and I'm sorry, but I've seen girls who cut themselves. I'll take the outward aggression any day of the week."

Well, she had a point. Before he could internalize that wonder-prize, she stood up, her face looming into his line of sight. As she leaned in to kiss his cheek, he lost track of her until she bobbed back into view. "See you later, brotherkynd." Her blush blasted through him like a wall of heat.

Darken, you lucky son of a bitch. To have that God-given gift at your fingertips? Kallen would take to kneeling every day to give thanks to his Creator.

The snick of the door told him Daniela had left, most likely to visit the rest of his brethren. Except Darken, who would hightail it to any part of the house where she wasn't. He avoided her, and with what Kallen had thought was good reason until today.

Daniela, in her uncanny perception, was right. The Kynd were in agony —*victims*—and rather than take it out on themselves, they poured their pain outward onto each other and this house. A fact Darken was striving to remedy one panel of sheetrock at a time.

Kallen would search him out when the moon finished working her magic. Already his locked muscles were loosening, the heat of the sun on his back losing strength. He wriggled his fingers though they were like cold sausages sitting on a plate awaiting the fire of the grill to unleash their potential. He strained to loosen his neck as if he was pulling a semi-truck with his head. All at once, day let go and so did his muscles.

Off balance, he staggered sideways, catching himself on the maple credenza before crashing to the floor. Thank shit the piece of furniture was built like a pig—legs on each corner and a low center of gravity. Otherwise, he'd be putting that on the list of things needing to be replaced.

Embarrassed, Kallen picked himself up from the floor and glanced around to make sure he didn't have an audience. What a show. A feared and reviled monster—according to the Others—falling on his ass like a one-man tribute to the Three Stooges.

Beauty, again. How many more instances would he get to dub with the sarcastic label before the night was out?

Brushing imaginary dirt from his jeans, he headed into the corridor. Halfway up the staircase, he caught the whisper of voices in the dining room and stepped down the stairs backward, retracing his steps as if rewinding the movie of himself.

He leaned his head around the archway. "Hey, Angelia. Guys. What gives?"

"Oh, hey, Kallen. Come on in." The aroma of cooked dough filled his nose, yet his stomach remained impassive, apathetic to the idea of food landing on its pad. Merrick piled another pancake onto an already impressive stack in front of him.

It wasn't charred black, so Angelia must have been at the helm of the stove.

Darken had a plate of peanut butter toast in front of him. Impeccably spread with the four sides still intact, no smile-shaped bite marks in the crust. Like the male had had an appetite then lost it after all the prepping.

"Grab a chair. We were just plotting ways to bring Daniela into the fold. Permanently." She nodded toward Darken. So, that explained the dive in his appetite. Nerves.

"Oh, yeah? Color me Accomplice." Kallen rubbed his hands together after pulling out a chair. The dining room table was back in the center of the room where it used to be when they'd first moved in. They'd shoved it against the wall to keep from breaking it during their frequent outbursts. A glance upward showed the chandelier was still in impeccable, shining form.

Funny, but fixing the inside of the house did make him feel like he was getting repaired, too. God bless Darken and his latest hobby. He'd been right.

"So, how are we pulling off the Heist of the Century?" He knew by the time the last word left his lips he'd dropped a bomb. By the looks of the dour pusses around the table, they were all thinking of Uri and his kidnapped Chosen.

Beauty number three.

Under the table, Merrick pushed his foot against his, an offer of touch. The Kynd equivalent of a pat on the back. They all missed their brotherkynd, and could only hope he was holding his own against a known killer. Uri's Chosen One was a hunter; how was that for an ironic twist for the bear chimera?

Aaaanyway. "Well?" Kallen glanced around the table. Angelia, bless her observant soul, dove on in.

"Daniela has her monthly girl-gathering with some college friends tonight. We're not sure where, yet, but I'm going to call her…" Kallen lost the rest as his brain packed a picnic for park What If.

What if he found his Chosen One, too? Would he have to go through the wringer like his brethren just to have her? Probably. God was like that. One twisted fuck with a penchant for dishing out hard lessons with their just rewards. Frigging asshat.

Was the outcome always going to be good like it was with Merrick and Angelia, or was the end result up to the individuals? True story that God loved his Free Will. So, most likely the odds for a fairy tale ending were fifty-fifty. Or, more realistically ninety-ten, given the Kynds' track record for landing in shit and coming out smelling like shit.

He caught himself just as his hand lifted to cover his eyes. A despairing gesture none of them needed to see.

"…prepared, and then we'll head out."

"I'm sorry. What?"

Angelia gave him a queer look. "I said, once we get Daniela and Darken hooked up, we'll get Drakus prepared, then we'll head for Violet's apartment."

*Drakus prepared.* Like they would need to truss him like a turkey…oh, wait. They probably would. Couldn't have those wings unfurling in public. Jesus, this was such a bad idea on a lot of levels. Why couldn't Angelia just convince him he could help from home or something. Seriously, and it was just a thought, but wouldn't a dragon in downtown Portland add to their overburdened cart that was already listing to port. Oh, and let's not forget the spastic wheel that wouldn't let them steer straight.

Kallen took a deep breath. "Yeah, sure." Over his dead body. "So, my brotherkynd, you're taking the plunge. Smart. And might I add about frigging time."

"I'm not even sure she'll say yes." Darken shot them all a glance, his gray eyes deep with a soup of emotions.

"No worries." Kallen got up and clapped a hand to Darken's lintel of a shoulder. Wide motherfucker. Daniela was no Twiggy, and he made her look delicate and precious as shit. "She won't be able to resist your charm. Trust me." With a parting wink, he left them to wonder if he was joking or not. A coyote's trick to keep them on their toes. And on their flipping rockers.

The sons of bitches. He loved them with all his might. He just wasn't sure how much longer his heart was going to hold out.

Or how pissed they were going to be when they discovered he'd taken Angelia's car. With Darken heading out to reunite with his Chosen, that would leave the rest of the crew without transportation and exactly where he wanted them.

Home safe. While he went to Violet's apartment without them.

---

*V*iolet didn't know what made her walk back into the cave with Urick, other than it seemed the right thing to do. The fact that he'd wrestled his stone-turning butt out into the coming daylight to make sure she was all right? Well, that pressed her sweet, little compassion button with cherub fingers.

While he'd been stone for the day, she'd worried over Jaime and the other kids. Now, though, she was ready to face the dragon, sword in hand. Whether she wielded it or not was up to the male sitting in front of her.

"How do you do it? Not talk for hours at a time?" It had been night for a while. Urick had remained in his corner after his stone curse had left him, silent, whiling away the precious hours she could have been using to make those sick kids feel better.

He shrugged, his broad shoulders rolling like waves way out in the middle of the ocean where the bottom is miles down. "I'm used to it."

Guess her question was rhetorical. Points for the chimera for answering at all. She sat up straighter. If she could get him talking, he'd probably loosen up a little. "Soooo…mind if I sit closer?" Urick shrugged again, but she caught the flash in his eyes now that she knew what to look for. He wanted it desperately. Unfolding herself from her cross-legged position, Violet reversed her motion, sitting face to face, and making sure her knees touched his.

He twitched like she'd zapped him then shifted a little as if to hide his response. Which was fine. The low-grade hum was vibrating through her, too. Sharp as she knew Kynd senses to be, Urick wouldn't have missed her reaction either.

They fidgeted for a while, struck silent by their closeness. At least, that's why she was tongue-tied. Urick, apparently, was used to saying nothing.

"You lived in this cave for a long time, didn't you?"

His gaze snapped to hers. "Why would you say that?"

"It's not like it would take Sherlock Holmes to figure it out. You prefer it here." She nudged him with her knee. "You feel safer."

Urick looked away, giving her his profile. Straight nose, clenched jaw with a hint of stubble. Having had to look at it for days upon days while she'd been trapped in his arms, she knew it wasn't a beard, but the hint of bear hide. As if it was always skimming the surface waiting to erupt full force.

It made him look roguish and rugged like the Marlboro Man of yesteryear.

When he looked back at her, his gray eyes were flat, emotionless.

"Nice trick. I suppose you had to learn it given—"

He growled then swallowed, pushed his knee harder to hers as if seeking balance. Good. He was touching her. Next step, getting him to the hospital.

"*Given* it was your only defense." Okay, so she nicked the dragon with her sword to get him to budge. Sue her.

"It's…in the past."

She snorted. "Right. In the past. Mind if I take a little bite then? I'm feeling peckish."

Urick flinched then smoothed out.

"Too late. I caught your reaction. You don't want my fangs anywhere near you."

"No." He looked to his left, revealing the other side of that strong face. "Yes." When his gaze touched upon hers again, black marbled into the gray. "I don't know."

"Since we're being honest, nobody has ever fed from me before." A heavy second lay between them then Urick crammed the heels of his hands to his forehead, his biceps bulging so hard it looked as if his skin might split.

Violet touched his knee with her fingertips. "Hey. Look at me." When he did, she admitted for reasons God alone knew, "I liked it."

"You don't have to say that."

"Why not? I did. I'd let you do it again." She waggled her eyebrows.

His lips twitched as if he was fighting a grin. "You remind me of my brotherkynd, Kallen."

"Yeah?"

"Yeah. He's always trying to make our troubles seem ridiculous." The suppressed grin made an appearance. "One time after a fight, we were standing in our poor frigging library, you know, sheaves of paper floating down around us like leaves or some shit, and he says, serious as all get out, '*I lost my page.*' Like his book had fallen off his knee to the floor, not cycloned by the rest of us losing our shit."

"You guys do that a lot? *Lose your shit?*"

"If I said *yes,* would you hate me more?"

She pursed her lips down on her smile but let it spark upward to her eyes. "Not possible."

"Yeah." He nodded a couple of times. "Yeah."

"So, about what I said. Would you try, you know, to feed from me again?"

His hand reached out for her but he pulled it back, fisting it. "God, what a question. Seriously? I don't know. I don't want to hurt you. You're my Chosen One. I'm not supposed to be able to, and I do when…" He swallowed around the words that lodged in his throat.

"No, you don't. Surprisingly, it feels good." She knew she blushed because it scorched her face like a frigging house fire.

"You're not lying."

As if rueful, she shook her head. "No. No, I'm not."

"I'm not sure I can return the favor without…you know, freaking the fuck out."

"That's all right. No books."

"Funny."

"I was trying to be." Their gazes locked. Violet licked her lips, her tongue skimming a sensitive fang. Man, talking with Urick like this was *stimulating*—to avoid a more risqué description that would sear the heated skin of her face even worse.

Riveting his gaze to hers, he said, "They chained me down. For centuries. Feeding off me in groups or alone."

"Jesus H. Christ."

"No. He wasn't anywhere around."

"I can't even joke about that." Mainly because she knew exactly what Urick was talking about. It was the second reason she needed to get her butt out of there. Pronto. She had a vampire to kill.

Urick slid his arm out, his palm up and open. Without glancing down, Violet placed her hand in his. "You feel that, too, yes?"

He nodded.

"You didn't lie about it, then, did you? We're connected in this weird way."

"I'm sorry."

"I'm not. Not really." Not if she could get him to help the kids.

"You should be. Connected to the Kynd? You were right to revile us. We're cursed."

"As are we all in some way."

They sat together like that for a while, her hand in his, the feel of it rough and warm.

"So. Will you go back to the hospital, even though…"

His sharp gargoyle teeth chewed at his bottom lip. "I could lose it?"

Violet nodded as she watched him closely.

Urick squeezed her fingers. "You'd take that risk?"

"The kids are worth it."

He seemed to assess her as if weighing the truth of her admission against the likelihood of his own. "Then, yeah. Yeah, I guess so." As he rose to his feet, he helped Violet to hers.

"Peachy." Her smile felt four feet wide. It was contagious, too. Urick smiled back at her, all sheepish with splashes of fear in his mercurial eyes.

---

*U*ri needed to keep touching her. Standing together as they were, his hands turned into locks unwilling to tumble free. His thumb was stroking the inside of her wrist, and he had to will it to stop, which was like trying to bend a spoon with his mind. "Violet."

She answered by lifting hooded lids to meet his gaze, her thousand-watt smile dimming to something more smoky. A shiver rippled through him, hardening his cock. *Holy Jesus.* He gripped her hand tighter and stepped closer. Dropping his head, he pressed his face to her hair, breathing her in.

"W-what are you doing?"

Sniffing her like his bear ass wanted a piece of the action, too. How frigging disgusting was that? The Others were like humans in their prejudices, right? No bestiality. Except sometimes Merrick's lion mane and claws crept forth and Angelia would twirl her fingers through the shag at the chimera's neck, play with his claws with her fingertips. They would disappear shortly after. Uri could guess where they went.

But still. Violet wasn't Angelia. If he needed a reminder, he could think back to when he'd first abducted her, when she'd called him nasty things. Words which had torn deep, ripping wide holes inside him. He was proud to be Kynd, even though she'd spewed poisonous words he'd heard countless Others say, too. They were monsters, and here he was gaining ground, proving there was more to him than grim legend, and he was suckling her scent like a freak.

"Do it again." She tilted her head, the motion dragging her hair along his cheek.

His insides coiled tighter, shrinking his skin. His grip tightened around her wrist. She wanted more? A low snarl eddied out of him as he tugged her closer, his hips pushing into her. Violet leaned in, her body pliant, her head dropping back so the tendons in her neck strained.

Thoughts scattering like a jar of marbles smashing to the floor, Uri curled himself around her, his arms wrapping her close as he pressed his lips to her neck. Against the flesh of his lips, the ligaments were taut cables encased in silk. He craved more of this contradiction, flicking his tongue for salty nibbles. Her jugular throbbed, a frenetic tempo marking the rhythm of her heart.

She grew excited. His own heart crashed, a giant bird thrashing in a too small cage. His breaths grew short, heated. Things became jungle-like about his face, moist, hot. He worked his mouth over the bone of her jaw and sucked when his lips found hers.

The moan riding through him was hers, fraying the fetters of his control. Uri clutched her tighter, his hips pushing as he lowered his hand to grip her tight ass. Violet dragged her leg up the side of his.

Holy Christ, the swelling at his nether region pained him. It needed assuaging. It needed the hot little vampire to touch it. A flicker of thought that he held a vampire so close struggled to flare up, but her scent swamped it, her need like a hard breath snuffing the trembling flame.

She was his Chosen One, a truth humming under his skin like a maddening reminder of why he was losing himself. She was his. A creature born for him. That she was of the race who had tortured and abused him was of no consequence. She was a shining star in a barrel of filth. An anomaly kept pure for him alone!

She tasted like life. Uri dug deeper, swallowed it, gorged upon it. When her claws pinched the skin of his back, he lifted her feet from the floor so as to lay her down. He craved to have her beneath him, her legs spread, her neck bared.

As he looked down upon his feast, she was…not looking at him but at the wall.

"Violet." His voice sounded thick, guttural. "Look upon me." Gently, he reached for her chin, tilting it so he could see her amber eyes. "What's wrong?"

For a few ponderous heartbeats, she didn't answer or look up at him, and doubt slid toward him like demon shadows, certain to swallow him in a chill, inky darkness. She didn't want him, after all. Now that they were getting more intimate, her old feelings of revulsion were returning, she was going to do something painful to him in order to get away.

Inwardly, Uri curled around his shriveling stomach; a preemptive act of self-defense. Not that he'd let Violet know how hard he was cringing. She'd take full advantage of his weakness. Except when she finally turned her face, he wanted to cup her cheek in his clawed hand and caress his thumb along her temple. She looked at him with wanting, her eyes glittering. Her lips were flushed red, her fang tips pressing the corners. She was hungry?

Oh, Jesus, Jesus. His blood ran cold. She was hungry in the way he'd been. Aroused and wanting a stronger connection. His blood flared hot. Like he had a fever, his burning skin shivered.

"I…" If he breathed, he'd blast an abhorred roar in her face. Like he'd done so many times before when the vampires had feasted.

*She isn't them.* The thought ushered through him like a soothing breeze, loosening his lungs so he could take a breath. This was Violet, who had fed from him before. She hadn't squirmed all over him like a snake, fangs twisting in his flesh, rending it with painful gashes. She had suckled gently, her eyes had been brimming with concern. And it had been right to give of himself to her.

Not only because she was his Chosen female, but for what she'd done with his blood in her veins. She'd sought to give succor to those in dire need. Mere children who faced death. So unfair that those innocent lives were but a blink, while his went on endlessly. For what end?

To remain tortured and bitter?

Uri gazed down upon Violet spread beneath him. She lay quiet, watching him as if aware of his struggle as if she cared that he wrestled his demons. She was giving him time, not thinking of ways to hurt him.

With a sigh, he rolled off her onto his back, pulling her on top of him so she straddled his hips. If she undid his pants, his erection would spring forth, his lust for her still riding him despite what he was about to let her do.

*Probably because of it.* Yeah, there was that. The vampire ached for its female.

"Take of me." He said the words, but his body remained rigid, his fear marking him for a liar, a coward.

Violet folded her arms. "Really?"

He nodded and stared off at the wall she'd been looking at.

"You're a real gem, aren't you?"

"What?" He stole a look from the corner of his eye.

"Look at you. *Take of me.* What a crock. I should suck you dry just for making me feel like the frigging leech I am. Which I'm not, by the way," she quickly corrected herself.

"You aren't a leech." He meant it with every fiber of his being. He turned his head to get a better look at her.

"Oh, no? Then why are you laying under me like a cow awaiting slaughter."

"A cow?"

"Yeah. Mooooo." She waggled her fingers at him.

He propped himself up on his elbows. Violet remained straddled across his hips. "I'm not a cow. I'm not scared."

"Well, now you're not. But five seconds ago?"

"Fine, I was, but I was going to let you feed from me."

"Oh, wow, sah! Surely you're so gen'rous!" Violet clasped her heart.

Uri bit down on his smile. "Cut it out."

She put her hands on his pecs, leaned in, and pushed him down. "Not until you do."

His muscles went wooden as a smokehouse Indian again. He fought to keep eye contact, but his peepers drifted to the ceiling, his brain needing to exit the scene.

"Hey. Look at me."

"I am."

She slapped his stomach. Hard. As he ooofed and curled in on himself, she said, "Cut it out. Look at me."

Uri leaned back, the sting on his belly reminding him of the here and now. "Okay. I'm looking at you."

"Better." She got up off him, wiping her hands across her ass once she stood up. "Now, let's go."

"To the hospital?" His dick deflated. Fear could do that.

*"To the hospital?"* She wagged her head as she mocked him, putting her hands on her hips. "Yeah, to the hospital. Where else?"

"But I haven't…we haven't…"

"No, we haven't, Captain Cripple, but my blood will do until you can figure out how to get your thumb out of your ass." Without looking back, she walked purposefully toward the exit.

"Wait. I…" Shit. He wasn't ready. He was ready. Shit. He exhaled like a bull preparing to charge, scraped his hands across his scalp. "Okay." He trotted after her, anxiety and excitement bubbling through him like a witch's brew.

By the time they burst out onto the desert night, he'd managed to gather his shit. Watching Violet's taunting butt could be the reason. God knew, he didn't want it far from his sight, and if he didn't yank his thumb out of his crack then Violet would indeed go without him.

Which scared him more than what he was about to do until she turned to face him, her lips lifted in a wondrous smile. His feet tripped to a stop, and suddenly he felt like one of those superheroes. Uri all but put his hands on his hips to survey his job well done.

Instead, he snagged her close, disappearing them to the hospital ledge. As they landed he held onto her, afraid she'd feel woozy and topple off the edge. Yeah, because she wasn't a vampire and hadn't been teleporting for ages.

He shut his mental pie hole, glad as hell to be touching her.

Violet stepped away, blowing into her hands to warm them. Uri curled his, not feeling the cold, but the emptiness. "I think I want to head back to where we were. Heck, it's freezing."

His heart rate spiked at the idea. She wanted to go back to the place he thought of as his own. *She's kidding, fidiot.* Everyone says things like that when they're faced with zero-degree temperatures. On the roof, a February wind whipped at his thin clothes though he didn't notice. Not when Violet was hopping from one foot to the other, rubbing her arms.

"O-okay, we should have discussed a game plan before we left." The bitter wind played with her hair, fluffing it about her face. Her cheeks were pale, her nose shiny and red at the tip. Her eyes watered, making the amber seem like sparkling gems.

"Sorry," he said, grabbing her again. This time he landed them inside, a mere foot from Jaime's bed.

In a raspy whisper, Violet gave him hell. "You shouldn't do that! What if she was awake?" She spun around to look at the girl.

"She wasn't. I checked. No one else is either."

Maybe it was her relief that made her relax into his space again, but he shut his eyes to savor the heat of her. It was wrapped in cold, but the contrast made her closeness that much more real to him.

It also shut out where they were, sort of. He could still hear the faint blips of the machinery hovering near, but Violet's presence dominated, his senses so tuned to her he could filter everything else.

"You checked? How in heck could you—" She waved it off. "Never mind." As she took a step closer to the bed with its aluminum railing, Uri's feet ushered him backward, two thieves trying to exit the crime scene.

Fear grew inside him like a hairy animal as his eyes stuck to the unfolding horror in front of him. He didn't stop until his radar registered he was about to hit something with his panicking ass. Like one of those scared-shitless girls in those human horror movies, he looked around himself slow-like, afraid fast movement might stir the monster stalking him.

Hell, and damnation. He'd gravitated to Winnie the Pooh's bed.

Guess he found the monster. It was him. A giant beast of a male who would scare what few months of life this poor kid had left if he woke to see him. Because come on. On a good day, Uri had claws and sharp teeth. Gargoyles looked human from far away, but close up? The damage was in the details.

The kid stirred under his ironed cotton blanket. The covering was blue, like his bruised eyelids, his arm thin as a chicken wing. God, how awful. The boy should be ruddy cheeked and robust from playing ball in the snow. He should be...not this. Not here. A wounded ghost of kids his age whose toys were bats and stick guns, while his were softer things such as stuffed animals.

Like Winnie the frigging Pooh, a bedraggled doll clutched and crushed to the sleeping boy's chest. Pooh's arms were stuck out as if stretching for freedom, his plastic eyes empty. Seeing them gave Uri the willies, like looking at a dead body.

He shuddered, fur poking from his skin along his back, tickling up his spine.

The last time he'd seen lifeless eyes, his hands and feet had been chained to a floor and his cell companion had succumbed to having his blood drained. Not sporting enough pints to keep the old ticker going could do that to you.

As could enough toxins.

Uri stared down at the child in the bed, his eyes traveling the looping road of a clear tube running up to the frail elbow, to where a band of tape veered it off to the pole standing ready, yet indifferently, at the head of the bed.

The smell of sickness was all over the boy as if his very blood was poisoned.

His Violet supped on this?

Oh, hell no. As Uri's world tipped sideways, he clamped his jaws down on

75

the growl welling up inside him. *Protect her.* Absofuckinglutely. But from what? Herself?

Hell, yes. Even if he had to lock her—scratch that. He'd imprisoned her more than he ever should have. It wasn't as if he didn't know all about the emasculation of helplessness. Peeling his gaze off the bed in front of him, Uri bounced his gaze to Violet, landing it on her like one of those Velcro dart board games. Target sighted and stuck.

She'd lowered the bars at the side of the bed and was now sitting with the girl. Thin legs encased in stiff blankets were like railroad tracks covered in sand dunes beside her. Fuck him, but the sight of them lurched his gut as if someone launched off the diving board of his stomach. The sac started bouncing under his ribcage, threatening to vault bile in a reverse swan dive up his throat.

Uri was across the room before the machines blipped out the passage of a second but stopped from grabbing her at the last instant. His body all *hey now* and swaying with the abrupt cease.

He didn't touch her. All he could do was watch the back of her head bob as she fed on the arm she held in her hands. As if flown by its own pilot, his hand fell to her back, gripping her shirt and fisting the fabric with a gentle squeeze.

# CHAPTER 5

*V*iolet knew Urick returned, not by the big hand splayed across her back, but by the low-grade hum hitting her like a couple of Alka-Seltzers, settling her with a plop-plop and a sizzle. She drank it in through her skin, glad for the unexpected relief his touch brought her.

As she kept sucking out the vile shit in Jaime's veins her hand reached out, patting around like a blind kitten. Wobbly and unsure but for one thing, mama's tit.

Not that this huge, hovering, and trembling male at her back reminded her of mama. But the offer of comfort was there, nonetheless. When she found it, she latched on so hard the bones of his hand rubbed together like chopsticks.

She'd say thanks, but her fangs were deep and working to keep the twin holes open so the blood would continue to ooze forth. It felt as if it was taking forever. Then again, it probably was. The girl was so sick her heart thumped as lazy as a dog's tail on a rug by the hearth.

The worst was over, at least. She'd punctured the skin, which for Violet was like biting into an overripe plum. Not that she compared Jaime to rotting fruit, but her skin, like everyone else's, was leather-like while inside the flesh was…well, fuck it, it was juicy.

Yet, the girl's blood didn't exactly spurt out. Violet had to suck hard, doing the heavy lifting Jaime's heart should have been doing. A few more tugs, though, and she could refuel that which she'd drained.

Urick's touch was like a few gallons of gas added to an empty tank, especially when the hand gripping her shirt started sliding over her spine in an easy rub. Back and forth, back and forth. Soothing, but the trembling in his palms told her to hurry the eff up.

How long he'd tolerate watching her feed was a game of craps in a back alley. No telling when the fun police would show up and ruin your lucky streak. She pulled her fangs out and swiped her tongue across the puncture wounds. With a squeeze to that big hand pushing into the bed, she bored twin holes into her own wrist and held the dripping elixir to the girl's lips.

"Hand me some of those tissues from that table, would you?" As she heard the piff piff of Kleenex serving it up from its continuous roll, she did a little math in her head. Would Urick hand over the tissues before the blood channeling down her arm spread its evidence onto the satin lining of Jaime's night dress?

The girl wasn't pulling on her vein the way she should. "Come on, baby, come on. Think of it as a milkshake." Since her hands were busy, Violet couldn't push the girl's bangs from her pale forehead, but it didn't mean she couldn't give comfort another way.

It was the best part of what she did. Yeah, she was going to vomit her guts out over the next several hours, but it was this nurturing that she loved and took as a just reward. As the tension in Jaime's brow eased, Violet felt the tug on her heart. The clap for a job not just well done, but done right. This comfort to others less fortunate allowed her to live with herself.

The tissues were daubed then pressed under her wrist by a hand still shaking. Directly over her shoulder, Urick's breaths came out calculatedly steady, as if he counted them in yogic calming techniques.

His heart was close enough to her back now she could feel the whump of the air between them. "Not long now," she whispered, though not sure if the words were for Urick or herself. Already she felt the sticky fingers of corrupted blood climbing up the back of her throat.

When her own heart started flailing like an albatross shot in the wing, she let Jaime have a few more pulls then took her arm away. She pushed her wrist to her lips, lapping to close the wounds.

"We're done here," Urick said and swept her up. Seconds later she was on the fire escape outside her kitchen window. In the bear chimera's arms, where else. Another blink of her eyes and she was inside getting lowered onto her sofa. "I'll be right back."

He released her slowly, as though reluctant to lose contact. But the moment he did, his heavy boots could be heard clomping down the wood floor of her hallway. As her defenses spiked her pulse, she listened as he stopped at her workout room door.

Before she could rally excuses, and battle the rising tide of Jaime's blood to her back molars he was back, holding an empty duffel. Keeping her jaw clamped shut, Violet pointed to the bag in his fist. "What's that for?" She let her hand flop back down onto the arm of the couch, resisting the urge to curl into the fetal position.

"For your things. After you pack, we're going back to the cave while you recuperate."

"I don't think—" She clapped her hand to her mouth and shoved passed him, gunning for the bathroom. She made a sloppy slide to her knees just as her guts heaved, splashing blood and bile into the bowl. Mostly.

Hands pushing her hair out of her face and elbows on the rim, she groaned a throaty *fuuuck* into the red soup in front of her. As she spit and swallowed, calloused hands caressed over hers, petting the loose tendrils back and gently pinching a pony tail at her nape.

A cold, wet cloth appeared in front of her. "Thanks." She pressed it to her forehead, not bothering to wipe her mouth because that wasn't her last hurl. No point in mopping up if you were just going to get things nasty again.

"This happens a lot?"

She nodded and spit. Urick's sigh added weight to the room. When she heaved another batch of her stomach contents, he muttered *fuck* for her, but kept hold of her hair. Violet lay her cheek on the cool porcelain while around her the air seemed to shimmer with Urick's body heat.

His hovering bulk would have been suffocating except that somehow it did the opposite, easing her throat so she could breathe a little easier between the spastic swallowing. It was several minutes before she could claim victory in that department, but at least her stomach felt calm enough to sit back on her ass.

Hands shaking and with cold sweat stuck to her skin, she held the wet cloth to her burning forehead. "I must look like a million bucks." Urick reached over her to flush the toilet. "And smell like it. Jesus."

When he helped her to her feet, she let him. It felt too comforting to have someone hold her when her body was made of Jell-O. Then ever so slowly he scooped her into his arms and set her on the edge of the tub. While the water gushed out of the spout behind her, Urick unlaced her boots.

Bent over in front of her, his back looked two yards wide. Muscles rippled under his t-shirt and yet he painstakingly dragged the laces through the eyelets, never once tugging too hard to unbalance her.

"I can do this, you know."

He didn't look up. "I know."

Right, she'd proven that when she'd bungled playing coy in front of him in the cave. "I'm just saying you don't have to...you know, pamper me."

His gaze flashed up and held hers. "Yes. Yes, I do."

"That Chosen thing?"

"That and others." Urick pulled her to her feet and began popping the buttons through the slots of her blouse. One. Two. She watched his clawed fingers flick the tiny, hard plastic buttons. Holy Lord, he shook. Three. Four...until he was done. Rough palms caressing her clavicles, he pushed the shirt off her shoulders.

The bathroom shrunk by the square yard.

"I...I can get my pants." Her hands went to the clasp at her waist. Urick stepped back, his head down as though being polite enough not to watch her undress. She slid her pants off and stepped into the steaming tub.

No bubbles to hide under. Figured.

"May I wash you?" His gaze flicked to her eyes again, holding her, the stubble of his jaw rolling across the clenching muscle.

"Ah..." If her mouth hung open any farther, she'd catch flies with it. "Yeah, um, yeah, sure." While her gaze bounced around looking for the soap and wash cloth—because, hey, she'd never been in her own tub before— Urick knelt beside her, the barrier of porcelain seeming as inadequate as a podium in one of those dreams where you're naked in front of an audience.

Yeah, okay, whatever. She was naked, and he was ready because he didn't have any sleeves to push up. Oh, and lookie, he already had a washcloth in his trembling hand. Bathing her meant this much to him?

Aw, shit. How tender was that? If she wasn't careful she was going to fall for this guy, Chosen thing or no. "You could join me." *What!* She did not just say that! "I mean, you can, you know, wash..." Oh, man, she had diarrhea of the mouth. And what do you know, the blood she'd swallowed earlier was climbing up her throat again. "S'cuse me!"

Sloshing water like a tanker coming in to dock too fast, she bolted for the toilet, skidding into a wet and naked heap just as blood spewed out of her mouth. When she finally became aware of the world outside of the red water in the bowl under her face, Urick was still right there with her holding her hair, caressing back the errant locks.

"God, I'm sorry. I probably should have told you this happens." Hand flapping to find the handle, she flushed without bothering to move. She watched the swirling water change from bright red to pink before it funneled down the drain.

"Great first date, huh." Another cold washcloth appeared in front of her face.

*U*rick couldn't answer her. She was trying to make light of this, and he was trying not to crawl out of his skin. After Violet took the cold cloth he offered her, he fisted his hand at his hip, fighting the urge to put that fist through the mirror above her sink. Or through her sink, for that matter. How could she do this to herself? She knew she'd be sick, and she went ahead and swapped blood with that girl? Pride infused itself into his anger, barely tempering it.

His Violet was strong, but Jesus Christ, he felt so fucking helpless. She was spewing up her stomach in great heaves, and with every splashing retch, the top of his head was going to blow off. While he wanted to hug the life out of her.

Granted, with her head in the toilet bowl, she couldn't see what this was doing to him. But another round of her cuddling the crapper and she was going to find out.

"You think this is funny?" His voice sounded weird in his ears like maybe he wasn't pushing it up his throat so much as threading it through a meat grinder.

With his fingers coiled into her hair, he felt her fall still. Then spit. Her attentive silence pushed the door on his temper ajar. "You think I enjoy watching you suffer? Watching and smelling that poison come out of you? When there is nothing, *nothing*, I can do about it?" His gaze swept down the knobs of her bare spine. Naked and undone as she was, she seemed delicate as a housecat.

"Let me go." She spit into the bowl again. "I said, let my hair go."

"Why? So that can be desecrated too?" The last word came out toooooo as Violet recoiled like a whip, discharging her fist with a crack into his face. With his head snapping back, it took out his girders. Uri crashed to his ass on the hard tile.

Like a frickin' trick rider at the rodeo, she leapt and straddled him, lowering her face to within inches of his. "You think I like the taste of blood? Think I do when it's flying out of my mouth? You son of a bitch...You have no idea!"

The second punch came at him like one of those Jack in the Box toys. He'd been listening to the music of her voice, all jammin' like she's humming Pop Goes the Weasel, when bam! She hit him so hard the back of his head cracked the floor.

Well, thank you God for making him with a thick skull. His Chosen packed a nuclear bomb in those fists and didn't the blast do wonders for his equilibrium. He might have been knocked to his seat cushions, and his head might be swimming a teensy bit, but day-am.

Uri wiped the blood off his grin.

Violet cocked her head. "What's the matter with you?"

"Nothing. Now."

She slid off him to sit with her back to the tub, elbows on her naked knees.

Rolling to his knees real slow and careful so his spinning head didn't give him his turn at the puke-fest, Uri rewet the washcloth with cold water and handed it back to his Chosen. "You still have a little blood." He daubed at the corner of his mouth to show her and realized he did too.

"So, ah, I wasn't expecting that." His smile wouldn't quit, the darn thing emanating out of the center of him, making him feel overfull in a sunny-meadow and hand-holding kind of way. Any second he expected birds to start chirping love songs. His Chosen One...was frigging awesome.

"You never are." She dabbed at the blood on her mouth, masking her emerging grin with the cloth. But he saw the shine in her eyes, the sight of it practically levitating him off the floor.

"True." He shrugged, making no excuses.

"Because I'm this Chosen thing, right?"

"No. You are no *thing.* You're my..." He almost blathered out *awesome female* like some pimple-faced kid in Junior High.

"Your what?" Suspicion made her body stiffen and she grew pale. The adrenaline leaving her body? Would she be sick again?

Uri waved her question off and lumbered to his size thirteens. He held a towel out to wrap around her, fingers pinched on each end as he gave it a welcoming shake. "Come on, before you get sick again." Impatient lest she catch a chill, he swept her up in the towel as he swung her up in his arms.

Careful not to bang her feet or any other part of her precious body on the narrow doorjambs or hallway walls, he took her to her bedroom and set her down on her unmade bed. "Sit here." When she opened her mouth, he said, "Please."

She slumped but stayed put. Uri rummaged in her closet for another duffel bag and found an old army backpack that had seen more miles than a courier's bicycle. Violet had done some traveling afoot? When? More important, why? A hollow feeling set up shop in his gut as he imagined her out in the world alone with nothing at her back but this battered canvas sack.

Uri rifled his hand around in the bag to make sure it was empty then left the closet and its door with about thirty coats of paint. As he yanked open the top drawer of her dresser, Violet leapt off the bed, making a beeline for him on legs wobbly as a baby deer's.

"That's my underwear drawer, perv." She elbowed him out of the way.

---

*J*n the eyes of the Lord, stealing was a sin, which was why Kallen was merely borrowing Angelia's Audi. It wasn't even like he was splitting hairs since he'd be returning the vehicle when his visit with Kristov was over.

Putting the sporty little SQ5 in Park, he stared through the windshield up at the Vampyre's house. To his right, the brick pathway to the front door looked as inviting as a dead dog's tongue. Then the wrought iron lamps came on, shining buttery welcome along the walkway's ess curves.

Well, he was here, right? Might as well make his entrance. Uri needed help and Kristov knew just what kind. Feeling ridiculous as he shoe-horned himself out of the mini SUV, Kallen pocketed his sissy nerves and trudged for the front entrance. Without Kronos at his side, the trip to the main door seemed to warp, like maybe he was on one of those Funhouse treadmills that kept you in place even though your legs were pistons trying to fire your ass to another section of tricksy fun.

Like going back into the Vampyre's home when he'd managed to leave it the first time without demolishing it.

Barely.

The house opened its maw as he heaved his heavy carcass up the granite stairs, a triangle of light fanning across the dark lawn behind him. From the step he was on, he and Kristov looked face to face. On even ground so to speak, Kallen saw the deadness in the Vampyre leader's eyes on a level he hadn't been able to before.

A cold shiver ran down his back like someone dropped an ice cube down his shirt. Filled with a sudden urge to kindle something in that awful gaze, Kallen stuck his hand out for a meet and greet, and sent a little spark of Kynd into the palm clasping his.

"What the—"

"Call it a gift." Kallen grinned, showing off his gargoyle choppers. "If you want to return the favor, pink's my favorite color."

"Pink, huh? I'll remember that." Kristov pulled his hand from Kallen's grasp and rubbed his knuckles. "That's just too—"

"Weird?"

Kristov flashed him a look. "I was going to say frightening."

"That would have been my second choice."

"You guys could power a city with that kind of current."

"Most likely." Kristov led him down a different hallway than the one they'd used last time and ushered him into a library of sorts. To their left was a neat as a pin Sheraton style desk. Directly across from it, placed so it would never be missed by the male seated behind that desk, was a stunning portrait of what had to be Kristov's mate.

Leaning in, Kallen fingered the gilded frame surrounding the oil painting of a female primped to the nines in peach silk. Her gown was corseted but flowed like mead all around her. The eyes gazing out from the canvas matched the dress, and her hair, black and shiny as a clarinet in the footlights, had been intricately piled so it seemed to spill upward even as the glittering gems woven through it cascaded down.

"She's beautiful."

Kristov stood behind him, still rubbing his hand. "Yes, she was the most beautiful woman I've ever known."

God, he wanted to drown himself. The Vampyre's sorrow hadn't been dulled by the passing of years. "Why are you showing me this." The last time he was here, he and Kronos had been ushered to the sitting room. This was about as far from formal as the ancient Vampyre probably got.

"To share, I suppose. I don't know." As if his knees lost their starch, Kristov folded into a damask chair. "I thought...hell, I don't know what I was thinking."

Kallen found a home in the chair beside the Vampyre, so they were both seated facing the portrait of Kristov's mate, who should still be warming the rooms of the house with her beating heart. "You think Uri will love his mate the way you love yours?"

"I don't know. Yes, I guess so."

"Why? Why show me this when obviously this Violet is nothing like..."

"Arabella." He said the name as though he had a rolled carpet crammed in his throat. "Her name is...was...Arabella."

They stared at the woman immortalized before them. She was beautiful in the way of ages past. Unlike this Violet, who was as modern as they came with her Lara Croft arsenal. How could someone like that fall for a male like Uri? Not that the guy wasn't the best male he knew, but come on. He was almost up there with Drakus, and that wasn't a compliment. If Uri lost his shit over wanting to mate a vampire like a vampire, this female wasn't going to clasp her heart and faint.

Dragging his thoughts out of that hellhole, he asked, "Did she love you the way you love her?"

Kristov shrugged. "I suppose she did. She was very distraught when faced with…"

Kallen waited for him to elaborate and got no fruits for his labor.

"What if she's harmed him? What if she doesn't return his love, rejects the idea of being his Chosen One?" Terror took up residence under his skin, and he got up to walk it off before he demolished the shrine of Kristov's love.

"I thought you and I could visit her apartment this night. You might pick up on something my friends and I may have missed."

"It's like you're reading my mind." Kallen waggled his eyebrows. "It's why I came over here tonight. I was hoping to talk you into coming with me. You know, be my vampire sidekick."

Kristov held in a long-suffering sigh. "I'll drive."

"What, you're not going to teleport me?"

"Your heavy ass?" This time when Kristov smiled there was a flash of warmth in his silver eyes, reminding Kallen a little of his brethren when they had their happy moments.

"Fine, but I pick the music."

"Not a chance." As they made their way to the garage, Kallen got a fast tour of Kristov's home. A woman's touch was evident throughout, and a pang stung his heart. Of its own volition, his hand went to rub the hurt in his chest.

*God, please let our home be like this. Let our females make their mark upon our lives as Arabella has done in Kristov's.* Scratching the grief and death part, of course. He sent his prayer heavenward, hoping God in his infinite wisdom knew what the hell He was doing.

---

*S*nagging the backpack as she shoved Urick's nosy nose away from her unmentionables, Violet willed the shakes out of her muscles. God, how embarrassing! He was going to see her not so special underwear. No frilly anythings with lacey straps or peekaboo silks.

Just boy shorts and cotton bras and camis. The sole exception had been the red thong bought in a moment of whimsy. How lucky that she'd been wearing it the night of her abduction. Kind of like being caught in Tuesday's panties on Tuesday.

Usually, she dressed for comfort. It wasn't as if her nights out involved seduction. Unless, of course, you counted her love affair with killing rogue vampires. Ridding the planet of them kind of turned her screw, got her blood revving.

Urick loomed behind her. When Violet spun around to hide the open drawer, his hands went up to fend off a hit. She couldn't help but smile as pride flushed through her to starch her sagging muscles. "That's right, Kynd, back off. This is private, so go over there." She flicked her fingers, shooing him off.

The oaf folded his arms and planted his feet.

"What now?" Even though he hadn't shifted, his stubborn refusal made her think of bears standing their ground. She tightened the knot on the towel.

"You're hiding something." Under his black t-shirt, his shoulders rolled like maybe he was trying to keep himself from swinging out with a big paw.

"Duh, I'm hiding something. It's called my underwear, and you can keep your observating ass away from them. So, go on now. Flee." She waggled her fingers at him again. When he didn't budge, she shoved him. He swayed like an oak tree in a summer breeze—barely bending. He smiled like she was amusing.

"Man, you really like getting punched, don't you?"

"No." But he nodded.

*What the frig?* He was more confounding than Twitter. "Then go over there while I pack, or I won't pack." She lifted her eyebrows as she squared her jaw, the taste of tainted blood riding over her tongue. She feigned indifference. *Strong front, Vi.*

Urick growled. An honest to goodness bear growl. She'd been right about the ursine thing. The crackerhead was a chimera, after all, his triple beastie-ass ever present. Which meant his vampire hovered at the edge of the stage waiting for its chance in the spotlight. A creature double feature.

Where, then, was the gargoyle?

With a shake of his head, Urick backed up to the window as if he'd just lobbed a coherent thought into his frontal lobe. Pulling the drapes aside he peered out, probably scanning for enemies.

There it was. The gargoyle watcher. The strike three in this game of… Oh, hell and tarnation. Violet spun back around to finish her packing. Cursing at herself, she shoved a tee and some undies into her sack then worked her way down the dresser, finishing off with a pair of cargo pants. Bag full, she went to toss it onto the bed while she got dressed, but fell still as her attention wandered to Urick lurking by the window instead.

He watched the street below, looking protective as hell—what with his imposing height, the width of his shoulders, and his thick, long legs made sturdier by the boots he was wearing. Oh, and she couldn't miss his flat stomach.

Three strikes, her ass. Overbearing tendencies aside, the hunk was growing on her. Tending her when she was vomiting like Old Faithful, undressing her gently as he ignored the crushing bulge in his jeans, looking at her—and here was the clincher—like she was his sun and he was stuck in her gravitational pull.

She spaced getting dressed. "Come on then, if we're going." Urick snagged a blanket from her bed and was wrapping it around her before she finished blinking. Pulling her close, he rasped in her ear, "You aren't too weak to teleport on your own, I just…"

With him stuck tighter than a June bug, it wasn't hard to feel him tense up.

"Want to do it because you're a control freak?"

He squeezed a little harder as though to squash her lie.

When their feet reappeared on the night sand, he kept hold of her arms to peer down at her. "No. Because you're my Chosen and mine to care for."

Son of a biscuit, he was…sweet. "Ah, so I'm your property, is that it?" She stepped from his embrace so he wouldn't feel her heart fluttering. Nor did she want him to know how weak she was. From being sick, yeah, but also because no way in hell could she have teleported so frigging far in one leap. At least, now that his blood no longer flowed through her veins.

Violet didn't know of any other vampires who could teleport that far, not even the ancient Triumvirate Vampyres. If Urick had been ignoring his vampire side, chances were good he didn't know that such a herculean feat was anything special.

Heart squeezing, she also figured he'd teleported her to safeguard her pride. He probably thought she had no problem going such huge distances, but couldn't this time because she was sick.

*Damn it.* Getting sappy would muddy the waters when she needed a clear head around this guy. "Whatever," she said, cutting off his response to her being his property. "Get us inside before the sun comes and I don't know… does its thing." Like fry her exhausted butt and turn his to stone.

Poor bastard. How awful to be struck helpless like that every dawn. She nipped the thought like a Doberman on a mailman's britches.

Once they were in the cavern, Urick peeled the blanket from her shoulders and spread it out on the floor near her corner, placing her bag on one end like a pillow. Still squatting, he twisted those wide shoulders to look up at her. "The water in the pool is always warm if you still want that bath."

Well, since she was standing there in a towel… "Yeah, I feel kind of gross."

Urick opened his mouth then shut it. Because he thought she wouldn't like what he had to say?

"Still want to bathe me?" A sympathy invitation. Truly. She headed for the shallow pool while images of his big, gentle hands caressing her skin assailed her. When he didn't follow, the water she lowered herself into slipped over her skin and somehow made her feel more naked.

He was still squatting and staring at her makeshift pallet when she turned to see why he hadn't come with her. His gaze hadn't followed her, either. Like maybe watching her bathe would've been too much? Silly lad. Didn't he know she'd let him help her?

She started to call him over when the sickness washed over her skin. The rotten blood gushed up her throat like a geyser, and she had just enough time to lurch her upper body out of the pool before it flew over her tongue and onto the dirt.

Urick was hovering in an instant. Half a cave away one second, holding her hair the next. "Shit. I thought I was done." Violet started to wipe her forearm across her mouth when he pressed his shirt into her hand, squeezing her hand in his.

"Use it."

"But you don't have another."

He shrugged, his gray eyes welling with...fear? "It's no matter."

She dabbed at her mouth and leaned her back against his stomach, the touch of their skin cloaking her in comfort. "It passes, Uri, it always does." She felt the shake of his head on the top of hers.

"It doesn't mean I have to like it."

No, it didn't. She didn't like the side effects of what she did, either. But the end result was always worth it. The kids got a few days of feeling better afterward before the cancer cells rallied the troops.

They sat together like that for a while, her upper body in his embrace while her legs floated weightless in the warm pool. "This is nice. Just what the doctor ordered." She sighed and relaxed further into his strong arms.

"Glad you like it." He stressed the *you*, implying his thoughts were anything but.

She pushed away from him and lifted herself out of the pool.

---

$\mathcal{U}$rick watched as she strode over to snag up the blanket to dry herself off with. He mourned the sudden loss of her bare skin, but couldn't deny the relief coursing through him that she felt well enough to get feisty.

She spun around, imperious in her makeshift robe. "Well, excuse me for thinking we were..." She waved her arm as if the physical gesture could make up for her loss of words, of her not admitting there was more than just a predetermined attraction between them.

Uri sat still as the stone he'd be very soon. *Say it*, he willed. *Just say it*. If she would admit to the budding of her feelings toward him, he might be able to take a full breath.

Instead, every comforting gesture he gave his Chosen was tearing his heart out. He was dripping concern like a melting popsicle, and she was sucking it up without giving much back. He might be new to these feelings and the way his body now responded to feminine flesh, but he wasn't a rube with a grass stem sticking out of his teeth.

He had seen love in the centuries before he'd been—aw, fuck. He so didn't need thoughts of his capture piled on top of what he was dealing with right now. He paced, hoping the movement would remind him of his freedom.

At least Violet watched his back and forth, as gripped by the action as any tennis fan. "Would you stand still? You're giving me a headache with all this..." This time it was clear what she meant as she jerked her arm back and forth.

Uri stopped to face her. "How did you expect me to react? You thought I'd love seeing you puke that vile shit. *Shit*, I'd like to remind you, you voluntarily sucked into your gut. So do I think this is nice? No. No, I fucking don't."

Sometimes dropping the eff bomb went a long way toward keeping his hands under control. The pulled cork on a bottle of bubbly, a verbal hit instead of a physical one.

"And another thing—while I'm pouring my heart out over this, the least you could do is 'fess up. Admit that we have a future beyond you using me."

"Using you?"

Oh, he'd touched a nerve with that one. Violet stalked toward him, broadcasting her intentions like her body was a bullhorn. She was going to nail him one. Uri braced himself.

"Using you!"

"What, you thought I wouldn't notice? I'm Kynd, remember. We see things others don't."

Anxiety crept across his skin as she stilled. Not wounded, but the viper on the scent of its prey, the spider on her web. "Oh, I know you're Kynd. It's hard to forget when you're always. Fucking. Touching me!"

The viper struck in a way he hadn't seen coming, her insult gutting him like a fish. He toppled to his knees, the claws on the ends of his fingers growing longer, sharper. His spine arched ceiling-ward as coarse hair sprouted along its curve.

She dared insult the only thing he was proud to be? The only thing making him feel…not like a cock-sucking meal on the paw? Uri roared, his face contorting as his snout protruded forth.

To his ever-loving horror, Violet didn't back down as he lost control. "Run." It was a gruff and guttural warning, but clear despite the shifting of his mouth.

"No. You started this, you damned coward, you stand up and finish it." She anchored her fists to her hips. "You're the one who kidnapped me, remember? My life was just fine and fucking dandy until you showed up."

Uri blinked and shook his head, his emerging ears wobbling on his fracturing skull. How dare she blame him when…

His blood simmered from its roiling boil as his gray matter processed her accusation.

She must have seen him blink. "That's right, asshole. I'm just doing what I have to do. What anyone would do in my shoes. And damn you, Kynd, for making me think less of myself for it. Damn you!" The tears welling in her eyes cracked his heart, sidelining his fit of rage like a tire spinning off its lug nuts.

Uri sat on his furring ass.

Violet picked up steam. "I'll have you know I freely chose to come back here. And sorry if I'm not all oooh, let's make love, but I'm trying to process here!" When she turned her back to him, the blanket curled around her legs. She'd trip if she moved, but she stood there facing the wall, her shoulders lifting as she rode her temper.

Like a coward, he surrendered to the momentum of his shift, letting the bear fully emerge. As volatile as grizzlies were known to be, there were times when wearing his fur brought him solace, as if his thick hide sheltered him from the searing pain of his heart.

This time was no different. Except maybe he could share that if Violet would let him.

Pushing up onto his four legs, he lumbered over to her, pressing his broad head against the backs of her thighs then sliding his furry cheek along her hip. Large as he was, her forearm rested between his ears, her arm bent at a right angle. He closed his eyes to the tickling of her fingers on his muzzle.

For long moments they just stood there, both of them facing the wall, a repetition of what they'd been doing at the pool. He didn't grow nervous as he felt the coming of the sun. Instead, he savored her touch despite her cruel words about his being Kynd and always, desperately needing contact.

When she finally spoke, his ears flicked like it was instinct to harken to her. "Patrick would love this."

He canted his head.

"Winnie the Pooh. The boy in the bed opposite Jaime's."

*Ah.*

"He loves bears." Her thoughts were never far from that hospital, those kids. And why would she come back here so readily? Surely it wasn't just because she was his Chosen One. There was more to this, more than she'd admitted in her anger. The puzzle niggled, yet he couldn't solve it.

Though did it matter as long as she fell into the reflex of touching him? Maybe if he ignored her motives she'd come around eventually. Accept him for who and what he was.

Fidiot. Maybe he'd sell himself the Brooklyn Bridge.

Despite chasing his thoughts, he was tuned into her enough to register her shaking before her knees unhinged themselves. Gently, he pressed to her side, the bulk of his shoulders and long fur giving her something to hold onto. She crumpled slowly, giving him the chance to get his paws adjusted so that by the time her body was kissing the floor, it wasn't. She was curled up on him instead.

A bear rug. How was that for sacrificing more of his pride for this female?

Though when he reached for his resentment, it wasn't there. As she sighed and snuggled in as if into a down comforter, his steady, becalmed heart told him he'd do this a billion times for her, however many times she needed it.

"Patrick would love this, too." With her cheek nestled against his thick fur, her warm breath wove straight to his skin, which rippled in response like a current. He felt more alive in this intimate scenario than he had in a long time.

It swelled his frigging heart, as if it was so full it capsized its contents. Making him feel bigger than the world and so much bigger than himself. Was this what Violet felt when she helped those kids? If so, then he had an inkling now to her motivation.

Because Uri wanted more of this feeling.

If he couldn't directly share his blood to make them better, maybe he could do this. With Violet's help, maybe he could let that sick, little boy cuddle up to him like he was an oversized teddy bear. Fulfilling a dream for a kid who didn't have much else and never would.

As his heart elbowed for more room in his chest, he lifted his head off the floor, anxious to get the day over with. He had something important to do, a purpose outside of his own selfish needs.

Funny how this eagerness scratched his itch and calmed him even more. For the first time in months, he did not raise his face in wretched fury at his Maker. He relaxed his body instead so that when he succumbed to the stone his Violet would still have a comfortable place upon which to sleep.

Or rise from.

He would not trap her within his stone embrace. He didn't yet know why she'd freely come with him to this cave, but he could suck it up and give her the space to tell him.

*Trust.* Holy shit, that's what was smoldering in his thickening blood. The seeds of a real relationship, where the soil was fertile and rich with trust, giving love a safe place to grow.

# CHAPTER 6

*P*arking places in downtown Portland at three in the morning were surprisingly hard to come by. But then, this was when humans were at home, so their cars lined the sidewalks like horses hitched outside the only saloon in town.

Kristov drove his Mercedes Benz G-Class down the center of the street like the vehicles on either side were the dangerous banks of the Amazon. Any second, a Toyota crocodile was going to slip onto the potholed pavement and swamp the SUV's ugly ass.

A dent would be an improvement. Man, the ride was square. In style and personality. Kallen would have thought an all-powerful, ancient Vampyre would drive something more representative. Not this David Attenborough wannabe. But then Kristov didn't need to flaunt his power. It oozed from his pores like a scent. Who needed Bugatti when you had that?

As they passed Violet's apartment a second time, Kallen squirmed his big ass behind the seatbelt Kristov had told him to wear. Like if they had a fender bender the nylon straps would save his immortal life. One more frigging pothole causing this wreck of style to jostle, and consequently, the strap to bite into his neck, and Kallen was going to put an end to someone else's immortality.

He looked across the cabin of the SUV. Kristov's driving gloved hands, no frigging joke, were gripped to ten and two. What. A. Frigging. Nerd. "No shit. Come on, stop and let me out. I can't take this anymore."

"The seatbelt is necessary. If we get pulled over by the police—"

"Trust me. We will not be getting pulled over in this."

"You don't like my automobile?"

"First, I'm new on this realm and even I know not to call this tin can an automobile. It's wheels, your ride, man. Now stop so I can get out of it. We're never going to find a place to park close to the apartment."

"It's not a good idea to have you walking farther than is necessary."

"*Farther than is necessary?* Do you hear yourself?" He shook his head, hiding his grin.

"I speak perfect English." Kristov pressed the volume button on the Bose.

"Nooo. You're making my ears bleed." Clapping his hands to his ears, Kallen laughed outright as *Seasons in the Sun* leaked out of the speakers. "Torture, man, this is torture."

Eyes on the road, Kristov kept the tin can creeping forward, his grip on the wheel tightening so his skin showed alabaster through the little holes on the knuckles of his driving gloves.

Was he fighting a laugh? "You're seriously twacked."

"Twacked? That's not even a word."

Maybe not, but *suave* was. Kristov glided the steering wheel to the right, sliding the square monstrosity into a slot then backing up to line it perfectly with the sidewalk. In front of them shivered a naked sapling. A fire hydrant peeked its domed head out of the dirty snowbank, its stubby arms encased in ice.

"Seriously."

Kristov's cheek twitched. "For a Kynd, you're not very observant. How many times did we drive by this space?"

"Twice, but who's counting." Kallen shouldered his door open and stepped out onto the brick sidewalk, the kernels of rock salt crunching under his boots. As the vapor of his breath encircled his head, he twisted to look up at Violet's third floor apartment.

The windows were black, which didn't mean anything. A vampire wouldn't exactly have lace curtains, now would she?

"Wait on the steps, and I'll buzz you in." Kristov materialized on the opposite side of the glass door. A few minutes later they were repeating the vampire version of B and E, with Kristov opening Violet's apartment door from the inside.

Kallen stepped into the little foyer, his senses firing up. Not sure why they were lighting up like a switchboard on Christmas Day, he made cat burglar and crept deeper into the female's living space. Uri's scent tickled more than his nose, it tingled over his skin. "He's been here."

Just as he was going to cross under the archway into her small living room he halted, turning his face right to look down the narrow hallway. "Jesus Christ." Instead of peeling back like he wanted to do, Kallen followed his curling nose. "What in hell died in here?"

Not Uri, or his heart and stomach would both be doing gymnastics. The male's scent grew stronger the farther he went down the hall. The stench of bad blood threatened to overwhelm his brotherkynd's presence, but Kallen kept in tune with the tingling sensation riding his dermis.

Otherwise? He eased the door to the bathroom open, peering in as his hand landed on his nose to cover it. "What the hell?" The smell of sickness bloomed like the tile and porcelain created a terrarium for the shit to grow. Kallen backed up into the hallway, as much to catch a lungful of clean air as to keep himself from adding to the stench.

Kristov peeked around him, a disgusted look on his stoical face. "I don't understand."

"Phrase of the day." Kallen wiped his arm across his offended nose and forced himself back into the tiny bathroom. He picked up a washcloth from the edge of the sink and sniffed, kicking his head back as he pushed the thing at arm's length. "Well, it's not Uri's, but I don't know whose it is."

"It's cancer. This is a sick person's blood." Kristov had taken the damp washcloth and was waving it under his nose like a perfume expert. A flick of his wrist and a quick sniff then a moment of contemplation. "What's it doing here?"

"Good frigging question." With no answers forthcoming in the john, Kallen shouldered his way farther down the hall.

And landed at ground zero. "They were both here." He took in the rumpled bed, the messy closet, and let his brain triangulate the mental math. "But not for long."

"How do you figure?" Kristov was clinging as persistent as lint from a dryer.

"Shh. You hear that?"

"What?"

"Shhh." Kallen tilted his ear to the hallway. "The kitchen. Someone's here."

"I don't hear—shit."

Kallen took off up the hallway like he'd been snapped by a slingshot. There was someone else snooping in the apartment and it wasn't anyone on his meager list of friends. Every Kynd instinct he had fired up, the hallway doors registering as blips on the blur of the beige walled hallway. In seconds, he was rounding into the kitchen, his boots tight as suction cups on the bare floor.

It was a flash of movement for the trespasser to bolt to attention. A second of time for him to hiss, baring his fangs.

*Vampire.* Kallen didn't slow to shake his hand. His brotherkynd was MIA, and if this fanged fucktard had anything to do with it the questions could come after, when he'd broken both his legs so he couldn't run. Forget teleporting. With a gargoyle sitting on his chest, the bloodsucker wouldn't be going anywhere with a poof!

Though Kallen's plans were for nothing. The fear on the vampire's face proved a little panic went a long way toward swizzle-sticking the neurons. He twisted as if he'd forgotten how to shake up his molecules, and ran for the window at the end of the kitchen like he was a letter headed for the mail slot and needed to send himself.

It took an instant for Kallen to get his hands on the male's arm, a mere breath more to yank him to his chest. Except the vampire found his wits, so when he crashed up against the wall of gargoyle, he slashed his claws across Kallen's neck.

"Son of a bitch!" Ignoring the burn and spurt, Kallen reached low to grab the male's thigh, breaking his legs taking on a whole new appeal now that he'd had his neck slashed. If the vampire thought that would go unpunished, he had a—

The bastard teleported, dragging Kallen out the window with him. Glass shattered in thin, wide wedges as they emergency-landed on the fire escape. Too heavy to take far, Kallen slid and bumped down the iron stairs with the vampire in his grip, the jagged edges of stairs and railings ripping and gouging his skin.

He'd feel the pain later when he had a moment to lick his wounds. Right then, he was a little preoccupied with nailing this eely bastard hard enough to immobilize him. As it was, gravity decided to work against him, pulling down with a nasty ten-foot drop looming between him, the tumbling vampire, and the icy sidewalk.

He had just enough time to see it coming when the freefall claimed his body. Kallen landed like the stone he was, the air knocked so far out of his lungs they worked like they did at dawn—they seized up. In his periphery, his quarry staggered upright, reeling until he hit the shadows and the brick wall of the apartment building.

"Kallen!" With a whir and flash that caused his stomach to lurch with his head, Kristov appeared at his side. "Are you all right?" All Florence Nightingale when what he should have been doing was the snag and grab on the vampire who was...

"Fuuuuck." Kallen let his head fall back onto the brick, his eyes closing on the empty space where the vampire had been. "You let him get away."

"It's not important." Kristov patted around his head, dabbing like he was finger painting or some shit.

Kallen slit one eyelid enough to see through. "It was important." He probably knew where Uri was. Or at least something about Violet, seeing as how he'd been raiding her apartment.

"Not enough to get noticed by the cops. Hear that? Sirens. We've got to get you out of here before someone sees you."

"Nervous Nellie." Sitting up put his head on the spin cycle. Kallen clutched it before it teetered off its axis.

Kristov shoved himself under his armpit, slinging his arm across his shoulders to keep him upright. "Come on. Let's get you to the…wheels."

"Close enough." After what seemed like a mile of lurch, thump, heave, and breathe, Kallen let his bones slop into the passenger seat of the SUV. A slide of nylon and a click later, he was tucked into the leather seat and Kristov materialized behind the wheel. Another second after that, the Vampyre had the G-class in Drive and they were lurching onto the car-lined street, executing a slick get away.

Behind them, Violet's apartment building came to life like the eyes of a candlelit pumpkin. "Well, that was close." Rubbing the back of his head, Kallen turned to his partner in crime. "I mean, we kind of bungled the reconnaissance, but all in all, it wasn't a total washout."

Kristov kept his eyes on the road, the streetlights making his skin seem paler than normal. "How do you figure? You almost got yourself exposed!" Elbow propped on the thin lip between the door and the window, he rubbed his eyebrows like he could smudge them out of existence. "If Anton and Godrick find out I have gotten myself mixed up with your drama…"

"Well, don't quit with the elaboration for my benefit. What are they gonna do, slap your wrists?"

Kallen found himself on the dagger end of a fierce glare. "We have risked everything for you and your Kynd. Everything! If the Others get wind of this, everything we've done in the name of the Triumvirate will be jeopardized. The treaties, the peace," he sliced his hand across the top of the steering wheel. "Done! Broken."

"Well, jeez, no need to get huffy about it. I mean, I did get us this."

Kristov sighed, his melodramatic hand finding its home back onto two o'clock. "What?"

"A prezzie." Kallen dangled his prize in the blue glow of the dash lights.

"Is that—"

"Yep. A flap of skin off the bastard's neck. I don't know what the tattoo represents, but I'm thinking we're going to find out."

"You sneaky, treacherous, creation of God. It's no wonder the ancient world feared you." Except pride sparked the Vampyre's otherwise dead eyes, and Kallen bared his sharp teeth in a fearsome grin.

"That's right, K. We're baaaaack." As he mimicked the crazy Chuckie doll, Kallen couldn't help but feel a hum of happiness all the way into his shitkickers. His Kynd were back, and it had felt damned fine to be in a scuffle for the good of his brethren.

Now, he just needed to get that piece of vampire hide into Angelia's hands. With the collective knowledge of the Literati at her fingertips, she was sure to find out what the tattoo meant. Once they had that it would be a matter of a little Sherlock Holmesing and bam!

Answers.

And, hopefully, a line to Uri's Chosen One. Who wouldn't be far from the brotherkynd. Kallen would bet his bruised but rock-hard ass on it.

---

"*Y*ou are out of your mind." Violet hauled herself out of the pool, shaking her head as much to rid her hair of water as to show Urick how opposed she was to his idea of taking his bear into the hospital. She'd awakened while he'd still been stone but had been too worn out to leave the body she was spooned against.

*Yeah, right.* She'd fallen right back to sleep, so the next time her lids lifted she was cradled in what was fast becoming her favorite spot. Uri's arms, damn him. No longer stone, he'd unloaded his idea without so much as a *Good evening.*

"I'd be doing something." He handed her the towel, and while she dried off with it, his gaze traveled along the places it didn't cover, his attention making her feel feminine in a way she never had. Hell, she was even aware of her damned nipples kissing the air, and the way her ass swayed when she walked.

She needed to concentrate on what they were talking about. It was too important to lose track. Because really, what kid was going to keep his mouth shut about touching a real frigging bear. "Hey, my eyes are up here." Violet puckered her lips to hide her grin. "And yeah, you'd be doing something all right. Like setting off alarms and blowing my chances to visit."

Urick's rapt attention remained on the path of the towel. His watching burned her skin, heating her from the inside out. Violet's grip on the terry loosened as she lowered her hand to touch herself.

Jaw grinding tight, Urick curled his fists, the tendons in his arms moving like steel bars beneath flesh. His biceps bulged, setting off a chain of physical events that ran all the way to the striated muscles of his shoulder. Without his shirt, he was giving Violet a show of her own, no glimpses necessary, thank you very much.

God, he was big. Thickly muscled without being bulky. His jeans, now pretty worn out, barely clung to his hip bones and provided a launching pad for her gaze to climb the stack of muscles quartering off his stomach.

Eight. Pack.

He made human males look positively lacking with their six little bulges.

"Like what you see?" His grin said he was pleased with her ogling.

Violet shrugged. "Maybe." The front of his jeans began to protrude, and Urick spread his feet to accommodate the growth. Jesus, even his nipples were turgid. A bead of cream slid down her inner thigh.

Urick's nostrils flared, his eyes pooling black.

"Ah…" Violet's gaping mouth clapped shut when he grabbed her, molding his hard, hot skin to the contours of her body. His roughly padded fingertips caressed her bare back, his tented jeans chafing her belly as he slowly circled his hips.

He gazed down at her more rabid than a male vampire. The snarl chain-sawing up his throat meant his bear craved a piece of her, too. Urick seemed to want to devour her, ravage her. She could barely breathe as he lowered his head. Entranced, Violet pushed herself up on her tiptoes to meet him.

When the kiss came, it wasn't the hard crashing of his mouth that she'd expected. His lips brushed hers before he pulled back to watch her reaction. "Another?"

Violet teetered forward. She meant to say *yes* but nothing came out of her parted lips.

Urick's grin was all pleasured male. Though when his lips touched hers again there was a weight to the kiss as if behind his holding back there was a pressure. Violet leaned closer, raising herself higher to meet him. Demanding more than his restraint.

The instant their lips sealed, his mouth dragged her in like an epic movie. She was on the edge of her seat, her body tense yet squirming. Squeezing his arms around her, Urick's big hand slid down her back to cup her ass as he moaned in her mouth. Violet pushed her hips into him, desperate to ease the throbbing between her legs with stroking herself on his constrained cock.

As her breaths came out of her like she was sprinting, it wasn't enough to caress his bare back. She needed to fist it, claw it. Fire licking through her, she broke the kiss but couldn't stand to have her mouth off him. She nipped and sucked on the burning skin of his chest, not caring where…loving where.

The salty taste of him engulfed her and still, she craved more. She dragged her tongue over him when she wasn't nibbling. Gripped tight to his butt when he wasn't shoving hard enough, wasn't penetrating her. He maddened her with his caution, with his harnessed aggression.

He was kissing her neck, scraping his hard-scrabble jaw on her skin, anywhere it seemed he could scent her, or taste her, his face was there. His hand was clasped onto her hipbone, claws digging in, his supremacy wetting her core, making it throb.

"Yes," she hissed against his chest and bit hard on his nipple. She tugged his hand off her to drag his fingers through her melting sex, her legs splaying as a current of electricity buzzed through her folds and across her clit. His touch was a vibrator triggered to high. The connection hummed straight through her, a purr zinging to every strung nerve.

On a growl, Urick flexed his arm, lifting her at the crotch. He wrapped his other arm around her back, hitching her closer while his thumb maddened her singing nub. When he worked two fingers inside her, he rocked his hips as if to thrust his erection into the place his hand was.

"Oh, God, yes. Fuck me." She couldn't get wetter, his fingers were slick and slipping along her folds.

"Need," was all he said as they dropped to the floor. Kneeling between her legs, he reared back, a stifled roar expanding his wide chest. He fumbled his wet fingers on his button while Violet played with herself, thrusting her hips as she pinched her clit.

Urick's eyes bloomed fully black, his fangs rupturing beyond his bottom lip. As he wrenched his jeans down his thighs, his dick dropped forth, sticking straight out in front of him, dark, veined, thick as a flagpole.

Violet snagged it in her grip, twisting to her knees so she could suck the head of his cock into her mouth. When the tight chamber of her mouth closed over the silk, Urick threw his head back and roared. Bucking once, he clasped the side of her head. "Jesus, Chosen!"

With her mouth stuffed and her cheeks hollow, Violet rolled her eyes up to watch him. Urick was all twitched and clamping muscle, his face aimed at the ceiling like when she'd first known him, when dawn had come and his fury had consumed him.

Only this time he wore an expression of stunned reverence. He seemed consumed by rapture, not by rage, as he slid his erection back and forth across her tongue.

With the musky taste of him filling her mouth, Violet clasped one palm to the back of his thigh and coiled the other around the base of his thick shaft. The moan rising from his throat was one of surrender as he anchored himself by gripping her head harder.

"No, God no." Urick's balls drew up tight and heavy as he started to drag himself free. Violet pushed her tongue to the underside of his engorged shaft, making the hole of her mouth even smaller. "Not in you, Chosen, blessed be thy God, not in your mouth!"

She didn't expect the force of the jet and nearly gagged. While she swallowed fast, his hands alternately caressed her head and gripped her hair, his hips twitching as he fought the carnal instinct to thrust during orgasm.

In his throes, he was beatific. Yet, as his breath left him in a shudder, he looked down upon her with a stern expression. Urick shook his head, lifting her with the touch of a bent knuckle beneath her chin. "You should not have…"

He didn't elaborate, but then with the salty musk of his come all over her tongue, he didn't have to.

Violet smiled sheepishly as she dabbed the corner of her mouth. "Yeah, well…" Seemed they were both finding it unnecessary to put the tails on their sentences.

"Come." He looked so fierce she didn't even joke about his word choice and let him pull her tight against his sweating chest. His breaths still labored, Urick curled her onto his lap. They sat there on the dirt of the cave floor, yet she'd never felt so cherished.

Even though he gazed down on her with those liquid ebony eyes and fangs almost too long for his mouth. The male vampire with his mate, but this wasn't like that at all. There was too much tenderness.

Too much touching.

His fingers smelled of her.

And suddenly she wanted to take of what he'd tried to give. She wanted to feel his mouth on her, to have him drag her to the surrendered heights of orgasm. The need built in her as heat, a fire she stoked the more she rocked her butt against his thighs.

Those black eyes hardened as though they strained with a fierce understanding.

"My female is unsatisfied." A Cheshire Cat grin spread Urick's sensual lips. As he leaned her onto the blanket he straightened it behind her, and in that moment, she knew he wasn't just any vampire.

He was a Kynd vampire, nothing at all like the usual males of her species.

Beneath his rages was a tenderness yearning to be nourished, to be protected in its fragile state of brokenness.

Violet's chest swelled tight. "Love me with your mouth, Uri."

---

*N*ever had five words sounded so beautiful to his ears. Never had anything looked so lovely. She was gazing up at him with affection, and Uri wanted to roar with triumph. He wanted to guarantee she would always look upon him thus.

With affection. And wanting. Something she sought from him, no one else. There was no glitter in her eye as before when she'd seduced—then reduced him—to escape. She could leave at any time and chose not to.

*She chooses to stay with me.* Laying before him, her beautiful body bared, he couldn't keep himself from touching. His fingers traced the curve of her stomach to her hip like she was a rare artifact.

To him, she was. She was precious beyond measure, and oh, so beautiful.

Her nipples were dusky and puckered tight. Mouthwatering, he bent to pull one into his mouth, his eyes shutting in reverence as he dragged the hard bud across his tongue. When she arched her back, pushing more of her breast to his face, he filled his hands with her creamy plumpness, the woman smell of them exciting him.

Though he craved to feel her dew upon the sensitive skin of his hardening length, his desire to pleasure her weighed upon him heavier. Lifting his face, he closed his eyes to better catch the tendrils of her heat.

God have mercy! Her scent stole into him and wound itself around his being, clenching it tight until it felt like a coil of...he didn't frigging know. All he could understand was that she was under him and drawing him in so that his body did things his inexperienced mind knew nothing about.

He shut off the fricking internal monologue and kissed and dragged his tongue in a trail to her springing curls. Such wonderful texture! He buried his nose as he breathed her in, closer than he'd ever been to her essence. Fingers digging into the mounds of her ass, he lifted her to his mouth, stroking his tongue in one, long lick through her folds.

She moaned, encouraging him with little thrusts in his hands. Uri delved deeper, learning her with his tongue, exploring the myriad ways he could lift her higher so her breathing quickened and she squirmed. "Uri...more."

God above, she was going to turn him into an animal with the way he devoured her. He flicked and licked at the hard bud while he suckled her juices. She seeped like a ripe peach, and mewled and writhed the faster and harder he delved.

"Yes, Uri, yes!" Her skin grew hot in his hands as she pumped her hips. When he thrust his finger into her she arched hard, her entire body stiffening as her breaths hitched then ceased, her feminine scent blooming around him.

With a heavy sigh, she relaxed beneath him, a smile curling beneath her rosy cheeks, her eyes glassy and hooded. As he looked up at her from between her bent knees, she absently twirled his hair in her fingers.

"That was wonderful." She giggled, tilting her head in order to see him watching her.

He wanted to crush her tight, so precious did she seem in that moment. His female sated and looking upon him now as some great thing. As if he alone could render her thus.

It made him feel special. Maybe not so twisted in the head. Uri sat up on his knees, pulling her to him so she straddled him, his length hotdogged between her melon cheeks. With slow strokes, he rubbed himself, nibbling at her ears, kissing her nose.

With her arms draped over his shoulders and her fingers once again playing with his hair, he surrendered to the goodness of male with female. The Chosen thing aside, Violet was a female he could well learn to be happy with in the centuries to come.

As she bit her bottom lip on a hitched breath when he pushed his erection a little firmer against her, he flushed with pride that he could be that male. She dripped and slipped around him, escalating his sense that he was the right male, that with her he could be a whole male.

Not a wounded one.

She certainly wasn't looking at him like he was fucked in the head. "Uri, do me."

His breaths coming faster and his skin slickening with sweat, he nuzzled the column of her neck. She tilted her head, and his heart thumped hard with hunger. Dragging his tongue along her pulsing vein, he loosened his jaw to make way for his fangs.

"Yes, Uri." Violet lifted her chin more, gripping him tighter while incongruously relaxing into him. He rubbed his nose along that enticing vein as he shook his head.

"Please." Snaking her arm down between them, she gripped his cock.

Uri hissed, his hunger spiking. Loving Christ, he was going mad. Attached by his shaft, he craved to have his fangs sunk deep, a connection that blew away cogent thought. He surrendered to the power of it, sliding his fangs along her skin before piercing her flesh.

As her blood erupted onto his tongue, his erection kicked in her gliding fist. Moaning, she raised up and pushed herself down over him, her inner walls hot and tight. Squeezing his eyes shut and pulling at her vein, Uri lost himself in sensation.

She was in him, on him, around him. He consumed, and yet he was being consumed. His body locking tight to the feminine flesh in his arms, he growled possessively. Then gulped, a growing euphoria building in him as if her blood coursed through his, as though she invaded his every vein and cell. He had to have more, he had to feel more of her. He was drowning, and she rode his shaft, driving him frightfully higher until he was maddened beast, pure instinct. Her cries spurred him on, and he plunged his hips faster and faster, his skin shrinking, his vision reduced to bursts of flashing light, banging, banging, banging, and then…

He wrenched his fangs from her neck to roar as lightning jolted up his spine and through his cock, and jets of his cum kicked into the burning, wet muscles clutching his length. Helpless to stop it, his bare ass clenched and unclenched over and over, the fine hairs tingling as he coasted down from his orgasm.

Opening his eyes, he muttered a curse. Less than a foot from his face was the cave wall. He'd screwed his precious Chosen One into a dirt wall. Ashamed, Uri glanced down. "Fuck!" Slipping his softening dick from between her legs, he clasped his palm over the draining wound on her neck. Blood seeped between his fingers.

"Take your hand away and lick it."

Uri blinked a half-dozen times to put the command into a string of understandable words. Beneath him, Violet slid her body along his, the motion flipping a switch in his brain. His female needed. He would obey.

Hand shaking, he removed it and lowered his head. The scent of her blood wended through him, awakening his mind, his body. She was inside him, his female an integral part of him. Uri's chest swelled, pushing aside his panic, and the fear that had sprouted upon seeing her harmed. Even if it had been done by him while they'd—

Uri's eyes popped wide. "We just made vampire love."

The smile curving Violet's lips swelled his chest more. "So, we did."

Bashful, he lowered his head so she wouldn't see him so vulnerable. "I…" Felt like a coward hiding his face in her hair. Uri lifted his gaze, holding hers boldly, prepared to die a thousand deaths if she didn't feel the same. "I liked it." He searched her face for any sign of horror, or at the very least, disapproval.

"Me, too."

A sigh gushed out of him as he pressed his forehead to hers. He had a thousand things to say, all of it pushing at once. If he opened his mouth to start, though, he'd babble like a fool and ramble on about healing and love and devotion. Instead, he rolled to his back, sweeping Violet up with him so she was no longer the one laying in the dirt.

She clasped her hands on his chest and rested her chin on them. Her amber eyes sparkled, her lids hooded above a small smile—the look of a sated female. Uri let his unspoken thoughts settle into his bones.

---

"*T*ell me you're joking." As Kallen stared Angelia down, his stomach tumbled south. "That was a glyph? A fucking mystical tattoo?" It had taken Angelia less than two hours to identify the mark on the strip of skin he'd torn from the neck of Violet's house guest.

From the window ledge, Drakus growled. Kallen didn't take his attention off the blonde seated in front of him. He pushed his fists into the desk separating them and leaned toward her. "You're telling me that Uri's Chosen One is connected to a sect of rogue vampires who have aligned themselves with the fae?"

In his peripherals, Drakus coiled himself tight, his boots and hands on the sill like the guy was giving in to baser trains of thought. Roughly translated, his reptilian brain. Drakus was about to lose his shit. The fucking fae. The dragon chimera's own tattoos bulged and contracted as the stained skin slid over tensing muscles.

They did not need another visit from T-Rex, thank you very much, but Angelia's bomb was raining shrapnel on a male who knew all too well the cruelty of the fae.

"If the name vaJacaka rings an old bell, it's because it's Sanskrit, literally meaning *rogue.*" Angelia pushed her chair out and made her way around the desk to Drakus. "It's also quite likely they've bargained for the glyph, which is why they're hidden in obscurity. With no evidence of them, history swallowed them, making it easy to do their thing without detection."

When Kallen looked to Merrick, the male shrugged, his thick shoulders rolling under his button down. Everything about it saying, *Who the hell knows when it comes to those tricky bastards.*

Folding his arms, Kallen parked his ass on the desk, his thoughts tumbling like ocean waves against the shore. In the background, like kids frolicking in the sand, Angelia's soothing gibberish filled the air. She was singing something from the Scriptum for Drakus.

While she and Merrick kept the dragon chimera's wheels on the track, Kallen left them to it, confident in the female's abilities. How many times had Angelia already coaxed Drakus from the edge? Enough so he wasn't worried this time. He let his thoughts sail on, not worried in the least for his brotherkynd behind him.

The one he worried about was Uri. If Uri's Chosen One was part of this sect, what did it mean for him besides his bear ass getting royally fucked?

Fear and frustration was a rock slide straight into agitation. Kallen's control slipped. "Hey, no offense, Drakus, but can we concentrate on what's really important here?" Seriously. The male could pull his tattooed head out of his ass for a second and think about their brotherkynd.

Drakus blinked, a clear layer of skin sliding over reptilian eyes. As the third eyelid seemed to swipe a speck of sanity back into him, Drakus looked back at Kallen with an eerie cunning. "That male could be dangerous for the both of them."

Ignoring the goose bumps galloping over his skin, Kallen pushed himself away from the desk. "And you've made this leap of logic because..."

Drakus curled his lip, exposing a sharp gargoyle fang as he glanced down at the offensive piece of flesh sitting on the desk. "Because that mark from the fae doesn't just represent a cult."

"It doesn't?" Drakus had a captive audience. The same question came out of three different mouths.

"No, it shows a member's status. That one," he pointed at the offender with a shaking hand, "says the male isn't of the highest order and never will be."

"And why's that?" Taking pity on his brotherkynd, who had managed to drag himself from the brink with some impressive self-control, Kallen took Drakus' hand in his, stroking his thumb over the male's knuckles.

Drakus shut his eyes, as soothed by the touch as he was by Angelia's humming. After a long exhale, he opened his eyes to look pointedly at all three of them. "He is a father."

Kallen ceased with the knuckle massage. "You think Uri's Chosen One is this scum's daughter?"

"It explains why he was in her apartment."

His blood pressure climbing, Kallen resumed rubbing his thumb along the bony ridge of Drakus' hand. "She's a hunter. Which means Uri's already good and fucked."

"Not necessarily." Angelia tried to lower the anxiety level in the room as it rose like water in a leaking submarine. Judging by the desperate expressions, they were all drowning—including Angelia—who was usually their life raft in times like these.

Kallen opened his mouth, but all that squeezed out was a low whine. He was a balloon squeaking air from his pinched neck, his body deflating to make room for the hot blast of wind he liked to call his rage. He dug his claws into the skin of Drakus' hand.

"Brotherkynd." A warning growl. Lifting his gaze from its inward spiral, Kallen glanced straight into a pair of slit pupils, the gray around them as slick as a slate roof in the rainy town of London. The sight of them was a chilled breath across his feverish skin.

Kallen eased off but didn't let go. How could he, when holding his fellow Kynd was a lifeline, an antidote to the disease of his rages. As it was for all of them. Merrick joined the knot, just as desperate for the connection despite the blessing of having his own Chosen One.

Except when his catcher's mitt of a hand topped their knot of fists, the hum of their union ran up Kallen's arm, sharp as an electric current. He hadn't felt anything like that since they'd—

"Holy fucking Christ." Instead of snatching his hand away, Merrick curled his clawed fingers for a tighter hold, the features of his face loose with reverence, his gray eyes bright. "Do you feel that? It's like it used to be."

Like he needed an answer? They were connected, for shit's sake. Of course, Kallen felt the strengthening of the vibration, much like if he bit onto a lamp cord plugged into the wall he'd feel a jolt. Drakus wrested his hand away, tucking it into his stomach as he backed away.

"No. No, no, no." Drakus shook his head, looking for all this world like the Rain Man having an autistic moment. "No. We mustn't, we can't. No." When the backs of his legs bumped the sofa, he launched forward like he'd been bit on the ass, slashing behind him as he leapt, gouging the leather bad enough it leaked its horse hair batting.

Merrick swore just as Kallen muttered, "Fucking fae bastards."

For the first time in millennia, the strength of their old power had resurfaced. Nothing to celebrate, though, as it careened the dragon into a frigging tailspin. Merrick lodged himself between the unraveling chimera and Angelia, who had started across the room the second Drakus started wringing his hands.

"No Kynd, no Kynd." Drakus' head shaking entered brain damage territory. Then he started gripping his buzz cut, his fingers slipping then gripping until he started punching his temple. "Don't hurt. Please, don't hurt, it hurts."

"Aw, fuck me." Tears blurred Kallen's vision, his heart squeezing so hard he couldn't catch a breath even if his open mouth was made of fly paper. "Brotherkynd." He stepped forward, hand out as if begging for alms.

Drakus reeled backward, tripping over the end table. "Noooo…" When his lungs finished leaking, he dragged in a breath so big it stretched his chest. Then he roared, his human jaw stretching as the dragon burst forth. Yet this time those magnificent leather wings didn't unfold to fill the room. They wound around Drakus as if to protect him from demons none of them could see. Coiled on the library floor, the dragon hissed as they tried to near him, to touch him the way he needed to be touched.

Poor, poor fucking Drakus. *No touching.* The rule had been tortured so deep into his psyche it overrode his Kynd instincts. Kallen wanted to bawl like a baby, the tears already slipping down his cheeks.

They were so, so fucked and broken. Every cursed one of them. Urick included, despite having found his Chosen One. As if the bear chimera hadn't suffered enough, the one female on the planet who could give him solace was the daughter of a rogue vampire who belonged to a cult known for their cruelty. With the evidence found in Violet's apartment, it was clear the apple hadn't fallen far from the poisonous tree.

Uri wasn't dead yet, but his days, if not already filled with pain, were most certainly numbered.

---

*a*s lovemaking went, there wasn't ever a bad session. A union with your soul mate was a blessed event, no matter how messy and awkward the stamp of it felt afterward. That's how Uri figured it, at any rate. Perfection was not in the flawless delivery of kisses and caresses and whispered sweet-nothings.

It was in the contented smiles of the lovers. The sated embraces. Though the muscles were jelly, the hearts beat strong. Uri snuggled Violet closer.

She buried her head under his chin, her cheek a warm press of silk to his chest as he trailed his fingers along her shoulder and down her arm. When his hand slid along hers, he lifted their coiling fingers to his lips, blissed out by—

How fucking pale she was. Uri's legs turned rocket launcher, jacking his ass off the floor with her still tucked safely in his arms. A fallacy for sure. There was nothing safe about him. He'd nearly drained her. Self-hatred bloomed as devastating as a mushroom cloud. Uri clutched Violet tight when what he wanted to do was rake his claws across his chest to rip his heart out.

God knew the traitorous thing was worthless.

From there, he'd yank off the dick that had come to life after thousands of years of lying dormant. To make love to his Chosen One?

Yeah, right. More like to lead him down a path of temptation and ruin.

"What the hell, Kynd?" Violet flailed in his arms.

As he lowered her to her feet, he cursed himself for savoring the slide of her skin along his. "I have taken too much." Stepping back and with his hands now free, Uri struck out at the wall behind him. The crunch of bone barely assuaged the sickness in his heart.

"Hey! Hey, what are you doing?" Violet grabbed his hand before he could smash it into the wall again. She caught him mid-swing, the momentum dragging her a bit, proving just how weak he'd made her by giving into his lusts. Shame weighing heavy as a house, he hung his head.

"What's this about, Uri?" Her voice came to him like the soft scent of meadow flowers, shaming him more.

"I have done the unspeakable."

"Oh, for shit's sake, quit being so dramatical." Gently she straightened the fingers of his broken hand, caressing the ravaged knuckles with her fingertips.

Uri let her, reminded again of how much she was like Kallen with her irreverence.

"What demons are haunting you now?"

"I have taken too much." Surely his ears had caught fire they burned so.

"Idiot." She dropped his hand, the throbbing starting up the instant gravity caused it to swell. "You did not. I'm fine."

He dared look at her. "You are pale. Weak."

She anchored her hands to her hips. "I am not."

"You are."

"Aren't."

"Are."

"Are."

"Ar—Cut that out. I'm right, and you're not."

"You're five years old, is what you are. Now, come here." She held her arms open, and his body obeyed. As they settled back into their earlier embrace with her head under his chin, he marveled at how well she ruled him even though his self-loathing still ate at him.

Like a cancer.

His thoughts ran on merry legs down that path. She wouldn't be able to help the kids now. She would resent him. At the worst, hate him for his spinelessness.

"Hey, where are you?" Her fingers combed through the little hairs surrounding his nipple.

"I'm here." Uri pressed his lips to the top of her head, breathing her in as he did so. Like her blood, her scent chased through his bloodstream, imprinting itself into his memory so she would always be inside of him, a part of him. Jesus, the intimacy. Logically he understood it, but to feel it? He nearly shuddered to refit himself around this new entity. "I was thinking of the kids at the hospital."

She lifted her chin to peer up at him. "Yeah?"

"Yeah." Wrapping the blanket around them he sat up, making sure Violet's skin didn't touch the ground. "I mean to do what I offered. Help the little Pooh kid."

"Look." Pushing off from his chest, she sat back to face him. "That's noble of you. But seriously, it's a risky stunt."

"And what you do isn't?"

"No."

"Bullshit."

"Bullshit? At least if someone comes I can slip into the shadows. Where would you go, huh? Lay flat and pretend you're a rug?"

"What the hell does that mean?" Uri stood up, wrapping the blanket around his female before letting her go.

As he punched his legs into his jeans, she rose behind him. "It means a bear isn't exactly something you normally find in a hospital."

"Oh, right. A vampire is."

She set her jaw.

He snagged his t-shirt from the floor of the cave, the smell of tainted blood and Vi's sickness wafting out at him—because he needed the frigging reminder. He balled the shirt in his fist and turned to her. "Oh, and this is really frigging normal."

She snatched it out of his hands. "Give me that."

He didn't let go. The t-shirt stretched between them. "Not until you agree."

Gaze locked to his, she leered up at him. "You're really frigging serious."

"Yes."

She released her end of the shirt. "Fine. But if this fucks up, it's on your head."

"I can shift back to gargoyle before anyone sees the bear."

"And what about Patrick? How can you be sure he won't blab?"

"Who's going to believe him?" As the plan took shape, it lifted him sure as if he had helium in his boots.

"This is so not healthy. What's that going to do for him, huh, when nobody believes something he knows to be absolutely frigging true?"

Aaaand Uri's zeppelin crashed and burned. He plunked his deflated ego, and his ass, onto a rock beside the pool. Staring into the crystalline water, it wasn't a stretch to think how it reflected the opposite of what Violet candidly pointed out was a shit idea. "Fuck."

When she remained quiet behind him, he turned. "What?"

She shrugged. "I don't know. You look defeated, I guess."

"Yeah, well, welcome to my—" The familiar sluggishness poured through him, eddying outward, the physical manifestation of his train of thought.

Violet put her hands on his solidifying shoulders. "Oh, shit. It's dawn." She stiffened when he curled his arm around her hips.

She feared being immobilized with him? Not that he would ever do that to her again. He'd only wanted to touch her one more time before he couldn't. Yet, who could fucking blame her? It was just that her resistance was like a slap to his face. It stung like a bitch, but the hurt came more from the humility.

She pulled away from him, shaking her head. "I'm sorry, but I can't. I just can't."

He knew all about the backing out. Hell, he was the king of the backslide. She was starving, thanks to him, so what could he say. Nothing as his muscles seized. Without his lungs working their magic of biology, he couldn't speak. What he had was one last burst of motion before his body completely surrendered to the stone.

Face thrown upward to his God, Uri silently roared his frustration.

# CHAPTER 7

The sight of it unnerved her. Violet had seen Uri turn to stone before, up close and personal even, but never like this. Not when her heart hurt watching him. Which was screwed up. He'd kidnapped her, he'd... kidnapped her.

Okay, so she was having trouble coming up with other crimes to pin on him, but God damn it, it hurt to see this quasi death. And make no mistake, his soul was trapped in that lifeless body of his, which made it worse than death. He was awake and aware behind those stone eyes, unable to react to the happenings around him.

Such as her refusal to be trapped with him. But come on. She wasn't the one who had been cursed, so why should she be a victim of it. Uri and the other Kynd had brought this on themselves. Hadn't they?

For Christ's sake, she didn't know anymore. Which came about when you learned something about the thing you loathed instead of operating on myth and legend. Her heart heavy, Violet walked up to the stone chimera and placed her palm on his shoulder.

He seemed so different to her now. Maybe because with her blood flowing in his veins, he was a part of her?

Shit. She was empathizing. With her kidnapper. Without thinking, she let her legs fold under her so she could sit between his. In this position, he hovered over her like he was protecting her. Which he kind of was really, what with secreting her away to this cave where other vampires couldn't come unless they hoofed it. And what were the chances of that?

Pretty good if her father ever figured out she was in here. The bastard. Last time she'd seen him he'd taken a nice hunk of flesh out of her neck before she'd gotten away from him. Granted, she'd been hunting him down to kill him. Just before she'd learned she was a Chosen One like her friend Daniela, as a matter of fact.

Just before Uri had kidnapped her.

She quit running her fingers up and down his thigh. God, what was she doing? It was as if she couldn't quit touching him. Was she infected somehow? Turning into a touchy-feely Kynd? Stranger things happened in this world. Hell, she couldn't deny the electric current she felt when she reached out for Uri, so if she wanted proof of weird shit, there it was in all its tingling glory.

What was up with that anyway? It wasn't like a set of claws or fangs, so what good was it. Another mystery surrounding the Kynd. Because they needed more lies circulated about them.

Aw, hell, she was falling hard for this male. Then again, maybe it was the loss of blood. Uri had been right, she was weak. She would have to feed again soon, and if he wasn't going to offer his vein again, she'd have to go elsewhere.

Right. A good plan. As soon as the sun set, she'd go. There had to be someone living around these parts. If not, there were always deer and other animals. Not great substitutes, but they'd get her through this dry patch with Uri.

Unless his reluctance wasn't a glitch, but an amputation to his psyche. He'd suffered horribly for centuries, so he may not ever let her feed from him without *losing his shit*, as he liked to say.

Which was a serious problem she wasn't sure she could live with. With Urick, she didn't mind being a vampire. He made her feel special, connected to another through blood in a way she hadn't thought possible. She took pleasure in having his fangs and his length lodged inside her.

Yet she couldn't ignore that one glitch preventing the full connection: her body taking in his in every way, too. Not like a parasite as it had always felt like before Uri, but more like a conduit. A continuation of self through another body.

Uri was the completion of herself.

The thought scared the bejesus out of her, the what-ifs rushing into her head like floodwaters. What if he couldn't get over his fear of having someone drink from him? What if he wouldn't let her feed from another source? What if she was always weak?

Oh, God. That couldn't happen. Not with Jaime and the others depending on her. Not with her hunting work unfinished.

Back to plan A then. Feed herself. Then live her life. Urick could either tag along, or he could huddle in this cave. The choice was his.

And there it was. An aspect of being a Chosen One she hadn't considered. Dread turned her skin cold. She'd grown to need him. If he couldn't heal the festering wounds of his captivity, he wouldn't choose to be with her. He wouldn't choose her.

Brilliant. She was beginning to see why he raised his face to God every morning. Their situation was a fucked-up mess she wanted to shriek at, and she didn't even turn to stone.

*V*iolet had taken time to settle down next to him, and though outwardly Uri did nothing, inside his stone casement he was alternately crawling with terror and raging against a God who could be so cruel. He couldn't see her, but shit, he'd felt her touch. From the absentminded stroking to the absence of those trailing fingertips.

It was the loss that tormented him most. Especially because she plucked them off him as if she realized what she was doing and snatched her hand away. Doubts of helplessness chewed on him like a river of piranhas, reducing him to bone.

An exoskeleton to be sure. The stone a mere casing for the emptiness inside. He'd been rendered hollow, a true shell of his former self.

Until she curled up between his spread feet and lay what he supposed was her head on his boot. He began to refill, to become whole as he did when he held her in his arms, his cock driven deep inside her as her blood slid by his fangs, the warm taste of her on his tongue.

He needed her. God almighty, did he need her. Not for the blood she freely gave, but because she gave it so willingly. To him. A beast filled with demons. A brute who took, but never gave. The miracle wasn't in having found his Chosen One, it would be having her stay with him of her own free will.

Fuck. He wasn't good enough. As his thoughts plunged into dankness, the tingling crept through his blood. Electric sunshine warming him within and finally without. Careful not to hurt the beauty at his feet, he stood quietly while movement returned to him. He filled his lungs and breathed steadily, waggled his fingers and wiggled his toes inside his boots.

All the while forcing himself to be calm, to wait to touch her when he could do it with coordination and tenderness. When he bent to comb her golden tresses from her cheek, her eyes were open, watching him. "You're awake."

Her smile was welcoming, her hair a little mussed, her lids puffy with sleep. The sight of her contentment blasted through him so fast and hard, Uri glanced at the ground to make sure he wasn't levitating. "I felt you move."

"How? I was being careful."

She shrugged. "I don't know. I just did."

Uri dropped both knees to the dirt and clasped his shaking hands to them. Everything about Violet made him timid as shit. She was so, so utterly beautiful, surely she couldn't want him?

And yet, she'd stayed. Because of the sun? She'd felt trapped in another way? Jesus Christ, he had to quit bringing her here. He had to get over himself so she didn't sleep in the dirt. Because of him, his bright ray of sunshine with the liquid amber eyes slept on the ground.

"Come here." He scooped his arms beneath her legs to lift her, then savored the slide of her body along his as he lowered her to her feet. "Are you ready? We'll go to your place and get you cleaned up, then head for the hospital."

She nodded, tucking a lock of hair behind her ear and glancing around her feet like she had a bedroll to tidy up. "Yeah, yeah, okay."

*Yeah, okay?* Was she still sleepy? He peered closer, the truth niggling until it bore through his stubbornness and stung his heart. She needed to feed.

"You ready?"

"Huh?" Uri yanked his head out of his self-pitying ass. "Yeah, of course. Let's go." It was the work of a concentrated thought to take them both back to her apartment clear across the continent. Like he had a superpower. Like his level of vampire was better because he had the strength of Kynd behind it.

He landed them in her living room this time. While she showered and put on warm clothes, he nosed around, his curious steps taking him into the kitchen. Peeling wide the refrigerator door, he leaned in to get a gander at the glass shelves and the barren white interior. The emptiness called to mind the appetites of his bear, and Uri put his hand to his stomach. All was quiet under his palm, making him think the grizzly had been as satisfied with Violet's offering as the vampire had been.

As he stared into the empty fridge, the cool air oozing out of its open maw never touched his skin, because happiness wafted out of him like a low-grade fever. "Holy shit." Uri looked around the kitchen as if to share this newfound feeling.

Which is when he realized, with a quick flop of his satisfied gut, that the bottom half of the window overlooking the fire escape had been boarded up with a piece of plywood. Calling to mind a similar patch job.

Nose leading him forward, Uri let it tell him what his eyes could not. When his hair lifted as if liberated by static, it took his brain all of a half second to know another vampire had been here. A growl eddied forth as more welcome scents permeated the building haze of fury.

*My brethren.* Kallen faintly, and Darken most recently. Sniffing closer, he settled down as he sifted the information. The scent of gargoyle was strong and all over the plywood, which meant his brotherkynd had come after the vampire to clean things up and make his Chosen's home secure once again.

Relief washed through him so fast it loosened his balls. As he straightened from his fighter's stance, he caught his reflection in the upper pane. In the shadows of his imperfect image, he couldn't tell if his eyes were black or gray, and understood in that same heartbeat he didn't care.

As the visit from his brethren confirmed, he was Kynd no matter what he was made up of. They had his back and then some. Peering closer, Uri lifted his upper lip. Sharp gargoyle teeth gleamed back at him, his fangs slightly longer because the vampire had jumped to the fore to protect his mate.

With an involuntary rock back on his heels, Uri realized he didn't care about that either. Grinning at himself, the crack in his visage allowed a chuckle to break forth. Then, as fissures in a dam will do, more spilled out of him, the pressure easing as he released his laughter.

"What are you doing?" Violet sauntered in. All grins and curious and dressed in a floor length wool coat. Heavy lugged boots stuck out from the hem, and a knit cap pulled down over her wet hair, topped off her outfit.

Uri's smile widened as he held out his arms. "Loving you, I guess."

His female stopped all forward motion, her smile slipping off her face.

As his heart fell from its casing, Uri's arms dropped to his sides as if the bubble of himself—of *them*—had popped. "Shit. Sorry. Let's go." He didn't want to hear her apologies or her excuses, and a second later they were mere particles in a vast Maine winter night.

---

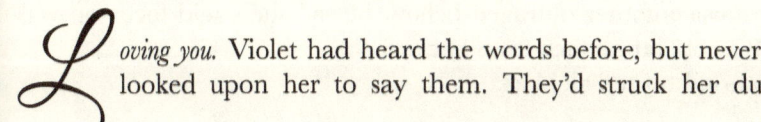 *oving you.* Violet had heard the words before, but never as someone looked upon her to say them. They'd struck her dumb. Having

longed to hear those very words for centuries upon centuries, when they finally came to her she simply hadn't known how to react.

She'd blown the moment the second Uri's open arms dropped to his sides, the awaiting hug and the expectation no longer offered. She wanted to blat. Instantly. Like a toddler. Which was, coincidentally, her earliest memory of wanting someone, anyone, to say those precious words to her.

When they hadn't come, she'd thickened her hide and built her walls. Uri, a frigging Kynd of all creatures, had been the one to work his way through her defenses to find her heart.

And she'd ruined it.

Feet growing solid on the tar and frozen snow, she just had time to notice they'd landed at her usual place by the cafeteria's dumpsters before Uri had her hand solidly in his and was tugging her toward the metal doors at the back of the hospital.

"How'd you do that?" She planted her feet, pulling him around to face her.

"Do what?"

"This. Put us here. I didn't think anyone knew about this spot." Cold as it was, her nose and eyes were already beginning to water as she looked up at him. He was still shirtless, wearing just his jeans and boots.

"I don't know." His cheeks flushed red. From the cold? Or was he that connected to her he could somehow sense her. It would explain his embarrassment like he thought he'd overstepped some line in the sand they had between them.

Oh, right. She'd etched that furrow when she'd stared at him like a ninny as he offered his heart to her.

"Maybe you—" There was a second or two where she couldn't understand why her words didn't come out of her mouth. She opened and closed her jaw like a landed fish, but nothing came. The panic struck when she tried to breathe and couldn't. Hands flying to her throat, she knew it was wet blood she felt, but even that took a second to register it was hers.

Three seconds. It took three seconds to realize her throat had been slashed. It took Uri a half second more to launch himself over the top of her as she fell to her knees, roaring like the enraged beast he was shifting into.

When the icy ground rose up to meet her, she knew it should hurt, that she should feel the cut of the frozen snowpack like razors on her skin. In the distance, there was another outraged bellow, but all she could focus on was the black of the cold tar an inch from her eyes.

Then her world turned all black.

*U*ri had always thought he came undone every dawn, until the moment he caught the flash of a silver blade sliding along his Violet's throat. He'd been gazing down on the female who owned him tooth and nail, and then she had a mortal wound. Just as fast, everything he knew about himself detonated.

And still he hadn't been fast enough, the assassin gone in less than a blink. *Dematerialized.*

A vampire had killed his Chosen One. He went from rational being to instinctual animal in one beat of the heart. A heart that was dying in his chest. He couldn't fucking breathe and didn't need to. Unable to track the assailant, he pivoted, his attention homing in on the only thing that did matter.

The form slumped on the ground beside the dumpster. "Violet!" Her name came to him on wings inside his head, spreading so wide she obliterated everything. The next image he beheld was her in his arms, her blood pulsing from the gash in her white throat. Frantic, he cradled her lolling head to his chest.

*Stop it. Stop it.* A mantra in his brain. The blood. Stop the flow of blood to save her life. With only his breaths as the vapor between their faces, and the steam rising from the spilling of her blood, Uri reacted.

Not to return her to the cave as he had done before when vampires threatened but to his brethren. Electrified by instinct, Uri teleported his beloved to the safe house.

*K*allen wasn't usually one for thinking his head would explode with too much information, but Drakus was pushing the boundaries by spewing off more fun fae facts than his cranium had the space for.

As the scenery of winter bare trees and the petticoats of evergreens dragged by at a snail's crawl, he gave serious thought to leaping out of the car even though he was the one behind the wheel.

Drakus sat in the passenger seat, his mouth rolling along with the tires. He hadn't stopped at the identification of the tattoo. Oh, no. Once he'd returned from the land of the deranged and conned them into letting him go for a ride in a vehicle, Drakus had babbled everything he knew about the fae.

Some facts were arcane, some useful, but all were cathartic for the poor bastard.

He talked like he unburdened himself, and Kallen guessed he did. Shitting out of his mouth, so to speak.

Kallen didn't have the heart to tease him about it. Hell, that lovely organ was lying in a broken mess by the gas pedal where he'd pick it up later. Drakus' stories of the fae were too horrid. Too fucking personal.

And all he could see every time he glanced to his right—to make sure his brotherkynd was handling the ride and didn't scatter his marble jar again—was his fucking tattooed face.

Which wasn't like the one he'd torn from the vampire at Violet's apartment. Drakus' dragon tattoo, which smothered nearly every inch of his skin, hadn't just been pinpricked in, it had been burned there. The flesh not only colored but mutilated. So even if the ink was erased, the shape of the dragon would remain etched in his skin. Forever.

"Wait. Back up. I was thinking of…" Kallen waved the words away. Did Drakus really need to know where his thoughts had traveled?

Can we have a big *Hell no*?

Kallen didn't need to pull the Audi off the road when he hit the brakes. Their driveway was so far down a barren track nobody bothered driving down it, not even in the summer. He could hog the road all he wanted. Pushing the stick up to P, he turned in his seat. "So, you're saying because the tat is mystical it will be as if I never tore it off his fugly neck?"

"Yes. He has traded a piece of himself for induction into the vaJcakas. As long as that piece remains in the possession of the fae he sold it to, then the tattoo will remain no matter how the host is damaged."

"Jesus."

"No. Daewon most likely. He's kind of the fae equivalent."

Kallen smiled. "That was rhetorical, buddy."

"If you say so. But know this. If you want to identify the owner of that mark, do not seek Daewon." The name came out on a screech like it was riding down the highway in a speeding car with no hind wheels. It was the dragon oozing out of him, but Kallen still expected to see a shower of sparks.

"Hey, shit, now. Come on." Kallen reached out then remembered how Drakus had taken a trip on the banana boat the last time they'd touched him. He drew his hand back and gripped the steering wheel in front of him. Not consoling his brotherkynd with touch made him feel helpless as shit.

Which was the point now, wasn't it? Torture the beast and eventually, he'll be as toothless as an old lion at the circus. Kallen torqued on the steering wheel as he wrestled with the urge to reach out and touch the fae with his fists. Their tactics hadn't just ruined Drakus, it had affected all Kynd.

Well, screw that. He needed contact as bad as the dragon recoiling against it. When another muffled screech hit his ears he grumbled, "Fuck it," and hauled his ass across the center console to flop onto Drakus' lap like a dramatic girlfriend, his legs stretching across the driver's seat because let's face it, Angelia's SUV was dinky.

But, so what. The Kynd were back together again and it was time to erase some of the fae damage. "Easy, man. You're safe now with your brethren." Of course, while he was cooing to his brotherkynd like a frigging dove, Kallen was seeing them as if he gazed in from the outside of the glass.

"Hey, look at me." Cupping that stained cheek, he turned Drakus' attention onto him. "Look at us." He waggled his eyebrows. "It's like you just proposed, and I said yes."

Drakus blinked. With his eyelids—and not the see-through one of the dragon, sending Kallen's meaty little heart a-thumping. "You did? You said yes?"

Dodging a sloppy kiss, Kallen smacked the side of his head on the windshield. "Cut it out, you cheeky bastard." But the laughter evened his keel. It didn't hurt to see the grin on the puss in front of him, either.

Rather than try to wedge his big ass back across the center divider and get the gear shift up his crack, Kallen fumbled for the door handle behind his back and spilled out onto the snow when the passenger door gave way.

"You crazy son of a bitch." Seeing Drakus' gray eyes was worth the swan dive. Shaking the snow out of his hair, he rounded the ass end of the SQ5 and slid back into the driver's seat. A forty point turn later and he and Drakus were leaving the two-track road and snow-sailing around the circular drive, nosing the SUV into the five bay garage.

With the engine ticking, they sat in the bucket seats staring at where the headlamps shined on the empty wall in front of them. The silence in the car was as subdued as the forest covered in snow. Drakus had gone quiet, and that itched Kallen like a wool sweater.

Mainly because the brotherkynd had more to say and wasn't spilling. It was as if his mouth had closed the same way the garage doors had trundled down. He'd bottled up, which wasn't good for any of them.

"Soooo..." Kallen kept his face forward but rolled his peepers to the right.

Drakus squirmed in the seat like he didn't fit. "It's complicated."

"I think that's the name of a movie. Give it another shot."

Making like he had ants in his pants, he tried again. "Uri's Chosen. Violet. The sect her father is a member of."

"The sect *she's* probably a member of."

Drakus sighed. "It's bad, Kal." Silence stretched between them like they lolled on an abandoned beach. All screeching gulls and roaring surf, and nothing else but the vast expanse of ocean and sky. "They take prisoners, too. Keep them." So now his mouth was constipated? At least it wasn't a total blockage.

"What are you driving at, Dray?"

"The prisoners. They take them from every realm. Every realm, Kallen. They don't discriminate."

"Meaning what, that you were their prisoner?" Even as he said it, he knew that wasn't what Drakus meant. His stomach gained about a thousand pounds, his skin growing clammy cold around it.

His brotherkynd shook his head. But that was all he needed to do, wasn't it? He meant Urick. Uri could have been one of their prisoners. Which explained his hatred of vampires and why he absolutely refused to acknowledge that part of him.

Kallen melted back into his seat while his anger came to life under his skin. "And his fucking Chosen One is part of this."

Drakus ran a palm up and down his arm like maybe his tattoo itched. Or was squirming with a life of its own. "We have to go back to her apartment. Search again. Find any clue we can. We can't lose him. Not like this. We can't lose him."

Kallen put his hand out, putting an end to Drakus' ironing routine. "Brotherkynd, stop. We won't lose him. We'll go inside, okay, and have a meeting. Get everybody together, yeah?"

Though Drakus kept his peepers looking straight ahead, he nodded, his Adam's apple taking a dip as he swallowed.

"All right. Come on." Kallen clapped his brotherkynd's shoulder before getting out, punching the fob with his thumb so the Audi would do that cute bleep-bleep thing as she winked at him.

As he opened the door into the hallway leading to the kitchen, he stepped aside so Drakus could go first. "Age before beauty."

"Funny."

Whiiiich might have been the wrong thing to say to a guy when half his face was stained. Thank Christ Drakus let it roll as his long legs carried him through the uterus of the pantry and spit him out into the kitchen.

"Hi, Angelia."

Her blonde hair swept up in a messy bun, Angelia turned from stirring a bubbling pot on the stove, a long wooden spoon in her hand. "Hey, guys."

"Hey, Blondie. What's cookin'?" Kallen wedged himself between her and Merrick, who was never more than two feet from his Chosen, no matter what she was doing.

Merrick growled.

"What?" Losing the staring match, Kallen pushed his ass off the counter and fiddled with some cheese smeared gadget. "Ow, son of a bitch!" He crammed his bleeding finger into his mouth.

"Serves you right." Merrick snatched the grater out of his hand and set it back onto the cutting board. "So, Drakus, how was the ride?"

"Fine."

"Fine? Your first ride ever and all you can say is—"

As if choreographed, all three males dropped to their knees, glanced at each other, then scrambled for the foyer, tripping and shoving off each other like criminals fleeing the Keystone Kops. They rounded out their dance routine with sloppy halts the instant they broke through the archway. Riding up his back because the momentum had to go somewhere, Drakus yelled, "Uri!"

So it was. Their beloved male was obviously alive, but the female in Uri's arms couldn't be. No effing way. Not with those limbs all loosy-goosey and spilling out from his arms. Uri's face cracked open as pain bled from every pore. "Brethren, help me."

So help him God, if Kallen lived ten thousand years more, he would never forget the sound of that plea or the horrorstruck visage of his brotherkynd. As Uri wobbled like death chewed on his heart, Kallen guessed the association wasn't far off.

He hadn't gotten a gander at Uri's Chosen One, but that had to be her. What else could make him feel as if a wrecking ball swung around them, laying waste to everything in its chained path? In front of them, spinning helplessly round and round as if he had no bearings, Uri bellowed and shrieked while his Chosen One's blood splattered.

"Help me, brethren, help me. Oh, so help me, Jesus, help me!" An apt plea. If that female was dead, the world had yet to see what real terror looked like, and then it would be on its knees praying.

While they stood dumb struck by the sight, Kronos, Darken, and Daniela spilled down the stairs, tripping and running just as he, Merrick, and Drakus had done.

"Holy motherfucker, move!" A sharp jab to his side tilted Kallen off his planted shitkickers, and Angelia burst into the circle. "Uri, set her down! Set her down!" Yanking on his blood smeared arms, she finally got the bear chimera's attention. "On the floor, Uri. Put her down!" As Angelia helped to speed things along by dragging the huge male to the floor, Daniela dove into the lowering mess.

"Violet! Violet, stay awake, okay. Stay awake. Kronos, your shirt!" Without looking away from the bloody female laying on the cold marble, Daniela flung out her hand, fully expecting the shirt to be delivered as prompt as a surgeon's scalpel. Kronos didn't disappoint.

If Kallen could step back, remove himself from the scene, he would notice there wasn't as much sound in the room as there was roaring through his head. It was just Angelia and Daniel barking orders back and forth with the background whine of Uri's keening.

And yet Kallen could barely hear the words spoken. Clearly, he saw lips take shape around words, but it seemed all around him was a great din, as if the battle against death was performed before a thundering crowd. Or perhaps, the thundering came from within his chest, where his heart fought to crash through bone.

Brown eyes stricken wide as she crammed Kronos' shirt to the Chosen's neck, Daniela turned to Angelia. "Tell me about vampires. If I stem the bleeding, will a vampire live?"

"Yes," Angelia answered with the conviction of the righteous. "She will, but she needs blood."

---

*T*he answer fell upon Uri's ears like the pronouncement of life spared on the operating table, and the doctor had come to give the good news to the grief-stricken family.

Vi would live with blood, and so she would live. Without a thought, he bared his fangs and sank them into his wrist then thrust the bubbling vein against Violet's parted lips. "Drink, love, drink." Whispered expressions of devotion as one would murmur when counting the rosary. Oddly, he grew aware of his bulk. While making sure to keep his wrist pushed against the lips of his beloved, he moved to the side so the women could tend the god-awful wound on her neck.

"More pressure." Daniela's voice came to him like street noise in the background of one's park bench reverie. But if he should blink and look around, he'd see he wasn't alone. "Kallen, in the second drawer beside the stove there's Saran Wrap. Grab it. Merrick, do you guys have a first aid kit?"

Bodies swarmed and hovered above and beside him, but all he could see was the face before him. Along with his blood sliding down her cheek from the corner of her mouth. "Vi?" Uri pressed harder, as though nudging her jaw would stimulate her to suckle upon his wrist.

"Uri, you're going to have to give us some space." He knew that voice, although the words made no sense. "Uri, you've got to move." Someone bumped his side, but none of that mattered, not when he was struck by how pale Violet was, how a twinge of blue grew around her lips.

"She's not breathing. She's not breathing."

"We know, Uri, but you've got to move."

"She's not breathing. Oh, holy Christ, she's not breathing."

"Hey, someone get him out of here! I can't see…"

Other things were said, though he knew not what. Hands fell upon him, faces appearing to block his view of his Chosen. "Urick, man, move back a little so the females can work. They need room to save her life."

Bodies nudged him, and hands gripped to pull on him. "Violet. She needs my blood. I have to give her my blood." Anger rose to accompany his fear. His body stiffened, refusing to be shoved aside as his brethren circled him, cutting him off from his line with his female.

"Listen, man. You have to give them a minute."

As his spine locked to give his muscles something to brace on, he could see his Chosen as he looked over the heads of the ones trying to separate him from the most important thing in his life. *Oh, God, help me.* She moved only when she was bumped or tended to. Otherwise, her legs remained straight out on the floor, her arms lifeless.

Fear sprouted like a tree inside him, its limbs unfurling to fill his.

"Jesus Christ, Uri, you've got to calm the fuck down!" Merrick's fanged face came into view, his black mane curling along his jaw. Uri brought his arms together and fisted that mane, lifting his brotherkynd off the floor to pull him closer.

He bellowed his terror straight into that face.

"Fuck a duck," he might have heard. Just before a blast of wind flattened his skin to his bones and a shriek cut his fury in half like a flaming sword—where it doubled as if the severing cloned it. He roared back, throwing Merrick away with a swift surge of power. As the male careened across the foyer, Uri launched himself at the dragon.

"Look what you've done! You see what you're doing?" For some strange reason, the fear resonating in that shout called to him, as though like harkened to like. As he and Drakus collided, Uri twisted toward that voice.

Darken straddled the females on the floor as if he was the last barrier to their safety. The sight of his brotherkynd bravely guarding the Chosen Ones stilled him as surely as if stone crept through his blood.

Sensing the change, Drakus' hold became a hug, the great tail sweeping round to snug him closer to that scaled body rather than send him flying the way Merrick had gone. It was as though Uri watched it from afar, but he still noticed that despite the immensity of the dragon, Drakus had maneuvered himself so as not to come anywhere near the females on the floor.

It was then he felt it. The humming. The electric current so much stronger than it had been when they'd reunited after millennia apart. This sensation reminded him of old, in the days when the Kynd had reason to be feared.

Floundering toward Violet while he dragged a two-ton dragon with him like cement shoes, Uri managed to get himself close enough to curl his hand to her ankle. The electrified hum circuited through him and Drakus and whipped into his Chosen like she was a grounding rod.

Drakus yanked away as the screech from behind Uri's head stabbed his eardrums with a thousand ice picks. He folded to the floor with his hands clapped to his head, the severing of touch shorting out the connection. The dragon crumpled beside him, his leather wings scraping along the floor as Drakus folded them around himself.

*Great Christ Almighty.* He was going to have a heart attack. Surely, he couldn't take any more. Too much pain engulfed him, too much power, and laying in the midst of it all were living miracles. Especially if the fleeting jolt he'd shared with Violet had actually done some good. If it hadn't, it was too late—the other males were hauling Drakus out of the room.

On his hands and knees, Uri could see the gentle ministrations of the two females to the One. Where before their movements were sharp and decisive, now they were kind and careful, their voices murmuring to the One laying face up. Violet's skin shined like alabaster behind the runnels of blood.

But it shined. So help him, her skin glowed with a life he'd thought lost. On sloppy limbs he crawled toward them, his beloved's face turning red and blurry. He slapped at his eyes to clear the blood tears, although it wasn't because he cared that someone would see his vampire tears. Nor did he care who saw him reduced in his need for his Chosen. She alone mattered. Only Violet mattered.

As he neared touching distance once again, he slowed, mindful of the sanctity of the space in which he moved. He was a brute, a beast, but the females were to be handled with great care now that his brain decided to kick instinct to the curb like the stray dog it was. With a trembling hand, he reached to touch his special One.

The other two females parted to make room for him. "Careful, Uri. The wound is barely closed." That little tidbit stopped him cold, his outstretched fingers curling into a fist. So, Drakus had pulled away too soon. "She will live, though, right? She'll live?"

His throat clotted tight enough to choke him, and he clung to the awaited answer like a man hanging over a ledge by his brittle fingernails.

"Yes. The connection was short, but it got her breathing again. Feed her now, though. Don't wait." Angelia turned away from him to look down as her patient started to gurgle.

"No. He...can't." The gargled words came from a throat that had been severed only moments before. The voice came from Heaven itself. Uri's fractured heart swelled, choking him up more. When he brought his wrist up to his mouth to pierce the skin anew, he saw how badly he was shaking.

What if it jostled the wound and tore it apart? He couldn't mask his fear as he glanced from Angelia to Daniela, two glorious and righteous females he could never repay even if he lived until the end of the world. And Drakus? He'd helped, after all. It didn't matter if Vi wasn't fully healed. She would be whole again with a little time.

Daniela's lips curled into a smile, her eyes knowing. "Just go slow and it will be okay." She took his calloused hand in hers and guided him closer. "Sit right here with her. Keep her back flat...that's right. Good." She pulled small rugs of fur up around them to immobilize Violet further.

Where in hell had she gotten those? As Angelia helped Daniela tuck them in tight, Uri really couldn't give a rat's ass. He was nestled in with his Chosen One, who was groping in search of...ah, there it was. As her fingers curled around his, the familiar cadence of their special hum vibrated through him.

When the little pinch between Violet's eyebrows eased, he knew she felt it, too. It made him want to sob like a sissy, seeing that this particular Kynd trait could offer comfort and solace to the female who meant everything to him.

Uri bit into his wrist again without hesitation. "Here, my love." As he lowered his arm, he tried not to drip blood onto her face, but a few droplets went rogue and left tiny marks upon her cheek like red snowflakes.

Mere drops compared to the rest of the blood smeared all over her, soaking into her clothes. With the emergency fading with every healing minute, Uri's anger simmered to a boil, the sight of so much blood elevating his fury toward the will to do murder.

He refused to think of the vampire who had done this. He had no place in this sacred sphere of healing. Uri closed his eyes to better sense the tugs on his wrist as Violet swallowed. Such dainty draughts, her lips soft as flower petals against his skin. Blessedly, his dick decided discretion was the better path and lay folded in his jeans, as flaccid as it used to be before he'd found his Chosen One.

When she stopped he urged her on, whispering at her ear, kissing the dainty seashell curve of it. "More, Vi. Take more." Now that he wasn't freaking out over it, giving Violet what she needed was so right, and every resistance and refusal before seemed a sin. He would never deny her again.

She pushed against his arm and tried to pull her head back.

"Shh. Easy now." Although the fur blankets were already laying on her, he pulled them tighter, fussing over her. She had so little strength, her pushing against him made him think of newborn fawns for some silly reason. "Had enough?"

"Yes."

Careful not to move her, he wriggled closer. Which is when he noticed they were alone in the huge foyer. When the other Chosen had left they'd dimmed the lights, as if to soften the edge of the trauma.

"Where are we?"

"Home, love. We're home."

# CHAPTER 8

*H*ome. God, how awful. He had teleported her to his home, and she wanted to cry. After the vampire attack, she knew what it must have cost him to bring her here and not to the safety of the cave. That he'd done so for her sake...

The tear, when it slid toward her ear, left a warm trail against her skin. She swallowed, glad for the slick of blood on the back of her damaged throat. The first sip had been like swallowing razor wire.

"Hey, you're all right. It's going to be all right."

Another tear chased the first. "No, it isn't." She swallowed, squeezing her eyes shut against the pain. "It's not." It had never been all right, and she'd been a fool to have pretended otherwise. She had escaped death because of the male who now lay close beside her, and she would do nothing but bring something far worse to him.

"My father—" A cough punched at her throat, and she tried to stifle it by holding her breath. As the pressure in her lungs built, the cough fought back, pushing harder on her healing flesh. "Shhh, Vi. Don't talk. Don't talk." As Uri finger-combed the blood caked hair from her temple, his strokes were gentle even though his hands shook. She closed her eyes and kept them shut as if she could stave off the truth if she couldn't see the male lying beside her.

She had brought his past straight to him, and he didn't know it yet. And when he learned the truth? Oh, God, he would shun her as he had every right to. Renouncing her would do more than break him, she knew that now, but to see her face every day? Looking at her would only remind him of his past tortures. They'd eat at him like maggots until there was nothing left but the husk of who he was.

Fuck. *Who he was.* She knew exactly the kind of male Uri was, and she didn't want to lose the happiness he'd brought to her life. Too late for regrets now. She couldn't change who her father was, although she had even more reason than before to assassinate the bastard.

Not because he'd tried taking her life—again—but that Uri had been one of his victims. She had no idea how the chimera had escaped. Usually, the only way prisoners left the convent was by getting their carcasses dragged out by the heels and burned to hide the evidence.

Violet shuddered. Sickened that she knew even that much, ashamed that she was connected to those atrocities even if she'd never taken part in the ritualistic feedings. Her entire life she'd felt tainted by her birthright. "I must tell you…who the…vampire is."

"Later, love. It's not important right now." Uri clenched his jaw, the muscle bulging like a baby's fist.

Riiiiight. Maybe not this second, but she'd bet her favorite backpack that the second she let sleep overtake her, he'd be out tracking that male down. And then he would come face to face with one of his old tormentors. "I must." With every swallow, her voice felt a little better, even if the sealed skin of the wound tugged like wet tissue paper every time she tried to talk. Violet struggled to sit up.

Uri pressed down on her shoulders. "Hey, settle down. It's okay." Without the strength to fight him she relented, letting him tuck the furs around her again. "We'll talk, but you need to lay here quietly, all right?"

She dipped her chin a smidge, afraid to nod lest she tear the wound open and bleed like a stuck pig again.

"So, then, what's so important it can't wait?"

Oh, God, she was really going to tell him. Violet closed her eyes so she wouldn't have to see the revulsion blooming on his face.

"Hey, bro, how's the female doing?"

Snapping her lids open and rolling her peepers toward the new voice, Violet got a gander at a pair of scuffed boots the Hulk would swim in. Lord, the Kynd were huge males.

"Kallen." Uri rose to hug his brother or whatever they called themselves. Brotherkynd, wasn't it? So far, the legends weren't exactly factual, so who knew? As the males whacked each other on the back, the new one glared down at her.

Goose bumps shivered over her skin. Violet knew exactly what that look meant—this Kallen knew all about her. But how? And was that really the important part? Uri wouldn't want to have anything to do with her no matter who delivered the news.

"It is so good to have you back. It's pretty much the only thing keeping Drakus tethered. She talking yet?" As the two males peeled apart, they locked hands and turned to look down at her. How appropriate. A souring thought, but there it was. She wasn't worthy enough to lick their gigantic boots.

Uri knelt beside her to stroke his fingers up and down her arm. As his fingertips hit the landing strip of her skin that familiar humming rippled through her, much stronger than she remembered. Sliding her gaze a little upward, she saw the answer hanging in front of her—Uri and Kallen were still holding hands.

Wow, and what the fuck? Apparently, when the Kynd were together they shared some kind of electricity. She squirmed to evade his touch and caught Kallen's glare again, everything about it promising if she wasn't already stabbed, he'd have a go.

Uri ignored it. "She's trying to speak." The look on his face was the polar opposite of the other male's, shining love and relief down on her despite the traces of admonishment. As the clomp of footsteps joined the party, Uri dragged his attention from her to the newcomer.

Shit. Make that plural. Three other males parked their shitkickers around her. A pair of stilettos and some high heeled boots stepped in to join the circle.

"She talking?"

Jesus, good thing she was wrapped in furs or the ice in that voice would freeze her nipples off.

Uri went still beside her. "What's going on?" His growl puckered her nipples in a different way. She felt the twist coil deep and tight down through her.

"Brotherkynd, we need a meeting." The male with the short black hair and the wide shoulders…oh, who the fuck was she kidding. They all looked the same. Ready to kill, and she was the one holding the short straw. This was the Kynd of legend, the ones who tore heads off newborn babes and raped their mothers.

At least the one with the craggy face didn't look as fiercely determined as the others. Then again, he wasn't even looking at her. Like maybe he didn't want to witness her execution? Naw. Surely, he was as bloodthirsty as the rest of them.

"Angelia and Daniela will stay with her while you come with us."

"I don't think so."

131

Urick's fingers quit the strolling up and down and curled around her bicep like the roots of a tree.

"Believe me, you'll want to." Kallen. And the names of the others? They hadn't even introduced themselves, so how was that for not boding well.

"No."

"Oh, for goodness' sake. *Men.*" The blonde flapped her hands, shooing the others away. "We'll tell him nicely, not like the frigging Inquisition. Or we can be even nicer and let her tell him herself."

"No effing way. We just got him back. I'm not about to lose him again."

"*Him* is right here, and I have no intention of going anywhere. Now tell me what in the hell is going on." Uri's intense gaze slid from one brotherkynd to another.

"She doesn't have any weapons on her, right? Owww, Darken." The one named Kallen winced and rubbed his upper arm.

"That's for being an insensitive dick."

As the other male shook out his fist, he reached for Daniela. *Ah, yes.* Now she recognized him. He was the gargoyle from the cellar, the one who'd planted himself between her and her only friend. He wasn't being so brazen about it now, but he draped his arm over Daniela's shoulders, subtly positioning himself in front of her in case Violet should heal instantly and attack her best friend out of the blue.

Asshats. Still though, it hurt.

"Violet," the blonde knelt down beside her. The other Kynd from the cellar clung to her backside, not being subtle in the least about protecting his female. God, if she wasn't the one with her head under the ax she'd admire the caring.

As Uri gave a gentle squeeze to her shoulder, she realized she had that. For now. In a few minutes, Uri was going to hate her with the venom of the wounded. Violet tried to concentrate on the pressure, so if she lived through this, she could remember what it had felt like to be coveted.

Blondie spoke to her again. "Violet, we want you to know that no matter what, you won't be harmed."

"No, we don't want her to know that. *Owww.* Jesus, Darken." Kallen scowled at his brotherkynd beside him, and if she wasn't laying on her back fresh from visiting death's door, Violet would think the two were a little comical.

Right then, she wasn't laughing. She was trying to sit up so she could get her feet under her. Fighting from the floor would be sloppy and laughable for about five seconds. Then they'd quit rubbing their shins and get down to the business of flinging her severed limbs to the four cardinal directions.

Besides, they were distracting her. Uri was the one she needed to be focused on. But when she lifted her chin to look at him, a wet warmth trailed down her neck and dripped from her nape.

"Oh, shit." When the mean one—Kallen—glanced down at her, his knees unlocked as his face paled out. "She's bleeding again. Oh, shit." Nervous gaze latching onto her protector, he said, "I'm sorry, Uri. I didn't mean—"

The roar from behind her was deafening. "Get out! All of you, get out!"

Even blondie backed off, the thick arms of her male draping around her as he said, "She heals, and then we talk."

"I'm staying." The chivalry came from the one with the craggy face, and the brotherkynd with blondie nodded like some secret code passed between them. Which was kind of like finding an empty roll beside you after you'd taken a slippery crap. She didn't want any of them there when she told Uri. Besides, with her flopped on the floor as helpless as a furry burrito, he wasn't going to need the frigging bodyguard.

Her throat was slit, not her brain. She could read between the lines just fine. But what was she going to do, argue about it when she rasped like Marlon Brando?

"I'm staying, too."

God bless Daniela. Violet reached out for her, the other woman's warm hand sliding into hers in an instant.

"If she stays, I stay." The one named Darken moved to stand behind her, legs spread in a military stance, arms folded.

"Well, that's hardly fair. I'm staying, too." Kallen joined his brotherkynd, mimicking the stance and everything.

"Oh, for the love of God, would you all just go? Please?"

If things weren't so dire, she'd laugh. As it was, when Daniela winked down at her, Violet nearly broke into a grin. She hid it by licking her lips.

"See! She's already preparing to—" The cuff to the back of Kallen's head came from blondie's guy. "Oh, that's it." He launched himself at the other male, the two of them going to the floor like tussling kittens. Gigantic tiger kittens.

"Oh, damn it, don't break anything!" Darken broke off from protection duty and joined the fray.

Daniela shook her head, her thick auburn hair shining like it was spun with strands of red gold in the low lighting. "Can you believe these guys?" She gave a reassuring squeeze to Violet's fingers. "They aren't bad, really. They just care." She glanced up at Uri. "We're glad you're back, but seriously, talk to each other as soon as you can. Angelia and I will try to keep them from barging in again, but I can't make promises." Getting to her feet, she turned to chase after the melee that had scuffled its way to the far side of the foyer.

"Glad you found her, Uri." Blondie—Angelia—pecked him on the cheek then left the same way Daniela did. A few shouts, thumps, and the sound of shattering glass, and the tumult exited, leaving the emptiness of the grand foyer in a vacuum.

Only Kronos remained, and he sat on the lowest step of the staircase silent as an ancient owl. If she rolled her eyes hard up at her forehead, she could just see Uri hovering behind her. It looked as if he was...

"Here, love. Feed." His dripping forearm came into view as he squatted closer.

She shook her head.

"You must, Vi. You're bleeding again and you have to heal." His words would have been commanding if they weren't so distraught.

"I'll help you heal her." The offer came from the foot of the stairs where the craggy faced Kynd was sitting, elbows on his knees, fists the size of those hammers used at carnivals to whack the bell hanging twenty feet aloft.

"Jesus, thank you, thank you, Kronos."

Since Violet figured he wasn't Jesus, then she'd just learned the name of another Kynd. She also realized something she hadn't picked up on earlier. Urick offered his blood to her without a case of the shakes. Careful not to kick the wheel out from under his apple cart, she touched his proffered wrist tentatively, cautious with her fangs as she pressed her lips to the punctured skin.

"That's right, love. That's good."

Though his arm was steady under her palms, he couldn't quite mask the quaver in his voice. Baby steps, she supposed and kept sucking. Kronos neared as cautiously as she'd reached for Uri, as if he was afraid things would go bombsville in a blink.

Uri didn't have to speak to express his relief. He showed it in the way he closed his hand around his brotherkynd's. Half a second later the vibration said hello. Violet's fingers clenched involuntarily, the strength of the zap surprising her. Yeah, she'd felt it earlier, but she'd still been a little out of it. With a fresh dose of Uri's blood coating her lips, her senses were singing back to life, spread wide open for the added oomph of Kronos' touch. Her skin at the wound on her neck felt as though it was crawling. She quit pulling on Uri's vein to scratch at it.

"Shh, easy. Just let it go."

*Let it go?* Not when her body was turning into a door buzzer. Kronos stayed kneeling beside them, his face averted so she couldn't read his reaction to all of this. Yeah, he'd volunteered and was taking it better than that Drakus guy, but by how much?

Licking her lips and swallowing, she didn't mask her surprise at how much the pain had receded, and let her eyes pop open. "Wow." Though the sound wasn't quite her usual voice, with a little use it'd be back to new. "That is frigging amazing." She wriggled to sit up. "Thank you."

"No bother." The short response came from the male who yanked his hand back the second she sat up, as if he'd endured enough, and now that she was well he could give in to his own problems. He curled his hand into his stomach as he stood. Clasping his other hand to Uri's shoulder, he held her gaze as he spoke. "She's beautiful. I'm glad you found her."

No chance to respond when he hightailed it for the door like his ass was on fire.

"Interesting brothers you have."

Uri rubbed the hand that had been holding the other male's and watched the archway like Kronos had left a comet tail behind his speedy exit. "Yeah. They're great, aren't they?" He meant it, despite having nearly battled them over her.

Too bad she wouldn't be sticking around to peel that onion. Picking at her blood caked hair, she said, "So, about what I was trying to tell you."

---

*W*ith euphoria revving through his veins, Uri nestled Violet to his chest. "Not yet, okay? How about we get you showered and into some clean clothes first." Whispering the words along her ear, they trailed off at the beginning of the fading scar, where he flicked his tongue to the puckered flesh.

"Sure. But we talk right after, okay?"

Uri nodded, rubbing his cheek along hers, loving the contrast of her silken skin to his stubble. At this point, he'd agree to anything that kept her with him. He knew what she wanted to tell him. Well, he suspected, and he wasn't eager to bring that toxic shit into their home. Not with her firm ass pressed against his livening cock. As his hips circled and she pushed against him, he groaned.

"So good," he rasped along her ear, nipping the lobe as he trailed his hand up under her shirt. Her blood-sticky shirt. Like a switch, his anger lit up, outshining his lust. The face of the vampire loomed into his conscience, and his hand gripped a handful of bulbous flesh.

"Easy, big boy. I know I have another one, but I kind of like the set."

*Shit.* He let go instantly, making a tent out of her shirt as he released. She pressed his hand back to her warm skin and worked circles until he took control. Pinching her taut nipple, he kissed down the slender column of her neck.

He smelled her drying blood and his mouth watered. Euphoric to have her in his arms, he surrendered to instinct. He lapped the copper stickiness, surprised by how good she tasted on his tongue.

"Keep that up and I won't have to shower."

No she wouldn't, and he didn't mind that at all. To prove it, he pushed his cock against her ass again. Until he caressed her hair back farther from her neck to lap some more of her blood and his fingers got stuck in the dry crust matting her soft locks.

He tamped down his fury the second it popped its ferocious little head up. This was about his Chosen One, not him. He would tend to her first and himself second. His vengeance resisted the cap he was cramming down on it, but the moment he had her sated and sleeping he would go hunting. Not a minute before.

As if they hadn't taken enough, somehow one of the vampire's who'd imprisoned him had found him and had tried to steal the most precious part of him. For his gall, the bastard would know pain. Uri would lay waste to everything precious to that monster, just to give him an inkling of the suffering Uri had known.

*Still know.*

Although as he trailed his fingertips over the rounded flesh of a delicate boob, down the valley between and back up over the other mound, suffering lay moored about a thousand miles off the coast of his heart. What filled him now made him want to growl, groan, and levitate off the fricking floor. He cupped the channel between Violet's thighs to keep his feet firmly planted on the marble.

Oh, right. They were still in the foyer. Sweeping her legs from under her, Uri ran up the stairs, taking two at a time. "What are you doing?" Surely Violet's laughter would unravel him at the seams. As it was, he was coming undone, his muscles twitching, his bones going loose.

God bless door handles. A door knob might have proven too slippery and sent him into fits. Mindful his Chosen was tucked out of the way, Uri pushed his shoulder against the door and stepped into his room.

"Holy shit."

Violet craned her newly healed neck to get a good look at his bedroom. "What? What's wrong?"

"That's just it. Nothing." In front of them, the bed looked freshly made, the ironed sheets turned down over a red duvet. There were about ten pillows of different sizes and colors arranged at the headboard, and the recessed lighting shined down like the bed was on grand display. He could smell fresh paint, and when he looked around he noticed the holes in the plaster were fixed, the gouges from his claws sanded out of the woodwork.

"I'm not following."

Like he was going to explain how he lost control and smashed shit. She'd seen it already. Bad enough he'd left rakings of his long claws in the stone and dirt of the cave, but for her to see them in something so nice? They were reminders of a time that was fast falling behind him. His future with Violet dawned brighter than that.

Without a doubt, his brethren and their Chosen had done this for him, for when he returned with Violet. The knot cinching his throat turned the room wavy as his eyes watered up.

Violet turned her attention from the room to look up at him. "Ah." A mountain of understanding put the weight on that one syllable. As he continued to suck in the scenery around them, Vi nudged him with her elbow. "Hey."

Uri glanced down over his cheekbones, worried that red rivers would drop from his eyes if he lowered his face.

"It's beautiful."

"So are you." He hadn't meant for the compliment to sound so fierce, but there it was.

Violet's lips parted and he slanted his mouth over hers. The moist heat of their joining washed through him like a cascading glass of bubbly, for surely his cup runneth over. Violet dragged her lips from his to run her tongue along one cheekbone, the tips of her little fangs peering out when she grinned shyly. "No sense in wasting them, right?"

He took her mouth with the fervor flaring inside him, tasting his scent on her tongue. Loving that it was there, he welcomed the lengthening of his fangs and shivered when one scraped across one of Violet's.

*Claim her.* The notion burned fierce, his erection weeping with its mushroom cap sticking out of the waist of his jeans. Yes. He would drink of her life's blood while he pumped his seed into her hot, welcoming sheathe. And she would take in his life's blood as she released her seed like a flower to a bee.

Claim and bestow. A vampire mating. As fundamentally right as holding her in his arms. Uri pulled back from the kiss to gaze down upon his female without shame. Slowly, too, he lowered her from his arms, unable to drag his attention from her as he set her feet on the floor. A floor which was now buffed free of scratches, the warm grains of oak branching out from under a thick, ornamental rug. Blown glass wall sconces glowed warmly into buttery corners.

With the utmost care he could manage with his trembling fingers, he plucked the individual buttons down the front of her stained shirt, caressing the satin softness of her shoulders as he pushed the cloth away.

Violet glanced up at him, her cheeks as ruby red as the real gems, yet infinitely more precious. "I'm…" She flushed more as she dipped her chin.

Uri hooked a finger under her chin to lift her gaze. "I am but a beast compared to you."

"No." The denial rode a breath.

Uri feathered his thumb over her temple. "Yes." He dropped to his knees, his big hands tracing a path down her waist. With a flick, he released the button of her cargo pants. Never had he heard a more erotic sound than the metal slide of her zipper. He pressed his lips to the hem of her cotton panties, her woman scent strong.

"Uri." Another breathless whisper as her fingers pushed into the hair above his ears.

"Let me love you." He didn't care that she'd denied him earlier. How could she love such a male as he, when he'd been enslaved, and used, and was all too familiar with degradation. A male who was still haunted, who was tainted and damaged beyond fixing. For him, it was enough that he loved her, that with her he was better than without.

He slid her pants down her legs, her hand on his shoulder holding her steady as she lifted a foot to step out of them. As he stood up, he wrapped her in his arms; arms so large he could cup the opposite elbows while he held her within his hug.

She was so fragile. And yet resilient in ways that had surprised him at first, and now filled him with pride. Carrying her to the bathroom, he set her down once again on the heated tile, his heart hammering hard against his sternum.

She was in his bathroom, his rooms. Standing naked and vulnerable, though full of trust. How fearless! Claiming her as his vampire mate would be the greatest thing he'd ever done.

---

iolet knew she couldn't hold out, not when she looked up at the male before her. A male who had once been ashamed of himself,

but who now gazed down at her with glistening black vampire eyes, the crimson of blood tears making them shine like city lights upon the ink of an ocean harbor.

Magnificent. A word lost in the rapid beat of her heart. He wanted to love her. With his vampire at the forefront, she knew what that meant. He wanted to claim her. As if being his Chosen One wasn't enough, he needed her to be a physical part of him, not just a spiritual one.

As Uri lowered himself to his knees before her, his bare back bowed with thick muscles, the breadth of his shoulders robbing her of breath. When he dragged his lengthened fangs across her hip hard enough to scratch, she creamed in her panties. An independent female, she'd never thought being claimed could feel so…necessary. She needed it as badly as he apparently did. As his big hands cupped her cotton-covered ass cheeks and squeezed hard, the truth turned her spine to mush. Being his Chosen One he wouldn't hurt her, but he came close as he embraced the vampire claiming.

Her fangs singing in her gums, she ached to sink them into flesh, too. His flesh. To taste this male who made her weak and brazen at the same time. Fingernails biting into his shoulders, she clamped them just a bit more to draw blood.

"God, Violet, it's…"

Oh, shit, she'd gone too far. As lust and love had consumed her, she'd forgotten he'd been tortured by vampires, that pain and blood were triggers for his rages. Violet eased up on her grip.

Uri snarled. "Harder."

Oh…yeaaah. She dug her nails back in when he snagged his sharp teeth on her panties and sucked in a deep breath. Then tore them down to the reinforced crotch. "Need to taste you." The words vibrated hot against her folds. Violet's knees trembled. When he pinched her throbbing nub, she sank her nails deep and folded over his shoulders, her fangs bared.

The need for Uri resonating deep, she pushed the sharp points of her lengthened fangs against the skin where his thick shoulders met his neck. "Yes." Another growl as he tipped his head.

She took a breath….*No.* What in hell was she doing? How about accepting an irrevocable vampire claiming with a male who would shun her when she told him who she really was. Lips twitching into a frown, she ignored the itching of her nose as more tears threatened. God, how she wanted him! Wanted to be loved the way he wanted to love her.

But, she couldn't do this to him. Not someone so noble and brave. Someone who fought to overcome his demons and had victory so near *she* could feel it. "Uri." His name came out as crushed as her throat felt. She'd barely eked it passed the knot in her windpipe.

He went still beneath her palms, yet when he looked up at her he grinned. The happiness in his ebony eyes cut through her heart like a serrated blade. "Right. Shower first." He reached behind her to turn on the shower. When he stood up to adjust the knobs, he pressed her close to the heat of his bare stomach, as though he couldn't stop touching her.

Dear God, he was going to be ruined no matter how this played out. With her hands clasped onto his lean waist, the notion that she was clinging to him kicked her in the gut. To ease the hurt, she ran her palm up the ripples of his stomach and tickled her fingers over his pebbled nipple.

He shuddered like a Saint Bernard sloshing up out of a pond, drawing her close as he buried his face against the column of her neck. "Clean first, little lady, then dessert." He noshed at her skin.

Oh, God! He was playful? Violet's heart cinched up so tight, those earlier tears that had been threatening were going to squeeze right out. The ferocious Kynd of legend were like puppies. Big, tenderhearted, funny around those they trusted—even when they were being serious.

"Uri...I..."

"Hey, hey now. What's this?" He pulled back but held her elbows in his warm hands.

Unable to face him, she hung her head and wished her hair was longer so she could hide behind it. Instead, he finger-combed a short tress behind her ear as he squatted in front of her. "Vi, it's okay. I swear it's going to be okay."

He'd grown courageous with his love for her, and she was going to demolish him. She nodded. "I know. I know." She sniffled to get her running nose under control and pasted on a brave smile. "It will be."

The smile he beamed back at her rotted her insides. She was lying to him, and he was trusting her with everything he had.

"I guess I'm more shook up about what happened than I thought."

"Yeah, yeah, of course." He squeezed her elbow and stood up. Her head fell back to keep him in her line of sight. Man, he was tall. And her news would fell him like a frigging oak. "One steaming hot shower coming up." Uri released her to yank open a cupboard door. With his fingers pinching the little knob he fished inside, his arm sturdy as a tree branch. "Here we go."

When he turned back around, he held a couple of red bath blankets out for her. "Poo's in the shower. It doesn't smell very womanish." He shrugged and gave her a shy grin.

"It'll be fine." She couldn't wait to slather herself in the scent of it, of him. Before she caved and ran into his arms and blabbed everything, she stepped into the shower with one ear listening behind her. He didn't follow. *Good.* So, why, then did she want to cry. Like a frigging sissy, not the warrior she'd raised herself to be.

This was just one more fight she had to face. A fight that would leave her utterly amputated. No heart, phantom limbs. Hollow. Violet put her face up to the spray to hide her tears, the blood of them mixing with the blood rinsing off her skin and hair.

---

*N*ever let it be said that opportunity didn't ring twice. Or was that the doorman? Who cared. On the third ringy-dingy, Kallen flipped open his phone and put it to his ear. "Hello?"

"Hello, Kallen."

"Uh, hello."

"You can't tell who this is, can you?"

Offended someone got the drop on him, he pulled the phone from his ear to stare at it, hoping the postage stamp sized screen or the itty-bitty buttons would give him a clue.

"...ov."

Too late to hear what the caller said as he put the device back up to his ear, he yanked the phone down again to glare at it. The tinny, faraway voice sounded familiar. "Kristov?"

"Yes, I said—wait. Put the phone back up to your ear."

As he did so, Kallen wondered if the Vampyre could see him and started to pull the phone down again until he caught what Kristov was saying.

"You'll catch up with the rest of the twenty-first century soon enough."

"I am caught up."

"You're not, but you're getting close."

Insufferable, observant Vampyre. So what if he was part of the venerable Triumvirate. He was still an asshat. "You rang?" The instant the words fog-horned out of his mouth, he knew he sounded like Lurch from the Addams Family. Who was not from the twenty-first century, damn it. He swore he could hear Kristov smiling.

"I did. I've already phoned Darken and Angelia, but I thought you'd want to hear the news first-hand, too."

"Yeah? What's so important that—"

"We were able to trace Violet's family tree and made some—shall we say startling—discoveries."

Yeah, he could. Kallen bet the descriptive *startling* didn't begin to cover what they'd found. Not after having his convo with Drakus. Most likely, Kristov wasn't going to be sharing anything they hadn't already figured out.

"Violet is the daughter of Dömötör Dali, a sixteenth century vampire who went underground like a rat."

"And this is important becaaauuuse…"

"Her mother was the Countess Elizabeth Báthory de Ecsted."

"Well, why didn't you just come out and say so. That was sarcasm, by the way. In case you missed it."

"I don't understand."

Kallen drew in a long-suffering sigh. "I was kind of preoccupied while the rest of the world continued turning. I could tell you exactly what I was doing that century, but I don't want to bore you with the details." In fact, he could recite what he'd been doing every century since his banishment. Not living with the rest of the world, fuck God very much. He wasn't just behind on the twenty-first century, but almost every damned one since recorded history.

"Right, of course. I am sorry."

Kallen waved it away even though he knew Kristov couldn't see through the phones. "It's nothing. Now tell me what's so important about Violet's lineage."

"Aside from an infamous mother, not much. What's important is where her father went after her mother's imprisonment."

*Imprisonment.* Uri's Chosen One was a fine specimen indeed. "He went to shake hands with the fae."

"Well, yes, but that's not all."

"Mr. Dali belongs to an illegal cult."

"Yes! But how did you—forget it. You're Kynd. Feared because you're observant sons of broomsticks."

"Sons of broomsticks?" Kallen barked out a laugh. They weren't sons of anyone, but what the hell, a broomstick had as much of a chance. "Any chance you know what the male looks like?"

"Godrick got his hands on a portrait done of him a few years before the Countess was brought to heel. He's not tall for this day and age, maybe five ten. Blond hair."

"Wow. The artist should be proud."

"I wasn't finished. We'll need you to see if he looks like the trespasser from Violet's apartment. Given how Dali disappeared at the same time records indicate the death of the Countess' seventh child, we assume it's Violet, that he absconded with her to keep the fact they were real vampires secret."

Big surprise. Nothing had changed since Kallen had lost touch with the world. Vampires were still a secretive lot. As were the rest of the Others, the Kynd included. Humans had a habit of burning and pitchforking species who were humanoid, but not all human. Intolerant sons of broomsticks.

"All right. I'm coming. When?"

"I believe we're coming to you. There was going to be a meeting on your end about it, but if I were to guess, I'd say tomorrow night. Things sounded imperative."

"You're batting a thousand with the modifiers. Keep up the good work." Kallen flipped his phone shut while his brain chewed on the word *imperative.* Yeah, he guessed that was as good a word as any, what with Uri's torturer under the same roof with him. Oh, wait. In the same bed with him.

Picturing that tipped Kallen's top off its spinning axis. Shoving the phone into his jeans' pocket, he pushed his hand all the way through the thin cotton. "Fuuuck." Because he needed one more dumbass wreck to keep him off balance.

Speaking of...where in hell was Kronos? He'd stayed behind to help Uri heal his Chosen, the rat fink. What a brown-noser. Though Kallen's anger over it took a nose dive when he remembered the determination on that craggy face. Maybe touching the Chosen Ones was the only thing keeping the poor bastard from screaming, no matter what Violet's past was with their brotherkynd.

God knew, the presence of the third Chosen somehow strengthened their Kynd bond. If he doubted it, he could visit a quivering Drakus, who had locked himself down in the basement for the good of everyone.

With only an hour until dawn, Kallen headed downstairs to find everybody. If there was going to be a meeting, they'd better get to it. As he dropped one foot in front of the other to descend the staircase, he looked over the rail to the foyer below where the furs were piled.

They'd been neatly piled once, but now looked like a giant moth had broken out of its cocoon, the browns, blacks, and whites of the furs making a haphazard patchwork quilt on the marble. So, Uri had taken the little murderess to his room.

As a chill shivered through the length of him, his boots parked it halfway down the staircase. What if she'd already slain Uri? Or had him tied down so she could suck him dry like members of the vaJcaka were expected to do? With panic setting up camp in his chest, Kallen threw out a call to his brotherkynd.

*W*aiting happened to be a skill Uri had honed down to a fine blade. He'd done plenty of it, what was a few minutes more? Legs stretched out in front of him and a mountain of pillows behind his back, he studied the tendrils of steam seeping out from under the bathroom door. Steam that was also curling around his female, caressing her skin…

Pushing his ass deeper into the mattress, he fought the urge to barge into that tiled room to find out what was taking her so frigging long. But she needed space, so he'd bench it and tick the passing of time in his head to keep himself preoccupied. The trouble was the click of those passing seconds. Each one tightened down on him like a ratchet, screwing his head tighter and tighter until it was going to explode with the pressure.

Ass gone wild, he sprung off the bed and paced. Every turn his gaze re-glued itself to the bathroom door. What could she be doing that was taking so long? *Lathering caked blood out of her sunshine hair.* With a growl rumbling through his chest, he gripped the doorjamb and hung his head.

Torn. He was so fucking split in half. The Kynd in him desperately needed to be in the other room touching her, comforting them both. The bear needed to be out chasing a scent while it still lingered on the night air. The vampire, so close to revenge, yearned so badly for retribution it crawled under his skin.

As another familiar tingle latched onto his awareness, Uri let it pass. *Kallen.* Checking in to make sure Violet hadn't killed him. Fidiot. If he had his own Chosen One, Kallen wouldn't be wringing his mitts over what his Vi did for a living.

Besides, because of his connection to her, Uri had turned Violet into the hunted like himself. The bastard who'd tried to kill her hadn't realized she was a Chosen One. His Chosen One. So when Uri had seen his life, his heart, his love crumpled on the frozen ground, he'd thrown his chance for justice away without a second look back.

Now, with his Chosen safe, justice beckoned like a siren's call. As did the stone, which stirred with the looming dawn, along with a twinge of panic. What if Violet wasn't all right in there? Well, there you go. A single thought like that and his fist was all about the bang, bang, bang on the door. Not waiting for her reply, he pushed the door open with his shoulder.

What he saw took the wind out of his bag, and his feet were crossing the floor before he could stop them. Slipping around the glass wall of the shower, Uri clapped his grip to the thick glass to keep himself from skidding all the way into the empty stall.

Head on a swivel, it took all of a half second to know she wasn't sitting on the can or hiding behind the clothes hamper. Like she was going to leap out and shout *Surprise!*

"Violet!" Her name tore out of his throat like his lungs were bellows squeezing out a rush of air. One of his last. Lungs growing inert as a concrete sidewalk, Uri pushed himself toward the bathroom window, dragging his two-ton legs as he silently swore to Christ that if Violet had leapt from that window, he'd—

Do abso-fucking-lutely nothing as his body betrayed his will. Hand reaching for the hasp, his shoulder locked into place just in time for him to play lawn jockey for the next twelve hours. Jesus Christ, he hoped nobody walked in. How humiliating. The only thing he needed was a towel draped over his extended arm.

While he stood like a plastic army man, his brain turned into a shrieking monkey rattling the bars of its cage. With his eyes stuck on the hasp of the window, he got a good long chance to study its beveled lines and utterly untouched lock.

Violet had dematerialized. Which explained why he'd stayed in the bedroom with visions of sugar plums dancing in his fucking head. So naively secure in his and Violet's budding…God, he wanted to say *love*.

Obviously, he'd read that one wrong. He'd been hearted eyes and candy assed, and she'd been waiting for the chance to hightail it. This close to dawn, he'd bet his left nut she had herself a hidey-hole for emergency moments like this. A place where she could hide from her enemies.

Oh, and yeah. From a male who had been ready to claim her with everything he had. His Kyndness, the bear, and the vampire. What a party. No wonder she'd bolted.

# CHAPTER 9

*A*shamed of her utter weakness, Violet had stepped out of the shower, put her crusty clothes back on, and colored herself gone so she wouldn't have to face the male who had become her heart.

Not that she went far. She managed to put her molecules back together in the foyer, right next to the haphazard pile of furs. Though the marble floor wasn't cold, she wriggled her bare feet into a pile of plush, her ass following suit when her knees caved under the weight of her heavy heart.

How cliché, but there she sat, plucking at the strands of a brown pelt she held to her stomach like it was a pet who'd crawled into her lap. As her fingers did the rub and slide over and over, it finally dawned on her there was something off about what she held to her belly for comfort.

The furs weren't fur. They were fakes, a truth that cut straight across her brooding heart. Without having to gawk around, she knew the potential cost of so much fur wasn't why the pile she sat in wasn't real. It was because the legendarily brutal Kynd hadn't had the callousness to use beasts for such a disgusting display of comfort.

"Hey, you all right?"

Violet almost dragged herself out of the pity party until she looked up at a familiar commiserating face. "Oh? Yeah." Except her head wouldn't nod and her chin fell back to its place on her chest.

Daniela sat down in front of her, a table-width distance between them. Kind of like back when they'd sit in the hospital cafeteria on long, empty nights when their heads were full of people they cared about.

Without coffee to share, though, Daniela developed a case of the yaks. "So, talk about a huge surprise."

Violet shrugged, her throat too tight to push out words. Her only friend… was still her friend. Violet pinched a tuft of fake fur as if to ease the stinging of her eyes. Like a disobedient child at the playground, a tear skated down her cheek anyway.

Daniela pressed a tissue into her hand. "Here. Pretty cool, by the way. Blood tears. I thought the blood on your face had been from your neck wound, but Darken said probably not all of it." A piff and a twist of her wrist and Daniela presented another tissue. With a nervous giggle, she said, "Don't even get me started on how amazed I am that you're healed already."

"I'm not healed." Did that sorry-ass lamentation come out of her mouth? Violet tried lifting her gaze, but her entire body just felt too frigging heavy. Daniela scooched a little closer and held out her hand.

Which was like the unfolding of a flower. Violet felt drawn to it, her hand reaching for what her friend offered. She tried to recall if Daniela had ever reached out like this before, but couldn't find a memory of it. Then again, Violet had never been the one who'd needed reassurance at the hospital. The abused women were.

*Ah.* How often had she sucked in the comfort of Daniela's quiet presence after her nights of hunting? When she'd been sore from fighting or her spirit too thin, and she'd sat with her friend while her tanks refueled enough for her to visit the kids.

"I'm pathetic." With Daniela squeezing her fingers, it was as if the gesture wrung the confession from her. "All those months we sat together. I didn't take your blood, but I fed off you in other ways." Although now that she'd purged the words, they didn't seem so horrible.

"How?" Violet looked up, the curiosity in her friend's voice drawing her out as surely as her touch had.

"All those months of sitting together I grew stronger."

"You mean you don't drink blood? You take energies?"

True curiosity with a touch of incredulity shone from the woman's face, the brown eyes sparkling. Violet's lip twitched like it wanted to reveal the smile building in her. "No. I need the blood. Some stories the humans spread are true."

Ignoring the strangeness that she was sitting with a real vampire, a parasite…Violet cut off her line of thinking the instant the insult popped into her thoughts. She wasn't a parasite. Uri had taught her that.

"A little confession, Violet. I took your energies, too." Daniela let her smile beam forth as she finger-quoted *energies*. "God, those poor women. And

I'd be feeling horrible and mad at the world and then I'd see you sitting at our usual spot in the caf. I bee-lined it for our table."

"But we never did things as friends, we——"

"Did exactly what friends do. We shared ourselves. We were there for each other when we needed someone the most."

"God, when you put it that way."

They were grinning at each other like idiots when the little hairs on Violet's arms tingled. The sensation made her think of winter when she put on sweaters fresh from the clothes dryer.

Daniela's whole body went light bulb. "Darken!" It took her all of one second to bounce to her feet, her love for the male beaming out of her with some serious wattage. "Violet and I were just catching up." She molded herself to the body behind those big, open arms. Arms that wrapped around her the instant the two of them came together.

Darken embraced his Chosen One the way Uri embraced her, as if he'd been dying to have her close. The relief on his face hit her like a punch to the stomach. She'd bet her finest blade Uri wore that same expression. And she was running from that?

It was either take off now or do it after seeing the disgusted look on his face. She'd rather remember his affection. Call it self-preservation.

"Hey, Violet, Darken's making breakfast. Want to join us?"

Why the hell not. She was stuck in this house until sunset, so she might as well get a look at the layout. Just in case she had to poof it to another room in order to get away from Uri and his protective brotherkynd.

Oh, right. Violet flicked her gaze a little higher. If Darken's jaw was any tighter he'd break his teeth. She opened her pie hole to say, *No.*

"I'm making toast. Please join us."

Well, slap her on the cheek and call her surprised. "Ah, yeah, okay. But you know I don't eat solid food, right?" She waited for the familiar self-loathing to rise up in her gut like a bubbling cesspool, but all remained calm below. Weird. She was finally getting used to being vampire after all these centuries.

*Uri.* His acceptance had rubbed off on her.

"I wondered about that. But come on, anyway. I've got a thousand questions about the Others, and I think I'm making Darken's head hurt." Daniela snuggled tighter against the huge male, her head tilting back as she laughed up at him.

Violet's chest squeezed tight. It wasn't just good to see her friend so happy, it was beautiful. Eyes riveted to their cuddled backsides, she missed most of the scenery as they made their way to the kitchen. After Darken and

Daniela reluctantly let each other go, he headed for the Subzero while her friend aimed for the coffee making station.

Violet parked her butt on a stool on the opposite side of the island, just in case Darken acted on his tethered aggression. She wasn't fooled by the loaf of bread in his hands. If he had anywhere near the speed of Uri, then he would be a fast son of bitch.

Except most of his attention lingered on Daniela like she was too far away, even though she was only down the length of the counter.

"You know, if I was going to hurt her, I'd have done it ages ago."

"What?" Darken dragged his eyes off his female.

"Possessive much?" She poked a snake but watching him watch Daniela bore an aching hole in her chest.

His lip lifted in a snarl, the gray of his eyes going flat and hard. "Another comment like that and I'll—" He pushed the tail end of the loaf of Country Kitchen's finest around so he could twist open the ruffled mouth. Gaze flicking to Daniela, he shoved his clawed hand into the sleeve, pulling out four slices with surprising gentleness.

"Oh, good. Coffee." Violet cranked around on the stool to see Angelia strutting into the kitchen. Strutting because she wore…slippers with heels? Lumbering in behind her was another Kynd, attached to the silk of her thigh high bathrobe. Or at least he was so close he might as well have been sewn to it.

"Morning, Angelia." Darken smacked the other Kynd's hand off the short stack of bread. "Merrick, you're not touching my toast. You'll burn it."

As Merrick cradled his wounded hand, he walked to the fridge with a sideways glare at Violet. "You tell him yet?" Thick muscles rolling under his t-shirt, he yanked open the stainless steel door to peer inside.

"No." Damn it, she answered like a scolded school girl, not the four-hundred-year old vampire hunter she was.

Merrick straightened, his grip on the fridge handle turning white. "Stop it, you goon." Angelia skated by to smack a kiss to his cheek. The male instantly softened, his grip on the bar relaxing to pet his Chosen One's rear.

Dear God, she felt like the fifth wheel on this love bus. And how sad was it that she yearned to be on it?

"I'm going—"

"Stay. We've got questions."

Before she could stop it, her body halted to the command, her attention zeroing in on Darken who stood on the other side of the island, his hands braced on the counter. "Where's Uri?"

"Back in his room, I guess." Her butt cheek sought the edge of the stool she'd been sitting on.

"You guess? Why isn't he here with you?"

"What do you mean?"

"He means, if you're his Chosen, he should be in this kitchen right now helping Darken ruin breakfast." Merrick set a bowl of eggs down next to the bread. Standing shoulder to shoulder, the males formed an impressive wall of ticked off muscle.

"I don't understand…" She looked from one to the other as if they'd written the answer on their foreheads, her instincts prickling to attention.

"In their oh-so-diplomatic-way, they're wondering why Uri is still stone if you're his Chosen One." Angelia strolled behind them, winking at her before rummaging through a lower cupboard. "Now, where did I put that large fry pan?"

Daniela hitched herself onto the stool next to her and slid a cup of steaming joe into her cold hands. "I wasn't sure if you drank coffee, since come to think of it, I don't remember you actually sipping from your mug at the caf. I took a chance."

Grateful for the warmth of the cup and the female sitting beside her, Violet shook her head, willing the urge to run out of her muscles. Because where did she want to run to? Uri. Even though he was stone, just like his brotherkynd said he was.

Ignoring that gnawing ache in her chest, she leveled as steady a gaze as she could muster on the two huge males in front of her. "Maybe I'm not his Chosen One." Though her throat threatened to seize, she managed to say it without squeezing the lie.

"Yeah, right." Angelia stood up, holding the fry pan up like a trophy hard won. She slid the heavy thing onto one of the cast iron grates of the stove.

"It's a valid point." Darken broke the wall of shoulders to drop two slices of bread into the toaster. Daniela watched him with a delicate curl of her lips, like a connoisseur of fine chocolates watching a confectioner work his magic.

Merrick cracked an egg into a bowl with a wet plop. "You're one to talk, Mr. I-let-my-Chosen-go. How'd that work out for you?"

"Pretty good, I'd say." Darken waggled his eyebrows at Daniela, his arm stretching to touch her before he realized there was an island separating them. "But I'm serious. How do we know Violet here is Uri's? Maybe she's supposed to be Kallen's or Kronos'."

"Violet here is a living thing who can make up her own mind, thank you." As she said it, doubt covered her like a second skin.

"Pfft, yeah, right." Merrick pointed at the ceiling. "It's already been decided, hence the term *Chosen One*. But Darken could be right. Maybe you're not Uri's."

Why did she want to argue this? If she and Urick weren't supposed to be together then all the better, right? Then why did the idea of running from him hurt like a bitch? Why was the hole in her chest getting bigger and more hollow as the day wore on?

Genius that she was, she could figure that out. She'd gotten to know Uri and had fallen for him. Uri was the Kynd she wanted. No other. Besides the vampire bonding thing, they fought well. A horrible thing to say, but he didn't back down from her temper, nor did she back down from his.

Rather than intensifying the antagonism, it forged them.

Oh, shit, she didn't want to leave. Not from Uri, and not from this motley family. If they'd let her, she could be a part of this. The banter, the moxie, the aggression that somehow worked the same way it did with her and Uri.

The Kynd were close. She saw their chumminess, the way their bodies moved with each other, the way they touched without thought. The habit of contact and comfort.

As Merrick whisked eggs in a bowl, Darken reached across him to grab the jar of peanut butter. The warm scent of toast and frying butter filled the kitchen.

"So, your father is a servant to Satan, huh?"

Aaaand this was why she had to go. Violet gripped her mug. "Something like that."

"Being his daughter, that makes you…" Darken circled the knife globbed with peanut butter, the hand roll her cue to fill in the rest.

"Out of here." Violet hopped off her stool, careful to keep her front facing her antagonists. Kynd were fiendishly quick and could get the drop on her even if she pasted her eyeballs to their feet.

"Wait. Merrick and Darken, cut it out." Angelia clacked across the tile and rounded the island. Quick as a cat, Merrick put himself between her and the row of stools.

Darken growled, warning Daniela to move back.

As though Violet would hurt her only friend? "Fuck you, asshole."

"Oh, you are Satan's spawn, no doubt about it." Darken leaned forward, ready to pounce over the acre of countertop between them.

"Yeah, I am. So back off." Violet reached for her hip. As her fingers brushed over nothing but the empty waist of her bloodstained cargo pants, fear tickled the back of her neck.

Weaponless, but not helpless, she placed her feet in a plumb line under her shoulders and hips. Now that she was balanced, she willed her muscles to relax, her gaze slicing like a knife from Merrick to Darken, assessing the greater threat.

"Uh-oh, brotherkynd. You've got yourself a hot one." Merrick teased. As though not in the least afraid of the damage she could inflict before they beat her to a bloody pulp. Yeah, he had every muscled, clawed, and fanged reason not to be worried. She was nothing but a fly pestering a water buffalo.

*Fuck*. Outgunned, Violet disintegrated the form of her molecules and willed herself back to the foyer. Ears honed, she took stock. Hallways and doors and stairs, each of them leading somewhere. A maze she could use to confuse her hunters until the sun went down.

---

*"W*ell, that was frigging brilliant." Kallen tugged at the knees of his jeans before he sat down on the sofa. Beside him and just as freshly showered, Kronos scooched over to make room for him. "That was sarcasm, by the way." He planted himself next to his brotherkynd, unfolding his arms across the back of the sofa, the fingers of his right hand resting on Kronos' shoulder.

It felt good to stretch his muscles after having them locked in place all day. It didn't feel good to be getting the news that Violet was hiding out somewhere in the safe house. All because his brethren had let her get one up on them.

"She's still here." Said the one who should know. Uri paced behind the sofa, his fists balled against his thighs. Kallen was surprised the guy could talk through the fangs sticking out past his bottom lip.

"How do you know?" Daniela, cute as a button sitting on Darken's lap, looked around at all of them, not just Uri.

Darken kissed her temple as he combed a thick lock of her hair behind her ear. "If we're quiet, we can feel her." Which was why Drakus was still in the basement chained to the cement floor, and they were all grouped in the library trying to talk Uri out of hunting the male vampire who had cut Violet's throat.

"Well, if she's not going to tell him, I will."

"Can it, Kallen. We scared her, all right. We just need to give her more time."

*More time*. So she could have ample opportunity to let her father know where she was, and where in turn, Uri was. The idea chafed him raw. Pushing his hands on his knees, he got up to pace alongside his brotherkynd.

"Which is why I should be out hunting. She's safe here."

"But you won't be. We wait for Kristov to show up and that's final."

Kallen would argue Merrick's bossy tone if the male wasn't talking sense. Uri didn't need to be out hunting those bastards alone. He'd been captured once, they weren't risking a second one. Finally back together, they were going to stay the fuck together.

"Besides, if that portrait he has turns out to be the same male Kallen ripped the tat from and who harmed Violet, we'll have to approach this problem from a different angle. The Triumvirate will need to be involved, or we're going to come across as an uncontrollable mob of vigilantes. We've got enough bad press without that."

The lovable bastard was right. Legends aside, with a preemptive strike of his scythe, Darken had chopped the head off the leader of the Literati. Aro might have been in charge of the greatest collection of Other knowledge, but he'd also tried to kill Angelia and Merrick. He'd deserved the head roll.

Image, however, was everything, and Darken's stunt had only reinforced how the Others felt about the Kynd. They had to tread carefully if they wanted to make it in this realm. And they had to. Daniela and Angelia couldn't live anywhere else, and there was no way in Hell they were parting from those two females.

Speaking of females. "Look who decided to join the party." Kallen stopped abruptly at the sight of Violet in the doorway. With her shoulders and back straight and her jaw pushed a little forward, she didn't look like she was there to be asked in.

Sure enough, she strode into the room. A bold move considering she didn't know their hostility was as harmless as a fart in the wind. As far as she knew, Kallen and his brethren could kill her for what they knew about her.

Yet in she walked, her eyes riveted on Uri, who was gripping his elbow so hard Kallen thought the bone might be bending. She stopped at the point she'd have to look up in order to maintain eye contact. Trying to make it seem like they were on equal footing? Not possible, but he had to admit the smarts behind it. Which only proved she wasn't some innocent novice, a fact which didn't give him much comfort.

Kallen moved to block her path to Uri. "What do you want?" He would have folded his arms over his chest if Uri hadn't been holding on. Instead, he accepted the contact, like having a knife in your boot for backup.

Violet narrowed eyes the color of whiskey. He bet they had a little bite to them, too. She looked right past him to Uri. "We have to talk."

"True." Nimble as shit, Uri nearly leapt over the top of him to get to his Chosen. "Fellas, let me know when the Triumvirate gets here." With that, he scooped Violet up in his arms like a bride and walked from the library so fast you'd have thought he was hot-footing across a bed of coals.

Merrick pushed back from the desk to watch them go. "Well, shit."

Kallen couldn't have summed up the situation better himself.

---

"*P*ut me down." Before he could deny her, Uri placed Violet's feet on the wool carpet of the bottom stair. With the eight inch lift, she could just about look him straight in the eye. She took advantage of it, poking her finger to his chest. "Don't lose your shit until I'm through. Come on." She snagged his hand and turned on the stairs.

Uri would have followed even if she hadn't been dragging him. He'd been royally pissed that she'd taken off, and would have blown the top off his stone skull if he hadn't still felt her presence in the house. That she sought him? When he'd seen her in the library doorway, his heart had almost executed a full somersault.

Stopping at his bedroom door, she turned toward him once again. Only this time she had to look up, her short hair sliding back from her exquisitely stubborn chin. "Promise me."

"Sure." He shrugged as the lie rolled off his tongue. If she meant to deny his vampire claim, she had another think coming. She pretended she wore a coat of armor over her heart, but he knew better. That shell was about as strong as a soap bubble. Violet wanted his love. Needed it, in fact. Of course, he'd fight for that. Lose his shit? That, too.

She led him into their bedroom. "All right." Releasing his hand, she walked over to the window to peer out like she needed the open view to organize her thoughts. Uri moved up behind her, wrapping his arms around her waist as he rubbed his cheek along the column of her beautiful, completely intact neck.

Vi clasped her fingers around the backs of his hands, holding him to her. "I never wanted any of this."

"No." Uri nuzzled her collarbone, skating kisses along the length of it as he let his thoughts take him back to that first night. The night he'd gripped onto her and had whisked her away from her life. She'd been spitting mad for weeks, the fuse on her temper matching the length of his.

"So, you know none of this was my idea."

He knew where she was going with this. None of what she'd say would matter, so he let her talk.

She drew away from him, their fingertips trailing until contact was lost. Vi sauntered around the room, picking up little things, setting them down. Which she did all of twice. There wasn't much in the way of knick knacks. Or personal items for that matter. The less to smash.

She stopped to touch a crystal vase with day old roses in it, the satin edges of the petals already peeling back. Her hand stopped as she spoke, her voice so low Uri had to tilt his head to hear her. "You might think you want me, but you don't. I'm not who you think I am. Yeah, I try doing the right things, but they don't erase my blood. They can't remove who I am to you."

"Of course not, Vi."

"Don't call me that." Her voice came out scratchy as if the thorns on the stems of the roses coated her throat.

"Why not? You're my Vi. I like the ring of it."

"Don't, Uri. *Urick.*" She heaved a sigh that came out heavier than a death rattle. "What I am to you isn't what you think."

"Then tell me. Who do you think you are to me, if not the female I love." He hadn't meant to announce it like that, but there it was. He wouldn't take it back and fumble it worse. "I love you, Vi. With all my heart. I don't care that you're a hunter, that you kill Others."

She gave him a sharp look like she was surprised he'd figured out what she used her weapons for. "You snooped in my rooms."

Uri shrugged, brushing it off. "It wasn't hard. Your place is small."

Leaning against his dresser, she crossed her arms over her chest. "Well, then. I guess you probably should have snooped a little further. Your brothers did. They found all kinds of dirt. Who I am, who my father is."

Ookay, this wasn't exactly the direction he thought she'd go.

"You don't care because you love me? Well, sit down, Urick, and hold the fuck on."

Uri narrowed his gaze, lining her up as if to put her in his sights.

"I'm not joking. Sit down on that bed and grip onto the bed post."

He did as she instructed, backing up slowly until the backs of his knees hit the mattress. He sat down and curled his hand around the tall post. Not liking how pale she turned, for good measure he dug his claws in.

"You know how I figured out you'd been held captive?"

"Yeeaah?"

"I figured it out because I was most likely there."

His lungs deflated, squeezing his heart. "No. I would have known it if you had."

She shrugged, dismissing his claim as he'd done to hers just a few moments ago.

"I would have smelled you, Vi. Everything about that place I remember.

*Everything.* And you sure as shit were never there." His anger building, Uri's body rose of its own accord from the bed.

Not backing off, Violet stood straight up, too. "You sure about that? You're so fucking sure that while you were chained to the walls and that stone floor, with dead or dying Others around you, that you didn't miss something?"

What she said set him back, his thoughts reeling into his past. "I must have told you about the bodies. Or you're guessing."

"Am I?"

"Yes." He knew it came out as a growl, but she'd been right. His anger was getting the better of him.

"I wouldn't know about the stone altar, either, where they would have chained you while they fed. While they writhed in ritual orgasm all over you, biting and licking—"

"Enough!" he roared, raking his grizzly claws through the bed post. The shredded end flew upward as it helicoptered across the room.

She didn't cower but stepped up to face him and his fury. "I know because one of those sons of bitches who fed on you was…is…my father. I am his daughter. Born of that monster's blood, made in his image."

"No!" Her words annihilated everything. His vision, his thinking. The only solid thing was the fact she was standing right in front of him. His Chosen…his gift from God Himself…was…he couldn't think straight, his reasoning flashed like brief explosions just before his fury H-bombed every coherent thought. "No!" he roared again.

All he could see was her face, the stain of blood tears trailing down her cheeks. Yet, the amber eyes he adored were hard as the fossils they resembled. "Yes, Urick. I am not your love."

He heard everything she said even though she swallowed as if choking on her words.

As he struck out to haul her against his heart, she disappeared before his very eyes, dematerializing to God only knew where but most certainly away from him.

---

*V*iolet couldn't breathe. Having landed on her kitchen floor on her hands and knees, she stayed there, heaving and gasping as droplets of blood plopped onto the linoleum. Her body frozen with grief, she didn't swipe at the tears streaming down her face, she didn't cover her mouth as she shrieked over and over.

At some point, she thought her neighbors would call the cops, but she couldn't bottle the screams belching out of her like poisonous gas. She was toxic. So, so fucking toxic. She thought she was someone who could be loved? Oh, God, she should have never let her guard down with Uri. It wasn't better to have loved and lost. Not by a long shot.

The slitting of her throat hadn't even felt this life threatening. She was dying, one wilting cell at a time, crumbling and imploding on herself. Her vision tunneled, and Violet crumpled to the floor.

With her blood tears still wet on her face, she knew she hadn't passed out for long. But it kicked her instinct for self-preservation into gear. Sluggish though it was, it spurred her ass off the linoleum, and she stumbled and banged into the hallway walls to her bedroom.

She couldn't stay in her apartment. There were too many people who could find her. The cops, Uri, her father, and his ghoulish cohorts. Although, if she had any luck at all—and she wasn't going to bank on it given her current status—her father would think she was dead.

His ignorance would have given her an edge, even if it was just while she got her shit together. Broken heart ticking like a peen hammer against her breast bone, Violet jabbed her legs into a clean pair of cargo pants, yanked a merino camisole on for warmth, and covered it with a thick, cotton hoodie. After lashing a pair of army boots to her feet, she snagged her old canvas backpack and marched for the most important room in her apartment—her armory.

The instant she stepped over the threshold she felt like Meryl Streep in *Sophie's Choice*. She needed to arm herself, but which of her beloved children did she sacrifice? She'd spent centuries caring for her weapons. This was the first time she'd never had the time to cache them properly, to store them in a safe place until she could come back for them.

She'd never let a vampire have her blood before, so in the past when she'd had to run, no one had been able to follow her blood trail. Until Uri. She was good at hiding when all she had to worry about were footprints, witnesses, and paper trails.

Uri posed a level of threat she didn't know how to elude. Well, she'd bought herself some time with the bomb she'd dropped. She'd been ruthless in the delivery to gain a head start. It wouldn't last, though. She'd learned how the Kynd were with their Chosen Ones. Those females were essential in a way she'd never seen before. It was as if they were the Kynds' only skin, and whenever it stretched beyond touching distance they grew vulnerable, uneasy without that protection.

An odd arrangement until you watched it play out. Kynd were potent bastards. They weren't just stronger and bigger than any Other, their senses were sharper than anything she'd ever come across. The only reason she'd ever gotten the drop on them was because she was…Chosen.

As her heart flopped, straining the arteries connected to her chest wall, the pain nearly leveled her. Violet put a hand out to steady herself, locking her knees as she gripped onto the door jamb. Breaths shallow until the pain eased enough for her take a full pull of air into her lung sacs, she waited for her thoughts to clear.

*Leaving Uri is for the best. Leaving Uri is for the best.* She'd repeat it until she believed it. While her instincts screamed *No!* her brain slogged through the syllables as it struggled to sort out which weapon would suit her needs best.

So far, she'd had success in killing members of her father's sect with a crossbow, three different knives, a short sword, a long sword, and a mace. Oh, and once with her hands, even though she'd had to finish the deed with the ax she'd found wedged into a nearby stump.

She'd been lucky that day, nothing more. Always have a blade of some sort. Although the mace had been effective, what with smashing the vampire's head until the mutilated skin ceded its hold on the shoulders.

Gruesome, yeah, but hammering away had been a kind of therapy. She wouldn't take that chance this time. Over the years her father had become her nemesis, proving tougher to kill than she'd thought. They'd clashed three times. Twice had been her doing, and the third was this latest when he'd sliced her an extra mouth.

Sneaky bastard. How he'd discovered her secret place behind the hospital, let alone where she lived, had trumped her ace. He now knew more about her than she did of him. But after centuries of hunting him, she did know her quarry. Her father would come back to make sure the blow he'd struck had been fatal. He had control issues, and he wouldn't leave that *i* without its dot.

Beyond ready to end their game, Violet plucked the rondel dagger from its velvet cradle and held it upon her fingertips. In the silver light of the winter night, the ivory handle with its intricate skull carvings looked sinister. The thin, glinting blade even more so. Twelve inches long and sharp as a razor from pommel to pointed tip, the dagger suited what she had in mind.

She wanted close. She wanted her father's death to be painful and slow, but quick if she needed it to be. What she desired most of all was to see his face the moment he realized death was unavoidable. She needed to see the agony of his wounds etched on his gruesome mouth and the fear in his eyes.

Exactly how Uri must have looked as her father had tortured him with his ritualistic feedings. She didn't need her imagination to picture it. She'd seen

Uri's face when the memories rose up as real as though he was chained once more.

Violet wanted her father dead for the thousands of souls he'd bled dry over the centuries, and for reminding her with every-one, who and what she was. Because of him, she grew up despising herself, always striving to be better than the leech she'd been born to be.

All of that had changed with the fucked up attention from a fucked up chimera.

Violet couldn't have been more grateful. Uri had taught her to see herself as beautiful and selfless—and as the killer she'd honed herself into. In a court of law, she'd be found as guilty as those she'd slain. Just as under the Triumvirate's rule, there was no room for vigilante justice. There was fairness with a tribunal, the opportunity to voice your objection to the accusations brought against you.

Screw that. The sect her father belonged to had remained hidden even from the Triumvirate's judicious leadership. Which suited her just fine. She'd been able to off each member without recrimination, rid the world of the parasitic bastards who gave vampires a bad name.

Huh! A new outlook. Uri had shown her that, too. Which gave her another reason to find her father and end their cat and mouse game, once and for all. Before, Violet had always hesitated that fraction of a second, her doubts about committing patricide slowing her hand.

Her father had shown no such reservations. His blade had been quick, proving he felt no pangs of guilt for killing his daughter. Violet didn't need a second reminder. Wrapping the rondel dagger in a chamois cloth, she tied it shut with a length of cord, and slid the bundle into her battered backpack.

Resolve lowered the flap and fastened the buckles. Resolve hoisted the pack over her shoulder. Love teleported her to the scene of her near death, where she hoped to pick up her father's cooling trail. Or await his return.

---

*A*s Uri roared, his radar blipped a tidbit of info—the sound blistering up his throat wasn't all bear. A shit-ton of pissed off vampire bellow had hit his ears. Then his room went spinning sideways as the floor rushed up for a meet and greet.

A body almost as heavy as his own landed on top of him, arms gripped around his chest like steel Saran Wrap. Frustrated, Uri roared again.

"Bear! Calm the fuck down!"

He knew that voice, remembered the arms, the scent of the male. *Darken.*

What the hell? He was supposed to be with his Chosen, not here when Uri's...wasn't. As fury welled for another rocket blast, those arms cinched tighter. "Bear, you've got to settle the fuck down." The words brushed close and warm against his ear.

*Settle down?* No effing chance. He needed to follow his female. The one who didn't want him. As despair swamped him, he recalled her face, how pale she looked, those amber eyes shining with tears.

It had hurt her to leave.

Pain sluiced through his body like a tendril of acid, and he sought relief by disintegrating into a billion unformed molecules.

"No way, Uri. Hold...on." Darken gritted the words through a clenched jaw as he locked his arms down tight as the hatch on a submarine. "You're not going anywhere."

The bastard, of course, was right, as he had too much determination to play anchor. Even as strong as he was as a Kynd vampire, Uri only dragged the lovable asshole across the rug to his dresser.

"That's gonna leave a mark," Darken hissed, his hold firmer than before with his legs locked around Uri's thighs.

"Get. Off. Me."

"Ah, almost full sentences."

Uri wriggled like a dying worm on the hook. "Get off me."

"Better. Now, say you're okay and promise not to George Jetson out of here."

Uri took a gander at the lack of dust bunnies under his bed, then twisted his face off the floor to get a look at his brotherkynd. "I'm staying put. I promise." *For now.* Darken hadn't forced a time limit.

"Your eyes are still black."

"Get the fuck off me." Uri heaved, sloughing Darken off like a sodden coat. As he climbed to unsteady feet, he rubbed his chest where his heart was burning a hole through the muscle. A few staggered steps and he surrendered to the unhinging of his knees. His ass slumped onto the edge of the bed, the mattress bowing under his weight. Much the same as his brain sagged with the pressure of too many thoughts.

Now that they weren't shooting off like the sharp reports of a semi-automatic rifle, Uri could process Violet's verbal attack. He'd call that spade a spade because it was an assault, meant to shake his new foundation. Or, now that he knew her, crack the ever-loving hell out of it, so he'd be crushed under what she thought was his house of cards.

Foolish female. There was nothing flimsy about the direction his heart had taken toward her. He could count the stars and pin every one with his reasons why.

Her courage alone he'd tag to a shining planet, something big and bright you could see without the aid of a telescope. God alive, Vi had the heart of a warrior. Though she was a stubborn thing, not trusting in his love for her.

Although if he were honest—and right then, sitting on his bed and blasted so wide open he could be—he apparently didn't trust his love for her, either. How could he, when he'd reacted so violently to her news.

At least it wasn't his balls she'd lain waste to, even though he'd left himself just as wide open this time. Like those other times, he hadn't seen this hit coming either, but he still felt hijacked, his guts reamed hollow. Uri folded his arms over his midsection, trying to fill some of the empty space.

Or to keep himself from puddling onto the floor in a sorry mess.

"Hey, you all right, Bear?" Fingers digging into his sides, Uri tilted his chin to watch Darken heave his carcass off the floor. "I couldn't help but overhear."

Uri stayed hunkered over and holding on, pretty sure that if he sat up straight his guts would tumble out between his knees. "No. I don't think I'm all right at all." When the mattress listed under Darken's weight, Uri turned to look at him, easing his grip a little when the comfort of a fellow brotherkynd hummed onto the radar. "You knew who she was, didn't you?"

"Yeah. Kristov told us."

"Fuck." His head fell between his shoulders like a cannonball in a nylon sock. "Explains why Kallen doesn't like her. Why he wouldn't help her."

Darken shrugged. "None of us wanted to, Bear. Honestly, while you were gone, we imagined her doing all sorts of horrible things to you. And after Drakus helped us put two and two together...you know...your captivity and shit...we were even more distrustful of her."

"But she never—"

"We know this now, but it's still hard to fully trust her. What if she's just trying to lure you back to her father?"

Well, just when Uri thought he might be feeling better. "She wouldn't."

"Yeah, well." Darken studied his claws. They remained on the bed, their shoulders touching as if the mattress conspired to push them together. "Kristov's here. He and the rest of the Triumvirate want Violet to ID the portrait, too."

"I guess they can wish in one hand and shit in the other. She's gone."

Darken's big frame peeled back in a WTF, his chest jutting out as if throwing his senses open. "Gone gone, or lurking in the house like she did before?"

"High tailed it. Two guesses to where." The absence of his brotherkynd's touch added to the size of the hole in Uri's gut. He bet if he dropped a coin into his stomach the metal would clang as it bounced down into the abyss.

"That's some messed up shit, her father trying to kill her."

"Was he? I don't fucking know anymore." The problem with not trusting someone was you believed all kinds of shit about them. By her own admission, Violet had known who had tortured him for all those centuries. Or at least she'd suspected, which was the same thing.

*Though not really.* Fuck. Uri released his midsection to clasp his hands to his cracking skull. To relieve the pain, he gripped shanks of his hair and pulled, one hurt distracting him from the worst one.

Darken's arm snagged him around the back and heaved them both to their feet. "Come on, Bear. Let's meet up with the others and make a plan."

Colossal mess that he was, he let the weight of that comforting arm steer him across the room and into the hall, down the stairs to grandmother's house they went. All the while, the emptiness throbbed with something more. Like maybe it wasn't just his own, but he was sensing Violet's, too.

Which couldn't be true, could it? He thought about how he could find her anywhere. Her blood coursing with his through his veins, tugging as if the cells were magnetic and yearned to be returned from whence they'd come, reuniting with the original source.

Jesus, he'd never thought of it like that. Was it this way with all vampire's, or just him because he was Kynd and she was his Chosen One? Well, one thing he did know. The feeling would pass over time. Vi's blood-hold on him would lessen.

One foot dropping in front of the other as he and Darken navigated the wide staircase to the foyer below, he tried to fathom how he felt about losing his connection to the female he loved in spite of how things had gone down. Right then, with the pain riding him and the hollowness giving his muscles the shakes, he still couldn't sort himself out.

Uri gave up, letting his brotherkynd lead him in the right direction.

# CHAPTER 10

*K*allen thought Darken had looked like shit when he'd let his Chosen One go? Uri sported a whole new level of fucked. Obviously, the female had told him who she was, and the brotherkynd hadn't hugged her to him and promised they'd work it out.

'Cause, hey, how did you fix something like that? You couldn't. She was who she was, and the only thing to remedy that would be a trip back in time. When Uri executed a slow motion fold onto the leather sofa as Darken released him, Kallen kind of wished they'd find a way to bend the curve.

Kronos instantly made like a security blanket and nestled the poor male against his side. Arm draped over those monstrously wide shoulders, Kronos bent his head to Uri's to whisper reassurances. Why the hell not? God knew miracles occurred.

"This doesn't look good." King of the understatement, Angelia's father, Anton, stood up straighter in his Desmond Merrion suit. As one of the leaders of the Triumvirate, he'd have reason to be concerned about Uri's state. If the brotherkynd couldn't help with this investigation, the pace would slow to a crawl, giving those leeches time to find a better hidey-hole.

"She's flown the coop." Darken wrapped himself behind Daniela, who placed her hands over his as they circled her belly. She settled back into him, and he welcomed her weight like a man stumbling onto paradise. Merrick had the same felled look on his puss with his Chosen perched on his thigh.

Like Uri's devastation might be contagious.

Maybe it was. If losing your Chosen could do this, they all might have been a little too hasty with passing judgment on Violet. They'd been harsh, and she'd done exactly what anyone would do. She'd painted herself out of there.

Shit.

Kristov knelt in front of the sofa. As if remembering what touching a Kynd could feel like, he kept his hands to himself. "Urick, we have to find her. Where are her usual haunts? She goes to the hospital, right? Would we find her there?"

Uri leveled him with a matte gray stare as if he couldn't even muster the gumption to shrug.

"Where, Uri?"

"I bet somewhere near the cafeteria." Every eye in the room turned to Daniela. "It's where we always met up."

Kristov turned back to Uri. "Where exactly?"

"By the dumpsters." A resigned growl. Exchanging meaningful looks, Anton and Godrick disappeared as if they'd never been standing in the library.

"Handy trick." Kallen pushed himself away from a wall of books, and for the first time in his long life, he was unsure about giving comfort to another Kynd because of a misunderstanding. He walked behind the sofa, attempting a casual drag of his fingertips along the back, uncertain how to close this divide he'd dug between himself and Uri. Those few inches of space yawned like a chasm inside him.

Desperate, his feet hit pause, and he lingered behind the couch like a frigging ghoul, sucking up the least little scrap of closeness he could get.

He'd been so, so wrong to alienate that female vampire.

"So now what, we wait?" Angelia slid from Merrick's knee and rounded the desk. Stopping behind it, she reached out to trail her fingers across the top cover of the Scriptum. With a freaky shiver, the ancient book flopped wide open like a gutted fish.

Giggling nervously, Angelia glanced up. "I don't think I'll ever get used to that." She dragged a finger down the open page, the ends of her eyebrows pinching together. "Hmm."

"Hmmm what, for God's sake." Jesus, he had bugs crawling under his clothes. The tension made him jittery, and without the touch of his brethren, Kallen was unraveling like a spool of thread.

Merrick growled.

"Oh, cut it out. I didn't mean any disrespect."

"Both of you stop it." Angelia laid a piece of ribbon in the crack and closed the book. "This isn't the time to indulge your...tendencies. Uri, look at the portrait Kristov brought. Does the man look familiar?"

"Of course he looks familiar. He's the male I—"

"For shit's sake, Kallen, would you watch some T.V.? Everyone knows you keep your trap shut so you don't taint the witness." Without his Chosen in his arms, Merrick was as testy as a wet house cat.

Which underlined just how bad Uri must be feeling. Kallen went back to his spot by the bookshelf. From there he got a clear shot of the bear as he raised himself up onto his oak tree legs. The bastard was big, but he trembled like a fart could blow him over. The closer his feet took him to the picture of Violet's father, the paler he grew.

Oh, he knew the guy all right. As Uri's claws lengthened and breaths puffed out of him like a steam engine cranking uphill, Kallen figured the antique portrait wasn't going to survive into the next century.

He should have bet on it. Just as Kristov back pedaled out of the way, a bear paw slatted the frame off the easel and sent the canvas clattering across the room. Uri roared, pivoting on his size thirteens to size up something else to smash. While Merrick and Darken bustled their females out of the room like a couple of mama ducks, Kronos started shrieking like he was reliving another nightmare.

Needing his hands for something besides clapping them to his ears, Kallen leapt for Kronos and latched on before the poor guy blew the hatches on his sanity. Real pain stretched those lids wide as Kronos looked up at him.

"Hurt." Kronos ground his jaw down before he discharged another shriek. He'd uttered one word, but no more were needed. He meant Urick, who wrestled with the mammoth desk like he was trying to wrap his arms around it.

Kronos drew back, his every muscle straining as he cracked his lips. "Hold."

"I am holding on!"

Kronos shook his head like a dog with a rat in its maw.

"The bear?" Who wasn't a bear at all anymore. When Kallen turned his head toward the sound of splintering wood, he knew exactly what Kronos meant. Uri wasn't trying to smash the desk. He was trying to hold onto it like a tidal wave victim to a tree.

Eyes as black and shiny as Satan's horns, Uri bellowed a toxic mix of frustration and fury. Without a thought to his earlier misgivings, Kallen abandoned Kronos to jump off the sofa and land behind Uri. The instant his feet hit the floor, he fell forward onto his brotherkynd, allowing not only his weight to cover him but his momentum as well.

Just as Anton and Godrick had done with their handy trick of dematerializing, Uri teetered on the cusp of doing the same. Obviously, he didn't want to. His disappearing act would be against his will, his loss of restraint manifesting in a far scarier way.

Without control, where in hell would he wind up? Not caring to find out, Kallen gripped onto him like a gorilla. He'd think it funny that he gave a whole new meaning to the term monkey on your back if Uri didn't seem so fucking shattered.

Well, no doubt about the positive ID. Sure as shit, the vampire was one of Uri's captors. Which meant the demon who had chained their brotherkynd had also sired one of their Chosen. Talk about not knowing God's plan with this train wreck.

But it didn't matter where the cars were going. For now, they just needed Uri stable. Oh, and yeah, getting Kronos leveled out would be a step in the right direction, too. Where in the hell were Darken and Merrick?

As Kallen craned his neck toward the door, who walked in was the last being he expected to see: Violet. Which was like bringing a propane tank to a bonfire. Real fucking smart. Except maybe as his Chosen One she could calm him down?

Riiiight. Because looking at her face wouldn't remind Uri of his past.

While Kallen played twenty questions with himself, Violet decided everything for him by launching across the room so fast she left Anton and Godrick in her metaphorical dust. He barely tracked her as she rounded the desk, skidding in like a base stealer.

With the deafening roars from Uri and the keening from Kronos, Kallen figured she had zero chance of snaring the male's attention. He figured wrong. As she touched her hand to Uri's, his brotherkynd fell eerily still, the only sound now coming from a final board snapping off the desk to the wooden floor, and Kronos' muffled moans.

Hands clasped so tight both their knuckles were ghostlike, Violet and Uri never moved. He just stood there humped over the demolished desk, and she remained prostrate on the floor looking up.

The hum between the three of them threatened to loosen the teeth from Kallen's gums.

"Jesus jumped up Christ." Shocked by the intensity, Kallen stumbled backward like he'd stuck a metal knife into the toaster. It had just been the three of them, but the charge reminded him of the old days. The way-old-days when they had free rein to redecorate the landscape.

Behind them, Godrick and Anton joined up with Kristov, forging once again the strength of the Triumvirate, a ruling body that held the discordant realms of the Others in tenuous harmony. For once, Kallen was happy for them to have their noses stuck in Kynd business.

They'd managed to wrestle Violet back. Now that Uri didn't need an anchor, Kallen turned to comfort Kronos, who hadn't left the leather sofa during all that turmoil. His brotherkynd welcomed him by opening his arms. Kallen pushed right in, as grateful for the contact as Kronos seemed to be.

"Hey, I thought I heard—" Merrick quit flapping his gums when he stepped farther into the library. "I guess I did." He didn't lift his gaze from the sight of his demolished desk and the dynamic duo still posing beside it like a still-life painting. Not even when Darken nearly ran up his back. Angelia and Daniela, clearly obeying the command that they stay out of harm's way, peered around the sides of their males.

Goody. The gang was all here. Time to get the three-ring circus on the road.

---

*V*iolet grasped Uri's big hand like she'd been sliding off a cliff and he was the last root between her hold and a three-hundred-foot free fall. As she lay on the floor looking up at him—his hand clasped just as tightly to hers—she thought the metaphor rather apt.

She had been falling. She just hadn't realized how hard and fast until Uri's fingers closed around hers. Now she lay on her belly as becalmed as a boat on a man-made pond. The serenity pissed her off, mostly because she'd dived headlong for it despite all the arguing she'd done with Crockett and Tubbs, the snazzy suits who'd arrived to drag her back to the safe house.

They were now standing with a third suit, and ding, ding, ding. They must be the ancient Vampyres who made up the Triumvirate. She'd never laid her peepers on them before but knew power when she felt it. The blond one, Anton, had teleported her like she weighed nothing more than a bag of popcorn. The only other vampire she knew who could do that was Uri, who didn't look like he could move anything more than his inky eyes.

Eyes he kept pinned on her like he would freefall, too. Though the darkest ebony, their depths drew her in as if her heart were trussed in strings. It tightened in her breast, her lower belly heavy and aching as heat rose under her skin. Uri's masculine scent wound through her, quickening her breaths.

"Thank God you held onto him, Kallen." As Merrick hugged the rat bastard, Kallen, Violet slipped her fingers from Uri's. It was like trying to pull her crushed hand from a car door.

Uri blinked as if turning the lights back on in the one-room apartment of his cranium, and released her. He staggered off to land in Darken's waiting embrace, the two males thumping heavily onto the battered sofa. A healthy distance away from her.

Good. Yeah, that was good. Nodding like the conversation was between her and someone else, she backpedaled into the wall. No, wait. The slight hum she felt at her heels wasn't the light socket. It was Kronos, the gargoyle with the craggy face.

As he lifted his arms to hold her, she stepped out of his reach, her heart jackhammering at the near miss. God, she'd forgotten how they needed to touch.

Riiiight. Which made her a royal bitch, now didn't it. Here was the male who'd healed her, and she repaid him by arching out of his reach like he was a leper.

Where was her trusty compassion? Just because she hadn't been able to revisit Jaime and the other kids, it didn't mean the shit had leaked out of her butt crack. Chagrined, Violet shuffled a return trip toward Kronos, stopping once their arms touched. Kronos leaned into her.

Uri remained on the couch, his hands curling into fists and releasing. If a wall was close, she'd bet her lengthened fangs he'd be punching it as he'd done back in the cave when he'd been furious and out of control.

*Because of me.* Three weeks later and nothing had changed. He was back to feeling betrayed and she was...devasta_determined. With the Triumvirate involved, it changed the outcome of killing her father, but sitting in a jail cell would be an all right place to count her coup.

Forcing her shoulders back and stretching her spine so she stood taller, she stepped forward. "All right, where's this portrait you wanted me to see." She struggled not to look at Uri, her gaze skidding over the sofa as she pretended to scan everywhere else in the room. "Ah." There it was, tilted against a chair, the wooden arm jabbed through the neck and lower jaw of the subject.

How fitting. Too bad that wasn't her dagger. For all the damage to the frame and canvas, the face remained unmarred, all Dorian Gray in its preservation. Violet's hand went to her throat, her fingertips caressing the faint line of scarring. "That's him." She glued her stare to the painted face in front of her as shame caught her cheeks on fire. "That's my father."

The room remained silent as if her confession had rendered the witnesses speechless. Violet stood alone, her back blessedly facing everyone so they wouldn't see the welling of tears along her lower lashes. She didn't have the guts to turn and look at Uri.

"It's decided then. Violet will be our bait to lure Dömötör Dali out of hiding."

"Still in agreement, Ms. Aster?"

"That I'll drink from him and let him go without killing him? Yeah. Yes, I can do that." If her father didn't kill her first. They had more faith in her fighting skills than she did, she'd give the Triumvirate that.

Behind her, she heard the squeak of leather and her heart fluttered, the wind of it filling her chest so she could barely breathe. From the corner of her eye, she watched Uri stride out of the room.

---

*B*ait. His Chosen One was nothing but bait, and so many pistons misfired in his brain it was a wonder his legs worked well enough to get him out of that godforsaken library. When he'd shot his ass off the leather, he hadn't known if his body would take him straight to Violet or drag him to a place where he could suck some much needed oxygen into his lungs.

He hadn't so much as taken a full breath after she'd pulled her hand from his. Craving to reconnect and recoiling at the idea, he'd sat there like his wires were crossed. Until he'd gotten an earful of the Great Plan. Then his filaments had sparked, and it was either destroy something or someone or get the hell out of there while he could still move without freaking out of his skin.

"Urick." And there she stood in all her fucking glory in the middle of the grand foyer. Like she was going to need the elbow room, just in case.

Uri stopped like his boots had suddenly become part of the floor. His heart halted right along with them. He didn't breathe either. He just stared at the female who owned every square centimeter of him, body and soul.

"It's for the best." Her pale face told him otherwise. "If I help, I'll be exonerated."

"From what?" The words came out like they rode a chain up his throat.

She shrugged. "Helping my father."

Uri's arm muscles twitched to reach for her, but he looked around for something to hit. Not finding anything close by, he dug his claws into his palms deep enough to draw blood. "You were never there."

Violet shrugged though her nostrils flared. Not so indifferent, after all—to him, to this frigging plan, and to being linked to the crimes of her father. She didn't deserve any of this, the certainty stemming from a side of him that had nothing to do with her being his Chosen One, and everything to do with his love for her.

With her sunshine hair mussed and her chin jutting with determination, his heart totally melted. He wanted to cry she was so precious. "Why are you doing this?"

"I must." Almost imperceptibly, she stuck her chin out more.

Uri was suddenly closer to her. Like he stood on a conveyer belt and cruised forward without moving his legs. One moment he couldn't reach her, and the next he was lifting his bloody hand to caress her cheek. "Vi, don't do this." His gaze fell to her lips. The bottom one was plumped, the tips of her fangs forming twin indentations. His cock stirred to life in his jeans, but he threw all of his concentration on her instead.

"You know I must." Her lips moved so enticingly, her little fangs beckoning. Uri roped an arm around her waist, hauling her against him. He tilted his head to kiss her as his brain calculated the feel of her in his arms. She was light, her bones thin.

Adding to the fact she wasn't in prime condition to fight. Sometimes he hated how quick and analytical his brain worked, but not now. He lowered her feet to the floor with a gentleness he had in heaping stores for her. "I can't let you do this."

"You have no say." Her voice wended through him on husky threads.

"To hell I don't." He bluffed, and Vi would know that, too. He wouldn't hinder her freedom. He'd done that, had had it done to himself. It was no way to live and certainly no way to nourish love. He'd let her to do as she wished no matter the consequences to himself.

"Uri." Upon her plea, her amber gaze flicked to his, locking them together on a visceral level. Planting Uri so profoundly he knew his feet had grown down through the floor.

He breathed in deeply, drawing her scent into him. "Then drink from me, Vi. Take from me so you'll be strong." His desire rode out on a gravelly breath, his arms trembling in his need to hug her closer, so he'd feel her heat against his belly and his thickening length.

Violet shook her head. "Just blood." She licked her lips. "No claiming."

"No." Though it killed him to say it.

"Your wrist." He knew what she meant, that she wouldn't get closer than she had to. She wouldn't snuggle up against him. She was the perfect size. When she placed her head along his neck, the valley between her thighs rested on his engorged shaft. She wouldn't do that now.

Uri swallowed a needful moan. "All right." As he drew his arms from around her she inched backward to put distance between them. A distance that filled with cold air or a thousand miles. To him, it was all the same. Although he shivered with her so close. His wires crossing again, Uri dragged in another breath.

When he offered his punctured wrist like a craven servant, he sucked in another lungful of air to strengthen his spine. He would be brave and strong for her. If this was what she needed in order to do what she thought she needed to do, then he could find the mettle like she always managed to.

Which served to remind him. "The children. Will you see them before you go?"

As her fingers closed around his wrist, she shook her head. "No. I left Jaime a little stronger, so she'll have to be all right."

Her courage leveled him, but he managed to lift his wrist to her lips. Of their own accord, his eyes closed as her mouth sealed around the dripping wound. He raised his face in benediction as her tongue pushed at the vein with her suckling.

So right. Everything about her mouth on him was so right. He wanted it everywhere, his body hers to use, to bite and suck and run her tongue all over. To run herself all over, to glide and grind her soft skin in contrast to his rough, smothering him with everything feminine while he drowned in the essence of her.

"Violet." Her name escaped his throat as his hips curled toward her. When she slid her fangs from his vein, he fought the bellow of being denied mushrooming in his chest. This giving had been for her. He repeated the words in his head until they grew so loud he could barely hear what she said.

---

*W*hen Uri's black eyes riveted on her, she knew she'd done the wrong thing. She should not have accepted his offer of blood. Not when she craved to be claimed by him, to be owned body and soul by this enormously strong, yet vulnerable Kynd. A vampire unlike any she'd ever known. He would treat her with care, would give her anything…

Oh, God! What was she doing? She was caving, and in turn ruining the greatest male she'd ever known. Uri didn't deserve this. He was healing, she saw it in the way he gave himself to her. He would allow their bodies to surrender to full-on vampire, to use and entwine and discover new pleasures and pains, and he would be blissed out by the joining.

Then consequently horrified once the heat cooled from their bloodied, yet sated bodies.

He would be reminded of his captivity, of the centuries where he'd been used in that way by vampires. *By my father.* She shoved herself away from him, her hands held up to ward him off as she backed up. "No. We can't do this. I can't do this." Though she wasn't exactly referring to their coming

173

together. She wasn't sure she could walk away from this male and never look back.

Uri took a step toward her. "Vi."

"Stop it. Don't come any closer, or I'll run, Uri. I will run." Her throat nearly closed on her words, her eyes stinging with unshed tears.

Uri halted, his arms falling to his sides. When she watched them drop, she saw the bulge sitting atop his thigh. Her tender folds moistened, her nub pulsing. Violet backed up farther even though there was no hiding her arousal from such an observant male.

The cords in his forearms flexed as he curled his claws into his palms. Uri growled then choked it off, aware he was crossing the line he'd sworn he wouldn't. He would do that. Sacrifice his wants and needs for her.

Dear God, if she stayed in his presence any longer, she would give in. She would selfishly ruin his life for her own pleasure.

She wasn't her father, though. The reminder hit her like an ice water bath. It cleared her head, taking her breath as if to kick start her lungs into breathing normally instead of the heated, shallow panting she'd been doing.

She had to rebuild the distance between herself and Uri. Though with his blood singing through her, she heard his heart thumping hard and fast in his chest, could smell not only his arousal but his fear.

Fear of her leaving?

No matter. Fear was an emotion as intense as passion, and as malleable as clay to anyone who knew how to manipulate it. Uri had appetites and demons—a brew easily turned to poison. She wasn't like her father, but if pressed she could do whatever it took to protect the ones she loved.

Compassion wasn't a weakness. Most times it was her greatest strength. Raking deep, she squared her shoulders, preparing to drop a bomb as she had done earlier. Was it only hours ago? Fuck, she felt ancient.

Shadows shifted into solidity behind Uri, and Violet glared over his shoulder just as he turned his chin, both of them sensing movement at the same time. A vampire with the deadest eyes she'd ever seen walked into the foyer. "Urick. Violet. We have to get started."

"Give us a minute, Kristov." Uri turned to look at her once again, his eyes alternating between gray and black, swirling with emotion.

Ignoring his distress, Violet strode passed him to the Vampyre leader. "I'm ready. Let's do this." As Uri faltered, giving her the space she needed to move by him, she reminded herself it was compassion driving her. She dug deep for a haughtiness she didn't feel.

Kristov fell in step beside her, offering his arm. Uri remained in the foyer as if he couldn't move.

*God help me, give me strength.* Swallowing a sob, she strode on, determined not to lean on her escort, her stiff back as solid as any slamming door in the face of the male she loved.

---

"*Y*ou think this is going to work?" Kallen stared out over the black of frozen tarmac. In the center and spotlighted by the fluorescent glare of the security lamps lay Uri's Chosen One, blood smeared and body akimbo, her whimpering like that of a stranded kitten. Along the edge of the paved area were the dumpsters for the cafeteria, dark green hulks hiding the Vampyres. Kronos and Merrick had taken to the roof.

"Fuck if I know." Shoulder pressed to Kallen's, Darken barely moved. They were well hidden behind a hospital employee's car, the odor of gas sharp in the cold of the predawn winter. Kallen tasted the petrol on his tongue, the fumes roiling around in his stomach.

"And the asshole better hurry. She's losing a lot of blood." Darken whispered into his ear, the moist heat welcome against his frigid skin. The temp hovered around twenty degrees, but that wasn't what gnawed into his bones. It was the damned dampness, inescapable in a port city.

How Violet ignored it to play the Writhing Dead proved she was a female with which one did not trifle. Which was probably why their prey hadn't shown up to take the bait. Mr. Dali was waiting for her to grow too weak to fight back.

Cunning bastard. Though Kallen had to hand it to Uri's Chosen One, who was proving to be every bit as crafty as her father. Still, though. "She's going to freeze to death first." Muscles picking up an itchy twitch, Kallen tugged his coat collar up around his ears. A nervous gesture, probably the first of many if this plan dragged out any longer.

Good thing Uri had stayed home with Drakus and the other Chosen. He'd be crazier than a shithouse rat by now.

"If Dali's not here soon, I'm calling this. I don't give a shit what Anton and the rest of them think. We can't let her suffer much longer. Daniela's going to hand me my ass as it is."

Kallen didn't have a female to read him the riot act, but he didn't need one. As much as he'd antagonized Violet, her commitment to this plan was eating at his animosity. "Maybe they're both just trying to make it look good. You know, Dali will swoop in at the last second and they'll run off together."

"Thought of that, but after watching her around Uri, I think she really cares about him. Besides, no matter where she goes, Uri can follow her."

"Well, duh, my point exactly. It's Uri they want, right?"

"You're forgetting her father tried to kill her."

"A ruse."

Darken set his jaw. "Violet doesn't even know where her father is now, let alone where this secret society of vampires is."

"So she says."

"Yeah, because she'd protect the male who carved a smiley face under her chin."

Kallen ignored the logic and abandoned his bid to turn Violet back into Satan's spawn. Violet's acting had begun to look a little too real. To be convincing, she'd nicked her own vein, arguing that her father would know if the blood was someone else's. Earning herself a round of respectful nods. "Fine. But how much longer are we going to torture ourselves watching this?"

Darken glanced up at the graying sky. "Not much longer, thank fuck."

As fed up as Darken, and ready to shed some of the guilt piling up, Kallen gave his twitchies full rein and started to push himself out from behind the piece of shit Camry they were crouched behind.

Darken yanked him down by the elbow. "Look."

As he took a gander to where his brotherkynd had nudged his chin, Kallen flattened himself out on the freezing pavement to make himself invisible. In three to four-yard increments, Dömötör Dali appeared and disappeared, as though the stealthy bastard sensed the trap as he closed the distance between himself and his daughter. If anyone lunged for him, he'd already be halfway gone.

With just a few more jumps for him to go, Violet flipped to her feet in a twist that defied physics and intersected him.

"Jesus on a popsicle stick!" Kallen bolted to his feet. "She broke his pattern!" Admiration flared inside him like a spark to gunpowder, and he lost a few seconds watching the female outmaneuver the older vampire. Man, she moved like a panther, all lithe grace and quick reflexes, striking with a one-two swipe of arms and legs that made seasoned ballerinas look positively clumsy.

"Oh, shit. She's going in for the bite." They'd known going in that taking Dali's blood would render her vulnerable. Violet would have to quit fighting, but that's where the rest of them were supposed to come in.

Their job was to protect her. Except things happened too fast, and Dali hadn't approached as they'd expected him to. All of them were running behind the eight ball, fractions of a second too slow. But in a fight like this one, a hair's breadth of time was all it took to end things.

"Go, go, go!" They couldn't lose her. She was a Chosen One. What in fuck had they been thinking? A wash of sickness rolled over Kallen, turning his muscles to cold jelly and sludging up his pistons.

Just as Kallen reached for Dali, his hand slammed into Uri's back. Someone off to his right, Godrick by the sound of it, shouted, "He's teleported in!" Meaning Uri, who was supposed to have stayed gone from there. The crunch of bone interrupted his internal bitch session—for exactly that reason. Dali had to get away. Having Uri in this part of the plan was like putting a juvenile delinquent in charge of a bag of kittens—you just knew things weren't going to turn out right.

Precious seconds flew by as Kallen maneuvered around his brotherkynd. He threw his arm out just in time to deflect Uri's blow to the vampire's skull. The hit pile-drived him to his knees. "Mother of Mary, that hurt," Kallen hissed as he fought the urge to retaliate.

The blow hadn't been meant for him, but son of a bitch. All those times they'd gone at each other in the safe house, Uri had been holding back. Now, he was off his chain. Which wasn't even a metaphor given who he unleashed himself upon.

Their plan to find the vaJcaka was going to derail like a train wreck.

Except two things happened in such quick succession, Kallen purposefully stood still to blink a few times to make sure his peepers were working right.

First, Kristov materialized, somehow inserting himself between Violet and Dali. Second, Godrick that blessed asshole, sandwiched Dali between himself and Kristov. Arms snaking around the vampire's waist so fast Kallen barely saw the blur, Godrick vanished, taking Dali with him.

They reappeared a few yards away, the Vampyre staggering off like he'd been struck. Dali disappeared right on cue.

"Fucking brilliant!" Flinching as he pumped his fist in the air, he pivoted around to take in the triumphant faces of the hunting party. Except there weren't any. Everyone was staring down where the center of the fight had been.

Violet was as flopped as she'd been earlier when she'd been playing bait, her arms and legs sticking out from Uri's possessively hunkered body. Only now she definitely wasn't acting. "Oh, baby Jesus." Kallen's stomach migrated south, his life draining out through his feet.

"She's going to be all right?" As his gaze bounced around the circle of witnesses, he sagged. The answer was stamped on the grim faces looking down, the strong bodies slumped under winter coats as if the draining of the Chosen's life sucked theirs out as well. "I'm going to be sick." Knees gone spastic, he gripped onto Darken's elbow to keep his ass from kissing the freezing ground.

Just as Dömötör Dali and several other vampires flashed in so suddenly it was as if they'd always been there. Rushing at Uri and Violet as cohesive as a pride of starving lions, their cloaked backs formed a solid wall so impenetrable that Kallen and the rest of them were left behind like the grimy ring on the sink after the dishwater drained away.

In the center of the surprise assault, Dali's expression was one of sheer delight. He'd duped them all—the legendary Kynd, the powerful Triumvirate. "Thanks, boys. We couldn't have done it without—" As parting shots went, the disrupted delivery would have been hilarious.

Except the vampires disappeared as quickly as they'd entered, leaving an empty space on the tarmac where Violet and Uri had been.

---

*U*ri knew several immediate things. First, he recognized his captors with a fury born from the smoldering cauldron of revenge. Second, he couldn't free himself from the way they shuffled his molecules, his body not wholly in his possession, so he couldn't fight them as he was.

Nor would he. Not while he summoned every ounce of his strength to hold Violet to him instead. They would not have her. They had stolen everything from him, but this they would not take. It was a determination he had never felt for himself, and the strength it infused into his muscles gave him hope that his will would hold fast.

Just so long as he held fast to her.

The instant he felt himself come back together, he curled his entire bulk around Violet to form an impenetrable wall of muscle and bone and skin. He prayed it was impervious, anyway. His living shield must have worked because he felt the all too familiar shackling of only one wrist and ankle, instead of the usual four.

And, blessedly, none on his Chosen. Though his heart turned to dry ice as soon as he realized why. She was no threat in the state of near death she was in. Besides, the bars were an alloy of metals no vampire could teleport through.

It's how Uri had learned those many years ago to find sanctuary in a cave where metals were mined. The knowledge had served him well. He hadn't been recaptured until he'd left the safety of the mine, and the security of his brethren's company.

Until Violet. For her, he'd risked everything. Including his sanity. Which she'd returned to him more intact than it had been for millennia. Even now with his body in chains once again, he could control the rage burning like an inferno under his skin, his frozen heart hanging in the epicenter.

When he heard the clang of the cage door shutting, he turned his back to his captors, the lengths of chain clinking along the stone floor as he shifted around. Ignoring the dread crawling across his skin, he caressed Violet's sunshine hair from her brow with his free hand. "Open your eyes, love. Please wake and open your eyes."

Her eyelashes fluttered as if she struggled to respond to his voice.

"That's right, Vi. You're okay." Uri raised his wrist to his mouth. He didn't care if his captors would soon drain him as they once used to do, he'd give Violet every drop she needed.

He pushed his wrist against her fangs, his blood bubbling around her lips. "Dear God, love, take it. Please take it." As though she heard his desperate whisper, she began to suckle. Weak pulls, but he welcomed them.

Her eyelids were bruised and her skin so pale it alarmed him, but for her, he pretended all was well, that as long as she fed she'd be all right. That they would both be all right. He'd keep her as safe as he could, and feed her often until her full strength returned. Something she'd not enjoyed since he'd kidnapped her.

And now look where he'd landed her. In the squalor of a cell he knew all too frigging well. Guilt chewing him a new asshole, Uri concentrated on the flush rising on her cheeks, and on the strength in her fingers as she curled them around his forearm.

"Soon you'll be strong enough. I promise." Though he kept from looking around him, at the rusty bars of their cage, the windowless and damp stone of the walls. Nothing had changed since the last time they'd held him here, except maybe a thicker growth of mildew. Most likely the rags used for their beds would be different, too, but the changes were like Mr. Gotrocks buying a new yacht—who gave a fuck?

Uri's gaze trailed from Violet's seashell ear to her temple. The flash of amber snagged his attention, and instantly he felt like a fucking idiot crouched in the cell with her in his arms, the cuffs and chains obvious. "Hi."

Violet licked her lips and brought her hand up to her head. "What happened?" As Uri readjusted his hold on her, she caught sight of the chains. Alarm annihilated the dozy gloss of her irises, and she bolted to her feet.

She would have staggered in a messy fall if Uri hadn't snagged her elbow. "Whoa, hold on. Easy."

"Easy? How can I be easy when we're in a frigging cage?" Her words tore across his heart like claws, but she let him sweep her body against his. He loved it when they stood like this—Vi's back curving along his stomach while he draped his arms around her protectively. From this vantage point, he could glide his erection along the crease of her ass as he nuzzled her neck.

"We'll get out." When she shook her head, the scent of her raked through him. His muscles tensed as he dragged his hips up her backside.

"Uri."

God, he loved it that she could be breathless for him, even in these circumstances. Uri pressed kisses to the column of her neck and nibbled when her fingers combed through his hair and held on.

"This is dangerous. If they know—"

As she turned in his arms, he sealed off her words with his tongue, slanting his lips over hers. The taste of her hit his joints like a shot of WD-40, swinging them loose so he had to steal a scrap of awareness from his singing cock and think about keeping himself standing. The floor was for later, after he had her blood rushing fast through her veins and her silken folds wet.

Violet pulled back, covering his mouth with her hand. "Uri, I'm serious. We have to get out of here." Her gaze drifted to the links tethering him to the wall. Fear stole into her usually courageous eyes.

Uri tamped down on the fury bubbling to the surface. "I have long since lost my fear of this place." Now he just wanted to destroy the bloodsuckers who had tortured him, to lay waste to anything they held dear. As they had done to his pride and would try to do again.

This time, though, Uri didn't feel powerless. He had his Chosen to fight for. He had Vi, who would fight strong beside him.

"Uri, you don't understand. He drugged me."

"Then he's a coward." Flexing his arm subtly so Vi wouldn't notice, he tested the strength of his chains. He'd grown much stronger since finding his love and feeding from her. He would still need to use all of his strength to stretch the links or drag the stone out of the wall, but he could do it when the time was right.

"My father stuck me with a needle to drug me and capture you. I'm only alive to keep you in line. They'll use me against you. To make you do those unspeakable things..." As though her fear turned to terror, Violet paced along the front of the cage where the bars were.

"Get away from there, Vi."

"Afraid they'll do something to me?"

Uri gave her one slow nod, his eyes riveted on where she stood, then sweeping along the passage on the other side of the bars.

"See? I make you afraid, Uri. Anytime you try to escape, they'll threaten me."

"They will try it once." Resolve seeped through him like his stone did every morning. *Oh, fuck.* His stone. He would turn statue, and Vi would be defenseless. They could do anything to her and he'd be powerless to stop it. His rage frothed over the lid and he strode forward, the chains yanking him off-kilter when he'd eaten the slack.

"Come back to me, Violet."

He no sooner said the words when three males he recognized materialized on the other side of the bars and snatched her hands.

---

*V*iolet felt the air stir just as something closed around her wrist and yanked her with a hard twist into the bars. The back of her head hit the rusted metal first, and a starburst of pain rolled her stomach in a wave of nausea.

As she winced, she caught sight of Uri lunging faster than she'd ever seen him do before. The momentum snapped his chains taut, flipping him sideways with a wrench so extreme she thought she heard muscles tear.

It didn't stop him. The instant he regained his feet he lunged again, and Violet heard a wet pop. "Your arm!" Uri backed up to throw himself forward again. "Stop! You're tearing your arm off!"

Eyes black as an abyss and aimed on the vampire males holding her against the cage door, Uri didn't seem to care. He was locked in, a mated vampire prepared to do anything to protect his female.

Yet it seemed even more intense than that. Uri's ferocity was that of the legendary Kynd, a Kynd who fought to protect his Chosen One. And she'd thought male vampires were possessive? If not for the pain she felt for him, she would have been flattered.

However. This wasn't going to get them out of there, not when vampires had tricksy in their DNA. She'd been brought along for a reason, left in the cage with Uri *for a reason.* Her father would turn him into a puppet simply by threatening her.

Having just witnessed him tear his arm out of its socket to protect her, and cease only when she'd told him to, she knew her father had nailed that one. Maybe Uri could muscle his way out of there. Hell, he'd done it before. Except she'd bet her only set of fangs his plate hadn't been cracked like it was right then.

They needed a different plan, one that didn't involve him disfiguring himself.

The idea that formed punched low and mean in her belly, and she had to gulp like a fish just to get air into her lungs. But the truth was, if Uri didn't care about her, they couldn't use her to bait him. And in order to accomplish that, she had to distance herself from him.

"Lock the other cuff and be done with her before the beast hurts itself."

Violet opened her mouth to tell them to go fly a kite with a friendly *fuck off* when she noticed the stone behind Uri. He was dragging it out of the wall, complete with bolt and rod.

So, their captors weren't worried Uri would hurt himself, they were afraid he'd get loose. Well, well, well. Seemed they had a shade more respect for him than she thought. While she stood feeling smug, a hand shoved at her back and sent her sprawling, her musings exploding from her head when she belly-flopped to the floor. With the chains taut, she couldn't catch herself and smacked her chin on the flagstone.

The second her lungs let go of their Ziploc seal to let in some air, she got to her feet and ran for her protector. And got yanked yet again by her own chains for the effort. "Son of a bitch." Could she just once look halfway competent? A threat in her own right? Oh, and how about using her brain. She'd just—*just*—formed a plan to separate herself from Uri.

She stood up and took stock, calculating that there was a spread of about three feet between herself and Uri. Eyes flicking up to see if he noticed, a spasm squirmed deep and low, her panties getting moist.

God, he was breathtaking. Like she needed to be drooling at a time like this? *Oh,* it wasn't drool, but her blood seeping from the cut on her chin. Without her hands to press the wound closed, it dripped like a lethargic clock ticking out the slow passage of time.

Keenly tuned to her, Uri had ceased struggling, his eyes no longer riveted on their captors, but on her. Broad chest rising and falling, and his voice scraping out of him with more gravel than a country road, he knelt to check the seeping cut. "You're hurt." He reached for her with his free hand.

Not wanting their captors to know how much Uri meant to her, and not wanting to back up toward them, Violet opted for a sidestep, going as far as her short leash would allow. Glancing over her shoulder when she felt her chains tauten more, she noticed they were fed through the bars and attached outside of the cage.

So they could pull her to them any time they wished.

Oh, goody. Escaping the cell was going to have more pitfalls than a game of Candy Land. An image of the kids at the hospital honed-in to steal some of her attention from the sitch at hand, but she blocked it immediately. She had enough to handle without adding that worry. As it was, Uri's hurt confusion was cutting her worse than her father's blade had done.

Yet she couldn't explain without jeopardizing her plan. She'd just have to pray their connection would be stronger than any lies she was about to choke out of her throat.

Uri watched her close for a few moments, then as if he fathomed her motives, he gave a sharp nod, his expression turning fierce. "Right. Smart. Stay away from them any way you can." The lovable idiot. She hadn't hurt him yet, but she was going to in three, two, one...

She turned to their jailors, who hadn't yet poofed their cloaked asses out of the dungeon. "Tell my father our plan is working. The beast will do anything he wants."

"Violet? What are you saying?" His confusion returning, Uri remained on his knees.

She couldn't look at him and continue this, not when her heart cracked so hard tears stung her eyes. "Tell him he can free me now. I'll tell him everything over a drink."

Even though she'd warned herself to keep looking away, she cast a glance at Uri from under lowered lids. His free arm lay on his thigh as if he hadn't the energy to hold it up. "Vi, whatever it is you're doing—don't. For the love of God, for the love of us, don't do this."

Swallowing the bile burning the back of her throat, she said, "Fool. There is no *us*. There never has been."

# CHAPTER 11

*D*id it matter which room they convened in? While the Vampyres of the Triumvirate situated themselves at one end of the dining room table—taking all the time in the world, for fuck's sake—the top of Kallen's skull threatened to fly off.

Why the almighty stooges thought they had to meet and discuss their next course of action sent Kallen's skin into a shrivel. Needing to move, he paced the length of the room, trying his heart out not to punch a hole through the wall.

"We're wasting valuable time. We need to follow—"

"And how is it you're going to do that, Kallen?" Merrick wasn't sitting either. The poor rhetorical bastard stood still like maybe a twitch of the wrong muscle might undo him. But he'd made his point. They couldn't follow their brotherkynd, not when he'd been teleported. Which was some serious fucking mojo, by the way. The Vampyres having their powwow at the other end of the table couldn't even do that, and they controlled an entire world of Others.

Frustrated gaze sliding around the room, he took stock of Kronos crouched in the corner. The male had one arm wrapped around himself, and a hand clapped to his jaw to keep his mouth shut. Darken leaned against the wall next to him, his outer thigh touching the other Kynd's shoulder for comfort.

Touch. Yeah, he could use some, but not to calm down in the usual

185

manner. Merrick looked loose enough to go a round or five, except then Kristov held up a hand as he leaned in for a last second nod with his cronies. Expectation sparking in his chest, Kallen's shitkickers locked onto the carpet. Godrick leaned back in his chair, Anton and Kristov following suit.

"Get Drakus in here. We'll need him."

Kallen rocked back like he'd been struck. "Oh, no. If you think you're going to use our brotherkynd for your—"

Godrick pulled a plastic vial from his coat pocket and held it out in front of him.

"What's that?"

"Dali's blood. I got it when we...scuffled."

"Son of a bitch." Kallen strode down the length of the room to get a closer look. Merrick and Darken joined him. "How?"

Godrick smirked like Kallen's disbelief amused him. He had a mind to knock those smarmy lips into the next century. "You think we'd trust Dali's daughter? We know nothing about her except she fights well. This was too important to simply cross our fingers and hope she would hold up her end of the bargain."

Jesus fucking Christ. If he didn't admire the strategy, Kallen wouldn't trust the Triumvirate, either. Oh, wait, he didn't. "So you had us all going in thinking the plan was for Uri's Chosen One to get the job done when all along you had something else in mind. Way to win our affection."

Godrick shrugged as if he couldn't care less.

"We felt the fewer of us who knew, the less likely it would be for Violet to get wind of it." Anton, ever the voice of reason, got off his ass and put a hand on his son-in-law's shoulder. "Merrick, it wasn't done out of distrust, but we know mated vampires, and their allegiance is to their mates."

"Uri isn't mated to her."

Anton offered a sympathetic smile. "She's Chosen, is she not?" When Merrick glared back at him, Anton squeezed his shoulder, his smile now one of pride. "You see how it is then. Kynd will do anything for the ones they love."

Well, wasn't that craptastic. "So, you're saying Uri can't be trusted either."

"We didn't say that," Godrick answered like his audience had juuust turned five years old.

"Yeah, you did. Now get on with whatever it was you were going to spout off about before I cave your forehead in with my fist."

"Kallen." Merrick stepped in front of him while pointing a finger at Godrick. "You. Sit down and stop taunting my brotherkynd. You know we're all on short fuses here. Quit trying to light his, or don't blame us for what happens."

"Hear that, Godfuck, sit down and shut—"

"You too, Kallen. This is too important to lose our heads over." Instead of bristling up to him, Merrick found a chair and parked his ass in it, proving by example he meant what he said. *Damn it.* His sitting down was like a yawn—contagious. Calming Kallen down a degree so he searched out a chair, too.

Forearms on the polished wood of the table, he leaned forward. "Okay, go on. Tell us your great plan."

Showing good faith, Anton and Kristov made Godrick sit down as well. Better. Godrick had a God complex as it was, lording it over them all the time, hoping the Kynd would slip up so he could tighten their leashes even more.

"Kristov will drink Dali's blood and follow its trail. Once he's found the source, he'll phone us with the coordinates. Which is why we need Drakus. Depending on where they're holding Urick, we might need the dragon to fly us in. A vehicle will be too slow."

So far, so good. Kallen kept his mouth shut like a good little boy.

"Once we're there, we'll reconvene. We've got no idea what we're getting into, but it's my guess we'll need every hand we can get."

"Angelia stays."

"Daniela isn't going anywhere near that place, either." Darken peeled himself away from Kronos to add his two cents.

"Just so." Anton agreed. "I wasn't even including them in this plan."

Well, don't let it be said Kynd were gender biased. If the two females in question weren't Chosen, none of the brethren would have batted their eyelashes at fighting side by side with a member of the opposite sex.

Woohoo. A mark in their favor.

"Where is my daughter anyway?" Anton looked to Merrick, as was right. If anyone would know it would be him, who usually had to be pried off Angelia just so she could use the bathroom in private.

"The ladies are with Drakus." Merrick didn't add anything more. Were they playing canasta? Shooting the breeze? Oh, hell, who was he kidding? If they were with Drakus in the basement, they were soothing the savage beast, not battling it out over a game of gin rummy.

"Good. Will Drakus be amenable to our plan?"

"We'll talk to him about it."

Godrick piped up. "The sooner the better. We don't want to waste any more time than—"

Merrick slammed his palm down on the table and pushed to his feet so hard his chair tipped over behind him. "I said we'd talk to him about it. Now, if you gentleman will excuse us, it's almost dawn and we have things to do before tomorrow night."

Effing right. Kallen rose to his feet, too, proud as a new dad with Merrick. He was protecting his brethren and hadn't hesitated, even if it offended the ruling Triumvirate. Though to be honest, the only one who looked like his undies had a burr was Godrick. Anton and Kristov had risen from their seats and were bowing their g'days.

Merrick held his hand out for Anton. "I'll tell Angelia that you and Marguerite send your love. We'll meet again here tomorrow evening at six?" After the cock-sucking sun fell from the sky.

As father and son in-law prattled away, Kallen stuck his hand out for Kristov. The Vampyre looked at it then up at him. Hesitantly, he took Kallen's and braced for the jolt of electric current.

"I'm holding back, old man. In good faith."

Kristov smiled, the spark of it almost reaching his eyes. "Thank you, Kallen. We'll meet tomorrow." Nodding, he departed. Kallen didn't hold his palm out for Godrick. If the guy wanted to be a prick, then he could stand out in the cold. The hum of electricity through touch was singularly Kynd, and Kallen had no intention of sharing something so special with an asshole.

Never let it be said the Kynd didn't have discriminating taste, as well.

------

*U*ri couldn't stop pacing. As long as his arms and legs moved, the lid on his anger didn't blow off. Of course, every time he changed direction he had to adjust his chains, a reality that parted the lid so a little pissed off spilled out. Uri just kept moving, righting it until the next time he changed direction.

Which came about every eight feet. So, in actuality, the lid on his kettle of fury was rattling on top of a full boil. When his chains tugged once more, he fisted them and pivoted, his fingers curling around the links and not letting go.

Violet sat off to the side of the cage away from the bars. She couldn't reach the wall, so she sat unprotected from all sides. Away from him. Uri's grip on the chains squeezed tighter. Though her beautiful amber eyes followed his back and forth, she said nothing to him for hours.

Which made him want to hold her to him even more. He knew what she was up to, but dear God in Heaven, she was killing him. Distancing herself?

She might as well reach down his throat and gut him. Oh, and tear his heart out of his chest while she was at it.

When his knees picked up a tremble, he knew he was going to lose it. He'd been fighting the urge to lash out indiscriminately, to save his strength for when his enemies showed their fanged faces.

His gaze once again drifted to Vi. "Your father is quite the honorable male."

She narrowed her lids like she was sighting him in for something unpleasant.

"First he cuts your throat then he drugs you. Nice plan. His idea, or did you come up with it together?"

She hugged her knees tighter to her chest, looking more forlorn than ever. The sight of it almost derailed him. Uri changed direction, his steps faltering midway through his track. He turned to face her, taking a deep breath when his chains snagged. Letting it out slowly, he forced his fingers to ease off on their death grip.

"When he comes to get you, tell my father in-law I send my love."

"He's not your father in-law."

"No, I suppose not, since I haven't officially claimed you in the vampire way."

Violet let go of her knees and straightened up. "He's not your fath—"

Uri waited for her to restart her sentence. And waited. He pinched his lips together with a fang to ruin his smirk. "What? No snappy comeback?"

Vi pulled her knees back up to her chest and wrapped her arms around them. Chin resting on her kneecaps, she shut her eyes. Uri deflated like the life oozed out of his skin. He caved to the shimmy in his legs and landed on his knees.

"Vi, look at me."

Nothing.

"Vi, please just look at me." Stubborn female. "I love you. I know you lo—"

She launched to her feet so fast Uri leaned back out of reflex, his hands cupping his nut sack. "Don't say it! Don't you dare say it." If she had a sword stuck to the end of her finger he'd be stabbed through three times by now. "I don't love you. I faked it all to get you here."

"No."

"Think about it, Urick. How could someone love you? Turning to stone, never in control. Yeah, that's great relationship material!" As if the rest of her tirade got stuck in her throat, Violet averted her face and dragged her chains back to where she'd been sitting. This time she turned her back to him.

189

Uri remained kneeling on the flagstone, guttering out like a candle flame. 'But those times we—"

"You stole my blood." She interrupted without turning around. Desire searing his hollowed insides, he eyed the curve of her spine, the row of knobs arcing to the delicate flare of her hips. She seemed so fragile he burned to take her in his arms, to shelter her.

"You gave it freely." He wouldn't play this game. She was in far more danger if they were separated than she realized. Proving she knew nothing of this place. Though he hadn't realized how her false confession had bothered him before, relief blew through him now, unlocking his lungs so he could take a breath.

"I was baiting you and it worked." Still not turning around, she talked to the bars.

"Yes. I'm as hooked as any fish, caught surer than a bear in a trap." He punned on purpose, hoping to draw her attention—and her body—back toward him with soft humor.

"Then more's the pity for you."

Uri ground his teeth.

"It's a done deal, chimera. You're caught, and I can go back to doing what I used to."

"Like throwing up every night."

Finally, she spun around. "Don't you dare bring those kids into this."

"No? Too bad. You leave this cage without me, and you're never going to see them again." Uri spoke the words without picturing the reality. If he did, he'd lose it.

"Such an ego. I imagine it's what got you kicked out of Heaven."

Their verbal swordplay grew sharper. He couldn't let her words sink in, either. "We were ousted for not taking sides. Scattered over the middle realm between Heaven and Hell as God's ironic punishment for not siding with Good. Tell your father that when you see him."

Vi stood up with a very faint wobble. Uri's heart lurched. If he hadn't been Kynd, he wouldn't have seen it, but she was weak. True fear crawled over his skin. He amped up the effort to change her mind. "The world got it wrong, Vi. Kynd were watchers. We were made to observe, to see and hear better than any other being. Our blood is strong."

Violet remained quiet, watching him.

"I wasn't captured, love. God put me here, and I hated Him for that. But now I understand why." As he spoke, the truth of his Lord's plan dawned as beauteously as the angels sang in Heaven. "He put me here for you, Vi. So I would find you."

"Bullshit."

"No. My vampire side had always been dormant. Kynd are vegetarian, I never partook of blood."

"So, God put you here to be tortured in order to love your vampire side? Sounds like a shitty lesson to me."

"If I hadn't had to struggle so fiercely, I would have ignored it. I wouldn't have been so furious at seeing you with the children. I'd have kept watching, afraid to go near you."

"Yeah, and look where it got you. Right back where you started. Great plan."

"It was. I wouldn't change any of it."

"Then you're a fool."

Uri shrugged off her insult. "Maybe. But I wouldn't take back a single thing if it meant we wouldn't be together."

"You're fucking serious? Look around you, Uri. You're a blood slave again." She struck her arm out to encompass their cell, and her chains rattled.

The hair on his nape shivered to attention, his anger at seeing her delicate arm in cuffs oozed away from his control. Uri screwed it down tight, afraid to spook her when he was gaining ground. She'd called him *Uri*. He bet she didn't even notice the slip. "True, but not for long. Don't go to your father." His command carried the low bass of a growl. Violet didn't seem the least worried by it, thank the baby Jesus.

"Why, because you think he's yours to kill? Think again."

"He'll kill you." Now he couldn't stifle his fear or his outrage. Uri stepped toward her, his own chains yanking taut. His hands curling into fists, he snapped them a couple of times as if he meant to punch something.

Violet, bless her staggering courage, never flinched. She braced up to him, testing the length of her chains, too. "Thanks for the compliment, you typical vampire asshole."

He opened his mouth to snarl back a retort when the faint whoosh of gathering molecules grabbed his attention. His body tensing and snapping against his restraints as he lunged to put Vi behind him, Uri roared his frustration and his warning.

Two vampires shimmered into solidity behind the safety of the bars. Vi stepped back then caught herself. Dragging in a breath, she ran toward them.

"No, Vi! Don't!" As his heart leapt up his throat, Uri thought he'd choke. Or was that his lungs seizing? She was really fucking doing this. "Violet, you don't know what you're doing! He'll kill you, Jesus-fuck! Don't do it!" With his lungs not working, he'd blasted out the last of his air.

Unable to talk, his body took command in a last-ditch effort to save his Chosen One.

The skin across Uri's shoulders erupted into a cape of six-inch fur, the longer outer hairs preceding the softer undercoat. The fangs of his vampire punched into his mouth. As he watched Violet raise her hands to the bars, his lungs jumpstarted like pneumatic bellows.

Uri blasted his utter outrage and swung a hand tipped with four-inch claws. He heard the grating of stone behind him as he gained a precious inch. "You will all pay if you touch her!"

Violet glanced back over her shoulder. Face pale, she mouthed *Trust me*.

Uri charged.

---

*G*od, she hoped Uri saw her desperate message to him, but she didn't have time to double check. Grasping onto the bars, she stuck her face right up to her vampire captors. "Release me. Take me to my father now!"

Even back when he'd first kidnapped her, she'd never seen Uri so magnificently terrifying. He seemed absolutely off his chain, which was going to be the case in real time in about five…four…three seconds. If she was going to kill her father and then the others, she needed out. Pronto.

As seemingly unstoppable as Uri looked right then, it wouldn't last. There was some kind of fae mojo in the works around this place. They'd taken him once, they could do it again. But not if she covertly cleaned house one sect member at a time.

Although Plan A, Part Two might work. She'd get out and Uri, in his fit of rage, would distract everyone from what she was doing. Kind of perfect, if she didn't feel like puking. It hurt her to hurt him, and she couldn't fix it yet. Not until they were free.

As Tweedle Dee and Tweedle Dum looked at each other then back at her, Violet didn't hesitate. Putting her face right up to the bars, she whispered so low she barely heard herself. Which was the point.

When Dee and Dum leaned forward for a better listen, she couldn't believe her luck. Violet snatched where the bottoms of their hoods met and yanked them close. She slammed Dum's face into the bars hard enough to stun him, then doubled her fun doing the same thing to Dee.

It wasn't pretty, but she managed to push her face through the bars far enough to sink her fangs into flesh. She bit and tore, praying she'd caught something vital in that neck. Before Dum could figure out what the hell their prisoner was up to, she did the same to him. Back and forth between the two until they went limp in her grip.

As they dropped to the floor, she fumbled for the keys in the folds of their cloaks.

Heart spiking when her fingers closed over metal, she held them up as if she was going to shout *Eureka!* Except silence was vital here. Taking a deep breath to steady her shakes, she didn't hurry as she unlocked her cuffs.

*Calm, Violet. Ignore what's going on outside of your mind and concentrate.*

Empty cuffs clanging to the floor, she massaged her sore wrists and looked over her shoulder at the reason she'd whispered the mantra in her head. *Uri.* "Holy Christ." He was resplendent in his rage.

Muscles carved and shining with sweat, he had his broad back to her, pulling with both hands on his chains. Trailing his spine was a vee of sleek bear fur, narrowing at the waist of his unbuttoned, low riding jeans. His shredded shirt hung like rags from his broad beam shoulders. Humma humma Hulk, anyone?

As if he heard her carnal thoughts, Uri released his chains and turned on her.

Violet gasped as a black, wrathful stare pierced her to her soul. Self-conscious, she wiped at the blood on her face. In a blink, Uri's eyes softened, the ebony as liquid as a well of ink. "Vi," he said through the biggest vampire fangs she'd ever seen.

Her body responded. Need pooled in her panties and her own fangs grew longer. Heart kicking her breastbone, her mouth dropped open.

"Unlock my chains, love." Uri tilted his chin as if embarrassed of his looks, then flicked his gaze back up to her.

Violet took a step forward before stopping herself and shook her head. "I can't."

As his muscles tensed and he faced her full on, Uri seemed to grow even bigger. He held out his hand palm up and wiggled some vicious looking claws. "Please."

God, he was so beautiful. Together they could lay waste to this place. They could...Violet's hunting instincts cut off her thoughts. There was fae magic at work here and she couldn't forget that.

She might be wrong, but as long as Uri remained bound no alarms would sound, and she could sneak about doing what she did best—assassinating those who needed it. As if she moved through a riptide, she turned her back on him and unlocked the cell door.

When she walked back inside she halted several feet away. "I'm sorry, Uri. I hope you can forgive me." She placed the key on the flat stones and ran.

---

*A*s days went, Kallen had had better. His mind, he decided—after hours of contemplating worst case scenarios—was his worst enemy. While sunbeams traveled across his bedroom floor, he imagined a thousand ways in which Uri could be tortured. Sometimes Violet played the role of the villain, just as he'd suspected her to be from the beginning.

Then he'd picture her flopped out on that freezing pavement with her blood seeping out of her, or in Uri's arms, and he'd visualize her being tortured to force Uri into surrendering to unspeakable things.

As the sun slipped under the horizon, Kallen's body came to life with a "Thank fuck" flying off his tongue. Shaking the remaining stiffness from his muscles, he headed for his bathroom on muscled legs that were more like pistons. Stepping into the double shower before cranking on the water, he didn't care about the temperature so much as cleaning off the residue of his day-mares.

He needed the baptismal, the cleansing of his body in symbolic gesture to his soul.

Blame and guilt were horrible demons which ate at the psyche and left festering wounds. The only way to heal them was to right the wrongs. Kallen planned to do just that. But first, he needed to scrub.

His hands not scraping the soap hard enough, he lathered up a washcloth and attacked his skin. He'd been wrong about Violet. They all had, except the other Chosen. Daniela and Angelia had sided with her all along, as if they'd known something none of the males had.

Which made absolute sense. If he hadn't had his head shoved so far up his over-critical and play-the-hero ass, he wouldn't have been so quick to judge a female who was obviously of more worth than he was.

Violet, at least, wanted what was best for Uri.

Kallen dragged the soapy cloth across his muscles, digging in for good measure. The pain gave him flashes of blessed relief. When his whole body burned and the spray of water on his skin felt more like pellets of acid, he cranked the shower off.

Shaking his hair out, he stepped onto the plush mat to snag a towel off the heated bar. Kallen ripped it across his body as he'd done the washcloth. Skin singing anew, he ruthlessly dragged the terry across his flaccid manhood, gasping as it yanked the useless flesh. The raw pain swamped him with a wave of nausea.

"Good." He swallowed and pushed through it, not bothering with the mirror, but heading straight for his dresser. Clothing. He'd not worn a stitch while he'd been exiled. He hadn't needed to. Isolated as he'd been, no one saw his nudity because no one saw him. Ever.

Relegated to his little slice of Purgatory, Kallen hadn't seen a living soul for more than...the calendar when he'd seen one for the first time had told him...more than two thousand years.

Two fucking thousand years where the world went on without him and he'd rotted in solitary confinement, free to toggle his sagging dick while he'd contemplated its use. Now he knew why the Kynd had one. But before? The Kynd might as well have been sexless for all the good that part of their anatomy had done them.

God and his wondrous, infinite vision. The game plan no one could fathom, not even His Archangels. Well, now that Merrick and Angelia had unlocked the secret of the Kynd and their Chosen Ones, they were gaining a clue.

Seeing his brethren with their females made him cup himself and give his saggy cock a wakey-wakey shake like he'd done before his days of getting dressed. Nothing. Though he'd seen the hardened flesh of his brethren, knew how it drove them the way it did other male beings.

Did Kallen want to be included in that madness? Sometimes. When he saw the dopey smiles and the intimacy of a secret language only couples seemed to share. Otherwise, letting his thoughts slip back into the groove of Uri's plight was all the warning he needed that finding your Chosen could go horrifically wrong.

Surely, Uri couldn't love a female who had brought him so low. Where was the salvation in God's plan for the Kynd with that level of suffering? Fucked if he knew. Pissed at the direction of his hamster wheel thoughts, Kallen yanked the knob on his closet door.

And tore the hardware right off.

Flicking the busted knob aside like a booger stuck to his finger, he jammed his claws into the edge of the door to peel it back and peered into the dark room. Slapping the light switch, he blinked until his eyes got used to the glare. Jeans and a no big deal t-shirt to start, then Kallen scanned the racks for a jacket that would hold up to the beating he was going to give it.

Taking more care than he had with the door, he shrugged the leather coat off its hanger and slipped his arms into it. The silk lined skin settled over his shoulders, calming him almost as well as the touch of his brethren. Minus the hum, of course.

But he'd take it along with the easier breath. A little adjustment here and there as he tweaked his back muscles, and he was ready to rescue Uri.

And Violet.

As guilt elbowed for room in his empty gut, Kallen ate up the distance toward the library where he and his brethren would meet to discuss a plan of attack. The voices grew louder as he neared. Stepping through the newly sanded door, his gaze fell on Drakus, who was perched on his usual spot by the window.

Not a real window anymore since the dragon had shattered the glass, but the plywood stand-in held up better. Speaking of holding up, Drakus looked like that was about all he was doing. Clawed hands gripped into a knot, he kept his stare on the floor beneath him as if facing the reality of this meeting would tear his seams.

It probably would. Kristov sat in Merrick's usual spot behind the desk, a shot glass of blood on the desk in front of him.

"You want a lime wedge with that, or are you good to go?" *Fake it 'til you make it, isn't that what Daniela advised?* Kallen latched onto his humor like the shield it was and plunked down on the center cushion of the sofa. No one occupied the empty space to his right, so he let himself relax against Kronos' side, the glorious vibration of touching another Kynd seeping into his bones like he was sunbathing.

Kronos exhaled long and slow beside him, as if the touch centered his rocking boat, too.

Eyeing Godrick the Prick, Kallen dared the Vampyre to make some snarky comment about how close he and Kronos were sitting. To his credit, the leader-of-his-people didn't rise to the bait.

Oh, and speaking of bait. "So, we're losing black sky. Throw what's in your glass back, Kristov, and let's get this party started."

"Hold up." With Angelia draped across his lap, Merrick didn't get up from the overstuffed chair, but he didn't have to. Every eye in the room rolled right to him, eager to offer all the attention he asked for. "I want it to be very clear that when we go in and don't like what we see, we're not going to wait around for your say so." He aimed his statement at the three Vampyres, aka the yankers of the Kynd leash.

Godrick, bless his unusual behavior, didn't open his mouth and looked to Anton to answer. Angelia's father pushed off the edge of the desk. "That's fair. When we split up, it's possible we'll be incommunicado anyway. Use your judgment."

What the fuck? "Have I missed something here?" Kallen sat up straighter.

"Yeah. Our Vampyre friends did some more digging now that they have something to work with. That strip of skin you took offered more clues than everyone first thought." Though it was good news, Darken's hand closed tighter over Daniela's thigh. The Chosen snuggled deeper into his lap, giving comfort automagically.

Kallen ignored the pinch to his heart. "And…"

"Shit might hit the fan." The words were hot when they hit his ear, as though Kronos' pent up breath had been cooking in his lungs.

"Well, all right! It's what we wanted, right?" Kallen sat forward.

"The Fae are definitely involved. It's their sorcery that allowed the vaJcaka to capture Uri."

A high-pitched keening leaked out of Drakus' lungs.

Dear God, they were going to rescue Uri with the finesse of a time bomb. No way Drakus was going to keep his shit together. Not when Angelia—their mother of calm and the direct channel to the sacred Scriptum—was staying behind in the safety of this house.

Kallen slapped his hands together and shoved himself to his feet. "Super! I don't know about you, Drake, but I've been dying to smash shit. No one reining us in? Sign me up." Though his stomach sat somewhere below his bellybutton, he hammed up the enthusiasm.

"I mean, come on, guys. This is our chance to go Kynd." When he finger-quoted the *go Kynd* portion of his pep rally, sparks and knowing smiles twitched to life on the otherwise dismal faces of his brethren. "Seriously, this is going to be awesome."

Godrick finally shed his Mr. Nice costume. "What in the hell does that mean?" As his gaze jumped from one face to another, he cursed. "If you Kynd think you're truly free to do what—"

"Godrick!" Anton slapped his palm on the desk, nearly knocking the precious glass of blood across the desk pad. Kristov snagged it before it tipped, and gulped it in one swig. A grimace revealed a glimpse of a bloody fang. Apparently, the nasty flavor of Dali's blood helped him ignore the drama unfolding between his two colleagues.

"It is their brotherkynd who suffers. Have you forgotten what it is to—"

"I have not forgotten!"

"Uh-oh. Trouble in Triumvirate Paradise." Kallen grinned broadly, knowing he revealed his strong and pointy gargoyle choppers. Thus poking a stick up Godrick's volatile ass.

Kristov tipped the drained shot glass in salute even though his eyes were even emptier than the bloodstained crystal pinched between his fingers. "I'll call when I find our destination." Kallen, like all Kynd could do, sensed the shimmer before Kristov dematerialized.

"Looks like the party's started." While Kallen leered at Godrick whenever the Vampyre turned his glare on him, the rest of them passed the time by deliberately ignoring the empty glass sitting on the blotter.

Angelia finally brought up what everyone else was most likely thinking. "What if it's daylight before he tracks Dali?"

"Let's hope it doesn't take that long, chickie." Anton squeezed his daughter's shoulder as he stopped pacing behind the chair she and Merrick were nestled in.

Angelia patted his hand. "In case it does, though, we need to discuss what to do while Kronos, Drakus, and Kallen still can."

"Way to keep—"

Kallen zipped his lip the instant Anton's phone ringy-dingied.

Thumbing send, he held it up so everyone could hear Kristov on the other end. As if he had to, he upped the volume because the male was whispering.

"You won't believe this, but they're close. Right here in the city. You can drive, but have Drakus come anyway. I think we're still going to need him."

"Where are you?" Godrick, the asshat, spoke from across the room. So much for stealth.

"The Promenade, due east. Stay in the vehicle." Instructions given, Kristov ended the call without so much as a good-bye and drive safely.

Anton slipped his phone back into his trousers' pocket. "All right. I guess we didn't have to wait long. It'll be cramped, but we can all fit in the Escalade."

"I'll go with Drakus if he doesn't mind stretching his wings." Kallen waggled his eyebrows at his brotherkynd. "I need some fresh air."

Drakus dropped off the windowsill to his bare feet and started unbuttoning his pants.

"Whoa, whoa, whoa, dude! There are ladies present. We'll go from the front lawn. Besides, I don't want anyone seeing your naked rear end but me."

Drakus snorted, but took Kallen's opened hand in his, squeezed it, then strode out of the room alone.

"Are we ready then?" Though Merrick and Darken hadn't smooched their babes so long yet, he knew they wouldn't dilly-dally either. Their faces mirrored his. Determined and grim despite his best effort at being funny. They wanted Uri home. Safe and as unharmed as he could possibly be.

And if he was guessing right, the reason Kristov wanted Drakus on hand was because Uri would probably need medical attention pronto, and it would take too long to travel home the modern way.

Fuck. A. Duck. This was going to be bad. Kallen filed out of the room with everyone else, zipping up his leather coat as he teamed up with Drakus in the foyer. "Ready to kick some fae ass, brotherkynd?"

Kallen's heart grew about ten times its size when Drakus locked his elbow with his. They stepped out into the freezing night, trudging through the deep snow to the center of the lawn. There a dragon could spread his wings without hitting anything. Kallen placed his hands over Drakus' talons as his boots lifted off the swirling snow.

Above him, the sparkling stars grew bigger the higher they climbed. As the warm lights of the safe house shimmered out of sight, and his breath left him in puffs of steam, Kallen thought about what they were going up against.

A small army of vampires with connections to the fae, and a brotherkynd who may or may not have his parts previously assembled. Just another night in the lives of the cursed Kynd.

Kallen turned his face toward the twinkling lights of Portland and the inkiness of the Atlantic Ocean blanketing its eastern shoreline. In a few minutes, they'd arrive where Kristov had instructed them to meet him.

As Drakus' great wings propelled them to their destination, Kallen mentally readied himself for the fuck show about to go down. The dragon wasn't going to wait for the others, not when the fae were involved in torturing Uri.

Parking them on a nearby roof ledge with backward strokes of his leather wings, Drakus settled himself as Kallen moved in close to the dragon's shoulders. "I don't see anything. I feel Uri close, but I don't see where he could be." As high as they were he could see a lot, even Kristov's nerd-car.

Drakus growled and nudged his chin before swinging it right.

Kallen followed the sweep of that great head. "The fucking fae." Below them spread the estates of the richest homes in Portland. Interlocked and completely invisible to the human eye stood a monstrosity of a stone fortress. With fae magic, the sect's stronghold had remained intact over the centuries, while industrious humans had built up inside and around it, creating a 3-D puzzle Escher-style where the vampires lived within, utterly unnoticed.

Drakus rolled the third eyelid over a slick gray iris. "Yeah, I trust you to get us into that maze." Kallen braced for the grip of talons. "Yippee ki-aye, motherfuckers!" It was the only warning he gave as he and Drakus smashed through the shimmering aura protecting the fortress.

Kallen tucked and rolled as he landed on the roof, glad for the protection of his leather jacket. Tumbling to his feet, he didn't wait for Drakus. No point in it. The dragon would make his own entrance, fuck you very much.

Grinning madly because he was excited as shit, Kallen kicked in the door to the roof.

---

*A*s far as escape attempts went, Uri's wasn't the most spectacular in history, but the punch of relief to his gut was a high note. Dragging the two stone blocks toward the key on the floor, he would have patted himself on the back if one of his arms wasn't swinging loose out of its socket.

As for his ankle, well, that would heal as soon as he found a living body to drain dry. His gut didn't even twinge at the idea, nor did his soul cower. No indeed. The salvaged thing wanted sustenance and would get it when his body would get blood.

Uri twisted the key and didn't wait for his cuffs to clank to the floor. He bolted for the cell door. And got yanked around like a junkyard dog on a short tether. He was chained again.

"What the…?" His outrage blinded him with an explosion behind his eyeballs, his brain obviously splatting against the inside of his skull. Shaking his head and rubbing his peepers with his free hand, he looked down at the impossible.

He was just as chained as if Violet had never left him the key.

"Violet!" He roared her name as a prayer, not a curse. She'd left him the key along with a plea. *Trust her.* To get them out of here? Absolutely. By herself? No effing way. He knew this place as well as the natives. Free of your bonds did not make you free of the walls. He'd learned that through hard experience and tortures that had made him curse his immortality.

To imagine Violet suffering the same? Uri jerked at his chains with savage tugs, his dislocated shoulder screaming in protest. But what was that compared to the pain in his heart?

He yanked, again and again, the returned stones sliding forth incrementally once more.

"Violet!" If her father or the other vampires laid a single finger on her, he would crush them under his fists and tear their limbs from their battered bodies. One finger. No longer was his fury about revenge. He wanted the vampires dead who had captured his Chosen. He hungered for their deaths so they could never harm his precious female ever again.

Her father? Would know the wrath of someone who loved. Uri would destroy him for Violet's sake. He wasn't fooled by her attempts to align herself with that evil dreg—Uri knew her cunning from personal experience.

The two she'd already slain hadn't. Not that they could regret it, what with their empty robes lying in a powdery residue upon the stone floor. God, he'd been reverently horrified by her trick, and so fucking proud. So turned on by how ferocious she was, his cock had sprung hard between his legs.

What a female! And she was his—if he could get free and save her from herself. Heart tripping into a frantic clunking, Uri renewed his assault on his chains, praying to God in Heaven that He would keep his Chosen One safe.

Because he couldn't. Right at the moment.

# CHAPTER 12

Violet counted twenty chairs lining the long table in the dining hall. They ranged from grand and ornate, to Shaker-esque the farther down the table they went and ended with nothing but wooden benches for the initiates. Goldilocks, anyone?

Six obnoxious throne-like chairs and a high gloss table sat up on a dais on the western end like high priests lorded it over the acolytes. A thirty-foot tapestry hung down the wall as a grisly background for the chiefs on high. Most likely to remind the underlings of their place in the order, and what would happen to them should they decide to grow disgruntled with the status quo.

Lovely. Where did one sign up?

Violet skirted the room, sticking to the shadows under the wall sconces. Her goal was the opposite side where flaming torches lit a lengthy hallway. So what, they didn't believe in electricity, preferring to remain in the Dark Ages? Egotistical maniacs.

Surely those flames led to living quarters. She'd just left the dungeon, so she knew she was steering the right course. Keeping the blade she'd stolen at her outer thigh, Violet treaded the width of the room.

Five down and…nineteen to go. Her father being one of the unfortunates left.

How lucky for her that he'd snatched her up along with Uri. She'd have never found this place on her own. She'd been looking for centuries, but their damned pact with the fae had kept them well hidden.

That bargain faded with every member she killed. She liked their dwindling advantage. Hopefully, it meant good news for Uri. Violet gripped the hilt of her blade tighter as her heart twisted so hard she almost cried out from the pain.

*God, Uri.* As if her thoughts conjured him, a bellow echoed around the chamber. Violet cringed as her name bounced off the cut stone and took shape. She hoped their captors would think they argued, not that the chimera called for her to return to him.

Not waiting to find out, she ran flat out for the hall with its vaulted ceiling and exposed beams, cursing the fae the entire time. She still couldn't trace, and didn't that just make her mission a tad bit dicier. Taking one step at a time didn't only suck ass, it slowed her down.

Peeking in through the first of several arched doors closing off secretive rooms, she refrained from clapping her hands. Unaware they had an assassin in their midst, three vampires knelt at an altar with wooden bowls fanned out in a semi-circle in front of them.

In the flickering candle flames, the contents looked congealed and inky, like old blood from vital organs. How gross. Violet didn't take time to gag. Lunging and spinning, she slit the throats of all three supplicants.

Nor did she stick around to watch them disintegrate to dust. Her count was up to eight, but there was a long way to go yet. Wiping her blade on the leg of her pants, she crept out of the room.

To follow voices. The deeper baritone she would have recognized blindfolded and screaming. Her father. The male who had set her on this path of her life's work—eliminating vampires who made her feel like she'd been born as nothing more than a dangerous parasite.

Violet leaned back against the wall and took a calming breath. Here she would slow down, plan her steps. For all she knew, her father had grown in power and occupied one of those six chairs on the dais. Wary, she crept along the wall toward the voices.

"...check on it every two hours. It's stronger than before. Better for us ritually, but it's not ever to be trusted. Go." On the dismissal, Violet flattened herself to the wall, sucking in her breath so as not release her scent.

Damn it. She hated decisions like this where the clock ticked. Exterminate the threat heading toward Uri, or get to her father while she could? Eenie, meenie, minie, moe.

Violet remained plastered to the shadows as the disciples marched from the room in two step formation like they were headed for the Ark and their subsequent salvation. There would be no deliverance for them, however. Once she was finished with Dad, she'd hightail it back to the dungeon.

This shouldn't take long. Measuring her breaths as she slinked around the jamb and into the room, Violet made friends with the shadows once more. Looking around to get her bearings, she plotted her path. A run along the southern wall of books shelved sky high to another one just like it. Then a cut west toward the gigantic fireplace. Providing Dali remained at his desk. As big as the room was, she should have no problem skirting the periphery and sneaking up behind him.

"Glad you could make it, darling daughter. Won't you have a seat."

Violet froze. As her nemesis turned a large leaf of paper across the desk without glancing up, her thoughts ran the wild track that maybe he hadn't seen her. That maybe he knew she was near, just not where in the room exactly. This wasn't a time to panic. Vi repeated that tidbit of advice several times before taking her first step.

Grip readjusted on her knife, she barely breathed as she inched along the wall of books.

Her father leaned back in his leather chair, pressing his fingertips together as if in prayer. He gazed out across his desk, missing her by ten feet. God, how she hated those eyes! From the moment she could register such things, they'd reminded her of the snakes she used to catch in the garden.

Slow in the cool air of the nights, snakes were easy to snatch once she found them. Their eyes had been glassy and cold, piercing the veil of her soul, and peering deep inside her. She'd cut their heads off as practice for the day she could do the same to her father.

In all the passing years, his reptilian gaze hadn't changed. Nor had her desire to sever his head.

"This game of ours grows wearisome. Step out of the shadows, Violetta."

She almost lifted her foot. Tricksy bastard. He didn't know where she was exactly. Breathing slow and measured, Violet sidestepped along her plotted path. Her father tilted his head as if to listen.

Exposing his jugular. If ever there had been a time for her to teleport! Well, if wishes were horses, she'd gallop her ass across the room and be done with this shit. Especially since the little hairs climbing her nape reduced her to the prey, not the hunter.

Steeling her nerves with a bitty breath, Violet turned her shoulder to slink along the next wall. Here her steps couldn't falter, nor could the light in the room change. If her father lit more candles, she'd be illuminated in their yellow glow. Just as assuredly, he'd hear her heart if she didn't slow the damned thing down.

Thank fuck vampires didn't sweat. Although Uri did. His glossy skin moved over his chiseled muscles like watered silk, the sheen arresting her eye and turning her into a hedonist. She could rub her body across those oceans of rippling muscle, be weightless in the strength of those waves.

*Shit.* What was she doing? *Focus. Masturbate later when he's forgiven you.*

Yeah, there was that. Violet refrained from the urge to lick her lips. Any extra movement...

She tucked and rolled away the instant she felt the breeze of molecules brush across her face. Her father materialized in time to grab her arm and plunge a short knife into her shoulder.

He missed bone but pierced the flesh of her armpit. Biting down on a hiss, Violet twisted, yanking her arm up and back as she landed on her feet. Facing her father now, she lunged low to swipe her blade across crucial tendons. Without support, he'd flop like a landed fish.

Too bad picturing it didn't make it true. Never one to leave herself exposed while she struck, she deflected Dali's strike to her neck, the clumsy attempt merely pissing her off. Her father grew sloppy in the growing of his ego, and she hated him all the more for it. Where she had striven to become the best fighter she could be, he had nurtured his smugness.

She punched his hand away, the arc of his arm baring his side. Violet plunged her knife. Her father dissolved half his torso and grinned down at her.

What the fuck? Too late she realized she'd underestimated him. She'd been a fool to think he'd grown slovenly. It had cost her. Striking down with the arm he kept whole, his gleaming blade slashed past the front of her face.

Violet flinched backward. Strong arms closed around her from behind as someone else grabbed her ankles. Other cult members tore at her clothes, brutally gripping as she writhed to wrench free. The crack of bone ushered in a tidal wave of nausea, and spots of red blurred the faces of the vampires attacking her. Though her wrist screeched in stabs of pain as she struggled, Violet didn't stop. She kicked out and twisted, clawing at the cloaks hard enough to pierce the fabric and reach skin.

"Are you children? Get those chains on her!"

"Sir, she's strong with the Kynd blood..."

Violet hadn't heard that accent since the horrific era of Salem, but the words renewed her hope. Unable to see past the cloaks heavy as drapes surrounding her, she kicked out. This time the crack of bone felt satisfying.

As a pained shriek clogged the close atmosphere of smothering bodies, Violet's fangs lengthened in triumphant outrage. She whipped her face around to bite the hands holding her left arm.

The blow to her head rocked it so far sideways the muscles in her neck stretched. Had it broken her spine? The second punch blasted her brain to black.

———

*T*hird time was always the charm, wasn't it? As Uri dragged the blocks of stone to where he'd dropped the key during the second return to his chains, the struggle to free himself had seemed easier.

Which shouldn't be. Though he didn't have time to stick his face inside that horse's mouth. Pinching the key between his claws, he unlocked his cuffs and then the door. Pushing the grate open he…found himself chained to the wall again.

"Fuck!" But he didn't waste time or energy on frustration. As sure as he knew he had bones in his body, he knew Violet was in trouble. If it hadn't found her yet, it was going to. He didn't need this fae conundrum to convince him.

Once again throwing everything he could against the chains bolted to the wall, relief slipped through him as the stones gave way even easier than before. The block higher up fell on one tug. Grinding his jaw against the agony in his ankle, he pulled again, his breath gushing from his lungs when the block followed him.

Reaching for the key, which had returned to the floor where Violet had first placed it, Uri released himself from the cuffs and charged out the cell door. He dragged his long claws along the stone to slow himself down as he rounded a corner. Not expecting it, he smashed into another wall.

With his ass double-bouncing on the cold floor, Uri glanced up just as Kallen swore. "Son of a bitch!"

Eye level and sitting on his ass, he'd never seen a more beautiful face. "Nope, I've got no mother." Though his right arm didn't rise as high as his left, and he limped so Kallen closed more distance than he did, Uri hugged his brotherkynd like a man long kept from his family.

"How'd you find me?" He leaned back but didn't let go.

"Long story, but Drakus is getting some me time."

"He's here?" Which explained the weakening of the fae spell. Uri would bet his soul Drakus was wreaking vengeance—dragon-style.

"Everyone else should be here soon, too. We took a shortcut."

Although he breathed like a freight train, Uri smiled wide.

"You're a scary looking bastard, Kynd. Where's your girl?"

"Somewhere in this lunatic asylum looking for trouble."

"I'm warming up to her already." Kallen slapped him on the back as he turned to leave.

As his heart squeezed tight and its temp rose a few notches, Uri grabbed his brotherkynd's shoulder. "Kal, don't let go. I need an anchor. I'm loose, but not for long. Maybe with your extra weight and Drakus killing vamps, the fae magic won't twitch me back to where I started."

Kallen grinned as he latched on. "You always were the needy one."

Uri dragged him forward without sassing back. Right then he felt as needy as fuck. As in he needed Violet. He needed her to be okay. He needed her out of this godforsaken place. Uri opened his senses wide. With his blood in her, she wouldn't be hard to find.

With the fae still protecting this place, he didn't bother disassembling his molecules for a speedier trip. He threw one foot in front of the other the old fashioned way. Kallen ran with him, their hands locked.

Bustling up the spiraling stone steps, Uri felt the familiar drag and lowered his shoulder as he plowed on. "Hang on, Kallen. Don't let go!" Their momentum slowed so radically Uri thought they might be going backward. He pushed harder, his broken ankle shrieking.

Kallen, bless his rosy old soul, squeezed an arm around his waist and dragged him on. By the time they reached a great dining hall, the pull on him lessened enough for his brotherkynd to let his body go but still hold his hand.

Uri didn't mind. The hum doled out comfort. With every cell in his body aching for his mate, he could use the reassurance. "We're getting close." No sooner had he spit the words out past his lengthened fangs than the most beautiful sight Uri had ever seen—Violet not included—spilled into the room from the north and east archways.

"My brethren!" Uri's heart lit up like a Christian Christmas tree as Merrick, Kronos, and Darken arrived as synchronized as Big Ben. Anton, Godrick, and Kristov hustled in from the southern entrance, punctual as the clock's second hand.

"Where's Drakus?" Relief may have softened his edges, but Merrick's tightened jaw proved how worried he was about their missing brotherkynd.

"Glad to see you, too." Jesting, Uri clapped Merrick on the back. Now that they were all together, he worried about Drakus, too. With the dragon's history with the fae, it was hard telling if he'd be working with all his pistons. Emotional scars had a way of axing your legs out from under you.

Uri ought to know. Yet, with Violet to worry about, his past seemed more like a mosquito buzzing in the room after you turned out the lights. Bothersome as shit, but you could deal.

"Kynd, you are without a doubt the ugliest son of a...no, wait, he is." Godrick redirected his pointy finger to Kronos.

"Godrick!" Anton and Kristov reprimanded him stereo-style.

Uri growled low in his chest as he draped an arm around Kronos' linebacker shoulders. "Yeah, and I'm mean as piss. You think as Vampyre you're strong? Insult my brotherkynd again and we'll find out whose vampire is the stronger." Uri snapped his longer fangs for effect.

Godrick bristled like maybe he wanted to do it right then. But they'd stood around long enough. Violet needed to be found. "Now, if you'll excuse me, my Chosen One needs me."

Uri grew too big for his skin when his brethren filed in behind him. "I'm guessing the Triumvirate can't dematerialize, or they'd have been at the meeting place before us." Merrick curled his fingers around Uri's elbow. "Can you trace?"

"No." And it chafed his ass that he couldn't. Striding down a long hall, he picked up the scent of his brethren and spilled blood. "You've already been here."

"We cleaned house, so to speak." Darken flanked his other side, leaving Kronos and Kallen to pull rear guard.

"No sign of Violet. We must be going the wrong way." Uri stopped, confused that the others hadn't found her when they'd swiped through. Yet, despite all evidence to the contrary, the urge to go in this direction pulled at him.

His brethren drew up close, Darken gripping his elbows. "Brotherkynd, we were wrong before, and we're sorry. We wouldn't leave her. We want to find her as badly as you do."

"Doubt that." Uri looked long and hard down each end of the hallway. With the flames of the wall sconces flickering bright, he had to squint to see into the shadows. "What, they can't afford electricity?"

Darken released him and stepped back with the others. "It would mess with the plane of existence and give them away. Off the grid, they can hide like a turtle in its shell. There, but not."

"No wonder they were getting away with murder." As visions of Violet chained to the altar flashed across his frontal lobe, Uri shouldered through the knot of his brethren. The only thing easing the lead weight on his lungs was the lessening of the fae magic on his bones. Which meant the parasitic disciples were dropping like flies.

Which meant fewer unholy bastards to torture his Chosen One. The bear fur across Uri's shoulders bristled, and he swiped at the wall with his claws.

"Shit, brotherkynd, you are one scary S.O.B., true enough." Merrick grinned with lion's fangs. A chimera complimenting a fellow chimera.

Uri's throat closed at the camaraderie. None of his brotherkynd cared he was part vampire. It had been his delusion all along that he wouldn't be one of them if he partook of blood. The proof in accepting himself for who he was? The hum vibrating stronger under his skin whenever they all touched skin to skin at the same time.

Their old power hovered in the wings. Not yet ready for its grand comeback, but close enough to advertise the coming attraction. "We need to find Drakus." And blow this mausoleum to the ground like in the old days.

"Kronos. You, Darken and Merrick backtrack the way we just came. Kallen and I will push forward. I know you found nothing, but…" As he massaged his hand across his chest muscles, Kronos hugged him.

"Find her." He grinned the only way he could—tight lipped and locked jawed in case the screams burst forth. But his gray eyes shined bright like the sun behind a passing storm cloud, and that was the only thing that mattered.

A screwed up, motley crew they were, yet a crew nonetheless. Uri's breath lodged in his tightening throat. "I love you, guys. With all my heart, I love you."

"Right back at you, Bear. Now go find your gal while we search for Drakus. We'll meet up again in the dining hall."

*iolet first became aware of sound. Murmuring voices chanting as though in prayer. When she wriggled, the throbbing in the bones of her neck reminded her what had happened in the way stubbing your toe reminded you to pay attention to where you put your feet.

"Ah, you're awake."

Violet blinked like a wet butterfly flapping its wings. The moment her lids parted, she wished like hell she'd kept her eyes closed. Peering down over her front, she wrestled against the leather straps holding her down. When her father's face loomed into view, his reptilian glare gnawed all the way into her soul, chilling her.

"So, my spawn knows the joy of feeding from Kynd." When he smiled, it was more like the peeling back of his lips. A darkness passed through her, while every survival instinct she possessed screamed to life. Violet threw herself against her bonds.

Dali continued on, hovering over her as if she lay calm and accepting. "For once I am glad you are not dead, Violetta. With what runs through your veins, sacrificing you has become more beneficial than I'd dreamed. Finally, a reward for not allowing those villagers to burn you in the sun."

Violet stilled, her eyelids peeling back in fear. In spite of the searing pain in her spine, she tossed her head from side to side as two more faces loomed into view across from Dali's. She panted around the leather strip cutting into the corners of her mouth.

Oh, God, Uri had been right. She couldn't have defeated this evil with stealth, and certainly, couldn't have defeated it alone. Having been held here before, Uri had known what she'd be up against, and she'd left him chained in that cell. More to the point, she'd turned her back on him and left him behind.

A hot tear slipped down her temple and pooled at her ear. *Uri*. Who had never questioned her motives despite who she was. Even when he'd despised her for being vampire, he'd never harmed her. He had sought to know her while the horrors of this place had battered him.

Presented upon this altar like the sacrificial lamb, now she understood. Uri had overcome his past to…love her.

A sob broke past the gag, her jaw breaking wide as if to make room for the bubble of sorrow forging from her throat. She cried his name though no word formed. Two more faces hovered near, one licking its sharpened fangs in a macabre display of hunger.

She would die on this platform, and she hadn't told Uri she loved him. He would remember her as cruel, and he would curse her name as they drained him of blood on this same slab of stone, the one tainted with the death of his Chosen.

Dali cocked his head as he peered down at her. "All these centuries I had thought you brave. Now you cry when you serve us best?" He licked his lips as his fingers curled around her forearm. Gaze falling to where he held her, his smile twisted into something worshipfully sinister.

As her father lowered his head, the others joined him. Licking snail trails across her skin, scraping their fangs, their mouths growing rabid until Dali bit through her skin. Violet screamed as the rest followed suit, not caring if they pierced her veins or not. All they sought was blood, eating her alive as they lapped and suckled wherever their fangs punctured her flesh.

Over and over they reverently murmured *Kynd*.

As Violet writhed, arching her back off the stone slab and curling her feet, her thoughts fled to Uri still chained in that dank cage. He had endured this for centuries and would endure it for centuries more because of her. As the mouths sucked upon her skin, she shuddered in horror, repulsed by what these vampires did. Ghoulish in their appetites, there was nothing of herself in the male who had moved up her arm and now pierced his fangs into her shoulder. When her father lapped his tongue along the bleeding holes, Violet jerked away.

She was nothing like this male, even though he'd sired her. She was nothing like any of these twisted vampires. Her entire life she'd driven herself to be their antithesis when all along her soul had never been tainted as theirs surely were.

Uri had seen beyond her lineage and had loved her anyway. Even when she'd shunned him to pretend to side with her father he had remained true in his love for her. If that's what it meant to have Kynd blood in her veins, then she was proud to be aligned with them. Let the rest of the world assume the worst about the Grotesques. She knew the love and affection of one and counted herself to be the most blessed female on Earth.

She'd been a fool not to let Uri claim her, and now she would die with that regret weighing down on her soul. If only she could see him once again. Tell him how much she loved him. How proud she was to be part of his Kynd family, how humbled she was that he would want her to be.

When he appeared in her vision as she turned her face away from the feeding disciples, she sent a silent prayer to God for letting her see his image one more time before she died. Her throat full of tears and her lips parted with the leather gag, she murmured to the figure of her Uri, "I love you."

As his handsome face contorted with rage, and another Kynd fell in beside him, Violet blinked away the blood tears blurring her vision. A vampire lapped her lashes, expunging the beatific image of her true mate. But her heart surged with the hope that what she'd seen had been real.

Had Uri freed himself? Had his brotherkynd stepped forward to stand with him?

She screamed his name before she could temper her relief.

He answered with a roar that stripped her of fear and filled her with a passion to live. To touch that beautiful beast again, to feel his strong arms embracing her. Violet threw herself against her bonds as her father and his acolytes ceased their worshiping and bolted upright, facing the sound of Uri's bellow.

For one disciple, it was his last movement. A grizzly's claws slashed across his throat, severing his head so forcefully, Violet lurched back on the slab. One second the male's face held an expression of surprise and the next his head flew away.

The second vampire had time to register horror before his head, too, departed his neck.

Uri roared again, magnificent in his swift charge.

"*T*his one is mine." A guttural claim but Uri was so deep in his protective fury it surprised him to hear coherent words come out of his mouth. Finding Violet strapped to the very altar he'd been chained to, and the bodies sliding along her bloody skin, unleashed his memories the way you unclipped the collar of a rabid Rottweiler. A cyclone of emotions and vision-scapes ripped through him so fiercely, he thought when he spread his jaws another bellow of outrage would spew forth.

Guess he still had his mind, after all. Dali straightened with fear wobbling his eyeballs.

Uri's charge was swift and calculated. As Violet's father disappeared, he opened his senses wide and immersed himself in his chimera, embracing his vampire to fight a vampire. Yep, sure enough, three seconds later Dali reappeared at his daughter's head with a gleaming blade in his fingers. Uri was already standing between him and his beloved Chosen.

Snatching Dali's wrist, he gloried in the grinding of bone. With all the air in his lungs, he blasted his promise in the male's stricken face. "You will never harm her again!" As fleeting as the whir of a hummingbird's wings, Uri realized he cared little about his own safety. It was Violet who mattered. If it meant another thousand years on that altar in return for her wellbeing, he would do it without hesitation.

The insight slowed his demolition. Grinding the shattered bones together, he lowered his arm as Dali cowered to his knees, the unused blade clanging to the flagstone. Behind them, Kallen cut the leather bonds to free Vi.

"Come to me, Vi." A pang of insecurity twisted in Uri's gut. Raging as a full vampire mate, he knew he sounded overbearing. With his bear and gargoyle uncontained, he knew how monstrous he looked. Would she want him now? That tic of apprehension had him wringing Dali's broken wrist harder until the male cried out.

The mewl sent a shiver of satisfaction rippling over his skin and riled the bear fur capping his shoulders. With all his heart, he wanted to share that feeling. Turning his chin, he sought Vi, who stood on solid legs although Kallen kept his arm around her.

So brave! Yet the sight of her blood streaming down her bare skin almost unchained his composure. Uri curled his claws into his palm to stay the blow to Dali's head. Blood dripping through his fingers, he said, "He is yours." Again, his voice rolled out of his mouth on nothing more than a base growl. But his words were lucid. This was Vi's triumph as much as his. She'd earned the right to stand over this male as much as he had.

Dragging Dali with him, he turned to look upon his Chosen full on. "So splendid." His long fangs slurred his esses, but Vi lit up as if she glowed. Gaze on his, she stepped from Kallen's arms.

Without a word, she bent to snatch the blade from the floor and flipped the hilt so it nested in her palm. She kept her gaze on Uri, the intensity of it shivering across his skin, softening his muscles to peanut butter.

His cock pumped in his torn jeans, snapping an electric current through his core. Uri shivered to lustful life. Vi's bravery made him hard as a rock and pining to sheathe himself through that precious gap between her thighs.

As she strode toward him, one long leg in front of the other, his eyes drifted to that winking gap, and his free hand dropped to cup himself. How shameful! He held their tormentor in his fist while he lusted for his mate. As Uri averted his avid gaze, Vi reached for his chin, turning his face so he would look at her.

"You love me, yes?"

He nodded gently so as not to lose the touch of her fingers on his skin.

Amber eyes brimming with blood tears, she stood with her chin lifted in pride. "Then your need is nothing like what they've done. I accept your offering as a mating gift." With a mere dip of her bitten shoulder, she passed the blade across Dali's throat, ending the monster's life with little more than a flick of steel. "Finish it." She gazed up at him with eyes like stone. "Take his head."

Uri blinked, hope ballooning inside him. "Mating gift?"

The hint of a smile quirked the corner of her lips. Ignoring the male who gushed blood at their boots, Vi stepped closer so he felt the brush of her heat. "If you'll have me."

The hope inside him erupted like the unfolding of Drakus' wings, filling him until he thought he'd burst. In his excitement, he stepped back. It was the work of a second to release his tormentor's wrist and twist off his head.

As with the others, the conquest gave him little joy. Not when compared to Vi. Everything paled next to her. As Dali shriveled to dust, Uri closed the distance between them with a stride so great, that as he swept her into his arms the momentum carried them forward.

Tendrils of dead vampire swirled about Kallen and the bloody altar as he clapped his hand to his heart. "So…romantic."

"Shut up, and come on." Uri's grin spread from the inside to the out as he put his arm under Vi's knees to sweep her into his arms. Her giggle tickled like raining flower petals inside him. Delighted, he pressed Vi closer.

"Hey, I'm not an accordion." But her arm went around his neck so she'd stay where he'd put her. Uri threw his head back and coughed a laugh. So full! With his brotherkynd beside him and his female in his arms, he had to concentrate to make sure his boots were touching the floor.

He was pretty sure they flew to the dining hall where his brethren awaited them, relief washing over their faces as he and Vi and Kallen stepped into the room. "You found her!" As Merrick and Darken rushed forward, Vi stiffened in his arms.

Uri's boots stuck to the floor as he curled a shoulder to shield her. His brethren halted.

"We would not harm her." Simultaneously, they lowered their heads as if shamed in the company of a queen. "We swear, brotherkynd. We would not."

Uri looked to Vi, his question unspoken, but he knew it shone in his eyes. It didn't matter if he believed them or not, this was Vi's choice. The Chosen's prerogative to choose. Not just him but all of them.

"Set me down, Uri." As he did so, she placed one hand in his and the other at her hip. Searching for her blade? Christ on the cross. Though she had every reason not to trust his brethren. Kallen had been the one to free her from the altar, but Darken and Merrick had given her little reason to believe in their change of heart.

He followed the trail of her gaze to Drakus and Kronos.

"What's wrong with him?" Violet nudged her chin.

Uri saw what she did. A broken male, stained not just on the outside, but inside as well. Kronos hovered near to offer comfort but didn't touch him, even though Drakus shook like a bobble head doll. With his arms wrapped tight around his knees, he looked like someone trying to hold his body together.

He probably was. Uri sucked in a lungful of air, hoping the oxygen would ease the tightening of his chest. "The fae." As if that explained everything.

Violet's eyebrows lifted then furrowed. "He came here knowing the vampires were protected by the fae?"

Wrapping an arm around her waist, Uri tugged her against the wall of his stomach, as much to offer her protection as to comfort himself with the feel of her skin. "We're Kynd. It's an all for one sort of thing."

She turned her perceptive gaze onto Kallen. "As Chosen, I'm one of you then." It wasn't an accusation. He felt the trembling of her hand in his and squeezed to reassure her. She gripped back. "All right. Consider yourselves on probation."

You'd have thought she'd granted them the keys to the city. Which in a way she had. With her acceptance, she'd unlocked the door on her heart to males who had yet to show her a kindness. Not a trifling gift.

"We deserve nothing more." Darken lowered to one knee, his shoulders rounding as he dropped his head. Merrick knelt beside him. The clanking of chains raised all their heads as Drakus and Kronos joined them.

Uri's heart plummeted like Icarus, as though he'd been soaring too close to the sun and reality, with its ever present drag of gravity, reclaimed him. "What is this, brotherkynd?"

*V*iolet leaned forward, anxious to hear why a free male would bind himself in chains. Yeah, he looked like he was chasing a serious head fuck, but still. To chain yourself?

Drakus lifted his chin. Peering out from his stained face, his eyes were as haunted as those she'd seen in the days of public executions. "I would touch the Chosen I killed for."

Holy. Shit. As if she'd say *no*? Her hand was already reaching out, a reflex to comfort one so shattered. Broken because he'd come to help her and couldn't bear the weight of consequence? Again, holy shit.

The moment his fingertips touched the skin on her forearm, her body became a conduit between Uri and the other Kynd. Drakus pressed his fingers deeper into her flesh as if he fought not to yank his hand away. With the buzz of a million flies vibrating through her, she could understand why.

She remembered how he'd shunned her before after he'd screamed to the rafters that touching her was a mortal sin. A sin he'd been violently punished for—by the fae. Assholes, every one. Without releasing Uri, Vi twisted her wrist so they locked forearms.

Drakus' eyes bulged wide, but he held on. When Kallen curled his fingers over their entwined arms, Drakus clamped his jaw as if to lock down the shrieking. Merrick and Darken stepped closer to Uri. "Anton and Godrick are teleporting in Daniela and Angelia." Violet barely heard Merrick over the hum's crescendo.

The males stood as if they braced against a strong wind. She felt like she was hooked up to the electric chair. "Hold on!" She barely heard Uri's shout, and she was pressed against him.

"Give us two minutes to get the rest of the prisoners out!" The Vampyre Anton thrust his face into the knot of their bodies. When the other Chosen snuggled in tight to their Kynd, the hum exploded into a shower of non-stop fireworks. The bursting was invisible, but the tremors were knocking Violet off her boots. How Angelia and Daniela—mere humans—were holding on was a testament to Darken's and Merrick's fierce connection to them.

Knowing her face mirrored the awed determination of the other Chosen, and afraid she'd spontaneously combust, Vi pressed her body tighter to the rock solid anchor of Uri's. The reprieve loosened her airway and she took a blessed breath, reconnecting with gravity at the same time she concentrated on the band of electricity she was joined to.

Which appeared to be maintaining, as if it had maxed out in strength and was content to hum along at this frantic intensity. Although it was clear Drakus, with his eyes squeezed shut and his chest heaving up and down like a San Francisco earthquake, wasn't going to hold up much longer.

Violet glanced around to catch all eyes on Drakus, too, like they knew where the weak link was. "Now!" It was her only warning. All that fierce energy burst outward, and the only image forming in her head was the televised version of an A-bomb test, where an abandoned house was flattened in a nanosecond, its beams and siding blowing apart like matchsticks. Then she was squished to an implacable body, with Daniela and Angelia joining her.

Uri held them together, his huge arms snugging tight like the armed seatbelts on a carnival ride. A flash later, and the fairway turned into the foyer of the safe house.

"What the hell?" Still a little dizzy, Violet pushed off as Uri released her.

"I'll be right back." He disappeared as if she'd imagined him. What she hadn't imagined was what he'd done. Uri had teleported three women and himself, something even the powerful Vampyres of the Triumvirate couldn't do.

"This is insane." Daniela paced like she had to work off the funsies. Hand on her forehead, she turned to Vi. "You do this all the time?" She was grinning like she'd won the Megabucks.

Violet shrugged, her mind still wrapping itself around Uri's feat and the bomb blast of their collective energy. "Yeah, but what the hell just happened?"

"The Kynd equivalent of a car bomb. Back up, more should be coming." Angelia spread her arms out like a woman slamming on the brakes and playing seatbelt with her passenger. Violet shimmied backward, snagging Daniela's wrist as she went. If Uri was coming in for a landing with the others, he'd need the space.

No sooner had they cleared the runway when in he came with Drakus, who still wore his chains. Uri didn't let him go. Good thing, since the male looked ready to do his own detonating. With his muscles straining against the iron cuffs, no way in hell were they going to hold against the strength of someone gone blitzo.

Drakus shrieked, the sound registering somewhere between the hopeless agony of a human and the outraged blast of a mythical flying beast. Though there wasn't anything fabled about the torment in the strains coming out of his stretched mouth.

"Come with me." Uri didn't wait to see who obeyed. Biceps bulging, he muckled Drakus in a Kynd version of the Heimlich and booked it for the door under the curved staircase.

Vi followed like she was sucked into his wake.

"Uri, what about Merrick?" Angelia dug in her loyal heels, refusing to circle the drain of Drakus' needs. Not without her man, at any rate.

"They're coming with Godrick. Your father and Kristov are with the prisoners. He said something about *triage*." Short sentences, but succinct enough to get the point across. There had been others in that dungeon. While Drakus and the Kynd had been a wrecking ball with the cult members upstairs, the Triumvirate had been helping prisoners escape from down below.

A two-front attack that had been executed as if it had been borrowed from the *Art of War*. Violet knew the sect had been annihilated because Uri had been able to teleport them out. The bargain with the fae had been severed along with a bunch of rogue vampire heads.

Too bad the same couldn't be said for the male Uri was ushering down to the basement. Still emotionally tied to what the fae had done to him, Drakus and his dragon had faced his greatest horror to free her and Uri. Violet owed that dragon more than her blood, she owed him and his brethren her entire future.

She followed like the bonds weren't just attached to Uri but to the other Kynd as well.

Not wasting time on thank you's, Uri barged down the column of stone steps ahead of her and stopped only when he was once again inside a cell. This time the prisoner shackled his own chains to the wall. Shaking his head, Uri risked a quick hug then backpedaled out, clanging the steel door shut. He plastered his front to it as he looked in through the face-sized hole cut into the top of the thick slab.

Shoulder muscles flexing, he gripped each side of the door. Violet placed her hand to the small of his broad back. It was bare now and sweaty, the thick coat of the grizzly that had been capping his shoulders and trailing his spine had retreated now that the threat was gone. "I'm sorry."

As if she'd sprung him loose from his thrall, Uri twisted in his boots and snagged her to him so tight a shoe horn would have failed to pry them apart. His hand cupped her head, and he rubbed his whiskered cheek along her hair as if drawing sustenance from the scent of her.

Violet dug her nails into the twin dimples sitting just above his tight butt. Need burned through her, and the only way to douse the forest fire consuming her was to rub all over the wonderfully smelling male in her arms. Pressing her forehead to his sternum, she moaned the words riding her hard. "Claim me." The command crept up her throat on a steamy sigh, her throat ground it into a wanton plea.

Mustering her shattered strength, Violet only just kept herself from dropping to the floor, where she wanted to writhe seductively, to arch her back and thrust her suddenly heavy breasts upward.

Uri growled as he pushed his hips against her, his bulge seeking. In a blink, they were in his bedroom, his big palms cupping her ass. He lifted her so she balanced on the tent in his jeans. Violet locked her legs around his waist as she looked up into his face.

A face chiseled with barely harnessed aggression. Yet she was captivated by his eyes. They were liquid black and brimming with the same need she felt. Uri took her mouth hard, their fangs locking then sliding past each other; his tongue slid along hers, teasing, promising, tasting the blood he'd nicked from her lip.

Fangs singing in her gums, Violet dragged her mouth from Uri's and struck his jugular as hard as he'd struck his kiss. He groaned, dropping to his knees as he pulled her closer. Hips rocking an age-old rhythm, he let his head fall back. "Yes, Vi, yes."

Violet forgot everything. Uri's past, her fears. Need engulfed her, and she surrendered herself to its rush—a female vampire under the thrall of an enormously strong mate.

---

*T*he little sucks of her mouth on his vein registered as a thumping in his shaft, as if Violet pulled his blood through the straw of his cock. Uri pressed her head to his neck so she wouldn't stop. With his other hand, he flicked his erection free and palmed it. The thing sprung heavy and thick and sang through his nuts, up into his guts. The hairs on his ass sprung to lively attention as he glided his rough palm down its silken length.

Craving Violet's small hand on his arousal, he released himself and sought her grip like his hand was a blind bird flailing around. Thank fuck she seemed to know what he begged for. Her fingers curled around his shaft and squeezed hard. Uri almost blew his seed. He let his jaw flop open to snarl *again* when it struck him that she should be riding this level of bliss.

Like an animal, he tore off her cargo pants so he could finger her slick cleft. Violet suckled harder, mewls escaping her throat after every swallow. Riding on instinct, he dragged his dripping fingers through his mouth, tasting the flavor of his mate. Her pungent scent slid down his throat and wafted up into his nose. Snarling, he milked her with flicking circles of his thumb as he dipped his fingers deeper. She pulsed and squeezed around his knuckles, her sheathe creaming.

God, he wasn't going to make it. The sensations were too much. Uri ground his teeth together, mining for control of his throbbing shaft. Violet's fangs in his neck was her claiming him, and he abandoned himself to the rightness of it. He was vampire, and this delectably scented and soft female in his arms was his. All his. He wanted to beat on his chest, he wanted to roar the power of his conquest.

What he did was hook his arm under her plump ass as he staggered to his feet so he could push his jeans down his thighs. Letting his knees unhinge, he lined himself up so that when his kneecaps banged to the floor, he thrust his hips at the same time he took hold of Violet's pelvic bones.

She slid down over his cock like a hot, wet fist.

Gripping hard as a drowning man to the gunnels of a lifeboat, Uri threw his head back and bellowed, his lips stretched wide over his fangs. Then he slashed the barrier of her camisole with a careful claw and sank his teeth into her bobbing breast.

With his mate sheathed around his ramming cock and her blood on his tongue, Uri spit his seed, his ass thrusting. The sucking at his neck synchronized with the kicking of his dick, and he groaned, lost in the sensation of ownership and of being owned.

He had never felt so entirely consumed. He wanted more. He needed more. Yet, he gently pulled his fangs from Vi's bulbous flesh and lapped to seal the punctures. Lids heavy, he gazed at his mark, a flush of pride suffusing his whole body.

Their mingled scents were everywhere. Inside him, outside, on her skin, radiating from it. Uri buried his nose in the slope of her neck as Vi's channel shuddered and clamped in little aftershocks around his softening shaft. Their juices wetted his balls, but he gloried in the spreading of their mated scent.

Lungs squeezing, he let out a shuddered breath. His hands shook as he caressed them up his mate's back, her skin so warm and soft in contrast to the roughened pads of his palms. Yet their bodies fit like locking puzzle pieces. He would swear he heard the click as her arms snaked around his neck, and she let her head fall upon his shoulder.

"I love you, Vi." The declaration tumbled from his lips and he fell still, awaiting…something. Her rejection. The accord as to how right they fit together. When she pulled back to look at him, he met her gaze straight on. He'd claimed her, the words a mere side salad to the meal of what had truly taken place.

He would never release her, not now—the vampire too possessive and plowing over his bear and gargoyle parts. Uri didn't care, not when Vi was his prize.

Violet held his gaze, her fangs still long from feeding, a teardrop of blood smeared at the corner of her lips. "You are mine, as well." Possessive little vampire. She placed her hand over his pounding heart and leaned in to brush her lips to his. "I love you, too, Uri."

Heart growing too big behind his ribs, he blurted, "I would have chosen you even if God had not."

Violet sat back on his thighs and cupped his jaw in her hands. Blood tears lined her lowered lids, but that wasn't what Uri saw. Joy shined from her amber eyes. Joy he'd given her just by being honest with her. And with himself.

"Now let me prove it, more gently this time." Uri leaned in to press his lips to hers and waited for her to soften, to open up to him. Exactly how he wanted their love to be—considerate, but above all else, accepting. He didn't even notice that the sun had been up for so long it had melted the icicles lining the eaves.

Violet spread her thighs as Uri nestled himself home.

Ω

# ACKNOWLEDGMENTS

*Acknowledgement*

Thanks to the usual suspects. You three know who you are.
My gratitude also extends to Sherri Good, my editor at Melange Books, who whips my work into viewing shape.
And finally, to J, R, and C, who respectfully left me in my private hell when my deadline loomed.
This story couldn't have been written without help.
As no man is an island, neither is an author alone on her journey.
Thank you all.

**THANK YOU FOR READING**

Did you enjoy this book?

We invite you to leave a review at the website of your choice, such as Goodreads, Amazon, Barnes & Noble, etc.

**DID YOU KNOW THAT LEAVING A REVIEW...**

- Helps other readers find books they may enjoy.
- Gives you a chance to let your voice be heard.
- Gives authors recognition for their hard work.
- Doesn't have to be long. A sentence or two about why you liked the book will do.

**Don't miss out on your next favorite book!**

**Join the Melange Books mailing list at**
www.melange-books.com/mail.html

**Subscriber Perks Include:**

- First peeks at upcoming releases.
- Exclusive giveaways.
- News of book sales and freebies right in your inbox.
- And more!

**Eager to hear what's next for S. C. Dane?**

*Join her mailing list!*

www.scdane.com

# ABOUT THE AUTHOR

© Leah Yetter, Photographer

S.C. Dane currently lives in Wyoming on a working cattle ranch. When she's not riding horses on the range, she's immersed in her second passion: writing. She loves traveling, too, and isn't sure what adventures her next move will find for her.

*You can get to know a little more about the author on her website*
www.scdane.com

## Also by S. C. Dane

### *Luna*
### *Book One of The Luna Chronicles*

Beth is a misfit struggling to be a responsible woman in human society. Then she meets Alec, a mysterious stranger, who knows by her scent that she is a rare Luna, the only being who can ensure the future of his wolf-pack.

When human beings injure Alec, Beth retreats from the stagnant safety of her human world and surrenders her fate to the wolf-man. Beth's and Alec's love for one another ignites the power of the Luna that courses through her veins, and she must learn the laws of being wild wolf if she is to live with Alec and his pack. But they are not the only wolf-people who covet the blood of Luna, and Beth must learn to harness the consuming power of her Luna and use it to safeguard her new family, even if it means giving up the very thing she was born to protect.

Set in the countryside of Maine, this novel unfolds as Beth surrenders her body to its absolute essence while she is protected by the loyal wolves she is destined to love. But their world is not only precious, it is also perilous, and Beth's freshened passion for life just may be the catalyst for her death.

---

### Prologue
### ~ Found ~

I shouldn't have been thinking I saw a wolf.

Not in Downeast, Maine. The area is famous for lobster boats and granite coastlines; not its wildlife, unless you're scouting for Atlantic puffins and sea ducks. It's not the hotbed of wolf sightings and has never been wolf territory, not even when the Pasamaquady people populated the shores.

Why, then, did I spot a large wolf-like animal while I was hiking out on the Great Heath that edges the inland border of my tiny coastal town? I followed the creature's paw prints without losing a single step, until that trail ended with a naked man standing within a thicket of alders, trying modestly to cover his lower half.

He was tall, and muscular; his hands clutching at the silver stem of an alder were beautiful. Long and oddly elegant compared to the rest of his scarred body. His chest heaved, as though he'd been running, and I swore I saw his heart pounding—it matched my own.

"What the... What are you doing out here?" I lashed out at him with my tongue hoping to scare the man off before he attacked me, or worse, raped me. Who knew what a naked stranger could do in the middle of the woods. He cocked his head as if my words made no sense to him.

"This is private property and you're trespassing." It wasn't, but he didn't need to know that.

The man tilted his head again, and gazed at me with golden eyes; then crouched down as if to pick something up off the ground. As soon as his fingers touched the earth, he thrust himself backward into the alder thicket where he was hidden by the swaying branches. Yet, it was the wolf I'd been tracking that dashed out of that thicket, not the naked man.

"Holy crap." My feet rooted to the ground and wouldn't move until the animal was long out of sight. My shaking hand went to my throat as I pushed my way into the alders for a closer look. I was being extremely stupid; I hadn't seen the man leave and he could've still been lingering.

Yet, I knew in my racing blood that the naked man wouldn't be anywhere around. Somehow, some improbable way, he was with the wolf.

I chased them until the tracks of the wolf disappeared into the mosses of the heath, knowing even before then I'd never catch up with them. I was a good runner, but no way could I have matched the speed of that wolf.

And the man? Not a trace, no matter how hard I scanned the area. I turned tail for home, telling myself I'd imagined the whole thing, that the sight of a man and a wolf together, especially in downeast Maine, was too bizarre for reality.

Wasn't it?

CHAPTER ONE

Early mornings were my favorite time of the day, when every sound was hushed in the predawn darkness. The coffee pot hissed on its plate and the kitchen clock clucked out the time in a monotonous echo. I liked to curl up, my bathrobe wrapped around me like a blanket, into my favorite chair and gaze out of the picture window.

For a time, I would stare at my reflection in the plated glass, where my features were distorted and shadowed, and some days I was intrigued by how beautiful the absence of light could make them. It was like studying a stranger; someone who wasn't me—the orphan whose bones had never molded to fit into society's box, the girl-child who preferred the comfort of the wave-worn rocks of the shoreline, or the alder-strewn thickets that curled like the fingers of the earth, where I pretended to be a baby bird cupped in its palm.

But the lovely image would fade as mourning doves cooed in the dawn, and it was then that my real life smothered itself upon me; I was no longer suspended in the glass, safe from the reproachful eyes of a small town.

The morning after I'd spotted the wolf and man had been no different. Except I wasn't serene, but vibrated with anticipation to get back out onto the heath, just in case that wolf-man combination had been real. And didn't that just reveal the truth of why I had to escape to the isolation of the woods to run every day. I still harbored a kernel of hope there was something more in this world than what was on its surface. Could there be something more mystical and untainted as the heath I retreated to?

The ringing of the phone startled me back to reality. It was Liz, wondering if I had to work that evening.

"Yeah, I'm filling in for Sarah. There's a game up at the high school." Baseball season was in full swing and since I was childless and had no vested interest, I often volunteered to change shifts with the other waitresses who did have families. "You going?"

"Probably. Zach won't want to miss it." Liz let out a sigh. As the only chauffer for her kids, she spent a lot of time at school functions she would have been happy to miss. It was social time for the kids, and not necessarily for their mother.

"Yeah, I figured. Why don't you guys drop in at the restaurant before the game for pie? My treat."

"Sounds good, I'll see ya then. Oh, wait, I almost forgot." Liz's voice returned to a normal level when she put the receiver back up to her ear. "Did you hear?"

"No, what?"

"Janet Faulkingham's daughter didn't get on the bus this morning."

"So." I forced an even register of tone into my voice as my mind raced back to the day before on the heath, where I'd seen the mysterious man.

"So? So, she didn't get on the bus, but she did go to the bus stop."

Surely, I prayed to any gods who might be listening, there was too much of a coincidence between what I'd seen in the woods and the Faulkingham girl's disappearance for there to be any connection. "She probably just wandered off," I replied, as much to console myself as Liz.

"That's what her parents think, too, so they've been scouring the town. Anyway, I've gotta go. I'll talk with ya later."

I hung up the phone but couldn't take my hand off the receiver. A missing girl, who probably had just gone to a friend's house and didn't tell her parents. Jonesport was a small town—where the crimes usually consisted of domestic disputes and petty thefts. But just to be sure, I promised myself I'd do some eavesdropping while I was waiting tables at the restaurant.

Right then I needed to get hiking out on the heath before I had to go to work. I had to have another look around, maybe find more tracks that led to the wolf or the man, because even after returning to my regular life, my innards still felt eerily unhinged, and my stomach knotted with the prospect of seeing them again.

Unable to do anything but heed my body's yearnings, I let go of the phone, booked it for the heath, and was swallowed up by the overgrown alders along the edge of the road in no time.

It felt supreme to stretch my muscles, and as they warmed, my pace quickened. I leapt and lunged from one uneven step of the path to the next, my steps squishing in the moss as water oozed up past the soles of my boots.

I didn't care which way I zigged and zagged until the trail abruptly ended and I stood amidst a cluster of smothering spruce boughs. My breaths steadied as I inhaled deep and exhaled slowly, feeling fresher with each spruce laden lungful of oxygen.

But the cadence of panting that filled my ears wasn't my own and my bladder constricted as I glanced through the thicket. The rapid breathing came from my left, about thirty feet away. I swirled around to face it but it was always to my left, as if circling.

"Who's there?" My voice was a violation in that wooded world.

The breaths slowed, became barely audible. They also stopped circling.

My mind scurried with a mental check of my pockets. They were pathetically empty, which meant I had nothing for a weapon except my panic. The curiosity I'd felt earlier abandoned me. I took a deep breath to calm myself and shifted my eyes from one dark bough to the next. Nothing. Not even the panting.

A chipmunk screeched from a higher branch and I flinched, then tore off down the trail and fled back the way I'd come. My pace didn't slow until the alders thinned and I could just make out Main Street. By the time I emerged from the woods I was walking, albeit still breathing pretty hard.

I chided myself for being such an ass. Here I was on the cusp of the fantasy I'd nurtured my entire life and I'd been afraid. Brilliant. But I'd get a second try. I knew myself well enough to know that I wouldn't stop hiking out onto the Great Heath; that I couldn't stop venturing out into the woods if I was going to keep my sanity.

I tried shoving the whole episode out of my mind. I headed home for a hot shower and got ready for work. Before I left the house, I put on my crappy, comfy sneakers since I would be standing on hard linoleum for the rest of the day. The restaurant was the only place to eat in town, which meant it was usually bustling. There would be the occasional lull, but that was when I refilled the sugars and anything else that had been emptied in the course of the day.

The interior of the restaurant was set up so the commercial fishermen could come in and sit at a communal table, drink coffee and shoot the breeze. Or argue and lie. They were fishermen, after all, and they came and went throughout the day, depending on the weather. If it was nice and no wind blew, I wouldn't see most of them until late afternoon when they clomped in for pie and coffee before they headed home to get out of their heavy rubber boots and fishy smelling clothes.

But the restaurant was also the hub of any gossip going around, so I kept a close ear on what was being said. Most of the talk, however, wound up being about the latest stranglehold the biologists were wrapping around the necks of the lobster fishermen. It was Liz who ended up filling me in on the Faulkingham girl's disappearance.

"Really?" I asked, once she was finished.

"Really." Liz eyeballed me as if I had two heads. "Where have you been?"

I didn't have the nerve to tell her what I'd been up to; that I'd seen a wolf and a naked man in the same day. In the same place. I knew Liz thought I was a tad strange as it was, even if she was a friend. Nobody in town hiked the heath like I did, so I kept my trap shut and taunted her instead.

"Obviously, not hanging around listening to gossip." I tilted my chin and gave Liz a challenging leer.

"Whatever. Anyways, Kristy still hasn't been found. I mean, where does a ten year old girl go?" She glanced at the booth behind her where her kids were stuffing pie into their faces, then leaned across the counter toward me. "Unless," she whispered, "she didn't go anywhere."

I knew what she meant, so I shoved the image of my hike out of my mind. "Are the police out looking for her now?"

"Of course! Jesus, Beth. The kid is missing. God, I wonder about you sometimes." Which she did. Even though Liz was a transplant and hadn't grown up in Jonesport, she'd managed to pick up on the fact I wasn't firmly attached to this town and its people. "But, listen. I gotta go. That game will start soon and if I don't get there by the first pitch..." She rolled her eyes as she slid off her stool.

"Yeah, yeah. If you don't get there when it starts, Zach will pitch a fit. I know."

Liz shouldered her purse and readied her one-ton wad of keys. "Come on you two." The kids thanked me for the pie and followed their mother out to the parking lot.

I got busy filling sugar containers, napkin holders, and taking orders. The men jabbered, but I heard nothing new about the Faulkingham girl. As the evening wore on, I'd completely forgotten about her.

By seven-thirty in the evening the place was relatively empty, save for a tourist couple eating fried clams in the back dining room. I was sweeping up for the night when someone came in through the door. I started giving him my spiel about the restaurant being ready to close before I looked up.

"The grill is turned off, but we can make you a san..." I glanced up and there he was. The man I'd seen out on the heath. This time, though, he had clothes on; which I barely noticed, because his almond-shaped eyes mesmerized me just as they'd done before. And just like our first encounter, I felt like I was standing on the rim of a deep chasm, my life tenuously suspended.

Holy. What a customer.

He stood as tall as I remembered, so I had to tilt my head back a bit. The way his eyes slid down my neck while he swallowed made me feel like my throat lay bared to a welcome predator; welcomed because my weight tipped to my toes and my heels lifted.

He leaned in a bit, too, dropping his wide shoulders as he cocked his chin as if to accept my invitation with his mouth.

Dearest God. It wasn't a kiss he wanted, even though my lips parted with the lifting of my jaw.

But he pulled back to speak instead, dispelling the silence that charged the room. His voice was throaty; the rasp of it stroking my skin like a caress, making it blush as if he'd touched me.

"A sandwich, please." He took a seat at the end of the counter, leaving me to stand by my pile of dirt like a scarecrow, the broom handle resting in the hand I forgot I had. From behind him where he couldn't see, I let my gaze feast on the cut of his muscled back that narrowed at his waist.

His sitting finally snapped my brain back to its purpose, and I rounded the counter to write his order on my pad while I checked out the curl of his sandy-silver hair along his jaw line.

He clenched that smooth cut of bone so hard the muscle bulged like a baby's fist, and he swallowed, shooting a quiver straight to my moistening loins.

Christ.

I bustled out to the cook, flipped him the order slip, filled a glass with milk and set it down in front of my mysterious customer, then grinned like an idiot.

"It's on the house," I said, because I couldn't possibly say anything more stupid, and grabbed my rag to wipe down a spotless counter. From the corner of my eye, I could see him tip the glass to his lips and drain it. Then he turned his chin and looked squarely at me, rushing me back to the alder patch, to where my heart had throbbed out of my chest.

"Thank you." The corners of his mouth lifted into a smile, and his eyes, a luminous gold, sparkled.

I dropped my gaze to keep my body from pooling to the floor, and rested my attention instead on his hand still holding the empty milk glass.

He followed my stare, then shoved those elegant hands into his coat pockets like they embarrassed him. I noticed a faint residue of dark soil, as if he were a gardener, perpetually close to the ground; a lover of the earth and its gifts.

The bell from the kitchen clanged from a hundred miles away, announcing his order was ready. I shot him a look of regret, and peeled myself away from him.

Once I was removed from his presence, I remembered my customers in the other dining room. I retrieved his plate from the kitchen, poured him another glass of milk, and presented his meal like I was the one who'd slaved to fix it for him, all breathy and shy, then retreated to the back to check on the clam-eating tourists before I made a bigger ass out of myself.

When I returned, my frantic stare went from the empty plate with the bills flattened out beside it to my stranger, who halted by the door and turned his face toward me, revealing his baby-fisted jaw.

"Thank you for the meal," he pushed through his clenched teeth as he lowered his head, those eyes pinning me via my pelvis just like his voice did, as if he actually brushed his fingers between my thighs.

I'd thought this man threatening? Uh-uh. I opened for him like I've never done for another living soul, and that shot my heart rate so high I felt my skin flush; I loathed to see him leave.

"Hey, I don't suppose we've met before, have we?" I asked, hoping to stall him.

Did he just stiffen and cringe?

"No," I muttered to ease him, of all things. "I suppose not."

My tall, mysterious stranger turned his broad back, stepped out through the door and disappeared into the night. No headlights left the parking lot; he'd come on foot. His hasty departure and his pained reaction to my question cleared up any doubts. We had met before. But, I had also just embarrassed the snot out of him. I couldn't wait for the next day so I could go out on the heath again to look for him. I told myself it was to apologize, but my heart knew the difference. I wanted to be in his presence again, to see myself reflected in those enthralling gold eyes, to feel the scrape of his voice.

I snatched up my broom and swept the nervous anticipation out of my body; then rang out my last customers of the night, shut off the lights, and locked up behind me.

---

The next morning, in spite of the heavy fog and the promise of rain, I was sitting at the kitchen table lacing up my boots. No way was I going to let a little rain keep me out of the woods. I donned my raingear and beat feet for the heath, barely noticing the easing of the darkness as dawn approached.

Once I crossed into the woods, I forced myself to slow my pace. I didn't want to make too much noise, even though my rain pants swished with every step. I kept my eyes peeled for movement of any kind as the forest woke around me. The damp air muted the noises of the woods, excepting the crows, who squawked boisterously. They were happy to be out and about early that morning, too.

I hiked on until all sounds from town had disappeared, then squatted on a stump to rest and just breathe in the forest air. A light drizzle started to fall, and the earthy aroma of the woods burgeoned so I could just make out the faint pungency of the peat on the heath. I wasn't far from the bog. I'd kept it to my left as I'd hiked, preferring instead to stick to the comfort of the thicker woods.

The drizzle increased to a steadier rain but I remained on my stump and listened to its patter. The morning was tranquil, the forest flushing my senses so even if I didn't see anyone special, the hike would've still been enough to soothe me. I closed my eyes to better smell and hear my surroundings.

When I finally opened them, I looked right at the wolf I'd seen the other day, and kicked myself backward onto my ass where I sat sprawl-legged on the ground with the nub of the stump between my knees.

Holy crap.

I hadn't even heard it approach, yet the thing sat less than twenty feet away under an old tamarack tree, gazing straight at me, its ears pricked forward as if registering every jabbing beat of my heart. The wolf's fur was matted from the rain, but its undercoat was fluffy and dry. It sat on its haunches, its front legs straight as iron I-beams.

Then it wagged the tip-end of its brushy tail, and for some unknown reason, I started to hum. Low at first, like a lullaby. The wolf laid its belly upon the spruce needles of the forest floor and cocked its head. Encouraged, I righted myself back onto my perch and hummed louder, crooned out every nursery song I could think of; combined the tunes to stretch out the ones I only knew the chorus to.

Still, the repertoire wasn't endless; and when I finally quit singing, the wolf sat up and yawned. Jesus, but it had big teeth. Every brain cell screamed for me to run, yet I must've grown roots into that stump because I couldn't get up.

The wolf could though, and it stepped cautiously toward me as if I would hurt it. Its ears swiveled toward every snap or chirp around us, yet I homed my focus on the eyes of the wolf, which were bright with flecks of gold, and their almond-shaped rims were lined with black, like the kohl on the eyes of an Indian prince.

The creature snuffled my shins, its furred lips puffing as its nostrils expanded, and a burning shiver zipped down my spine when its nose touched my hand. The wolf lurched backward as if shocked, but it didn't run. Instead, it stepped closer again and lowered its head, stringing every nerve in my body taut.

I'd seen that same gesture the night before at the restaurant.

Emboldened by that slightest coincidence, I whispered a soft hello.

The wolf cocked its head. Then it stiffened and curled its claws into the earth, as if it were trying to grab pawfuls of dirt. Then, with a flinch and a flick, it pivoted and bounded off toward the heath, vanishing into the spruce boughs in a few short strides.

Holy mother. I didn't bother chasing the wolf this time. I ripped my roots out of the stump and made my way for home, where a hot shower awaited. I replayed the event over and over as the steaming water spit down on me, and still I shivered with the excitement of having touched a wild wolf. But, was it really a wolf?

Did I honestly think, based on the similarities of a gesture, the wolf and the man were the same creature? Impossible, right? Except I couldn't ignore the replacement of that disjointed feeling I'd had previously with the tight coiling of my belly, as if a sunbaked snake had taken up residence, warming me from within. I shut off the shower and got myself ready for work out of sheer habit.

I wound up being a useless waitress and asked my boss to let me off early. I told him I might be coming down with the flu, but what I really wanted to do was just go home and burrow into bed with the blankets hauled around my ears. Turns out, it was a good plan. I immersed myself in the images of the wolf and the man, then dropped into a heavy slumber as if I were curled into the safest place on earth, like I was that baby bird in the alders of my childhood.

The jangling of the telephone woke me up the next morning and I cracked an eye against the sunshine streaming into the bedroom. For the first time in years, I'd slept until mid-morning, and scraped the crust from my eyes as I reached for the phone beside the bed.

"You're alive." It was Liz on the other end.

My mind cartwheeled to the day before. How did she know?

"Sarah at the restaurant told me you had the flu or something."

Ah. I put my feet onto the floor and stood up. My head felt thick, like I'd been on a bender the night before. Maybe I really did have the flu.

Liz continued, unaware I hadn't said a word yet.

"Anyways, they found the Faulkingham's girl. They found Kristy."

Oh, Jesus. Liz's anxious tone poked a sharp finger into my worst fear: the wolf had killed the girl. "What happened?" I got a flush of heat that always comes just before I throw up.

Liz's voice came from far away. "She was attacked. Killed. The police aren't saying anything yet, but my God, Beth, it could've been Trish."

I heard the panic in her voice, her hysteria rising. My encounter with the wolf the day before popped crisply into focus. "Do they have a suspect?" I croaked out the question, afraid of the answer.

"Not yet, and that's got everybody scared."

I sat down on the edge of the bed; the exhale of relief deflating me. My reaction to this was all wrong. I should have been frightened, angry, or concerned for my friend. I shouldn't have cared whether they strung that wolf up by its bushy tail. Or the man. But, no matter how much I tried to think he or it was responsible, I couldn't. My instincts railed against the idea they, he, or it was guilty. Reason told me one encounter did not an expert make, but I couldn't shake my conviction.

"Are you still there, Beth?"

"Yes, I'm here. Listen, Liz, everything will be fine. Why don't you come by for coffee?"

"Actually, I was thinking I'd take the kids to Ellsworth to go shopping or something. Take their minds off things, you know. Want to come?"

"No, I think I have to work today, but I've got to check the schedule. You guys have fun." We said our good-byes, and I hung up the receiver then crawled back into bed. For the second time in less than a day, I'd purposefully lied to someone. I didn't have to work; I was headed back out into the woods. It occurred to me I was as hopelessly snared as the Faulkingham girl and would probably wind up just as dead.

I got dressed anyway, laced up my boots and for good measure put my jackknife in my pants' pocket. I wasn't that stupid. I was a grown woman, after all, and fully capable of defending myself. Armed and potentially dangerous, I jogged toward the heath.

By the time I was sheltered by the crowding alders my head had cleared. I ran and dodged, rejoiced in every stride of my legs, lost myself in the sensations my straining muscles awakened within me. Until I skidded to a tiptoed halt so I wouldn't slam into my mysterious stranger.

He was clothed, not clutching an alder branch, nor was he breathing hard; it was as if he'd been waiting for me on the trail. He stood several feet away, but he might as well have been inches, his body felt so close to mine.

Christ Almighty, how the hell? "Hey, fancy meeting you here." That was clever, Beth. Apparently, the blood I needed to nourish my brain still coursed through my legs.

My stranger didn't say a word, but poked his face upward and moved it back and forth like he was sniffing me out. Then he lowered his head and dropped his arms to his sides, and my affected nonchalance disintegrated, as did the edge in my voice.

"Are you okay?"

He cocked his head as he gazed at me. Holy mother, I hadn't imagined it —his eyes were golden.

I took a step toward him. "You understand me, right?"

He stepped back, keeping the distance between us the same, so I halted.

"Yes, yes I understand you." His voice rumbled deep, as if it had been mined from the depths of his chest, and it lapped my skin as it penetrated my clothes like it had physical substance. "I'm known as Alec." This time he moved toward me, albeit cautiously, and extended his hand.

I gaped down at it like the social moron I'd always been. "You have beautiful hands." My sincerity got tangled in the knotting of his hands as he pulled them away, cupping one within the other. As usual I'd fumbled my social graces and forgot he'd been shy about them. Dearest God, people were right. I should be a pariah. Especially since the sight of his unusual hands tickled that basking snake in my belly so I gushed a genuine smile at him, instead of an apology.

Unlike the typical response to my blunder I'd expected, the tension eased in my stranger's broad shoulders, and he offered me his hand again as he swallowed. My eyes dipped and lifted with his Adam's apple as I rocked forward, my body seeking contact like a sock charged with static cling.

I kept my mouth shut, reached for him, and met his eyes as our hands clasped. My spine zapped the full length of my back with enough shock to quiver my knees.

He smiled, revealing teeth as straight and white as I'd ever seen. I couldn't believe how wildly gorgeous he was up close, or how utterly comfortable I felt with him, even with the singing of my spine writhing straight to my core.

Unexpectedly he yanked his hand from mine, backed toward the thicker trees, and covered his mouth with that palm I'd been touching, as if he was hiding a sneer.

Don't go. "I'm sorry. Did I do something wrong?" I stepped toward him, but he scuttled further away from me. "I mean, if I..." That was all I could say before he disappeared into the protective canopy of the thicker forest. A plane swooped low overhead, the sun glinting off the orange Coast Guard lettering on its metal side—the authorities looking for a killer. In the woods.

Right. Yet, I longed to follow the stranger named Alec. His retreat had taken with it the rising joy that had blossomed under my skin, so I stood yearning for him, for his wild smile he'd shared with me.

The plane hadn't flushed a killer; it had buried my rare moment of connection with another person. Resentment roiled in my chest and I grinded my teeth on its building pressure, then jogged back toward town. Back to where people were who would have never smiled at, nor forgiven, my accidental insult.

---

The following afternoon found me earning my keep at the restaurant instead of traipsing out on the heath in search of my handsome stranger. At least there was a Regional Championship baseball game going on at the high school, which meant practically everyone in town would be at the ball field, leaving me to myself. I even offered to fill in for the cook, as well as wait tables, since there wouldn't be many customers anyway.

Yet, the lack of customers only contrasted with the way Alec's presence had quickened me, and my thoughts jaunted right back to our encounters in the woods, to the memory of his smile. For the first time in my life, I longed for the company of another person—Alec.

I dawdled over filling the saltshakers and wiping down the stools at the counter, anything to keep myself busy and my feet from tripping out the door toward the Great Heath in search of my well-built stranger. In spite of my determination to stay preoccupied, I kept snatching glances toward that tempting door, hoping Alec would materialize like he had before.

Then in he walked, as if he'd been aware of my anticipation, and I stood there smiling at him like he was the apparition brought to life by my wanting. He dipped his cheek and grinned his shy smile he'd used the first time he'd come into the restaurant, and my world immediately tilted aright.

"Well, hello there. Long time no see," I strolled over to him like I was Mae West and he was a handsome cowboy needing a whiskey to quench his dusty throat.

"Hello." His voice was as deep as I'd remembered it; it vibrated the length of my spine. He cast his eyes down and lowered his head without losing his shy grin, and his bashfulness made me blush; I felt the heat of it ignite my skin.

Alec clenched his jaw, then looked up and nailed me with those odd golden eyes, so when he reached for me all I could do was gawp up at him like a teenager stunned by her riotous hormones.

His fingers tickled for mine, their brushing touch an electric current that pulsed a quiver through my stomach and to my feet, where I rooted into the linoleum.

My lips parted, but not to speak, and he leaned down from his broad shouldered height as if to take my mouth with his, the lids of his eyes hooded the gold flecks, softening them. Yet he paused, and straightened to cock his head as if he heard sounds. His entire body stiffened as a wall of heat enveloped my tingling skin like a dryer-warmed blanket.

Did he just growl?

Then he backed away and slipped out through the door as if it had been a magical portal sucking the life out of me.

What the hell?

My exasperation melted once I heard the cook walk in through the back door. Somehow, Alec knew we weren't alone anymore, just as he'd known about the airplane. Silently, I cursed the intrusion of normal life; but within minutes, fans from the game flooded the restaurant, and I had no more time to linger over the stimulating effects of the slow burn that smoldered beneath my skin.

I worked hard, went home, and nestled deep under the covers to covet the enduring warmth.

Sunrise found me in my usual spot in front of the picture window, sipping my coffee and gazing at my reflection as I fantasized about the stranger named Alec. I was running into him a lot, and he seemed to be searching me out as often as I was looking for him. No guy or teenage horny-toad had ever pursued me, not even out of curiosity. So, why didn't I find the whole situation unusual?

Because this man's interest stirred me like I'd only dreamed about. I wanted him. Scratch that. I craved him. Hell, I was getting goosebumps just sitting in my chair thinking about him. It was all I could do to keep myself from throwing my virginity at him.

So, I had to be careful. I had no experience in this sort of thing, and I sure as shit didn't want to scare him off with my weirdness. Forget I thought the guy could be a wolf. That was just me fantasizing again. The reality was, I was the freak, so if Alec found me interesting, I was going to have to act as normal as I could muster. Which meant not stalking him like a hungry predator.

Which reminded me I needed to hunt down some groceries if I was going to eat anything besides fried food from the restaurant. Right. Reality and its chores. I pulled my attention off the pane of glass, and gazed outward as the sun sliced an orange line between dark sky and ocean. Another day was beginning.

Lucky for me, the local grocery store opened early, given it did business in a fishing community and everyone was up and moving about at the crack of dawn. I pulled my red hair into a loose ponytail, threw some water on my face, and gathered up my canvas bags.

The place was only about a mile away and was an easy walk done in less than ten minutes. I strolled through the aisles, meandered to the produce section, bumped into Muriel Alley who was selling raffle tickets, then finally halted my cart by the deli.

There was a new guy behind the counter who I hadn't seen around before, but it was summer in a coastal town; people came and went with the season. He was about my height, so when he turned around to ask if I needed any help, we looked each other straight in the eye. His voice might have been friendly and accommodating, but his eyes were like glass that could cut flesh to ribbons, and the hair on the back of my neck prickled upright.

"I...I don't see any sirloin. Do you have any prepackaged?"

The man's lids lowered into hard slits. Then he smiled at me and revealed a row of shining white teeth, the likes of which I'd only seen on one other person. My pulse quickened.

No way was there two of them.

I tried to convince myself it was impossible, I was reading into things way too deeply; but his next gesture cemented my certainty and my heart plummeted.

I'd seen the maneuver before from Alec. The strange man's face moved from side to side as he pushed his nose around in the air.

He's getting my scent!

As if he'd heard my thoughts, he sneered and then disappeared through the heavy plastic curtain behind him. He was back before I could do a one-eighty with my cart and flee.

"Your meat." His voice was syrupy, too accommodating; and when he reached over the counter to give me the styrofoam plate of beef I couldn't take it. My knees wobbled, but the rest of me froze, because the meat was clutched in a pair of hands I'd also seen before. Only these fingernails weren't lined with dark earth; they shined as if polished.

I managed to look at his face and thought I caught his lip curl to one side in a snarl. I gathered my wits long enough to snatch the steak from him, muttered an obligatory thank you and made tracks for the safety of the check-out line, where other people were herded in a line.

When I looked back over my shoulder, he was standing on the aisle side of the deli counter, looking in my direction. He knew I was staring at him because he wagged his long index finger as if in warning and shook his head side to side, signaling the word No. Not a single black hair on his head moved out of place.

I paid my bill with shaking hands and walked home so fast I might as well have been running. I slammed and locked the front door once I'd scurried inside. Then instantly changed my mind about hiding in the house.

"Holy shit, I've got to find Alec."

I was at the edge of the heath scanning the expanse of low shrubbery before I knew it; but I saw nothing, so I waded in further. It occurred to me I was again connecting the two creatures together: I was physically searching out the spots where I'd seen the brown wolf, but I definitely had Alec on my mind. Forget the self-flogging about my fantastical daydreams; I had to take my chances maybe the two of them were linked somehow.

My mind back-pedaled to my encounter with the other man, and tossed around the possibility the two men were brothers. My heart told me no. The physical similarities may have been there, but that's where their likenesses ended. They were too different in one crucial way. The comfortable feeling I'd felt around Alec flared in stark contrast to the danger I'd felt in the presence of the dark haired man at the store.

I took my bearings and continued squishing my way to the eastern side of the heath, toward the spruce forest. I was too preoccupied to appreciate the beauty around me or the pungency of moss and spruce tickling my nose.

"Alec," I whispered with a voice foreign and intrusive in this natural landscape. I tried again, and this time put my diaphragm into it. "Alec!" Crows squawked their disapproval, but I yelled again. "Alec!"

Out by the northeast line of the heath I could make out a small form skulking close to the tree line. I held my breath, daring to hope it was the brown wolf, and as it trotted closer, there was no doubt. I watched as its sleek body rose and fell with the contours of the heath; it was grace personified and I wondered how human beings could have found so much menace in its beauty. The wolf dipped out of sight as it veered into an alder thicket. Or dare I dream Alec veered toward that cluster of alders?

I didn't fantasize long, even though my brain didn't believe what my eyes beheld. Emerging from the south end of the alder thicket was a very human Alec, naked all the way to his toes. When he glanced up, he hesitated, as if unsure of himself.

My heart flooded and grew. "Alec."

He stepped forward at the mention of his name.

"Alec, please," I muttered, not knowing what else to say. I couldn't even think where to begin; especially since I'd just witnessed some miracle of nature; something of pure magic. My words tripped over one another as I blurted out my reason for calling him. "I...you...There's something wrong. I don't know, it's..."

Alec stepped closer, his stride long and ground covering, until he stood only a few feet from me. My nerves unraveled as tears stung my eyes.

"Goddamn it, I'm such a mess." I swiped at my wet cheeks.

Alec gripped my eyes with his and a wave of calm enveloped me. I bubbled an involuntary laugh and he smiled at my reaction; it was then I realized he hadn't said a word since he'd shown up.

As if we shared the thought, he uttered a gruff "Hi." Then he hit me with an expectant expression, tilting his cheek into his shy grin that melted me.

I drowned in his gaze while I groped for his hand. He gripped mine in his as if to steady me, but the electric force of it nearly buckled my knees. He pulled me closer to hold me upright by my upper arms, and his chest, which was now only inches from my face, blasted heat like a radiator. I was going to swoon like some corseted heroine.

From some cavernous recess of my brain, I could hear my inner voice yelling at me to get a grip, but holy lord, I protested, he's overwhelming. I tried to focus on a long, white scar arcing just below his nipple, but my vision tunneled, and the world went black.